I0576734

John Milton

**Milton's Paradise Regained**

John Milton

**Milton's Paradise Regained**

ISBN/EAN: 9783744791304

Printed in Europe, USA, Canada, Australia, Japan

Cover: Foto ©Andreas Hilbeck / pixelio.de

More available books at **www.hansebooks.com**

# MILTON'S

# PARADISE REGAINED;

### WITH

## *SELECT NOTES SUBJOINED:*

#### TO WHICH IS ADDED

## A COMPLETE COLLECTION

#### OF HIS

## MISCELLANEOUS POEMS,

#### BOTH

## *ENGLISH AND LATIN.*

### ·LONDON:

Printed by T. Bensley;

FOR T. LONGMAN, B. LAW, J. JOHNSON, C. DILLY, G. G. AND J.
ROBINSON, W. RICHARDSON, W. OTRIDGE AND SON, R. BALDWIN,
F. AND C. RIVINGTON, J. SCATCHERD, OGILVY AND SPEARE,
W. LOWNDES, G. AND T. WILKIE, G. KEARSLEY, VERNOR AND
HOOD, T. CADELL, JUNIOR, AND W. DAVIES, AND S. HAYES.

1796.

# PREFACE.

THE firſt volume contained the jewels of Milton's tranſcendant genius, regularly ſet and wrought into one grand complete work, forming a ſuperb diadem or brilliant necklace of exquiſite workmanſhip in the compoſition, as well as of immenſe value in the materials.

The preſent volume is enriched with diamonds and pearls of equal beauty, though ſcattered and detached; and may be compared to thoſe ſmaller pieces which the Dædalean hand of the ſame artiſt condeſcends to execute in miniature.

To praiſe the well known and univerſally admired poems which fill this volume would be pointing out the luſtre of the ſun, or the beautiful colours of the rainbow. Deſcription indeed muſt ever fail in attempting to give adequate ideas of thoſe delicate and refined excellences which are perceived by the ſenſibility of taſte. Who can communicate by words the fragrance of the hyacinth or honeyſuckle?

Milton's Latin poems have never been ſufficiently commended. They are beautiful beyond moſt of the poetical productions in modern Latin. They are

# PARADISE REGAINED.

I, who ere while the happy garden fung,
By one man's difobedience loft, now fing
Recover'd Paradife to all mankind,
By one man's firm obedience fully try'd
Through all temptation, and the tempter foil'd
In all his wiles, defeated and repuls'd,
And Eden rais'd in the wafte wildernefs.

Thou Spi'rit, who ledft this glorious eremite
Into the defert, his victorious field,
Againft the fpiritual foe, and brought'ft him thence
By proof th' undoubted Son of God, infpire,
As thou art wont, my prompted fong, elfe mute;
And bear through height or depth of nature's bounds
With profp'rous wing full fumm'd, to tell of deeds
Above heroic, though in fecret done,
And unrecorded left through many an age;
Worthy t' have not remain'd fo long unfung.

Now had the great Proclaimer, with a voice

More awful than the found of trumpet, cry'd
Repentance, and Heav'n's kingdom nigh at hand
To all baptiz'd: to his great baptifm flock'd
With awe the regions round, and with them came
From Nazareth the fon of Jofeph deem'd
To the flood Jordan, came as then obfcure,
Unmark'd, unknown; but him the Baptift foon
Defcry'd, divinely warn'd, and witnefs bore
As to his worthier, and would have refign'd
To him his heav'nly office, nor was long
His witnefs unconfirm'd: on him baptiz'd
Heav'n open'd, and in likenefs of a dove
The Spi'rit defcended, while the Father's voice
From Heav'n pronounc'd him his beloved Son.
That heard the Adverfary; who, roving ftill
About the world, at that affembly fam'd
Would not be laft, and with the voice divine
Nigh thunder-ftruck, th' exalted man, to whom
Such high atteft was giv'n, a while furvey'd
With wonder; then with envy fraught and rage
Flies to his place, nor refts, but in mid air
To council fummons all his mighty peers,
Within thick clouds and dark ten-fold involv'd,
A gloomy confiftory; and them amidft
With looks aghaft and fad he thus befpake.
    " O ancient Pow'rs of air, and this wide world;
For much more willingly I mention air,
This our old conqueft, than remember Hell,
Our hated habitation; well ye know
How many ages, as the years of men,      ·
This univerfe we have poffefs'd, and rul'd

In manner at our will th' affairs of earth,
Since Adam and his facile confort Eve
Loft Paradife, deceiv'd by me; though fince
With dread attending when that fatal wound
Shall be inflicted by the feed of Eve
Upon my head: long the decrees of Heav'n
Delay, for longeft time to him is fhort;
And now too foon for us the circling hours
This dreaded time have compafs'd, wherein we
Muft bide the ftroke of that long threaten'd wound,
At leaft if fo we can, and by the head
Broken be not intended all our power
To be infring'd, our freedom and our being,
In this fair empire won of earth and air;
For this ill news I bring, the woman's feed,
Deftin'd to this, is late of woman born:
His birth to our juft fear gave no fmall caufe,
But his growth now to youth's full flow'r, difplaying ·
All virtue, grace, and wifdom to achieve
Things higheft, greateft, multiplies my fear.
Before him a geat prophet, to proclaim
His coming, is fent harbinger; who all
Invites, and in the confecrated ftream
Pretends to wafh off fin, and fit them fo
Purified to receive him pure, or rather
To do him honour as their king: all come,
And he himfelf among them was baptiz'd,
Not thence to be more pure, but to receive
The teftimony' of Heav'n, that who he is
Thenceforth the nations may not doubt: I faw
The prophet do him reverence; on him, rifing

Out of the water, Heav'n above the clouds
Unfold her cryftal doors; thence on his head
A perfect dove defcend, whate'er it meant;
And out of Heav'n the fov'reign voice I heard,
This is my Son belov'd, in him am pleas'd.
His mother then is mortal, but his fire
He who obtains the monarchy of Heaven;
And what will he not do to' advance his Son;
His firft-begot we know, and fore have felt,
When his fierce thunder drove us to the deep:
Who this is we muft learn, for man he feems
In all his lineaments, though in his face
The glimpfes of his father's glory fhine.
Ye fee our danger on the utmoft edge
Of hazard, which admits no long debate,
But muft with fomething fudden be oppos'd;
Not force, but well couch'd fraud, well woven fnares:
Ere in the head of nations he appear
Their king, their leader, and fupreme on earth.
I, when no other durft, fole undertook
The difmal expedition to find out
And ruin Adam, and th' exploit perform'd
Succefsfully; a calmer voyage now
Will waft me; and the way found profp'rous once
Induces beft to hope of like fuccefs."
     He ended, and his words impreffion left
Of much amazement to th' infernal crew,
Diftracted and furpris'd with deep difmay
At thefe fad tidings; but no time was then
For long indulgence to their fears or grief:
Unanimous they all commit the care

And management of this main enterprize
To him their great dictator, whofe attempt
At firft againft mankind fo well had thriv'd
In Adam's overthrow, and led their march
From Hell's deep-vaulted den to dwell in light,
Regents, and potentates, and kings, yea gods
Of many a pleafant realm, and province wide.
So to the coaft of Jordan he directs
His eafy fteps, girded with fnaky wiles,
Where he might likelieft find this new-declar'd,
This man of men, attefted Son of God,
Temptation and all guile on him to try;
So to fubvert whom he fufpected rais'd
To end his reign on earth, fo long enjoy'd:
But contrary unweeting he fulfill'd
The purpos'd counfel pre-ordain'd and fix'd
Of the moft High, who, in full frequence bright
Of Angels, thus to Gabriel fmiling fpake.
    " Gabriel, this day by proof thou fhalt behold,
Thou and all Angels converfant on earth
With man or men's affairs, how I begin
To verify that folemn meffage late,
On which I fent thee to the Virgin pure
In Galilee, that fhe fhould bear a fon
Great in renown, and call'd the Son of God;
Then told'ft her, doubting how thefe things could be
To her a virgin, that on her fhould come
The Holy Ghoft, and the pow'r of the Higheft
O'er-fhadow her: this man born and now up-grown,
To fhow him worthy of his birth divine
And high prediction, henceforth I expofe

To Satan; let him tempt and now affay
His utmoft fubtlety, becaufe he boafts
And vaunts of his great cunning to the throng
Of his apoftafy; he might have learnt
Lefs overweening, fince he fail'd in Job,
Whofe conftant perfeverance overcame
Whate'er his cruel malice could invent.
He now fhall know I can produce a man
Of female feed, far abler to refift
All his folicitations, and at length
All his vaft force, and drive him back to Hell;
Winning by conqueft what the firft man loft
By fallacy furpris'd.   But firft I mean
To exercife him in the wildernefs;
There he fhall firft lay down the rudiments
Of his great warfare, ere I fend him forth
To conquer Sin and Death, the two grand foes,
By humiliation and ftrong fufferance:
His weaknefs fhall o'ercome Satanic ftrength,
And all the world, and mafs of finful flefh;
That all the Angels and ethereal Powers,
They now, and men hereafter may difcern,
From what confummate virtue I have chofe
This perfect man, by merit call'd my Son,
· To earn falvation for the fons of men."
   So fpake th' eternal Father, and all Heaven
Admiring ftood a fpace, then into hymns
Burft forth; and in celeftial meafures mov'd,
Circling the throne and finging, while the hand
Sung with the voice, and this the argument.
   " Victory' and triumph to the Son of God

Now entering his great duel, not of arms,
But to vanquifh by wifdom hellifh wiles.
The Father knows the Son; therefore fecure
Ventures his filial virtue, though untry'd,
Againft whate'er may tempt, whate'er feduce,
Allure, or terrify, or undermine.
Be fruftrate all ye ftratagems of Hell,
And devilifh machinations come to nought."
  So they in Heav'n their odes and vigils tun'd:
Mean while the Son of God, who yet fome days
Lodg'd in Bethabara where John baptiz'd,
Mufing and much revolving in his breaft,
How beft the mighty work he might begin
Of Saviour to mankind, and which way firft
Publifh his God-like office now mature,
One day forth walk'd alone, the Spirit leading,
And his deep thoughts, the better to converfe
With folitude, till far from track of men,
Thought following thought, and ftep by ftep led on,
He enter'd now the bord'ring defert wild,
And with dark fhades and rocks environ'd round,
His holy meditations thus purfu'd.
  " O what a multitude of thoughts at once
Awaken'd in me fwarm, while I confider
What from within I feel myfelf, and hear
What from without comes often to my ears,
Ill forting with my prefent ftate compar'd !
When I was yet a child, no childifh play
To me was pleafing; all my mind was fet
Serious to learn and know, and thence to do
What might be public good; myfelf I thought

Born to that end, born to promote all truth,
All righteous things: therefore above my years,
The law of God I read, and found it fweet,
Made it my whole delight, and in it grew
To fuch perfection, that ere yet my age
Had meafur'd twice fix years, at our great feaft
I went into the temple, there to hear
The teachers of our law, and to propofe
What might improve my knowledge or their own;
And was admir'd by all: yet this not all
To which my fpi'rit afpir'd; victorious deeds
Flam'd in my heart, heroic acts, one while
To refcue Ifrael from the Roman yoke,
Then to fubdue and quell o'er all the earth
Brute violence and proud tyrannic power,
Till truth were freed, and equity reftor'd:
Yet held it more humane, more heav'nly firft
By winning words to conquer willing hearts,
And make perfuafion do the work of fear;
At leaft to try, and teach the erring foul
Not wilfully mifdoing, but unware
Mifled; the ftubborn only to fubdue.
Thefe growing thoughts my mother foon perceiving
By words at times caft forth inly rejoic'd,
And faid to me apart, ' High are thy thoughts
O Son, but nourifh them and let them foar
To what height facred virtue and true worth
Can raife them, though above example high;
By matchlefs deeds exprefs thy matchlefs Sire.
For know, thou art no fon of mortal man;
Though men efteem thee low of parentage,

Thy father is th' eternal King, who rules
All Heav'n and Earth, Angels and fons of men;
A meffenger from God foretold thy birth
Conceiv'd in me a virgin; he foretold
Thou fhould'ft be great, and fit on David's throne,
And of thy kingdom there fhould be no end.
At thy nativity a glorious quire
Of Angels in the fields of Bethlehem fung
To fhepherds watching at their folds by night,
And told them the Meffiah now was born
Where they might fee him, and to thee they came,
Directed to the manger where thou lay'ft,
For in the inn was left no better room:
A ftar, not feen before, in Heav'n appearing,
Guided the wife men thither from the eaft,
To honour thee with incenfe, myrrh, and gold,
By whofe bright courfe led on they found the place,
Affirming it thy ftar new grav'n in Heaven,
By which they knew the king of Ifrael born.
Juft Simeon, and prophetic Anna, warn'd
By vifion, found thee in the temple', and fpake
Before the altar and the vefted prieft,
Like things of thee to all that prefent ftood.'
This having heard, ftraight I again revolv'd
The law and prophets, fearching what was writ
Concerning the Meffiah, to our fcribes
Known partly, and foon found of whom they fpake
I am; this chiefly, that my way muft lie
Through many a hard affay ev'n to the death,
Ere I the promis'd kingdom can attain,
Or work redemption for mankind, whofe fins

Full weight muſt be transferr'd upon my head.
Yet neither thus diſhearten'd or diſmay'd,
The time prefix'd I waited, when behold
The Baptiſt (of whoſe birth I oft had heard,
Not knew by ſight) now come, who was to come
Before Meſſiah and his way prepare.
I as all others to his baptiſm came,
Which I believ'd was from above; but he
Straight knew me, and with loudeſt voice proclaim'd
Me him (for it was ſhewn him ſo from Heaven)
Me him, whoſe harbinger he was; and firſt
Refus'd on me his baptiſm to confer,
As much his greater, and was hardly won:
But as I roſe out of the laving ſtream,
Heav'n open'd her eternal doors, from whence
The Spi'rit deſcended on me like a dove,
And laſt, the ſum of all, my Father's voice,
Audibly heard from Heav'n, pronounc'd me his,
Me his beloved Son, in whom alone
He was well pleas'd; by which I knew the time
Now full, that I no more ſhould live obſcure,
But openly begin, as beſt becomes
Th' authority which I deriv'd from Heaven.
And now by ſome ſtrong motion I am led
Into this wilderneſs, to what intent
I learn not yet, perhaps I need not know;
For what concerns my knowledge God reveals."
  So ſpake our Morning Star then in his riſe,·
And looking round on every ſide beheld
A pathleſs deſert, duſk with horrid ſhades;
The way he came not having mark'd, return

Was difficult, by human fteps untrod;
And he ftill on was led, but with fuch thoughts
Accompanied of things paft and to come
Lodg'd in his breaft, as well might recommend
Such folitude before choiceft fociety.
Full forty days he pafs'd, whether on hill
Sometimes, anon in fhady vale, each night        .
Under the covert of fome ancient oak,
Or cedar, to defend him from the dew,
Or harbour'd in one cave, is not reveal'd;
Nor tafted human food, nor hunger felt
Till thofe days ended, hunger'd then at laft
Among wild beafts: they at his fight grew mild,
Nor fleeping him, nor waking, harm'd; his walk
The fiery ferpent fled, and noxious worm,
The lion and fierce tiger glar'd aloof.
But now an aged man, in rural weeds,
Following, as feem'd, the queft of fome ftray ewe,
Or wither'd fticks to gather, which might ferve        ` _
Againft a winter's day when winds blow keen,
To warm him wet return'd from field at eve,
He faw approach, who firft with curious eye
Perus'd him, then with words thus utter'd fpake.
    " Sir, what ill chance hath brought thee to this
        place
So far from path or road of men, who pafs
In troop or caravan? for fingle none ·
Durft ever, who return'd, and dropt not here
His carcafe, pin'd with hunger and with drought.
I afk the rather, and the more admire,
For that to me thou feem'ft the man, whom late

Our new baptizing Prophet at the ford
Of Jordan honor'd fo, and call'd thee Son
Of God; I faw and heard, for we fometimes,
Who dwell this wild, conftrain'd by want, come forth
To town or village nigh (nigheft is far)
Where ought we hear, and curious are to hear,
What happens new; fame alfo finds us out."
    To whom the Son of God: " Who brought me
        hither,
Will bring me hence; no other guide I feek."
   " By miracle he may," reply'd the fwain,
" What other way I fee not, for we here
Live on tough roots and ftubs, to thirft inur'd
More than the camel, and to drink go far,
Men to much mifery and hardfhip born; '
But if thou be the Son of God, command
That out of thefe hard ftones be made thee bread,
So fhalt thou fave thyfelf and us relieve
With food, whereof we wretched feldom tafte."
   He ended, and the Son of God reply'd:
" Think'ft thou fuch force in bread? is it not written
(For I difcern thee other than thou feem'ft)
Man lives not by bread only, but each word
Proceeding from the mouth of God, who fed
Our fathers here with Manna? in the mount   '
Mofes was forty days, nor ate nor drank;
And forty days Elijah without food
Wander'd this barren wafte; the fame I now:
Why doft thou then fuggeft to me diftruft,
Knowing who I am, as I know who thou art?"
   Whom thus anfwer'd th' Arch-Fiénd now undifguis'd.

" 'Tis true, I am that Spirit unfortunate,
Who leagu'd with millions more in rafh revolt
Keep not my happy ftation, but was driven
With them from blifs to the bottomlefs deep;
Yet to that hideous place not fo confin'd
By rigour unconniving, but that oft
Leaving my dolorous prifon I enjoy
Large liberty to round this globe of earth,
Or range in th' air, nor from the Heav'n of Heav'ns
Hath he excluded my refort fometimes.
I came among the fons of God, when he
Gave up into my hands Uzzean Job
To prove him, and illuftrate his high worth;
And when to all his Angels he propos'd
To draw the proud king Ahab into fraud
That he might fall in Ramoth, they demurring,
I undertook that office, and the tongues
Of all his flattering prophets glibb'd with lies
To his deftruction, as I had in charge,
For what he bids I do: though I have loft
Much luftre of my native brightnefs, loft
To be belov'd of God, I have not loft
To love, at leaft contemplate and admire
What I fee excellent in good, or fair,
Or virtuous, I fhould fo have loft all fenfe.
What can be then lefs in me than defire
To fee thee and approach thee, whom I know
Declar'd the Son of God, to hear attent
Thy wifdom, and behold thy Godlike deeds?
Men generally think me much a foe
To all mankind: why fhould I? they to me

Never did wrong or violence; by them
I loft not what I loft, rather by them
I gain'd what I have gain'd, and with them dwell
Copartner in thefe regions of the world,
If not difpofer; lend them oft my aid,
Oft my advice by prefages and figns,
And anfwers, oracles, portents, and dreams,
Whereby they may direct their future life.
Envy they fay excites me, thus to gain
Companions of my mifery and woe.
At firft it may be; but long fince with woe
Nearer acquainted, now I feel by proof,
That fellowfhip in pain divides not fmart,
Nor lightens ought each man's peculiar load.
Small confolation then, were man adjoin'd:
This wounds me moft (what can it lefs?) that man,
Man fall'n fhall be reftor'd, I never more."

To whom our Saviour fternly thus reply'd.
" Defervedly thou griev'ft, compos'd of lies
From the beginning, and in lies wilt end;
Who boaft'ft releafe from Hell, and leave to come
Into the Heav'n of Heav'ns: thou com'ft indeed,
As a poor miferable captive thrall
Comes to the place where he before had fat
Among the prime in fplendour, now depos'd,
Ejected, emptied, gaz'd, unpitied, fhunn'd,
A fpectacle of ruin or of fcorn
To all the hoft of Heav'n: the happy place
Imparts to thee no happinefs, no joy,
Rather inflames thy torment, reprefenting
Loft blifs, to thee no more communicable;

So never more in Hell than when in Heaven.
But thou art ferviceable to Heav'n's King.
Wilt thou impute to' obedience what thy fear
Extorts, or pleafure to do ill excites?
What but thy malice mov'd thee to mifdeem
Of righteous Job, then cruelly to' afflict him
With all inflictions? but his patience won.
The other fervice was thy chofen talk,
To be a liar in four hundred mouths;
For lying is thy fuftenance, thy food.
Yet thou pretend'ft to truth; all oracles
By thee are giv'n, and what confefs'd more true
Among the nations? that hath been thy craft,
By mixing fomewhat true to vent more lies.
But what have been thy anfwers, what but dark,
Ambiguous, and with double fenfe deluding,
Which they who afk'd have feldom underftood,
And not well underftood as good not known?
Who ever by confulting at thy fhrine
Return'd the wifer, or the more inftruct
To fly or follow what concern'd him moft,
And run not fooner to his fatal fnare?
For God hath juftly giv'n the nations up
To thy delufions; juftly, fince they fell
Idolatrous: but when his purpofe is
Among them to declare his providence
To thee not known, whence haft thou then thy truth,
But from him or his angels prefident
In every province? who themfelves difdaining
T' approach thy temples, give thee in command
What to the fmalleft tittle thou fhalt fay

C

To thy adorers; thou, with trembling fear,
Or like a fawning parafite, obey'ſt;
Then to thyſelf aſcrib'ſt the truth foretold.
But this thy glory ſhall be ſoon retrench'd;
No more ſhalt thou by oracling abuſe
The Gentiles; henceforth oracles are ceas'd,
And thou no more with pomp and ſacrifice
Shalt be inquir'd at Delphos or elſewhere,
At leaſt in vain, for they ſhall find thee mute.
God hath now ſent his living oracle
Into the world to teach his final will,
And ſends his Spi'rit of truth henceforth to dwell
In pious hearts, an inward oracle
To all truth requiſite for men to know."

    So ſpake our Saviour: but the ſubtle Fiend,
Though inly ſtung with anger and diſdain,
Diſſembled, and this anſwer ſmooth return'd.

    " Sharply thou haſt inſiſted on rebuke;
And urg'd me hard with doings, which not will
But miſery hath wreſted from me: where
Eaſily canſt thou find one miſerable,
And not enforc'd oft-times to part from truth;
If it may ſtand him more in ſtead to lie,
Say and unſay, feign, flatter, or abjure?
But thou art plac'd above me, thou art Lord;
From thee I can and muſt ſubmiſs endure
Check or reproof, and glad to 'ſcape ſo quit.
Hard are the ways of truth, and rough to walk,
Smooth on the tongue diſcours'd, pleaſing to th' ear,
And tuneable as ſylvan pipe or ſong;
What wonder then if I delight to hear

Her dictates from thy mouth? moft men admire
Virtue, who follow not her lore: permit me
To hear thee when I come (fince no man comes)
And talk at leaft, though I defpair to' attain.
Thy Father, who is holy, wife, and pure,
Suffers the hypocrite or atheous prieft
To tread his facred courts, and minifter
About his altar, handling holy things,
Praying or vowing; and vouchfaf'd his voice
To Balaam reprobate, a prophet yet
Infpir'd: difdain not fuch accefs to me."

To whom our Saviour with unalter'd brow.
" Thy coming hither, though I know thy fcope,
I bid not, or forbid; do as thou find'ft
Permiffion from above; thou canft not more."

He added not; and Satan bowing low
His grey diffimulation, difappear'd
Into thin air diffus'd: for now began
Night with her fullen wings to double-fhade
The defert; fowls in their clay nefts were couch'd;
And now wild beafts came forth the woods to roam.


THE END OF THE FIRST BOOK.

THE

## SECOND BOOK

OF

# PARADISE REGAINED.

# PARADISE REGAINED.

## BOOK II.

MEANWHILE the new-baptiz'd, who yet remain'd
At Jordan with the Baptift, and had feen
Him whom they heard fo late exprefsly call'd
Jefus Meffiah Son of God declar'd,
And on that high authority had believ'd,
And with him talk'd, and with him lodg'd, I mean
Andrew and Simon, famous after known,
With others though in holy writ not nam'd,
Now miffing him their joy fo lately found,
So lately found, and fo abruptly gone,
Began to doubt, and doubted many days,
And as the days increas'd, increas'd their doubt:
Sometimes they thought he might be only fhown,
And for a time caught up to God, as once
Mofes was in the mount, and miffing long;
And the great Thifbite, who on fiery wheels
Rode up to Heav'n, yet once again to come.
Therefore as thofe young prophets then with care

Sought loft Elijah, fo in each place thefe
Nigh to Bethabara; in Jericho
The city' of palms, Ænon, and Salem old,
Machærus, and each town or city wall'd
On this fide the broad lake Genezaret,
Or in Peræa; but return'd in vain.
Then on the bank of Jordan, by a creek,
Where winds with reeds and ofiers whifp'ring play,
Plain fifhermen, no greater men them call,
Clofe in a cottage low together got,
Their unexpeƈted lofs and plaints out breath'd.
  " Alas, from what high hope to what relapfe
Unlook'd for are we fall'n! our eyes beheld
Meffiah certainly now come, fo long
Expeƈted of our fathers; we have heard
His words, his wifdom full of grace and truth;
Now, now, for fure, deliverance is at hand,
The kingdom fhall to Ifrael be reftor'd:
Thus we rejoic'd, but foon our joy is turn'd
Into perplexity and new amaze:
For whither is he gone? what accident
Hath rapt him from us? will he now retire,
After appearance, and again prolong
Our expeƈtation? God of Ifrael,
Send thy Meffiah forth, the time is come:
Behold the kings of th' earth how they opprefs
Thy chofen, to what height their pow'r unjuft
They have exalted, and behind them caft
All fear of thee: arife and vindicate
Thy glory, free thy people from their yoke.
But let us wait; thus far he hath perform'd,

Sent his Anointed, and to us reveal'd him,
By his great Prophet, pointed at and fhown
In public, and with him we have convers'd:
Let us be glad of this, and all our fears
Lay on his providence; he will not fail,
Nor will withdraw him now, nor will recall,
Mock us with his bleft fight, then fnatch him hence;
Soon we fhall fee our hope, our joy return."
  Thus they out of their plaints new hope refume
To find whom at the firft they found unfought:
But to his mother Mary, when fhe faw
Others return'd from baptifm, not her fon,
Nor left at Jordan tidings of him none,
Within her breaft though calm, her breaft though
      pure,
Motherly cares and fears got head, and rais'd
Some troubled thoughts, which fhe in fighs thus clad.
  " O what avails me now that honour high
To have conceiv'd of God, or that falute,
Hail highly favour'd, among women bleft!
While I to forrows am no lefs advanc'd,
And fears as imminent, above the lot
Of other women, by the birth I bore,
In fuch a feafon born when fcarce a fhed
Could be obtain'd to fhelter him or me
From the bleak air; a ftable was our warmth,
A manger his; yet foon enforc'd to fly
Thence into Egypt, till the murd'rous king
Were dead, who fought his life, and miffing fill'd
With infant blood the ftreets of Bethlehem;
From Egypt home return'd, in Nazareth

Hath been our dwelling many years; his life
Private, unactive, calm, contemplative,
Little fufpicious to any king; but now
Full grown to man, acknowledg'd, as I hear,
By John the Baptift, and in public fhown,
Son own'd from Heaven by his Father's voice;
I look'd for fome great change; to honor? no,
But trouble, as old Simeon plain foretold,
That to the fall and rifing he fhould be
Of many in Ifrael, and to a fign
Spoken againft, that through my very foul
A fword fhall pierce; this is my favor'd lot,
My exaltation to afflictions high;
Afflicted I may be, it feems, and bleft;
I will not argue that, nor will repine.
But where delays he now? fome great intent
Conceals him: when twelve years he fcarce had feen,
I loft him, but fo found, as well I faw
He could not lofe himfelf; but went about
His Father's bufinefs; what he meant I mus'd,
Since underftand; much more his abfence now
Thus long to fome great purpofe he obfcures.
But I to wait with patience am inur'd;
My heart hath been a ftore-houfe long of things
And fay'ings laid up, portending ftrange events."

　　Thus Mary pond'ring oft, and oft to mind
Recalling what remarkably had pafs'd
Since firft her falutation heard, with thoughts
Meekly compos'd awaited the fulfilling:
The while her fon tracing the defert wild,
Sole but with holieft meditations fed,

Into himfelf defcended, and at once
All his great work to come before him fet;
How to begin, how to accomplifh beft
His end of being on earth, and miffion high:
For Satan with fly preface to return
Had left him vacant, and with fpeed was gone
Up to the middle region of thick air,
Where all his potentates in council fat;
There without fign of boaft, or fign of joy,
Solicitous and blank he thus began.
    " Princes, Heav'n's ancient fons, ethereal thrones,
Demonian fpirits now, from th' element
Each of his reign allotted, rightlier call'd
Pow'rs of fire, air, water, and earth beneath,
So may we hold our place and thefe mild feats
Without new trouble; fuch an enemy
Is rifen to invade us, who no lefs
Threatens than our expulfion down to Hell.
I, as I undertook, and with the vote
Confenting in full frequence was impower'd,
Have found him, view'd him, tafted him, but find
Far other labour to be undergone,
Than when I dealt with Adam firft of men,
Though Adam by his wife's allurement fell,
However to this man inferior far,
If he be man by mother's fide at leaft,
With more than human gifts from Heav'n adorn'd,
Perfections abfolute, graces divine,
And amplitude of mind to greateft deeds.
Therefore I am return'd, left confidence
Of my fuccefs with Eve in Paradife.

Deceive ye to perſuaſion over-ſure
Of like ſucceeding here; I ſummon all
Rather to be in readineſs, with hand
Or counſel to aſſiſt; leſt I who erſt
Thought none my equal, now be over-match'd."

So ſpake th' old Serpent doubting, and from all
With clamour was aſſur'd their utmoſt aid
At his command; when from amidſt them roſe
Belial, the diſſoluteſt ſpi'rit that fell,
The ſenſualeſt, and after Aſmodai
The fleſhlieſt incubus, and thus advis'd.

" Set women in his eye, and in his walk,
Among daughters of men the faireſt found;
Many are in each region paſſing fair
As the noon ſky; more like to goddeſſes
Than mortal creatures, graceful and diſcreet,
Expert in amorous arts, enchanting tongues
Perſuaſive, virgin majeſty with mild
And ſweet allay'd, yet terrible t' approach,
Skill'd to retire, and in retiring draw
Hearts after them tangled in amorous nets.
Such objeƈt hath the pow'r to ſoft'n and tame
Severeſt temper, ſmooth the rugged'ſt brow,
Enerve, and with voluptuous hope diſſolve,
Draw out with credulous deſire, and lead
At will the manlieſt, reſoluteſt breaſt,
As the magnetic hardeſt iron draws.
Women, when nothing elſe, beguil'd the heart
Of wiſeſt Solomon, and made him build,
And made him bow to the gods of his wives."

To whom quick anſwer Satan thus return'd.

" Belial, in much uneven ſcale thou weigh'ſt
All others by thyſelf; becauſe of old
Thou thyſelf doat'dſt on womankind, admiring
Their ſhape, their colour, and attractive grace,
None are, thou think'ſt, but taken with ſuch toys.
Before the flood thou with thy luſty crew,
Falſe titled ſons of God, roaming the earth
Caſt wanton eyes on the daughters of men,                    ⸺
And coupled with them, and begot a race.
Have we not ſeen, or by relation heard,
In courts and regal chambers how thou lurk'ſt,
In wood or grove by moſſy fountain ſide,
In valley or green meadow, to way-lay
Some beauty rare, Caliſto, Clymene,
Daphne, or Semele, Antiopa,                                    .
Or Amymone, Syrinx, many more
Too long, then lay'ſt thy ſcapes on names ador'd,
Apollo, Neptune, Jupiter, or Pan,
Satir, or Faun, or Sylvan? But theſe haunts
Delight not all; among the ſons of men,
How many have with a ſmile made ſmall account
Of beauty and her lures, eaſily ſcorn'd
All her aſſaults, on worthier things intent!
Remember that Pellean conqueror,
A youth, how all the beauties of the eaſt
He ſlightly view'd, and ſlightly overpaſs'd;
How he firnam'd of Africa diſmiſs'd
In his prime youth the fair Iberian maid.
For Solomon, he liv'd at eaſe, and full
Of honour, wealth, high fare, aim'd not beyond
Higher deſign than to enjoy his ſtate;

Thence to the bait of women lay expos'd:
But he whom we attempt is wifer far
Than Solomon, of more exalted mind,
Made and fet wholly on th' accomplifhment
Of greateft things; what woman will you find,
Though of this age the wonder and the fame,
On whom his leifure will vouchfafe an eye
Of fond defire? or fhould fhe confident,
As fitting queen ador'd on beauty's throne,
Defcend with all her winning charms begirt
T' enamour, as the zone of Venus once
Wrought that effect on Jove, fo fables tell;
How would one look from his majeftic brow
Seated as on the top of virtue's hill,
Difcount'nance her defpis'd, and put to rout
All her array; her female pride dejecft,
Or turn to reverent awe! for beauty ftands
In th' admiration only of weak minds
Led captive; ceafe to' admire, and all her plumes
Fall flat and fhrink into a trivial toy,
At every fudden flighting quite abafh'd:
Therefore with manlier objects we muft try
His conftancy, with fuch as have more fhow
Of worth, of honour, glory', and popular praife;
Rocks whereon greateft men have ofteft wreck'd;
Or that which only feems to fatisfy
Lawful defires of nature, not beyond;
And now I know he hungers where no food
Is to be found, in the wide wildernefs;
The reft commit to me, I fhall let pafs
No' advantage, and his ftrength as oft affay."

He ceas'd, and heard their grant in loud acclaim;
Then forthwith to him takes a chofen band
Of fpirits likeft to himfelf in guile,
To be at hand, and at his beck appear,
If caufe were to unfold fome active fcene
Of various perfons, each to know his part;
Then to the defert takes with thefe his flight;
Where ftill from fhade to fhade the Son of God
After forty days fafting had remain'd,
Now hung'ring firft, and to himfelf thus faid.

" Where will this end? four times ten days I've pafs'd
Wand'ring this woody maze, and human food
Nor tafted, nor had appetite; that faft
To virtue I impute not, or count part
Of what I fuffer here; if nature need not,
Or God fupport nature without repaft
Though needing, what praife is it to endure?
But now I feel I hunger, which declares
Nature hath need of 'what fhe afks; yet God
Can fatisfy that need fome other way,
Though hunger ftill remain: fo it remain
Without this body's wafting, I content me,
And from the fting of famine fear no harm,
Nor mind it, fed with better thoughts that feed
Me hung'ring more to do my Father's will."

It was the hour of night, when thus the Son
Commun'd in filent walk, then laid him down
Under the hofpitable covert nigh
Of trees thick interwoven; there he flept,
And dream'd, as appetite is wont to dream,
Of meats and drinks, nature's refrefhment fweet.

Him thought, he by the brook of Cherith ſtood,
And ſaw the ravens with their horny beaks
Food to Elijah bringing ev'n and morn,
Though ravenous, taught t' abſtain from what they
    brought:
He ſaw the prophet alſo hòw he fled
Into the deſert, and how there he ſlept
Under a juniper; then how, awak'd,
He found his ſupper on the coals prepar'd,
And by the Angel was bid riſe and eat,
And eat the ſecond time after repoſe,
The ſtrength whereof ſuffic'd him forty days;
Sometimes that with Elijah he partook,
Or as a gueſt with Daniel at his pulſe.
Thus wore out night, and now the herald lark
Left his ground-neſt, high tow'ring to deſcry
The morn's approach, and greet her with his ſong:
As lightly from his graſſy couch up roſe
Our Saviour, and found all was but a dream;
Faſting he went to ſleep, and faſting wak'd.
Up to a hill anon his ſteps he rear'd,
From whoſe high top to ken the proſpect round,
If cottage were in view, ſheep-cote or herd;
But cottage, herd, or ſheep-cote none he ſaw,
Only' in a bottom ſaw a pleaſant grove,
With chant of tuneful birds reſounding loud;
Thither he bent his way, determin'd there
To reſt at noon, and enter'd ſoon the ſhade
High roof'd, and walks beneath, and alleys brown,
That open'd in the midſt a woody ſcene;
Nature's own work it ſeem'd (nature taught art)

And to a fuperftitious eye the haunt
Of wood-gods and wood-nymphs; he view'd it round,
When fuddenly a man before him ftood,
Not ruftic as before, but feemlier clad,
As one in city', or court, or palace bred,
And with fair fpeech thefe words to him addrefs'd.

" With granted leave officious I return,
But much more wonder that the Son of God
In this wild folitude fo long fhould bide
Of all things deftitute, and well I know,
Not without hunger.   Others of fome note,
As ftory tells, have trod this wildernefs;
The fugitive bond-woman with her fon
Out-caft Nebaioth, yet found here relief
By a providing angel; all the race
Of Ifrael here had famifh'd, had not God
Rain'd from Heav'n manna; and that prophet bold,
Native of Thebez, wand'ring here, was fed
Twice by a voice inviting him to eat:
Of thee thefe forty days none hath regard,
Forty and more deferted here indeed."

To whom thus Jefus. " What conclud'ft thou hence?
They all had need, I, as thou feeft, have none."

" How haft thou hunger then?" Satan reply'd.
" Tell me if food were now before thee fet,
Would'ft thou not eat?" " Thereafter as I like
The giver," anfwer'd Jefus.  " Why fhould that
Caufe thy refufal?" faid the fubtle fiend.
" Haft thou not right to all created things?    ⸺
Owe not all creatures by juft right to thee
Duty and fervice, not to ftay till bid,

But tender all their pow'r? nor mention I
Meats by the law unclean, or offer'd firſt
To idols, thoſe young Daniel could refuſe;
Nor proffer'd by an enemy, though who
Would ſcruple that, with want opprefs'd? Behold,
Nature aſham'd, or better to exprefs,
Troubled that thou ſhould'ſt hunger, hath purvey'd
From all the elements her choiceſt ſtore
To treat thee as befeems, and as her lord
With honour, only deign to fit and eat."
    He ſpake no dream, for as his words had end,
Our Saviour lifting up his eyes beheld
In ample ſpace under the broadeſt ſhade
A table richly ſpread, in regal mode,
With diſhes pil'd, and meats of nobleſt ſort
And favour, beaſts of chaſe, or fowl of game,
In paſtry built, or from the ſpit, or boil'd,
Gris-amber-ſteam'd; all fiſh from ſea or ſhore,
Freſhet, or purling brook, of ſhell or fin,
And exquiſiteſt name, for which was drain'd
Pontus, and Lucrine bay, and Afric coaſt.
    Alas how ſimple, to theſe cates compar'd,
Was that crude apple that diverted Eve!
And at a ſtately ſide-board, by the wine
That fragrant ſmell diffus'd, in order ſtood
Tall ſtripling youths rich clad, of fairer hue
Than Ganymed or Hylas; diſtant more
Under the trees now tripp'd, now ſolemn ſtood
Nymphs of Diana's train, and Naiades
With fruits and flow'rs from Amalthea's horn,
And ladies of th' Hefperides, that feem'd

Fairer than feign'd of old, or fabled fince
Of faery damfels met in foreft wide
By knights of Logres, or of Lyones,
Lancelot, or Pelleas, or Pellenore :
And all the while harmonious airs were heard
Of chiming ftrings, or charming pipes, and winds
Of gentleft gale Arabian odours fann'd
From their foft wings, and Flora's earlieft fmells.
Such was the fplendour, and the Tempter now
His invitation earneftly renew'd.
    " What doubts the Son of God to fit and eat?
Thefe are not fruits forbidden; no interdict
Defends the touching of thefe viands pure;
Their tafte no knowledge works at leaft of evil,
But life preferves, deftroys life's enemy,
Hunger, with fweet reftorative delight.
All thefe are fpi'rits of air, and woods, and fprings,
Thy gentle minifters, who come to pay
Thee homage, and acknowledge thee their lord:
What doubt'ft thou Son of God? fit down and eat."
    To whom thus Jefus temp'rately reply'd.
" Said'ft thou not that to all things I had right?
And who withholds my pow'r that right to ufe?
Shall I receive by gift what of my own,
When and where likes me beft, I can command?
I can at will, doubt not, as foon as thou,
Command a table in this wildernefs,
And call fwift flights of angels miniftrant
Array'd in glory on my cup to' attend:
Why fhouldft thou then obtrude this diligence,
In vain, where no acceptance it can find?

And with my hunger what haft thou to do?
Thy pompous delicacies I contemn,
And count thy fpecious gifts no gifts but guiles."
    To whom thus anfwer'd Satan malecontent.
" That I have alfo pow'r to give thou feeft;
If of that pow'r I bring thee voluntary
What I might have beftow'd on whom I pleas'd,
And rather opportunely in this place
Chofe to impart to thy apparent need,
Why fhouldft thou not accept it? but I fee
What I can do or offer is fufpect;
Of thefe things others quickly will difpofe,
Whofe pains have earn'd the far fet fpoil." With that
Both table and provifion vanifh'd quite
With found of harpies wings, and talons heard;
Only the impórtune Tempter ftill remain'd,
And with thefe words his temptation purfu'd.
    " By hunger, that each other creature tames,
Thou art not to be harm'd, therefore not mov'd;
Thy temperance invincible befides,
For no allurement yields to appetite,
And all thy heart is fet on high defigns,
High actions; but wherewith to be achiev'd?
Great acts require great means of enterprife;
Thou art unknown, unfriended, low of birth,
A carpenter thy father known, thyfelf
Bred up in poverty and ftraits at home,
Loft in a defert here and hunger-bit:
Which way or from what hope doft thou afpire
To greatnefs? whence authority deriv'ft?
What followers, what retinue canft thou gain,

Or at thy heels the dizzy multitude,
Longer than thou canſt feed them on thy coſt?
Money brings honour, friends, conqueſt, and realms:
What rais'd Antipater the Edomite,
And his ſon Herod plac'd on Judah's throne,
(Thy throne) but gold that got him puiſſant friends?
Therefore, if at great things thou would'ſt arrive,
Get riches firſt, get wealth, and treaſure heap,
Not difficult, if thou hearken to me;
Riches are mine, fortune is in my hand;
They whom I favour thrive in wealth amain,   .
While virtue, valour, wiſdom ſit in want."
To whom thus Jeſus patiently reply'd.
" Yet wealth without theſe three is impotent
To gain dominion, or to keep it gain'd.
Witneſs thoſe ancient empires of the earth,
In height of all their flowing wealth diſſolv'd:
But men endued with theſe have oft attain'd
In loweſt poverty to higheſt deeds;
Gideon, and Jephthah, and the ſhepherd lad,
Whoſe offspring on the throne of Judah ſat
So many ages, and ſhall yet regain
That ſeat, and reign in Iſrael without end.
Among the heathen, (for throughout the world
To me is not unknown what hath been done
Worthy' of memorial) canſt thou not remember
Quintius, Fabricius, Curius, Regulus?
For I eſteem thoſe names of men ſo poor
Who could do mighty things, and could contemn
Riches though offer'd from the hand of kings.
And what in me ſeems wanting, but that I

May alfo in this poverty as foon
Accomplifh what they did, perhaps and more?
Extol not riches then, the toil of fools,
The wife man's cumbrance, if not fnare, more apt
To flacken virtue, and abate her edge,
Than prompt her to do ought may merit praife.
What if with like averfion I reject
Riches and realms; yet not for that a crown,
Golden in fhow, is but a wreath of thorns,
Brings dangers, troubles, cares, and fleeplefs nights
To him who wears the regal diadem,
When on his fhoulders each man's burden lies;
For therein ftands the office of a king,
His honour, virtue, merit, and chief praife,
That for the public all this weight he bears.
Yet he who reigns within himfelf, and rules
Paffions, defires, and fears, is more a king;
Which every wife and virtuous man attains:
And who attains not, ill afpires to rule
Cities of men, or headftrong multitudes,
Subject himfelf to anarchy within,
Or lawlefs paffions in him which he ferves.
But to guide nations in the way of truth
By faving doctrine, and from errour lead
To know, and knowing worfhip God aright,
Is yet more kingly; this attracts the foul,
Governs the inner man, the nobler part;
That other o'er the body only reigns,
And oft by force, which to a generous mind
So reigning can be no fincere delight.
Befides to give a kingdom hath been thought

Greater and nobler done, and to lay down
Far more magnanimous, than to aſſume.
Riches are needleſs then, both for themſelves,
And for thy reaſon why they ſhould be ſought,
To gain a ſceptre, ofteſt better miſs'd."

THE END OF THE SECOND BOOK.

THE

## THIRD BOOK

OF

# PARADISE REGAINED.

# PARADISE REGAINED.

So ſpake the Son of God, and Satan ſtood
A while as mute confounded what to ſay,
What to reply, confuted and convinc'd
Of his weak arguing, and fallacious drift;
At length collecting all his ſerpent wiles,
With ſoothing words renew'd, him thus accoſts.
   " I ſee thou know'ſt what is of uſe to know,
What beſt to ſay canſt ſay, to do canſt do;
Thy actions to thy words accord, thy words
To thy large heart give utterance due, thy heart
Contains of good, wiſe, juſt, the perfect ſhape.
Should kings and nations from thy mouth conſult,
Thy counſel would be as the oracle
Urim and Thummim, thoſe oraculous gems
On Aaron's breaſt; or tongue of ſeers old
Infallible: or wert thou ſought to deeds
That might require th' array of war, thy ſkill
Of conduct would be ſuch, that all the world

Could not fuftain thy prowefs, or fubfift
In battle, though againft thy few in arms.
Thefe god-like virtues wherefore doft thou hide,
Affecting private life, or more obfcure
In favage wildernefs? wherefore deprive
All earth her wonder at thy acts, thyfelf
The fame and glory, glory the reward
That fole excites to high attempts, the flame
Of moft erected fpi'rits, moft temper'd pure
Ethereal, who all pleafures elfe defpife,
All treafures and all gain efteem as drofs,
And dignities and pow'rs all but the higheft?
Thy years are ripe, and over-ripe; the fon
Of Macedonian Philip had ere thefe
Won Afia, and the throne of Cyrus held
At his difpofe; young Scipio had brought down
The Carthaginian pride; young Pompey quell'd
The Pontic king, and in triumph had rode.
Yet years, and to ripe years judgment mature,
Quench not the thirft of glory, but augment.
Great Julius, whom now all the world admires,
The more he grew in years, the more inflam'd
With glory, wept that he had liv'd fo long
Inglorious: but thou yet art not too late."
    To whom our Saviour calmly thus reply'd.
" Thou neither doft perfuade me to feek wealth
For empire's fake, nor empire to affect
For glory's fake, by all thy argument.
For what is glory but the blaze of fame,
The people's praife, if always praife unmix'd?
And what the people but a herd confus'd,

A mifcellaneous rabble, who extol
Things vulgar, and well weigh'd, fcarce worth the
     praife?
They praife, and they admire they know not what,
And know not whom, but as one leads the other;
And what delight to be by fuch extoll'd,
To live upon their tongues and be their talk,
Of whom to be difprais'd were no fmall praife?
His lot who dares be fingularly good.
Th' intelligent among them and the wife
Are few, and glory fcarce of few is rais'd.
This is true glory and renown, when God
Looking on th' earth, with approbation marks
The juft man, and divulges him through Heaven
To all his angels, who with true applaufe
Recount his praifes: thus he did to Job,
When to extend his fame through Heav'n and Earth,
As thou to thy reproach may'ft well remember,
He ask'd thee, ' Haft thou feen my fervant Job?'
Famous he was in Heav'n, on Earth lefs known;
Where glory is falfe glory, attributed
To things not glorious, men not worthy' of fame.
They err who count it glorious to fubdue
By conqueft far and wide, to over-run
Large countries, and in field great battles win,
Great cities by affault: what do thefe worthies,
But rob and fpoil, burn, flaughter, and inflave
Peaceable nations, neighb'ring, or remote,
Made captive, yet deferving freedom more
Than thofe their conquerors, who leave behind
Nothing but ruin wherefoe'er they rove,

And all the flourifhing works of peace deftroy,
Then fwell with pride, and muft be titled gods,   .
Great Benefactors of mankind, deliverers,
Worfhipp'd with temple, prieft and facrifice;
One is the fon of Jove, of Mars the other;
Till conqu'ror death difcover them fcarce men,
Rolling in brutifh vices, and deform'd,
Violent or fhameful death their due reward.
But if there be in glory ought of good,
It may by means far different be attain'd
Without ambition, war, or violence;
By deeds of peace, by wifdom eminent,
By patience, temperance: I mention ftill
Him whom thy wrongs with faintly patience borne· ·
Made famous in a land and times obfcure ;
Who names not now with honour patient Job?
Poor Socrates (who next more memorable?)
By what he taught and fuffer'd for fo doing,
For truth's fake fuffering death unjuft, lives now
Equal in fame to proudeft conquerors.
Yet if for fame and glory ought be done,
Ought fuffer'd; if young African for fame
His wafted country freed from Punic rage,
The deed becomes unprais'd, the man at leaft,
And lofes, though but verbal, his reward.
Shall I feek glory then, as vain men feek,
Oft not deferv'd? I feek not mine, but his
Who fent me', and thereby witnefs whence I am."
    To whom the Tempter murm'ring thus reply'd.
" Think not fo flight of glory; therein leaft
Refembling thy great Father: he feeks glory,

And for his glory all things made, all things
Orders and governs; nor content in Heaven
By all his angels glorify'd, requires
Glory from men, from all men good or bad,
Wife or unwife, no difference, no exemption;
Above all facrifice, or hallow'd gift
Glory' he requires, and glory he receives
Promifcuous from all nations, Jew, or Greek,
Or barbarous, nor exception hath declar'd;
From us his foes pronounc'd glory' he exacts."
  To whom our Saviour fervently reply'd.
" And reafon; fince his word all things produc'd,
Though chiefly not for glory as prime end,
But to fhew forth his goodnefs, and impart
His good communicable to every foul
Freely; of whom what could he lefs expect
Than glory' and benediction, that is thanks,
The flighteft, eafieft, readieft recompenfe
From them who could return him nothing elfe,
And not returning that would likelieft render
Contempt inftead, difhonour, obloquy?
Hard recompenfe, unfuitable return
For fo much good, fo much beneficence.
But why fhould man feek glory, who' of his own
Hath nothing, and to whom nothing belongs
But condemnation, ignominy', and fhame?
Who for fo many benefits receiv'd
Turn'd recreant to God, ingrate and falfe,
And fo of all true good himfelf defpoil'd,
Yet, facrilegious, to himfelf would take
That which to God alone of right belongs;

Yet fo much bounty is in God, fuch grace,
That who advance his glory, not their own,
Them he himfelf to glory will advance."

    So fpake the Son of God; and here again
Satan had not to anfwer, but ftood ftruck
With guilt of his own fin, for he himfelf
Infatiable of glory had loft all,
Yet of another plea bethought him foon.

    " Of glory, as thou wilt," faid he, " fo deem,
Worth or not worth the feeking, let it pafs:
But to a kingdom thou art born, ordain'd
To fit upon thy father David's throne;
By mother's fide thy father; though thy right
Be now in powerful hands, that will not part
Eafily from poffeffion won with arms:
Judea now and all the promis'd land,
Reduc'd a province under Roman yoke,
Obeys Tiberius; nor is always rul'd
With temp'rate fway; oft have they violated
The temple, oft the law with foul affronts,
Abominations rather, as did once
Antiochus: and think'ft thou to regain
Thy right by fitting ftill or thus retiring?
So did not Maccabeus: he indeed
Retir'd unto the defert, but with arms;
And o'er a mighty king fo oft prevail'd,
That by ftrong hand his family obtain'd,
Though priefts, the crown, and David's throne ufurp'd,
With Modin and her fuburbs once content.
If kingdom move thee not, let move thee zeal
And duty; zeal and duty are not flow;

But on occasion's forelock watchful wait.
They themselves rather are occasion best,
Zeal of thy father's house, duty to free
Thy country from her heathen servitude;
So shalt thou best fulfil, best verify
The prophets old, who sung thy endless reign;
The happier reign the sooner it begins;
Reign then; what canst thou better do the while?"
    To whom our Saviour answer thus return'd.
" All things are best fulfill'd in their due time,
And time there is for all things, Truth hath said:
If of my reign prophetic writ hath told,
That it shall never end, so when begin
The father in his purpose hath decreed,
He in whose hand all times and seasons roll.
What if he hath decreed that I shall first
Be try'd in humble state, and things adverse,
By tribulations, injuries, insults,
Contempts, and scorns, and snares, and violence,
Suffering, abstaining, quietly expecting,
Without distrust or doubt, that he may know
What I can suffer, how obey? who best
Can suffer, best can do; best reign, who first
Well hath obey'd; just trial ere I merit
My exaltation without change or end.
But what concerns it thee when I begin
My everlasting kingdom, why art thou
Solicitous, what moves thy inquisition?
Know'st thou not that my rising is thy fall,
And my promotion will be thy destruction?"
    To whom the Tempter inly rack'd reply'd.

                        E

" Let that come when it comes; all hope is loft
Of my reception into grace; what worfe?
For where no hope is left, is left no fear:
If there be worfe, the expectation more
Of worfe torments me than the feeling can.
I would be at the worft; worft is my port,
My harbour and my ultimate repofe,
The end I would attain, my final good.
My errour was my errour, and my crime
My crime; whatever for itfelf condemn'd,
And will alike be punifh'd, whether thou
Reign or reign not; though to that gentle brow
Willingly I could fly, and hope thy reign,
From that placid afpéct and meek regard,
Rather than aggravate my evil ftate,
Would ftand between me and thy Father's ire
(Whofe ire I dread more than the fire of Hell)
A fhelter and a kind of fhading cool
Interpofition, as a fummer's cloud.
If I then to the worft that can be hafte,
Why move thy feet fo flow to what is beft,
Happieft both to thyfelf and all the world,
That thou who worthieft art fhould'ft be their king?
Perhaps thou linger'ft in deep thoughts detain'd
Of th' enterprife fo hazardous and high;
No wonder, for though in thee be united
What of perfection can in man be found,
Or human nature can receive, confider
Thy life hath yet been private, moft part fpent
At home, fcarce view'd the Galilean towns,
And once a year Jerufalem, few days

Short fojourn; and what thence could'ft thou obferve?
The world thou haft not feen, much lefs her glory,
Empires, and monarchs, and their radiant courts,
Beft fchool of beft experience, quickeft infight
In all things that to greateft actions lead.
The wifeft, unexperienc'd, will be ever
Timorous and loath, with novice modefty,
(As he who feeking affes found a kingdom)
Irrefolute, unhardy, unadvent'rous:
But I will bring thee where thou foon fhalt quit
Thofe rudiments, and fee before thine eyes
The monarchies of th' earth, their pomp and ftate,   ——
Sufficient introduction to inform
Thee, of thyfelf fo apt, in regal arts,
And regal myfteries, that thou may'ft know
How beft their oppofition to withftand."

   With that (fuch pow'r was giv'n him then) he took
The Son of God up to a mountain high.
It was a mountain at whofe verdant feet
A fpacious plain out-ftretch'd in circuit wide
Lay pleafant; from his fide two rivers flow'd,
Th' one winding, th' other ftrait, and left between
Fair champain with lefs rivers intervein'd,
Then meeting join'd their tribute to the fea:
Fertile of corn the glebe, of oil and wine;
With herds the paftures throng'd, with flocks the hills;
Huge cities and high towr'd, that well might feem
The feats of mightieft monarchs, and fo large
The profpect was, that here and there was room
For barren defert fountainlefs and dry.
To this high mountain top the Tempter brought

Our Saviour, and new train of words began.

" Well have we fpeeded, and o'er hill and dale,
Foreft and field and flood, temples and towers,
Cut fhorter many a league; here thou behold'ft
Affyria and her empire's ancient bounds,
Araxes and the Cafpian lake, thence on
As far as Indus eaft, Euphrates weft,
And oft beyond; to fouth the Perfian bay,
And inacceffible th' Arabian drouth:
Here Nineveh, of length within her wall
Several days journey, built by Ninus old,
Of that firft golden monarchy the feat,
And feat of Salmanaffar, whofe fuccefs
Ifrael in long captivity ftill mourns;
There Babylon, the wonder of all tongues,
As ancient, but rebuilt by him who twice
Judah and all thy father David's houfe
Led captive, and Jerufalem laid wafte,
Till Cyrus fet them free; Perfepolis
His city there thou feeft, and Bactra there;
Ecbatana her ftructure vaft there fhows,
And Hecatompylos her hundred gates;
There Sufa by Choafpes, amber ftream,
The drink of none but kings; of later fame
Built by Emathian, or by Parthian hands,
The great Seleucia, Nifibis, and there
Artaxata, Teredon, Ctefiphon,
Turning with eafy eye thou may'ft behold.
All thefe the Parthian, now fome ages paft,
By great Arfaces led, who founded firft
That empire, under his dominion holds,

From the luxurious kings of Antioch won.
And juſt in time thou com'ſt to have a view
Of his great pow'r; for now the Parthian king
In Cteſiphon hath gather'd all his hoſt
Againſt the Scythian, whoſe incurſions wild
Have waſted Sogdiana; to her aid
He marches now in haſte; ſee, though from far,
His thouſands, in what martial equipage
They iſſue forth, ſteel bows, and ſhafts their arms
Of equal dread in flight, or in purſuit;
All horſemen, in which fight they moſt excel;
See how in warlike muſter they appear,
In rhombs and wedges, and half-moons and wings."
    He look'd, and ſaw what numbers numberleſs
The city gates out-pour'd, light armed troops
In coats of mail and military pride;
In mail their horſes clad, yet fleet and ſtrong,
Prauncing their riders bore, the flow'r and choice
Of many provinces from bound to bound;
From Arachoſia, from Candaor eaſt,
And Margiana to the Hyrcanian cliffs
Of Caucaſus, and dark Iberian dales,
From Atropaſia and the neighb'ring plains
Of Adiabene, Media, and the ſouth
Of Suſiana, to Balſara's haven.
He ſaw them in their forms of battle rang'd,
How quick they wheel'd, and fly'ing behind them ſhot
Sharp ſleet of arrowy ſhow'rs againſt the face
Of their purſuers, and overcame by flight;
The field all iron caſt a gleaming brown:
Nor wanted clouds of foot, nor on each horn

Cuiraffiers all in fteel for ftanding fight,
Chariots or elephants indors'd with towers
Of archers, nor of lab'ring pioneers
A multitude with fpades and axes arm'd
To lay hills plain, fell woods, or valleys fill,
Or where plain was raife hill, or overlay
With bridges rivers proud, as with a yoke;
Mules after thefe, camels and dromedaries,
And waggons fraught with utenfils of war.
Such forces met not, nor fo wide a camp,
When Agrican with all his northern powers
Befieg'd Albracca, as romances tell,
The city' of Gallaphrone, from thence to win
The faireft of her fex Angelica
His daughter, fought by many proweft knights,
Both Paynim, and the peers of Charlemain.
Such and fo numerous was their chivalry;
At fight whereof the Fiend yet more prefum'd,
And to our Saviour thus his words renew'd.

" That thou may'ft know I feek not to engage
Thy virtue, and not every way fecure
On no flight grounds thy fafety; hear, and mark
To what end I have brought thee hither and fhown
All this fair fight: thy kingdom though foretold
By prophet or by angel, unlefs thou
Endeavour, as thy father David did,
Thou never fhalt obtain; prediction ftill
In all things, and all men, fuppofes means,
Without means us'd, what it predicts revokes.
But fay thou wert poffefs'd of David's throne
By free confent of all, none oppofite,

Samaritan or Jew; how could'ft thou hope
Long to enjoy it quiet and fecure,
Between two fuch inclofing enemies
Roman and Parthian? therefore one of thefe
Thou muft make fure thy own, the Parthian firft
By my advice, as nearer, and of late
Found able by invafion to annoy
Thy country', and captive lead away her kings
Antigonus, and old Hyrcanus bound,
Maugre the Roman: it fhall be my tafk
To render thee the Parthian at difpofe;
Choofe which thou wilt by conqueft or by league.
By him thou fhalt regain, without him not,
That which alone can truly reinftall thee     ·
In David's royal feat, his true fucceffor,
Deliverance of thy brethren, thofe ten tribes
Whofe offspring in his territory yet ferve,
In Habor, and among the Medes difpers'd;
Ten fons of Jacob, two of Jofeph loft
Thus long from Ifrael, ferving as of old
Their fathers in the land of Egypt ferv'd,
This offer fets before thee to deliver.
Thefe if from fervitude thou fhalt reftore
To their inheritance, then, nor till then,
Thou on the throne of David in full glory,
From Egypt to Euphrates and beyond
Shalt reign, and Rome or Cæfar not need fear." /
     To whom our Saviour anfwer'd thus unmov'd.
" Much oftentation vain of flefhly arm,
And fragil arms, much inftrument of war
Long in preparing, foon to nothing.brought,

Before mine eyes thou' haft fet; and in my ear
Vented much policy, and projects deep
Of enemies, of aids, battles, and leagues,
Plaufible to the world, to me worth nought.
Means I muft ufe, thou fay'ft, prediction elfe
Will unpredict and fail me of the throne:
My time I told thee (and that time for thee
Were better fartheft off) is not yet come;
When that comes, think not thou to find me flack
On my part ought endeavouring, or to need
Thy politic maxims, or that cumberfome
Luggage of war there fhown me, argument
Of human weaknefs rather than of ftrength.
My brethren, as thou call'ft them, thofe ten tribes
I muft deliver, if I mean to reign
David's true heir, and his full fceptre fway
To juft extent over all Ifrael's fons;
But whence to thee this zeal, where was it then
For Ifrael, or for David, or his throne,
When thou ftood'ft up his tempter to the pride
Of numb'ring Ifrael, which coft the lives
Of threefcore and ten thoufand Ifraelites
By three days' peftilence? fuch was thy zeal
To Ifrael then, the fame that now to me.
As for thofe captive tribes, themfelves were they
Who wrought their own captivity, fell off
From God to worfhip calves, the deities
Of Egypt, Baal next and Afhtaroth,
And all th' idolatries of Heathen round,
Befides their other worfe than heath'nifh crimes;
Nor in the land of their captivity

Humbled themſelves, or penitent beſought
The God of their forefathers; but ſo dy'd
Impenitent, and left a race behind
Like to themſelves, diſtinguiſhable ſcarce
From Gentiles, but by circumciſion vain,
And God with idols in their worſhip join'd.
Should I of theſe the liberty regard,
Who freed, as to their ancient patrimony,
Unhumbled, unrepentant, unreform'd,
Headlong would follow'; and to their gods perhaps
Of Bethel and of Dan? no, let them ſerve
Their enemies, who ſerve idols with God.
Yet he at length, time to himſelf beſt known,
Rememb'ring Abraham, by ſome wond'rous call
May bring them back repentant and ſincere,
And at their paſſing cleave th' Aſſyrian flood,
While to their native land with joy they haſte,
As the Red Sea and Jordan once he cleft,
When to the promis'd land their fathers paſs'd;
To his due time and providence I leave them."
   So ſpake Iſrael's true king, and to the Fiend
Made anſwer meet, that made void all his wiles.
So fares it when with truth falſehood contends.

THE

FOURTH BOOK

OF

PARADISE REGAINED.

# PARADISE REGAINED.

## BOOK IV.

Perplex'd and troubled at his bad fuccefs
The Tempter ftood, nor had what to reply,
Difcover'd in his fraud, thrown from his hope
So oft, and the perfuafive rhetoric
That fleek'd his tongue, and won fo much on Eve,
So little here, nay loft; but Eve was Eve,
This far his over-match, who, felf-deceiv'd
And rafh, beforehand had no better weigh'd
The ftrength he was to cope with, or his own:
But as a man who had been matchlefs held          10
In cunning, over-reach'd where leaft he thought,
To falve his credit, and for very fpite,
Still will be tempting him who foils him ftill,
And never ceafe, though to his fhame the more;
Or as a fwarm of flies in vintage time,
About the wine-prefs where fweet muft is pour'd,
Beat off, returns as oft with humming found;
Or furging waves againft a folid rock;

Though all to ſhivers daſh'd, th' aſſault renew,
Vain batt'ry, and in froth or bubbles end;
So Satan, whom repulſe upon repulſe
Met ever, and to ſhameful ſilence brought,
Yet gives not o'er, though deſp'rate of ſuccefs,
And his vain importunity purſues.
He brought our Saviour to the weſtern ſide
Of that high mountain, whence he might behold
Another plain, long but in breadth not wide,
Waſh'd by the ſouthern ſea, and on the north
To equal length back'd with a ridge of hills,
That ſcreen'd the fruits of th' earth and ſeats of men
From cold Septentrion blaſts, thence in the midſt
Divided by a river, of whoſe banks
On each ſide an imperial city ſtood,
With tow'rs and temples proudly elevate
On ſev'n ſmall hills, with palaces adorn'd,
Porches and theatres, baths, aqueduĉts,
Statues and trophies, and triumphal arcs,
Gardens and groves preſented to his eyes,
Above the height of mountains interpos'd:
By what ſtrange parallax or optic ſkill
Of viſion multiply'd through air, or glaſs
Of teleſcope, were curious to inquire:
And now the Tempter thus his ſilence broke.
  " The city which thou ſeeſt no other deem
Than great and glorious Rome, queen of the earth
So far renown'd, and with the ſpoils enrich'd
Of nations; there the capitol thou ſeeſt
Above the reſt lifting his ſtately head
On the Tarpeian rock, her citadel

Impregnable, and there mount Palatine,      *50*
Th' imperial palace, compafs huge, and high
The ftructure, fkill of nobleft architects,
With gilded battlements, confpicuous far,
Turrets and terraces, and glitt'ring fpires.  `
Many a fair edifice befides, more like
Houfes of gods, (fo ,well I have difpos'd
My aery microfcope) thou may'ft behold
Outfide and infide both, pillars and roofs,
Carv'd work, the hand of fam'd artificers
In cedar, marble, ivory, or gold.      *60*
Thence to the gates caft round thine eye, and fee
What conflux iffuing forth, or ent'ring in,
Pretors, proconfuls to their provinces
Hafting, or on return, in robes of ftate;
Lictors and rods, the enfigns of their pow'r,
Legions and cohorts, turms of horfe and wings:
Or embaffies from regions far remote
In various habits on the Appian road,
Or on th' Æmilian, fome from fartheft fouth,
Syene', and where the fhadow both way falls,    *70*
Meroe Nilotic ifle, and more to weft,
The realm of Bocchus to the Black-moor fea;
From th' Afian kings and Parthian among thefe,
From India and the golden Cherfonefe,
And utmoft Indian ifle. Taprobane,
Dufk faces with white filken turbans wreath'd;
From Gallia, Gades, and the Britifh weft,
Germans and Scythians, and Sarmatians north
Beyond Danubius to the Tauric pool.
All nations now to Rome obedience pay,      *80*

To Rome's great emperor, whofe wide domain
In ample territory, wealth and power,
Civility of manners, arts and arms,
And long renown, thou juftly may'ft prefer
Before the Parthian; thefe two thrones except,
The reft are barb'rous, and fcarce worth the fight,
Shar'd among petty kings too far remov'd;
Thefe having fhown thee, I have fhown thee all
The kingdoms of the world, and all their glory.
90 This emp'ror hath no fon, and now is old,
Old and lafcivious, and from Rome retir'd
To Capreæ an ifland fmall but ftrong
On the Campanian fhore, with purpofe there
His horrid lufts in private to enjoy,
Committing to a wicked favourite
All public cares, and yet of him fufpicious,
Hated of all, and hating; with what eafe,
Indued with regal virtues as thou art,
Appearing, and beginning noble deeds,
100 Might'ft thou expel this monfter from his throne
Now made a ftye, and in his place afcending
A victor people free from fervile yoke?
And with my help thou may'ft; to me the power
Is giv'n, and by that right I give it thee.
Aim therefore at no lefs than all the world,
Aim at the high'eft, without the high'eft attain'd
Will be for thee no fitting, or not long,
On David's throne, be prophefy'd what will."
    To whom the Son of God unmov'd reply'd.
110 " Nor doth this grandeur and majeftic fhow
Of luxury, though call'd magnificence,

More than of arms before, allure mine eye,
Much lefs my mind; though thou fhould'ft add to tell
Their fumptuous gluttonies, and gorgeous feafts
On citron tables or Atlantic ftone,
(For I have alfo heard, perhaps have read)
Their wines of Setia, Cales, and Falerne,
Chios, and Crete, and how they quaff in gold,
Cryftal and myrrhine cups imbofs'd with gems
And ftuds of pearl, to me fhould'ft tell who thirft
And hunger ftill: then embaffies thou fhow'ft
From nations far and nigh; what honour that,
But tedious wafte of time to fit and hear
So many hollow compliments and lies,
Outlandifh flatteries? then proceed'ft to talk
Of th' emperor, how eafily fubdued,
How glorioufly; I fhall, thou fay'ft, expel
A brutifh monfter: what if I withal
Expel a devil who firft made him fuch?
Let his tormenter confcience find him out;
For him I was not fent, nor yet to free
That people victor once, now vile and bafe,
Defervedly made vaffal, who once juft,
Frugal, and mild, and temp'rate, conquer'd well,
But govern ill the nations under yoke,
Peeling their provinces, exhaufted all
By luft and rapine; firft ambitious grown
Of triumph, that infulting vanity;
Then cruel, by their fports to blood inur'd
Of fighting beafts, and men to beafts expos'd,
Luxurious by their wealth, and greedier ftill,
And from the daily fcene effeminate.

F

What wife and valiant man would feek to free
Thefe thus degenerate, by themfelves inflav'd,
Or could of inward flaves make outward free?
Know therefore when my feafon comes to fit
On David's throne, it fhall be like a tree
Spreading and overfhadowing all the earth,
Or as a ftone that fhall to pieces dafh
All monarchies befides throughout the world,
And of my kingdom there fhall be no end:
Means there fhall be to this, but what the means,
Is not for thee to know, nor me to tell."
        To whom the Tempter impudent reply'd,
" I fee all offers made by me how flight
Thou valueft, becaufe offered, and rejeсt'ft:
Nothing will pleafe the difficult and nice,
Or nothing more than ftill to contradiсt:
On th' other fide know alfo thou, that I
On what I offer fet as high efteem,                    .
Nor what I part with mean to give for nought;
All thefe which in a moment thou behold'ft,
The kingdoms of the world to thee I give;
For giv'n to me, I give to whom I pleafe,
No trifle; yet with this referve, not elfe,
On this condition, if thou wilt fall down,
And worfhip me as thy fuperior lord,
Eafily done, and hold them all of me;
For what can lefs fo great a gift deferve?"
        Whom thus our Saviour anfwer'd with difdain.
" I never lik'd thy talk, thy offers lefs,
Now both abhor, fince thou haft dar'd to utter
Th' abominable terms, impious condition;

But I endure the time, till which expir'd,
Thou haſt permiſſion on me.  It is written
The firſt of all commandments, Thou ſhalt worſhip
The Lord thy God, and only him ſhalt ſerve;
And dar'ſt thou to the Son of God propound
To worſhip thee accurs'd, now more accurs'd
For this attempt bolder than that on Eve,
And more blaſphemous? which expect to rue.
The kingdoms of the world to thee were given,
Permitted rather, and by thee uſurp'd; ·
Other donation none thou canſt produce:
If giv'n, by whom but by the king of kings,
God over all ſupreme? if giv'n to thee,
By thee how fairly is the giver now
Repaid? But gratitude in thee is loſt
Long ſince.  Wert thou ſo void of fear or ſhame,
As offer them to me the Son of God,
To me my own, on ſuch abhorred pact,
That I fall down and worſhip thee as God?
Get thee behind me; plain thou now appear'ſt
That evil one, Satan for ever damn'd."
      To whom the Fiend with fear abaſh'd reply'd.
" Be not ſo ſore offended, Son of God,
Though ſons of God both angels are and men,
If I to try whether in higher ſort
Than theſe thou bear'ſt that title, have propos'd
What both from men and angels I receive,
Tetrarchs of fire, air, flood, and on the earth
Nations beſides from all the quarter'd winds,
God of this world invok'd and world beneath;
Who then thou art, whoſe coming is foretold

To me fo fatal, me it moft concerns.
The trial hath indamag'd thee no way,
Rather more honour left and more efteem;
Me nought advantag'd, miffing what I aimed.
Therefore let pafs, as they are tranfitory,
The kingdoms of this world; I fhall no more
Advife thee; gain them as thou canft, or not.
And thou thyfelf feem'ft otherwife inclin'd
Than to a worldly crown, addiĉted more
To contemplation and profound difpute,
As by that early aĉtion may be judg'd,
When flipping from thy mother's eye thou went'ft
*Alone into the temple; there waft found
Among the graveft rabbies difputant
On points and queftions fitting Mofes chair,
Teaching not taught; the childhood fhows the man,
As morning fhows the day. Be famous then
By wifdom; as thy empire muft extend,
So let extend thy mind o'er all the world
In knowledge, all things in it comprehend:
All knowledge is not couch'd in Mofes law,
The Pentateuch, or what the prophets wrote;
The Gentiles alfo know, and write, and teach
To admiration, led by nature's light;
And with the Gentiles much thou muft converfe,
Ruling them by perfuafion as thou mean'ft;
Without their learning how wilt thou with them,
Or they with thee hold converfation meet?
How wilt thou reafon with them, how refute
Their idolifms, traditions, paradoxes?
Errour by his own arms is beft evinc'd.

Look once more ere we leave this fpecular mount
Weftward, much nearer by fouthweft, behold
Where on the Ægean fhore a city ftands
Built nobly, pure the air, and light the foil,
Athens the eye of Greece, mother of arts
And eloquence, native to famous wits
Or hofpitable, in her fweet recefs,
City' or fuburban, ftudious walks and fhades;
See there the olive grove of Academe,
Plato's retirement, where the Attic bird
Trills her thick-warbled notes the fummer long;
There flow'ry hill Hymettus with the found
Of bees induftrious murmur oft invites
To ftudious mufing; there Iliffus rolls
His whifp'ring ftream: within the walls then view
The fchools of ancient fages; his who bred
Great Alexander to fubdue the world,
Lyceum there, and painted Stoa next:
There thou fhalt hear and learn the fecret power
Of harmony in tones and numbers hit
By voice or hand, and various-meafur'd verfe, .
Æolian charms and Dorian lyric odes,
And his who gave them breath, but highcr fung,
Blind Melefigenes thence Homer call'd,
Whofe poem Phœbus challeng'd for his own.
Thence what the lofty grave tragedians taught
In chorus or Iambic, teachers beft
Of moral prudence, with delight receiv'd
In brief fententious precepts, while they treat
Of fate, and chance, and change in human life;
High actions, and high paffions beft defcribing:

Thence to the famous orators repair,
Those ancient, whose refiftlefs eloquence
Wielded at will that fierce democratie,
Shook th' arfenal and fulmin'd over Greece,
To Macedon and Artaxerxes throne:
To fage philofophy next lend thine ear,
From Heav'n defcended to the low-rooft houfe,
Of Socrates; fee there his tenement,
Whom well infpir'd the oracle pronounc'd
Wifeft of men; from whofe mouth iffued forth
Mellifluous ftreams that water'd all the fchools
Of Academics old and new, with thofe
Surnam'd Peripatetics, and the fect
Epicurean, and the Stoic fevere;
Thefe here revolve, or, as thou lik'ft, at home,
Till time mature thee to a kingdom's weight;
Thefe rules will render thee a king complete
Within thyfelf, much more with empire join'd."
    To whom our Saviour fagely thus reply'd.
" Think not but that I know thefe things, or think
I know them not; not therefore am I fhort
Of knowing what I ought: he who receives
Light from above, from the fountain of light,
No other doctrine needs, though granted true;
But thefe are falfe, or little elfe but dreams,
Conjectures, fancies, built on nothing firm.
The firft and wifeft of them all profefs'd
To know this only, that he nothing knew;
The next to fabling fell and fmooth conceits;
A third fort doubted all things, though plain fenfe;
Others in virtue plac'd felicity,

But virtue join'd with riches and long life;
In corporal pleafure he, and carelefs eafe;
The Stoic laft in philofophic pride,
By him call'd virtue; and his virtuous man,
Wife, perfect in himfelf, and all poffeffing,
Equals to God, oft fhames not to prefer,
As fearing God nor man, contemning all
Wealth, pleafure, pain or torment, death and life,
Which when he lifts, he leaves, or boafts he can,
For all his tedious talk is but vain boaft,
Or fubtle fhifts conviction to evade.
Alas! what can they teach, and not miflead,
Ignorant of themfelves, of God much more,
And how the world began, and how man fell
Degraded by himfelf, on grace depending?
Much of the foul they talk, but all awry,
And in themfelves feek virtue, and to themfelves
All glory arrogate, to God give none,
Rather accufe him under ufual names,
Fortune and Fate, as one regardlefs quite
Of mortal things.    Who therefore feeks in thefe
True wifdom, finds her not, or by delufion
Far worfe, her falfe refemblance only meets,
An empty cloud.    However many books,
Wife men have faid, are wearifome; who reads
Inceffantly, and to his reading brings not
A fpirit and judgment equal or fuperior,
(And what he brings, what needs he elfewhere feek?)
Uncertain and unfettled ftill remains,
Deep vers'd in books and fhallow in himfelf,
Crude or intoxicate, collecting toys,

And trifles for choice matters, worth a fpunge;
As children gathering pebbles on the fhore.
Or if I would delight my private hours
With mufic or with poem, where fo foon
As in our native language can I find
That folace? All our law and ftory ftrow'd
With hymns, our pfalms with artful terms infcrib'd,
Our Hebrew fongs and harps in Babylon,
That pleas'd fo well our victors ear, declare
That rather Greece from us thefe arts deriv'd;
Ill imitated, while they loudeft fing
The vices of their deities, and their own
In fable, hymn, or fong, fo perfonating
Their gods ridiculous, and themfelves paft fhame.
Remove their fwelling epithets thick laid
As varnifh on a harlot's cheek, the reft,
Thin fown with ought of profit or delight,
Will far be found unworthy to compare
With Sion's fongs, to all true taftes excelling,
Where God is prais'd aright, and god-like men,
The Holieft of Holies, and his Saints;
Such are from God infpir'd, not fuch from thee,
Unlefs where moral virtue is exprefs'd
By light of nature not in all quite loft.
Their orators thou then extoll'ft, as thofe
The top of eloquence, ftatifts indeed,
And lovers of their country, as may feem;
But herein to our prophets far beneath,
As men divinely taught, and better teaching
The folid rules of civil government
In their majeftic unaffected ftyle

Than all the' oratory of Greece and Rome.
In them is plaineſt taught, and eaſieſt learnt,
What makes a nation happy', and keeps it ſo,
What ruins kingdoms, and lays cities flat;
Theſe only with our law beſt form a king."

   So ſpake the Son of God; but Satan now
Quite at a loſs, for all his darts were ſpent,
Thus to our Saviour with ſtern brow reply'd,

   " Since neither wealth nor honour, arms nor arts,
Kingdom nor empire pleaſes thee, nor ought
By me propos'd in life contemplative,
Or active, tended on by glory', or fame,
What doſt thou in this world? the wildernefs
For thee is fitteſt place; I found thee there,
And thither will return thee; yet remember
What I foretel thee, ſoon thou ſhalt have cauſe
To wiſh thou never hadſt rejected thus
Nicely or cautiouſly my offer'd aid,
Which would have ſet thee in ſhort time with eaſe
On David's throne, or throne of all the world,
Now at full age, fulneſs of time, thy ſeaſon,
When prophecies of thee are beſt fulfill'd.
Now contrary, if I read ought in Heaven,
Or Heav'n write ought of fate, by what the ſtars
Voluminous, or ſingle characters,
In their conjunction met, give me to ſpell,
Sorrows, and labours, oppoſition, hate
Attends thee, ſcorns, reproaches, injuries,
Violence and ſtripes, and laſtly cruel death;
A kingdom they portend thee, but what kingdom,
Real or allegoric I diſcern not,

Nor when, eternal fure, as without end,
Without beginning; for no date prefix'd
Directs me in the ftarry rubric fet."
　　So fay'ing he took (for ftill he knew his power
Not yet expir'd) and to the wildernefs
Brought back the Son of God, and left him there,
Feigning to difappear.　Darknefs now rofe,
As day-light funk, and brought in louring night
Her fhadowy offspring, unfubftantial both,
Privation mere of light and abfent day,
Our Saviour mcek and with untroubled mind
After his aery jaunt, though hurricd fore,
Hungry and cold betook him to his reft,
Wherever, under fome concourfe of fhades,
Whofe branching arms thick intertwin'd might fhield
From dews and damps of night his fhelter'd head,
But fhelter'd flept in vain, for at his hcad
The Tempter watch'd, and foon with ugly dreams
Difturb'd his fleep; and either tropic now
'Gan thunder, and both ends of Heav'n, the clouds
From many a horrid rift abortive pour'd
Fierce rain with lightning mix'd, water with fire
In ruin reconcil'd: nor flept the winds
Within their ftony caves, but rufh'd abroad
From the four hinges of the world, and fcll
On the vex'd wildernefs, whofe talleft pines,
Though rooted deep as high, and fturdieft oaks
Bow'd their ftiff necks, loaden with ftormy blafts,
Or torn up fheer: ill waft thou fhroudcd thcn,
O patient Son of God, yet only ftood'ft
Unfhaken; nor yet ftay'd the terrour there,

Infernal ghofts, and Hellifh furies, round
Environ'd thee, fome howl'd, fome yell'd, fome fhriek'd,
Some bent at thee their fiery darts, while thou
Sat'ft unappall'd in calm and finlefs peace.
Thus pafs'd the night fo foul, till morning fair
Came forth with pilgrim fteps in amice grey,
Who with her radiant finger ftill'd the roar
Of thunder, chas'd the clouds, and laid the winds,
And grifly fpeftres, which the Fiend had rais'd
To tempt the Son of God with terrours dire.
And now the fun with more effeftual beams
Had cheer'd the face of earth, and dry'd the wet
From drooping plant, or dropping tree; the birds,
Who all things now behold more frefh and green,
After a night of ftorm fo ruinous,
Clear'd up their choiceft notes in bufh and fpray
To gratulate the fweet return of morn;
Nor yet amidft this joy and brighteft morn
Was abfent, after all his mifchief done,
The prince of darknefs, glad would alfo feem
Of this fair change, and to our Saviour came,
Yet with no new device, they all were fpent,
Rather by this his laft affront refolv'd,
Defp'rate of better courfe, to vent his rage,
And mad defpite to be fo oft repell'd.
Him walking on a funny hill he found,
Back'd on the north and weft by a thick wood;
Out of the wood he ftarts in wonted fhape,
And in a carelefs mood thus to him faid.

" Fair morning yet betides thee, Son of God,
After a difmal night; I heard the wrack

As earth and fky would mingle; but myfelf
Was diftant; and thefe flaws, though mortals fear them
As dang'rous to the pillar'd frame of Heaven,
Or to the earth's dark bafis underneath,
Are to the main as inconfiderable,
And harmlefs, if not wholefome, as a fneeze
To man's lefs univerfe, and foon are gone;
Yet as being oft times noxious where they light
On man, beaft, plant, wafteful and turbulent,
Like turbulences in th' affairs of men,
Over whofe heads they roar, and feem to point,
They oft fore-fignify and threaten ill:
This tempeft at this defert moft was bent;
Of men at thee, for only thou here dwell'ft.
Did I not tell thee, if thou didft reject
The perfect feafon offer'd with my aid
To win thy deftin'd feat, but wilt prolong
All to the pufh of fate, purfue thy way
Of gaining David's throne no man knows when,
For both the when and how is no where told,
Thou fhalt be what thou art ordain'd, no doubt;
For Angels have proclaim'd it, but concealing
The time and means: each act is rightlieft done,
Not when it muft, but when it may be beft.
If thou obferve not this, be fure to find,
What I foretold thee, many a hard affay
Of dangers, and adverfities, and pains,
Ere thou of Ifrael's fceptre get faft hold;
Whereof this ominous night that clos'd thee round,
So many terrours, voices, prodigies
May warn thee, as a fure fore-going fign."

So talk'd he, while the Son of God went on
And ftay'd not, but in brief him anfwer'd thus.

" Me worfe than wet thou find'ft not; other harm
Thofe terrours which thou fpeak'ft of, did me none;
I never fear'd they could, though noifing loud
And threat'ning nigh; what they can do as figns
Betokening, or ill boding, I contemn
As falfe portents, not fent from God, but thee;
Who knowing I fhall reign paft thy preventing,
Obtrud'ft thy offer'd aid, that I accepting
At leaft might feem to hold all pow'r of thee,
Ambitious fpi'rit, and would'ft be thought my God,
And ftorm'ft refus'd, thinking to terrify
Me to thy will; defift, thou art difcern'd
And toil'ft in vain, nor me in vain moleft."

To whom the Fiend, now fwoln with rage, reply'd.
" Then hear, O Son of David, virgin-born;
For Son of God to me is yet in doubt:
Of the Meffiah I have heard foretold
By all the prophets; of thy birth at length
Announc'd by Gabriel with the firft I knew,
And of th' angelic fong in Bethlehem field,
On thy birth-night, that fung thee Saviour born.
From that time feldom have I ceas'd to eye
Thy infancy, thy childhood, and thy youth,
Thy manhood laft, though yet in private bred;
Till at the ford of Jordan whither all
Flock'd to the Baptift, I among the reft,
Though not to be baptiz'd, by voice from Heaven
Heard thee pronounc'd the Son of God belov'd.

Thenceforth I thought thee worth my nearer view
And narrower fcrutiny, that I might learn
In what degree or meaning thou art call'd
The Son of God, which bears no fingle fenfe;
The Son of God I alfo am, or was,
And if I was, I am; relation ftands;
All men are fons of God; yet thee I thought
In fome refpect far higher fo declar'd.
Therefore I watch'd thy footfteps from that hour,
And follow'd thee ftill on to this wafte wild;
Where by all beft conjectures I collect
Thou art to me my fatal enemy.
Good reafon then, if I before-hand feek
To underftand my adverfary, who
And what he is; his wifdom, pow'r, intent;
. By parl, or compofition, truce, or league
To win him, or win from him what I can.
And opportunity I here have had        .
To try thee, fift thee, and confefs have found thee
Proof againft all temptation, as a rock
Of adamant, and as a centre, firm,
To th' utmoft of mere man both wife and good,
Not more; for honours, riches, kingdoms, glory,
Have been before contemn'd, and may again:
Therefore to know what more thou art than man,
Worth naming Son of God by voice from Heav'n,
Another method I muft now begin."
    So fay'ing he caught him up, and without wing
Of hippogrif bore through the air fublime
Over the wildernefs and o'er the plain;

Till underneath them fair Jerufalem,
The holy city lifted high her towers,
And higher yet the glorious temple rear'd
Her pile, far off appearing like a mount
Of alabafter, topt with golden fpires:
There on the higheft pinnacle he fet
The Son of God, and added thus in fcorn.

" There ftand, if thou wilt ftand; to ftand upright
Will afk thee fkill; I to thy Father's houfe
Have brought thee', and higheft plac'd, higheft is beft,
Now fhow thy progeny; if not to ftand,
Caft thyfelf down; fafely, if Son of God:
For it is written, He will give command
Concerning thee to his angels, in their hands
They fhall uplift thee, left at any time
Thou chance to dafh thy foot againft a ftone."

To whom thus Jefus; " Alfo it is written,
Tempt not the Lord thy God: he faid, and ftood:"
But Satan fmitten with amazement fell.
As when earth's fon Antæus (to compare
Small things with greateft) in Iraffa ftrove
With Jove's Alcides, and oft foil'd ftill rofe,
Receiving from his mother earth new ftrength,
Frefh from his fall, and fiercer grapple join'd,
Throttled at length in th' air, expir'd and fell;
So after many a foil the Tempter proud,
Renewing frefh affaults, amidft his pride
Fell whence he ftood to fee his victor fall.
And as that Theban monfter that propos'd
Her riddle', and him, who folv'd it not, devour'd,

That once found out and folv'd, for grief and fpite
Caft herfelf headlong from th' Ifmenian fteep;
So ftruck with dread and anguifh fell the Fiend,
And to his crew, that fat confulting, brought
Joylefs triumphals of his hop'd fuccefs,
Ruin, and defperation, and difmay,
Who durft fo proudly tempt the Son of God.
So Satan fell; and ftraight a fiery globe
Of angels on full fail of wing flew nigh,
Who on their plumy vans receiv'd him foft
From his uneafy ftation, and up bore
As on a floating couch through the blithe air,
Then in a flow'ry valley fet him down
On a green bank, and fet before him fpread
A table of celeftial food, divine,
Ambrofial fruits, fetch'd from the tree of life,
And from the fount of life ambrofial drink,
That foon refrefh'd him wearied, and repair'd
What hunger, if ought hunger had impair'd,
Or thirft; and as he fed, angelic quires
Sung heav'nly anthems of his victory
Over temptation, and the Tempter proud.
   True image of the Father, whether thron'd
In the bofom of blifs, and light of light
Conceiving, or remote from Heav'n, infhrin'd
In flefhly tabernacle, and human form,
Wand'ring the wildernefs, whatever place,
Habit, or ftate, or motion, ftill exprefling
The Son of God, with godlike force indued
Againft th' attempter of thy Father's throne,

And thief of Paradife; him long of old
Thou didft debel, and down from Heaven caft
With all his army, now thou haft aveng'd
Supplanted Adam, and by vanquifhing
Temptation, haft regain'd loft Paradife;
And fruftrated the conqueft fraudulent:
He never more henceforth will dare fet foot
In Paradife to tempt; his fnares are broke:
For though that feat of earthly blifs be fail'd,
A fairer Paradife is founded now
For Adam and his chofen fons, whom thou
A Saviour art come down to reinftall
Where they fhall dwell fecure, when time fhall be,
Of Tempter and temptation without fear.
But thou, infernal Serpent, fhalt not long
Rule in the clouds; like an autumnal ftar
Or lightning thou fhalt fall from Heav'n, trod down
Under his feet: for proof, ere this thou feel'ft
Thy wound, yet not thy laft and deadlieft wound,
By this repulfe receiv'd, and hold'ft in Hell
No triumph; in all her gates Abaddon rues
Thy bold attempt; hereafter learn with awe
To dread the Son of God: he all unarm'd
Shall chace thee with the terrour of his voice
From thy demoniac holds, poffeffion foul,
Thee and thy legions; yelling they fhall fly,
And beg to hide them in a herd of fwine,
Left he command them down into the deep
Bound, and to torment fent before their time.
Hail Son of the Moft High, heir of both worlds,

G

Queller of Satan, on thy glorious work
Now enter, and begin to fave mankind.

Thus they the Son of God our Saviour meek
Sung victor, and from heav'nly feaft refrefh'd
Brought on his way with joy; he unobferv'd
Home to his mother's houfe private return'd.


END OF PARADISE REGAINED.

# SAMSON AGONISTES.

A

## DRAMATIC POEM.

Τραγωδια μιμησις πραξεως σπυδαιας, &c.

TRAGŒDIA EST IMITATIO ACTIONIS SERIÆ, ETC. PER
MISERICORDIAM ET METUM PERFICIENS TALIUM
AFFECTUUM LUSTRATIONEM.

ARISTOT. POET. CAP. 6.

# OF THAT SORT OF DRAMATIC POEM

## WHICH IS CALLED TRAGEDY.

.

TRAGEDY, as it was anciently compofed, hath been
ever held the graveft, moraleft, and moft profitable of
all other poems: therefore faid by Ariftotle to be of
power by raifing pity and fear, or terrour, to purge the
mind of thofe and fuch like paffions, that is, to temper and reduce them to juft meafure with a kind of
delight, ftirred up by reading or feeing thofe paffions
well imitated. Nor is Nature wanting in her own ef-
fects to make good his affertion: for fo in phyfic things
of melancholic hue and quality are ufed againft melan ·
choly, four againft four, falt to remove falt humours.
Hence philofophers and other graveft writers, as Cicero, Plutarch, and others, frequently cite out of tragic poets, both to adorn and illuftrate their difcourfe.
The apoftle Paul himfelf thought it not unworthy to
infert a verfe of Euripides into the text of Holy Scripture, 1 Cor. xv, 33; and Paræus commenting on the
Revelation, divides the whole book as a tragedy, into
acts diftinguifhed each by a chorus of heavenly harp-
ings and fong between. Heretofore men in higheft
dignity have laboured not a little to be thought able to

compose a tragedy. Of that honour Dionysius the elder was no less ambitious, than before of his attaining to the tyranny. Auguftus Cæfar alfo had begun his Ajax; but unable to pleafe his own judgment with what he had begun, left it unfinifhed. Seneca the philofopher is by fome thought the author of thofe tragedies (at leaft the beft of them) that go under that name. Gregory Nazianzen, a father of the church, thought it not unbefeeming the fanctity of his perfon to write a tragedy, which is entitled Chrift Suffering. This is mentioned to vindicate tragedy from the fmall efteem, or rather infamy, which in the account of many it undergoes at this day with other common interludes; happening through the poets errour of intermixing comic ftuff with tragic fadnefs and gravity; or introducing trivial and vulgar perfons, which by all judicious hath been counted abfurd; and brought in without difcretion, corruptly to gratify the people. And though ancient tragedy ufe no prologue, yet ufing fometimes, in cafe of felf-defence, or explanation, that which Martial calls an epiftle; in behalf of this tragedy coming forth after the ancient manner, much different from what among us paffes for beft, thus much before hand may be epiftled; that chorus is here introduced after the Greek manner, not ancient only but modern, and ftill in ufe among the Italians. In the modelling therefore of this poem, with good reafon, the ancients and Italians are rather followed, as of much more authority and fame. The meafure of verfe ufed in the chorus is of all forts, called by the Greeks Monoftrophic, or rather Apolelymenon, without regard had to Strophe, Antiftrophe or Epod, which were a kind of ftanzas framed only for the mufic, then ufed with the chorus that fung; not effential to the poem, and therefore not material; or being divided into ftanzas or paufes, they may be called Allæoftropha. Divifion into act and fcene referring chiefly to the ftage (to which this work never was intended) is here omitted.

It fuffices if the whole drama be found not produced beyond the fifth act. Of the ftyle and uniformity, and that commonly called the plot, whether intricate or explicit, which is nothing indeed but fuch economy or difpofition of the fable as may ftand beft with verifimilitude and decorum; they only will beft judge who are not unacquainted with Æfchylus, Sophocles, and Euripides, the three tragic poets unequalled yet by any, and the beft rule to all who endeavour to write tragedy. The circumfcription of time, wherein the whole drama begins and ends, is according to ancient rule, and beft example, within the fpace of twenty-four hours.

# THE ARGUMENT.

Samſon made captive, blind, and now in the priſon at Gaza, there to labour as in a common workhouſe, on a feſtival day, in the general ceſſation from labour, comes forth into the open air, to a place nigh, ſomewhat retired, there to fit a while and bemoan his condition. Where he happens at length to be viſited by certain friends and equals of his tribe, which make the Chorus, who ſeek to comfort him what they can; then by his old father Manoah, who endeavours the like, and withal tells him his purpoſe to procure his liberty by ranſom; laſtly, that this feaſt was proclaimed by the Philiſtines as a day of thankſgiving for their deliverance from the hands of Samſon, which yet more troubles him. Manoah then departs to proſecute his endeavour with the Philiſtian lords for Samſon's redemption; who in the mean while is viſited by other perſons; and laſtly by a public officer to require his coming to the feaſt before the lords and people, to play or ſhow his ſtrength in their preſence; he at firſt refuſes, diſmiſſing the public officer with abſolute denial to come; at length perſuaded inwardly that this was from God, he yields to go along with him, who came now the ſecond time with great threatenings to fetch him: the Chorus yet remaining on the place, Manoah returns full of joyful hope, to procure ere long his ſon's deliverance: in the midſt of which diſcourſe an Hebrew comes in haſte, confuſedly at firſt, and afterwards more diſtinctly relating the cataſtrophe, what Samſon had done to the Philiſtines, and by accident to himſelf; wherewith the tragedy ends.

# THE PERSONS.

SAMSON.

MANOAH, THE FATHER OF SAMSON.

DALILA, HIS WIFE.

HARAPHA OF GATH.

PUBLIC OFFICER.

MESSENGER.

CHORUS OF DANITES.


THE SCENE BEFORE THE PRISON IN GAZA.

# SAMSON AGONISTES.

A LITTLE onward lend thy guiding hand
To thefe dark fteps, a little further on;
For yonder bank hath choice of fun or fhade :
There I am wont to fit, when any chance
Relieves me from my talk of fervile toil,
Daily' in the common prifon elfe injoin'd me,
Where I a prifoner, chain'd, fcarce freely draw
The air imprifon'd alfo, clofe and damp,
Unwholefome draught: but here I feel amends,
The breath of Heav'n frefh blowing, pure and fweet,
With day-fpring born ; here leave me to refpire.
This day a folemn feaft the people hold
To Dagon their fea-idol, and forbid
Laborious works ; unwillingly this reft
Their fuperftition yields me; hence with leave
Retiring from the popular noife, I feek
This unfrequented place to find fome eafe,
Eafe to the body fome, none to the mind
From reftlefs thoughts, that like a deadly fwarm

Of hornets arm'd, no fooner found alone,
But rufh upon me thronging, and prefent
Times paft, what once I was, and what am now.
O wherefore was my birth from Heav'n foretold
Twice by an angel, who at laft in fight
Of both my parents all in flames afcended
From off the altar, where an offering burn'd,
As in a fiery column charioting
His godlike prefence, and from fome great act
Or benefit reveal'd to Abraham's race?
Why was my breeding order'd and prefcribed
As of a perfon feparate to God,
Defign'd for great exploits; if I muft die
Betray'd, captiv'd, and both my eyes put out,
Made of my enemies the fcorn and gaze;
To grind in brazen fetters under tafk
With this Heav'n-gifted ftrength? O glorious ftrength
Put to the labour of a beaft, debas'd
Lower than bondflave! Promife was that I
Should Ifrael from Philiftian yoke deliver;
Afk for this great deliverer now, and find him
Eyelefs in Gaza at the mill with flaves,
Himfelf in bonds under Philiftian yoke:
Yet ftay, let me not rafhly call in doubt
Divine prediction; what if all foretold
Had been fulfill'd but through mine own default,
Whom have I to complain of but myfelf?
Who this high gift of ftrength committed to me,
In what part lodg'd, how cafily bereft me,
Under the feal of filence could not keep,
But weakly to a woman muft reveal it,

O'ercome with importunity and tears.
O impotence of mind, in body ftrong!
But what is ftrength without a double fhare
Of wifdom, vaft, unwieldy, burdenfome,
Proudly fecure, yet liable to fall
By weakeft fubtleties, not made to rule,
But to fubferve where wifdom bears command!
God, when he gave me ftrength, to fhow withal
How flight the gift was, hung it in my hair.
But peace, I muft not quarrel with the will
Of higheft difpenfation, which herein
Haply had ends above my reach to know:
Suffices that to me ftrength is my bane,
And proves the fource of all my miferies;
So many, and fo huge, that each apart
Would afk a life to wail, but chief of all,
O lofs of fight, of thee I moft complain!
Blind among enemies, O worfe than chains,
Dungeon, or beggary, or decrepit age!
Light the prime work of God to me' is extinct,
And all her various objects of delight
Annull'd, which might in part my grief have eas'd,
Inferior to the vileft now become
Of man or worm; the vileft here excel me,
They creep, yet fee, I dark in light expos'd
To daily fraud, contempt, abufe, and wrong,
Within doors, or without, ftill as a fool,
In pow'r of others, never in my own;
Scarce half I feem to live, dead more than half.
O dark, dark, dark, amid the blaze of noon,
Irrecoverably dark, total eclipfe

Without all hope of day!
O firſt created Beam, and thou great Word,
Let there be light, and light was over all;
Why am I thus bereav'd thy prime decree?
The fun to me is dark
And ſilent as the moon,
When ſhe deferts the night
Hid in her vacant interlunar cave.
Since light ſo neceſſary is to life,
And almoſt life itſelf, if it be true
That light is in the ſoul,
She all in every part; why was the ſight
To fuch a tender ball as th' eye confin'd,
So obvious and ſo eaſy to be quench'd?
And not as feeling through all parts diffus'd,
That ſhe might look at will through every pore?
Then had I not been thus exil'd from light,
As in the land of darkneſs yet in light,
To live a life half dead, a living death,
And bury'd; but O yet more miſerable!
Myſelf my ſepulchre, a moving grave,
Bury'd, yet not exempt
By privilege of death and burial
From worſt of other evils, pains, and wrongs,
But made hereby obnoxious more
To all the miferies of life,
Life in captivity
Among inhuman foes.
But who are theſe? for with joint pace I hear
The tread of many feet fteering this way;
Perhaps my enemies who come to ftare

At my affliction, and perhaps t' infult,
Their daily practice to afflict me more.

CHORUS.

This, this is he; foftly a while,
Let us not break in upon him;
O change beyond report, thought, or belief!
See how he lies at random, carelefsly diffus'd,
With languifh'd head unpropt,
As one paft hope, abandon'd,
And by himfelf given over;
In flavifh habit, ill-fitted weeds
O'er-worn and foil'd;
Or do my eyes mifreprefent? Can this be he,
That heroic, that renown'd,
Irrefiftible Samfon? whom unarm'd
No ftrength of man, or fierceft wild beaft could with-
        ftand;
Who tore the lion, as the lion tears the kid,
Ran on imbattl'd armies clad in iron,
And weaponlefs himfelf,
Made arms ridiculous, ufelefs the forgery
Of brazen fhield and fpear, the hammer'd cuirafs,
Chalybean temper'd fteel, and frock of mail
Adamantean proof;
But fafeft he who ftood aloof,
When infupportably his foot advanc'd,
In fcorn of their proud arms and warlike tools,
Spurn'd them to death by troops. The bold Afcalonite
Fled from his lion ramp, old warriors turn'd
Their plated backs under his heel;
Or grov'ling foil'd their crefted helmets in the duft.

Then with what trivial weapon came to hand,
The jaw of a dead afs, his fword of bone,
A thoufand forefkins fell, the flow'r of Paleftine,
In Ramath-lechi famous to this day.
Then by main force pull'd up, and on his fhoulders
    bore
The gates of Azza, poft, and maffy bar,
Up to the hill by Hebron, feat of giants old,
No journey of a fabbath-day, and loaded fo;
Like whom the Gentiles feign to bear up Heaven.
Which fhall I firft bewail,
Thy bondage or loft fight,
Prifon within prifon
Infeparably. dark?
Thou art become (O worft imprifonment!)
The dungeon of thyfelf; thy foul
(Which men enjoying fight oft without caufe com-
    plain)
Imprifon'd now indeed,
In real darknefs of the body dwells,
Shut up from outward light
T' incorporate with gloomy night;
For inward light alas
Puts forth no vifual beam.
O mirrour of our fickle ftate,
Since man on earth unparallell'd!
The rarer thy example ftands,
By how much from the top of wond'rous glory,
Strongeft of mortal men,
To loweft pitch of abject fortune thou art fall'n.
For him I reckon not in high eftate

Whom long defcent of birth
Or the fphere of fortune raifes;
But thee whofe ftrength, while virtue was her mate,
Might have fubdued the earth,
Univerfally crown'd with higheft praifes.

### SAMSON.

I hear the found of words, their fenfe the air
Diffolves unjointed ere it reach my ear.

### CHORUS.

He fpeaks, let us draw nigh. Matchlefs in might,
The glory late of Ifrael, now the grief;
We come thy friends and neighbours not unknown
From Efhtaol and Zora's fruitful vale
To vifit or bewail thee, or if better,
Counfel or confolation we may bring,
Salve to thy fores; apt words have pow'r to fwage
The tumours of a troubled mind,
And are as balm to fefter'd wounds.

### SAMSON.

Your coming, friends, revives me, for I learn
Now of my own experience, not by talk,
How counterfeit a coin they are who friends
Bear in their fuperfcription, (of the moft
I would be underftood) in profp'rous days
They fwarm, but in adverfe withdraw their head,
Not to be found, though fought. Ye fee, O friends,
How many evils have inclos'd me round;
Yet that which was the worft now leaft afflicts me,
Blindnefs, for had I fight, confus'd with fhame,
How could I once look up, or heave the head,
Who like a foolifh pilot have fhipwrack'd

H

My veffel trufted to me from above,
Glorioufly rigg'd; and for a word, a tear,
Fool, have divulg'd the fecret gift of God
To a deceitful woman? tell me, friends,
Am I not fung and proverb'd for a fool
In every ftreet? do they not fay, how well
Are come upon him his deferts? yet why?
Immeafurable ftrength they might behold
In me, of wifdom nothing more than mean;
This with the other fhould, at leaft, have pair'd,
Thefe two proportion'd ill drove me tranfverfe.

### CHORUS.

Tax not divine difpofal; wifeft men
Have err'd, and by bad women been deceiv'd;
And fhall again, pretend they ne'er fo wife.
Dejeɕ not then fo overmuch thyfelf,
Who haft of forrow thy full load befides;
Yet truth to fay, I oft have heard men wonder
Why thou fhouldft wed Philiftian women rather
Than of thine own tribe fairer, or as fair,
At leaft of thy own nation, and as noble.

### SAMSON.

The firft I faw at Timna, and fhe pleas'd
Me, not my parents, that I fought to wed
The daughter of an infidel: they knew not
That what I motion'd was of God; I knew
From intimate impulfe, and therefore urg'd
The marriage on; that by occafion hence
I might begin Ifrael's deliverance,
The work to which I was divinely call'd.
She proving falfe, the next I took to wife

(O that I never had! fond wifh too late,)
Was in the vale of Sorec, Dalila,
That fpecious monfter, my accomplifh'd fnare.
I thought it lawful from my former act,
And the fame end; ftill watching to opprefs
Ifrael's oppreffors: of what now I fuffer
She was not the prime caufe, but I myfelf,
Who vanquifh'd with a peal of words (O weaknefs!)
Gave up my fort of filence to a woman.

#### CHORUS.

   In feeking juft occafion to provoke
The Philiftine, thy country's enemy,
Thou never waft remifs, I bear thee witnefs:
Yet Ifraël ftill ferves with all his fons.

#### SAMSON.

   That fault I take not on me, but transfer
On Ifrael's governors, and heads of tribes,
Who feeing thofe great acts, which God had done
Singly by me againft their conquerors,
Acknowledg'd not, or not at all confider'd
Deliv'rance offer'd: I on th' other fide
Us'd no ambition to commend my deeds,
The deeds themfelves, though mute, fpoke loud the
     doer;
But they perfifted deaf, and would not feem
To count them things worth notice, till at length
Their lords the Philiftines with gather'd pow'rs
Enter'd Judea feeking me, who then
Safe to the rock of Etham was retir'd,
Not flying, but forecafting in what place
To fet upon them, what advantag'd beft:

Mean while the men of Judah, to prevent
The harafs of their land, befet me round;
I willingly on fome conditions came
Into their hands, and they as gladly yield me
To the uncircumcis'd a welcome prey,
Bound with two cords; but cords to me were threads
Touch'd with the flame: on their whole hoft I flew
Unarm'd, and with a trivial weapon fell'd
Their choiceft youth; they only liv'd who fled.
Had Judah that day join'd, or one whole tribe,
They had by this poffefs'd the tow'rs of Gath,
And lorded over them whom now they ferve:
But what more oft in nations grown corrupt,
And by their vices brought to fervitude,
Than to love bondage more than liberty,
Bondage with eafe than ftrenuous liberty;
And to defpife, or envy, or fufpect
Whom God hath of his fpecial favour rais'd
As their deliverer; if he ought begin,
How frequent to defert him, and at laft
To heap ingratitude on worthieft deeds?

CHORUS.

Thy words to my remembrance bring
How Succoth and the fort of Penuel
Their great deliverer contemn'd,
The matchlefs Gideon in purfuit
Of Midian and her vanquifh'd kings:
And how ungrateful Ephraim
Had dealt with Jephtha, who by argument,
Not worfe than by his fhield and fpear,
Defended Ifrael from the Ammonite,

Had not his prowefs quell'd their pride
In that fore battle, when fo many dy'd
Without reprieve adjudg'd to death,
For want of well pronouncing Shibboleth.

#### SAMSON.

Of fuch examples add me to the roll,
Me eafily indeed mine may neglect,
But God's propos'd deliverance not fo.

#### CHORUS.

Juft are the ways of God,
And juftifiable to men;
Unlefs there be who think not God at all:
If any be, they walk obfcure;
For of fuch doctrine never was there fchool,
But the heart of the fool,
And no man therein doctor but himfelf.

Yet more there be who doubt his ways not juft,
As to his own edicts found contradicting,
Then give the reins to wand'ring thought,
Regardlefs of his glory's diminution;
Till by their own perplexities involv'd
They ravel more, ftill lefs refolv'd,
But never find felf-fatisfying folution.

As if they would confine th' Interminable,
And tie him to his own prefcript,
Who made our laws to bind us, not himfelf,
And hath full right to' exempt
Whom fo it pleafes him by choice
From national obftriction, without taint
Of fin, or legal debt;
For with his own laws he can beft difpenfe.

He would not elfe, who never wanted means,
Nor in refpect of th' enemy juft caufe
To fet his people free,
Have prompted this heroic Nazarite,
Againft his vow of ftricteft purity,
To feek in marriage that fallacious bride,
Unclean, unchafte.

    Down reafon then, at leaft vain reafonings down,
Though reafon here aver
That moral verdict quits her of unclean:
Unchafte was fubfequent, her ftain not his.

    But fee here comes thy reverend fire
With careful ftep, locks white as down,
Old Manoah: advife
Forthwith how thou oughtft to receive him.

### SAMSON.

    Aye me, another inward grief awak'd
With mention of that name renews th' affault.

### MANOAH.

    Brethren and men of Dan, for fuch ye feem,
Though in this uncouth place; if old refpect,
As I fuppofe, tow'ards your once glory'd friend,
My Son now captive, hither hath inform'd
Your younger feet, while mine caft back with age
Came lagging after; fay if he be here.

### CHORUS.

    As fignal now in low dejected ftate,
As erft in high'eft, behold him where he lies.

### MANOAH.

    O miferable change! is this the man,
That invincible Samfon, far renown'd,

The dread of Ifrael's foes, who with a ftrength
Equivalent to Angels walk'd their ftreets,
None offering fight; who fingle combatant
Duell'd their armies rank'd in proud array,
Himfelf an army, now unequal match
To fave himfelf againft a coward arm'd
At one fpear's length.   O ever failing truft
In mortal ftrength! and oh what not in man
Deceivable and vain? Nay what thing good
Pray'd for, but often proves our woe, our bane?
I pray'd for children, and thought barrennefs
In wedlock a reproach; I gain'd a fon,
And fuch a fon as all men hail'd me happy;
Who would be now a father in my ftead?
O wherefore did God grant me my requeft,
And as a bleffing with fuch pomp adorn'd?
Why are his gifts defirable, to tempt
Our earneft pray'rs, then giv'n with folemn hand
As graces, draw a fcorpion's tail behind?
For this did th' Angel twice defcend? for this
Ordain'd thy nurture holy, as of a plant
Select, and facred, glorious for a while,
The miracle of men; then in an hour
Infnar'd, affaulted, overcome, led bound,
Thy foes derifion, captive, poor and blind,
Into a dungeon thruft, to work with flaves?
Alas methinks whom God hath chofen once
To worthieft deeds, if he through frailty err,
He fhould not fo o'erwhelm, and as a thrall
Subject him to fo foul indignities,
Be it but for honour's fake of former deeds.

Appoint not heav'nly difpofition, Father;
Nothing of all thefe evils hath befall'n me
But juftly; I myfelf have brought them on,
Sole author I, fole caufe: if ought feem vile,
As vile hath been my folly, who' have profan'd
The myftery of God given me under pledge
Of vow, and have betray'd it to a woman,
A Canaanite, my faithlefs enemy.
This well I knew, nor was at all furpris'd,
But warn'd by oft experience: did not fhe
Of Timna firft betray me, and reveal
The fecret wrefted from me in her height
Of nuptial love profefs'd, carrying it ftraight
To them who had corrupted her, my fpies,
And rivals? In this other was there found
More faith, who also in her prime of love,
Spoufal embraces, vitiated with gold,
Though offer'd only, by the fcent conceiv'd
Her fpurious firft-born, treafon againft me?
Thrice fhe affay'd with flattering pray'rs and fighs,
And amorous reproaches, to win from me
My capital fecret, in what part my ftrength
Lay ftor'd, in what part fumm'd, that fhe might know;
Thrice I deluded her, and turn'd to fport
Her importunity, each time perceiving
How openly, and with what impudence
She purpos'd to betray me, and (which was worfe
Than undiffembled hate) with what contempt
She fought to make me traitor to myfelf;
Yet the fourth time, when muft'ring all her wiles,

With blandifh'd parlies, feminine affaults,
Tongue-batteries, fhe furceas'd not day nor night
To ftorm me over-watch'd, and weary'd out,
At times when men feek moft repofe and reft,
I yielded, and unlock'd her all my heart,
Who with a grain of manhood well refolv'd
Might eafily have fhook off all her fnares:
But foul effeminacy held me yok'd
Her bond-flave; O indignity, O blot
To honour and religion! fervile mind
Rewarded well with fervile punifhment!
The bafe degree to which I now am fall'n,
Thefe rags, this grinding is not yet fo bafe
As was my former fervitude, ignoble,
Unmanly, ignominious, infamous,
True flavery, and that blindnefs worfe than this,
That faw not how degenerately I ferv'd.

MANOAH.

I cannot praife thy marriage choices, Son,
Rather approv'd them not; but thou didft plead
Divine impulfion prompting how thou might'ft
Find fome occafion to infeft our foes.
I ftate not that; this I am fure, our foes
Found foon occafion thereby to make'thee
Their captive, and their triumph; thou the fooner
Temptation found'ft, or over-potent charms
To violate the facred truft of filence
Depofited within thee; which to' have kept
Tacit, was in thy pow'r: true; and thou bear'ft
Enough, and more, the burden of that fault;
Bitterly haft thou paid, and ftill art paying

That rigid fcore.   A worfe thing yet remains,
This day the Philiftines a popular feaft
Here celebrate in Gaza; and proclaim
Great pomp, and facrifice, and praifes loud
To Dagon, as their God who hath deliver'd
Thee, Samfon, bound and blind into their hands,
Them out of thine, who flew'ft them many a flain.
So Dagon fhall be magnify'd, and God,
Befides whom is no God, compar'd with idols,
Difglorify'd, blafphem'd, and had in fcorn
By the idolatrous rout amidft their wine;
Which to have come to pafs by means of thee,
Samfon, of all thy fufferings think the heavieft,
Of all reproach the moft with fhame that ever
Could have befall'n thee and thy father's houfe.

SAMSON.

   Father, I do acknowledge and confefs
That I this honour, I this pomp have brought
To Dagon, and advanc'd his praifes high
Among the Heathen round; to God have brought
Difhonour, obloquy, and op'd the mouths
Of idolifts, and atheifts; have brought fcandal
To Ifrael, diffidence of God, and doubt
In feeble hearts, propenfe enough before
To waver, or fall off and join with idols;
Which is my chief affliction, fhame, and forrow,
The anguifh of my foul, that fuffers not
Mine eye to harbour fleep, or thoughts to reft.
This only hope relieves me, that the ftrife
With me hath end; all the contéft is now
'Twixt God and Dagon; Dagon hath prefum'd,

Me overthrown, to enter lifts with God,
His deity comparing and preferring
Before the God of Abraham.   He, be fure,
Will not connive, or linger, thus provok'd,
But will arife and his great name affert:
Dagon muft ftoop, and fhall ere long receive
Such a difcomfit, as fhall quite defpoil him
Of all thefe boafted trophies won on me,
And with confufion blank his worfhippers.

### MANOAH.

With caufe this hope relieves thee, and thefe words
I as a prophecy receive; for God,
Nothing more certain, will not long defer
To vindicate the glory of his name
Againft all competition, nor will long
Indure it doubtful whether God be Lord,
Or Dagon.   But for thee what fhall be done?
Thou muft not in the mean while here forgot
Lie in this miferable loathfome plight
Neglected.   I already have made way
To fome Philiftian lords, with whom to treat
About thy ranfom: well they may by this
Have fatisfy'd their utmoft of revenge
By pains and flaveries, worfe than death inflicted
On thee, who now no more canft do them harm.

### SAMSON.

Spare that propofal, Father, fpare the trouble
Of that folicitation; let me here,
As I deferve, pay on my punifhment;
And expiate, if poffible, my crime,
Shameful garrulity.   To have reveal'd

Secrets of men, the fecrets of a friend,
How heinous had the fact been, how deferving
Contempt, and fcorn of all, to be excluded
All friendfhip, and avoided as a blab,
The mark of fool fet on his front?
But I God's counfel have not kept, his holy fecret
Prefumptuoufly have publifh'd, impioufly,
Weakly at leaft, and fhamefully: a fin
That Gentiles in their parables condemn
To their abyfs and horrid pains confin'd.

MANOAH.

Be penitent and for thy fault contrite,
But act not in thy own affliction, Son;
Repent the fin, but if the punifhment
Thou canft avoid, felf-prefervation bids;
Or th' execution leave to high difpofal,
And let another hand, not thine, exact
Thy penal forfeit from thyfelf; perhaps
God will relent, and quit thee all his debt;
Who ever more approves and more accepts
(Beft pleas'd with humble' and filial fubmiffion)
Him who imploring mercy fues for life,
Than who felf-rigorous choofes death as due;
Which argues.over-juft, and felf-difpleas'd
For felf-offence, more than for God offended.
Reject not then what offer'd means who knows
But God hath fet before us, to return thee
Home to thy country and his facred houfe,
Where thou may'ft bring thy offerings, to avert
His further ire, with pray'rs and vows renew'd?

### SAMSON.

His pardon I implore; but as for life,
To what end fhould I feek it? When in ftrength
All mortals I excell'd, and great in hopes
With youthful courage and magnanimous thoughts
Of birth from Heav'n foretold and high exploits,
Full of divine inftinct, after fome proof
Of acts indeed heroic, far beyond
The fons of Anak, famous now and blaz'd,
Fearlefs of danger, like a petty God
I walk'd about admir'd of all and dreaded
On hoftile ground, none daring my affront.
Then fwoll'n with pride into the fnare I fell
Of fair fallacious looks, venereal trains,
Soften'd with pleafure and voluptuous life;
At length to lay my head and hallow'd pledge
Of all my ftrength in the lafcivious lap
Of a deceitful concubine, who fhore me
Like a tame wether, all my precious fleece,
Then turn'd me out ridiculous, defpoil'd,
Shav'n, and difarm'd among mine enemies.

### CHORUS.

Defire of wine and all delicious drinks,
Which many a famous warrior overturns,
Thou couldft reprefs, nor did the dancing ruby
Sparkling, out-pour'd, the flavour, or the fmell,
Or tafte that cheers the heart of Gods and men,
Allure thee from the cool cryftalline ftream.

### SAMSON.

Wherever fountain or frefh current flow'd
Againft the eaftern ray, tranflucent, pure

With touch ethereal of Heav'n's fiery rod,
I drank, from the clear milky juice allaying
Thirſt, and refreſh'd; nor envy'd them the grape
Whoſe heads that turbulent liquor fills with fumes.

### CHORUS.

O madneſs, to think uſe of ſtrongeſt wines
And ſtrongeſt drinks our chief ſupport of health,
When God with theſe forbidd'en made choice to rear
His mighty champion, ſtrong above compare,
Whoſe drink was only from the liquid brook.

### SAMSON.

But what avail'd this temp'rance, not complete
Againſt another object more enticing?
What boots it at one gate to make defence,
And at another to let in the foe,
Effeminately vanquiſh'd? by which means,
Now blind, diſhearten'd, ſham'd, diſhonour'd, quell'd,
To what can I be uſeful, wherein ſerve
My nation, and the work from Heav'n impos'd,
But to ſit idle on the houſhold hearth,
A burd'nous drone; to viſitants a gaze,
Or pity'd object; theſe redundant locks
Robuſtious to no purpoſe cluſt'ring down,
Vain monument of ſtrength; till length of years
And ſedentary numbneſs craze my limbs
To a contemptible old age obſcure?
Here rather let me drudge and earn my bread,
Till vermin or the draff of ſervile food
Conſume me, and oft-invocated death
Haſten the welcome end of all my pains.

### MANOAH.

Wilt thou then ferve the Philiftines with that gift
Which was exprefsly giv'n thee to annoy them?
Better at home lie bed-rid, not only idle,
Inglorious, unemploy'd, with age outworn.
But God who caus'd a fountain at thy prayer
From the dry ground to fpring, thy thirft t' allay
After the brunt of battle, can as eafy
Caufe light again within thy eyes to fpring,
Wherewith to ferve him better than thou haft;
And I perfuade me fo; why elfe this ftrength
Miraculous yet remaining in thofe locks?
His might continues in thee not for nought,
Nor fhall his wondrous gifts be fruftrate thus.

### SAMSON.

All otherwife to me my thoughts portend,·
That thefe dark orbs no more fhall treat with light,
Nor th' other light of life continue long,
But yield to double darknefs nigh at hand:
So much I feel my genial fpirits droop,
· My hopes all flat, nature within me feems
In all her functions weary of herfelf,
My race of glory run, and race of fhame,
And I fhall fhortly be with them that reft.

### MANOAH.

Believe not thefe fuggeftions which proceed
From anguifh of the mind and humours black,
That mingle with thy fancy.  I however
Muft not omit a father's timely care
To profecute the means of thy deliverance
By ranfom, or how elfe: mean while be calm,

And healing words from thefe thy friends admit.

SAMSON.

O that torment fhould not be confin'd
To the body's wounds and fores,
With maladies innumerable
In heart, head, breaft, and reins;
But muft fecret paffage find
To th' inmoft mind,
There exercife all his fierce accidents,
And on her purer fpirits prey,
As on entrails, joints, and limbs,
With anfwerable pains, but more intenfe,
Though void of corporal fenfe.
    My griefs not only pain me
As a ling'ring difeafe,
But finding no redrefs, ferment and rage,
Nor lefs than wounds immedicable
Rankle, and fefter, and gangrene,
To black mortification.
Thoughts my tormentors arm'd with deadly ftings
Mangle my apprehenfive tendereft parts,
Exafperate, exulcerate, and raife
Dire inflammation, which no cooling herb
Or medicinal liquor can affuage,
Nor breath of vernal air from fnowy Alp.
Sleep hath forfook and giv'n me o'er
To death's benumming opium as my only cure:
Thence faintings, fwoonings of defpair,
And fenfe of Heav'n's defertion.
    I was his nurfling once and choice delight,
His deftin'd from the womb,

Promis'd by heav'hly meſſage twice defcending.
Under his fpecial eye
Abſtemious I grew up and thriv'd amain;
He led me on to mightieſt deeds
Above the nerve of mortal arm
Againſt th' uncircumcis'd,  our enemies:
But now hath caſt me off as never known,
And to thofe cruel enemies,
Whom I by his appointment had provok'd,
Left me all helplefs with th' irreparable lofs
Of fight, referv'd alive to be repeated
The fubje&t of their cruelty or fcorn.
Nor am I in the liſt of them that hope;
Hopelefs are all my evils,  all remedilefs;
This one prayer yet remains, might I be heard,
No long petition, fpeedy death,
The clofe of all my mifcries, and the balm.

CHORUS.

Many are the fayings of the wife
In ancient and in modern books inroll'd,
Extolling patience as the trueſt fortitude;
And to the bearing well of all calamities,
All chances incident to man's frail life,
Confolatories writ
With ftudy'd argument, and much perfuafiou fought
Lenient of grief and anxious thought:
But with th' afflicted in his pangs their found
Little prevails,  or rather feems a tune
Harfh, and of diffonant mood from his complaint;
Unlefs he feel within
Some fource of confolation from above,

I

Secret refreſhings, that repair his ſtrength,
And fainting ſpirits uphold.

God of our fathers, what is man!
That thou tow'ards him with hand ſo various,
Or might I ſay contrarious,
Temper'ſt thy providence through his ſhort courſe,
Not ev'nly, as thou rul'ſt
Th' angelic orders and inferior creatures mute,
Irrational and brute.
Nor do I name of men the common rout,
That wand'ring looſe about
Grow up and periſh, as the ſummer flie,
Heads without name no more remembered,
But ſuch as thou haſt ſolemnly elected,
With gifts and graces eminently adorn'd
To ſome great work, thy glory,
And people's ſafety, which in part they' effect:
Yet toward theſe thus dignify'd, thou oft
Amidſt their height of noon
Changeſt thy count'nance, and thy hand with no regard
Of higheſt favours paſt
From thee on them, or them to thee of ſervice.
Nor only doſt degrade them, or remit
To life obſcur'd, which were a fair diſmiſſion,
But throw'ſt them lower than thou didſt exalt them
    high,
Unſeemly falls in human eye,
Too grievous for the treſpaſs or omiſſion;
Oft leav'ſt them to the hoſtile ſword
Of Heathen and profane, their carcaſes
To dogs and fowls a prey, or elſe captiv'd;

Or to th' unjuſt tribunals, under change of times,
And condemnation of th' ungrateful multitude.
If theſe they ſcape, perhaps in poverty
With ſickneſs and diſeaſe thou bow'ſt them down,
Painful diſeaſes and deform'd,
In crude old age;
Though not diſordinate, yet cauſeleſs ſuff'ring
The puniſhment of diſſolute days: in fine,
Juſt or unjuſt alike ſeem miſerable,
For oft alike both come to evil end.

   So deal not with this once thy glorious champion,
The image of thy ſtrength, and mighty miniſter.
What do I beg? how haſt thou dealt already?
Behold him in this ſtate calamitous, and turn
His labours, for thou canſt, to peaceful end.

   But who is this, what thing of ſea or land?
Female of ſex it ſeems,
That ſo bedeck'd, ornate, and gay,
Comes this way ſailing
Like a ſtately ſhip
Of Tarſus, bound for th' iles
Of Javan or Gadire
With all her bravery on, and tackle trim,
Sails fill'd, and ſtreamers waving,
Courted by all the winds that hold them play,
An amber ſcent of odorous perfume
Her harbinger, a damſel train behind;
Some rich Philiſtian matron ſhe may ſeem,
And now at nearer view, no other certain
Than Dalila thy Wife.

SAMSON.

My Wife, my Traitrefs, let her not come near me.

CHORUS.

Yet on fhe moves, now ftands and eyes thee fix'd,
About t' have fpoke, but now, with head declin'd
Like a fair flow'r furcharg'd with dew, fhe weeps,
And words addrefs'd feem into tears diffolv'd,
Wetting the borders of her filken veil:
But now again fhe makes addrefs to fpeak.

DALILA.

'With doubtful feet and wavering refolution
I came, ftill dreading thy difpleafure, Samfon,
Which to have merited, without excufe,
I cannot but acknowledge; yet if tears
May expiate (though the fact more evil drew
In the perverfe event than I forefaw)
My penance hath not flacken'd, though my pardon
No way affur'd.   But conjugal affection
Prevailing over fear, and timorous doubt,
Hath led me on defirous to behold
Once more thy face, and know of thy eftate,
If ought in my ability may ferve
To lighten what thou fuffer'ft, and appeafe
Thy mind with what amends is in my power,
Though late, yet in fome part to recompenfe
My rafh but more unfortunate mifdeed.

SAMSON.

Out, out Hyæna; thefe are thy wonted arts,
And arts of every woman falfe like thee,
To break all faith, all vows, deceive, betray,

'Then as repentant to fubmit, befeech,
And reconcilement move with feign'd remorfe,
Confefs, and promife wonders in her change,
Not truly penitent, but chief to try
Her hufband, how far urg'd his patience bears,
His virtue or weaknefs which way to affail:
Then with more cautious and inftructed fkill
Again tranfgreffes, and again fubmits;
That wifeft and beft men full oft beguil'd,
With goodnefs principled not to reject
The penitent, but ever to forgive,
Are drawn to wear out miferable days,
Intangled with a pois'nous bofom fnake,
If not by quick deftruction foon cut off
As I by thee, to ages an example.

### DALILA.

Yet hear me, Samfon; not that I endeavour
To leffen or extenuate my offence,
But that on th' other fide if it be weigh'd
By' itfelf, with aggravations not furcharg'd,
Or elfe with juft allowance counterpois'd,
I may, if poffible, thy pardon find
The eafier towards me, or thy hatred lefs.
Firft granting, as I do, it was a weaknefs
In me, but incident to all our fex,
Curiofity, inquifitive, importune
Of fecrets, then with like infirmity
To publifh them, both common female faults:
Was it not weaknefs alfo to make known
For importunity, that is for nought,
Wherein confifted all thy ftrength and fafety?

To what I did thou fhow'dft me firft the way.
But I to enemies reveal'd, and fhould not:
Nor fhould'ft thou have trufted that to woman's frailty:
Ere I to thee, thou to thyfelf waft cruel.
Let weaknefs then with weaknefs come to parle
So near related, or the fame of kind,
Thine forgive mine; that men may cenfure thine
The gentler, if feverely thou exact not
More ftrength from me, than in thyfelf was found.
And what if love, which thou interpret'ft hate,
The jealoufy of love, pow'rful of fway
In human hearts, nor lefs in mine tow'rds thee,
Caus'd what I did? I faw thee mutable
Of fancy, fear'd left one day thou would'ft leave me
As her at Timna, fought by all means therefore
How to indear, and hold thee to me firmeft:
No better way I faw than by importuning
To learn thy fecrets, get into my power
The key of ftrength and fafety: thou wilt fay,
Why then reveal'd? I was affur'd by thofe
Who tempted me, that nothing was defign'd
Againft thee but fafe cuftody, and hold:
That made for me; I knew that liberty
Would draw thee forth to perilous enterprifes,
While I at home fat full of cares and fears,
Wailing thy abfence in my widow'd bed;
Here I fhould ftill enjoy thee day and night
Mine and love's prifoner, not the Philiftines,
Whole to myfelf, unhazarded abroad,
Fearlefs at home of partners in my love.
Thefe reafons in love's law have paft for good,

Though fond and reafonlefs to fome perhaps;
And love hath oft, well meaning, wrought much woe,
Yet always pity' or pardon hath obtain'd.
Be not unlike all others, not auftere
As thou art ftrong, inflexible as fteel.
If thou in ftrength all mortals doft exceed,
In uncompaffionate anger do not fo.

SAMSON.

How cunningly the forcerefs difplays
Her own tranfgreffions, to upbraid me mine?
That malice not repentance brought thee hither,
By this appears: I gave, thou fay'ft, th' example,
I led the way; bitter reproach, but true;
I to myfelf was falfe ere thou to me;
Such pardon therefore as I give my folly,
Take to thy wicked deed; which when thou feeft
Impartial, felf-fevere, inexorable,
Thou wilt renounce thy feeking, and much rather
Confefs it feign'd: weaknefs is thy excufe,
And I believe it, weaknefs to refift
Philiftian gold: if weaknefs may excufe,
What murderer, what traitor, parricide,
Inceftuous, facrilegious, but may plead it?
All wickednefs is weaknefs: that plea therefore
With God or Man will gain thee no remiffion.
But love conftrain'd thee; call it furious rage
To fatisfy thy luft: love feeks to' have love;
My love how could'ft thou hope, who took'ft the
     way
To raife in me inexpiable hate,
Knowing, as needs I muft, by thee betray'd?

In vain thou ftriv'ft to cover fhame with fhame,
Or by evafions thy crime uncover'ft more.

DALILA.

Since thou determin'ft weaknefs for no plea
In man or woman, though to thy own condemning,
Hear what affaults I had, what fnares befides,
What fieges girt me round, ere I confented;
Which might have aw'd the beft refolv'd of men,
The conflanteft, to' have yielded without blame.
It was not gold, as to my charge thou lay'ft,
That wrought with me: thou know'ft the magiftrates
And princes of my country came in perfon,
Solicited, commanded, threaten'd, urg'd,
Adjur'd by all the bonds of civil duty
And of religion, prefs'd how juft it was,
How honourable, how glorious to intrap
A common enemy, who had deftroy'd
Such numbers of our nation: and the prieft
Was not behind, but ever at my ear,
Preaching how meritorious with the Gods
It would be to infnare an irreligious
Difhonourer of Dagon: what had I
To' oppofe againft fuch pow'rful arguments?
Only my love of thee held long debate,
And combated in filence all thefe reafons
With hard conteft: at length that grounded maxim
So rife and celebrated in the mouths
Of wifeft men, that to the public good
Private refpects muft yield, with grave authority
Took full poffeffion of me and prevail'd;
Virtue, as I thought, truth, duty fo injoining.

SAMSON.

I thought where all thy circling wiles would end;
In feign'd religion, smooth hypocrify.
But had thy love, ftill odioufly pretended,
Been, as it ought, fincere, it would have taught thee
Far other reafonings, brought forth other deeds.
I before all the daughters of my tribe
And of my nation chofe thee from among
My enemies, lov'd thee, as too well thou knew'ft,
Too well, unbofom'd all my fecrets to thee,
Not out of levity, but overpower'd
By thy requeft, who could deny thee nothing;
Yet now am judg'd an enemy. Why then
Didft thou at firft receive me for thy hufband,
Then, as fince then, thy country's foe profefs'd?
Being once a wife, for me thou waft to leave
Parents and country; nor was I their fubject,
Nor under their protection but my own,
Thou mine, not their's: if ought againft my life
Thy country fought of thee, it fought unjuftly,
Againft the law of nature, law of nations,
No more thy country, but an impious crew
Of men confpiring to uphold their ftate
By worfe than hoftile deeds, violating the ends
For which our country is a name fo dear;
Not therefore to be' obey'd. But zeal mov'd thee;
To pleafe thy Gods thou didft it: Gods unable
T' acquit themfelves and profecute their foes
But by ungodly deeds, the contradiction
Of their own deity, Gods cannot be;
Lefs therefore to be pleas'd, obey'd, or fear'd.

Thefe falfe pretexts and varnifh'd colours failing,
Bare in thy guilt how foul muft thou appear?

DALILA.

In argument with men a woman ever
Goes by the worfe, whatever be her caufe.

SAMSON.

For want of words no doubt, or lack of breath;
Witnefs when I was worried with thy peals.

DALILA.

I was a fool, too rafh, and quite miftaken
In what I thought would have fucceeded beft.
Let me obtain forgivenefs of thee, Samfon,
Afford me place to fhow what recompenfe
Tow'rds thee I intend for what I have mifdone,
Mifguided; only what remains paft cure
Bear not too fenfibly, nor ftill infift
T' afflict thyfelf in vain: though fight be loft,
Life yet hath many folaces, enjoy'd
Where other fenfes want not their delights
At home in leifure and domeftic eafe,
Exempt from many a care and chance to which
Eye-fight expofes daily men abroad.
I to the lords will intercede, not doubting
Their favourable ear, that I may fetch thee
From forth this loathfome prifon-houfe, to abide
With me, where my redoubled love and care
With nurfing diligence, to me glad office,
May ever tend about thee to old age
With all things grateful cheer'd, and fo fupply'd,
That what by me thou' haft loft thou leaft fhalt mifs.

*E. F. Burney del.*  *I. Fittler sculp.*

*Dal. Let me approach at least, and touch thy hand.*
*Sams. Not for thy Life, lest fierce Remembrance wake*
  *My sudden rage to tear thee joint by joint.*
       *Sams. Agonistes p. 123.*

*Published 1st May 1796, for C. Dilly, in the Poultry, and the rest of the Proprietors.*

SAMSON.

No, no, of my condition take no care;
It fits not; thou and I long fince are twain:
Nor think me fo unwary or accurs'd,
To bring my feet again into the fnare
Where once I have been caught; I know thy trains
Though dearly to my coft, thy gins, and toils;
Thy fair inchanted cup, and warbling charms
No more on me have pow'r, their force is null'd,
So much of adder's wifdom I have learn'd
To fence my ear againft thy forceries.
If in my flower of youth and ftrength, when all men
Lov'd, honour'd, fear'd me, thou alone could'ft hate
          me
Thy hufband, flight me, fell me, and forego me;
How wouldft thou ufe me now, blind, and thereby
Deceivable, in moft things as a child
Helplefs, thence eafily contemn'd, and fcorn'd,
And laft neglected? How wouldft thou infult,
When I muft live uxorious to thy will
In perfect thraldom, how again betray me,
Bearing my words and doing to the lords
To glofs upon, and cenfuring, frown or fmile?
This jail I count the houfe of liberty
To thine, whofe doors my feet fhall never enter.

DALILA.

Let me approach at leaft, and touch thy hand.

SAMSON.

Not for thy life, left fierce remembrance wake
My fudden rage to tear thee joint by joint.
At diftance I forgive thee, go with that;

Bewail thy falſehood, and the pious works
It hath brought forth to make thee memorable
Among illuſtrious women, faithful wives:
Cheriſh thy haſten'd widowhood with the gold
Of matrimonial treaſon: ſo farewel.

DALILA.

I ſee thou art implacable, more deaf
To pray'rs, than winds and ſeas, yet winds to ſeas
Are reconcil'd at length, and ſea to ſhore:
Thy anger, unappeaſable, ſtill rages,
Eternal tempeſt never to be calm'd.
Why do I humble thus myſelf, and ſuing
For peace, reap nothing but repulſe and hate?
Bid go with evil omen and the brand
Of infamy upon my name denounc'd?
To mix with thy conccrnments I deſiſt
Henceforth, nor too much diſapprove my own.
Fame if not double-fac'd is double-mouth'd,
And with contrary blaſt proclaims moſt deeds;
On both his wings, one black, the other white,
Bears greateſt names in his wild aery flight.
My name perhaps among the circumcis'd
In Dan, in Judah, and the bordering tribes,
To all poſterity may ſtand defam'd,
With malediction mention'd, and the blot
Of falſehood moſt unconjugal traduc'd.
But in my country where I moſt deſire,
In Ecron, Gaza, Aſdod. and in Gath,
I ſhall be nam'd among the famouſeſt
Of women, ſung at ſolemn feſtivals,
Living and dead recorded, who to ſave

Her country from a fierce deſtroyer choſe
Above the faith of wedlock-bands, my tomb
With odours viſited and annual flowers;
Not leſs renown'd than in mount Ephraim
Jael, who with inhoſpitable guile
Smote Siſera ſleeping through the temples nail'd.
Nor ſhall I count it heinous to enjoy
The public marks of honour and reward
Conferr'd upon me, for the piety
Which to my country I was judg'd to' have ſhown.
At this who ever envies or repines,
I leave him to his lot, and like my own.

CHORUS.

She's gone, a manifeſt ſerpent by her ſting
Diſcover'd in the end, till now conceal'd.

SAMSON.

So let her go, God ſent her to debaſe me,
And aggravate my folly, who committed
To ſuch a viper his moſt ſacred truſt
Of ſecreſy, my ſafety, and my life.

CHORUS.

Yet beauty, though injurious, hath ſtrange power,
After offenſe returning, to regain
Love once poſſeſs'd, nor can be eaſily
Repuls'd, without much inward paſſion felt
And ſecret ſting of amorous remorſe.

SAMSON.

Love-quarrels oft in pleaſing concord end,
Not wedlock-treachery indang'ring life.

CHORUS.

It is not virtue, wiſdom, valour, wit,

Strength, comeliness of shape, or amplest merit
That woman's love can win or long inherit;
But what it is, hard is to say,
Harder to hit,
(Which way foever men refer it)
Much like thy riddle, Samson, in one day
Or fev'n, though one should musing fit.

   If any of these or all, the Timnian bride
Had not so soon preferr'd
Thy paranymph, worthless to thee compar'd,
Succeffor in thy bed,
Nor both so loofely difally'd
Their nuptials, nor this laft fo treacheroufly
Had fhorn the fatal harveft of thy head.
Is it for that fuch outward ornament
Was lavifh'd on their fex, that inward gifts
Were left for hafte unfinifh'd, judgment fcant,
Capacity not rais'd to apprehend
Or value what is beft
In choice, but ofteft to affect the wrong?
Or was too much of felf-love mix'd,
Of conftancy no root infix'd,
That either they love nothing, or not long?

   Whate'er it be, to wifeft men and beft
Seeming at firft all heav'nly under virgin veil,
Soft, modeft, meek, demure,
Once join'd, the contrary fhe proves, a thorn
Inteftine, far within defenfive arms
A cleaving mifchief, in his way to virtue
Adverfe and turbulent, or by her charms
Draws him awry inflav'd

With dotage, and his fenfe deprav'd
To folly' and fhameful deeds which ruin ends.
What pilot fo expert but needs muft wreck
Imbark'd with fuch a fteers-mate at the helm?

   Favour'd of Heav'n who finds
One virtuous rarely found,
That in domeftic good combines:
Happy that houfe! his way to peace is fmooth:
But virtue which breaks through all oppofition,
And all temptation can remove,
Moft fhines and moft is acceptable above.

   Therefore God's univerfal law
Gave to the man defpotic power
Over his female in due awe,
Nor from that right to part an hour,
Smile fhe or lour:
So fhall he leaft confufion draw
On his whole life, not fway'd
By female ufurpation, or difmay'd.

   But had we beft retire, I fee a ftorm?

SAMSON.

Fair days have oft contracted wind and rain.

CHORUS.

But this another kind of tempeft brings.

SAMSON.

Be lefs abftrufe, my riddling days are paft.

CHORUS.

  Look now for no inchanting voice, nor fear
The bait of honied words; a rougher tongue
Draws hitherward, I know him by his ftride,
The giant Harapha of Gath, his look

Haughty as is his pile high-built and proud.
Comes he in peace? what wind hath blown him hither
I lefs conjecture than when firft I faw
The fumptuous Dalila floating this way:            ·
His habit carries peace, his brow defiance.

SAMSON.

Or peace or not, alike to me he comes.

CHORUS.

His fraught we foon fhall know, he now arrives.

HARAPHA.

I come not, Samfon, to condole thy chance,
As thefe perhaps, yet wifh it had not been,
Though for no friendly' intent.  I am of Gath,
Men call me Harapha, of ftock renown'd
As Og or Anak and the Emims old
That Kiriathaim held, thou know'ft me now
If thou at all art known.  Much I have heard
Of thy prodigious might and feats perform'd
Incredible to me, in this difpleas'd,
That I was never prefent on the place
Of thofe encounters, where we might have try'd
Each other's force in camp or lifted field:
And now am come to fee of whom fuch noife
Hath walk'd about, and each limb to furvey,
If thy appearance anfwer loud report.

SAMSON.

The way to know were not to fee but tafte.

HARAPHA.

Doft thou already fingle me? I thought
Gyves and the mill had tam'd thee.  O that fortune
Had brought me to the field, where thou art fam'd.

To' have wrought fuch wonders with an afs's jaw;
I fhould have forc'd thee foon with other arms,
Or left thy carcafe where the afs lay thrown:
So had the glory' of prowefs been recover'd
To Paleftine, won by a Philiftine
From the unforefkin'd race, of whom thou bear'ft
The higheft name for valiant acts; that honour
Certain to' have won by mortal duel from thee,
I lofe, prevented by thy eyes put out.

SAMSON.

Boaft not of what thou wouldft have done, but do
What then thou wouldft, thou feeft it in thy hand.

HARAPHA.

To combat with a blind man I difdain,
And thou haft need much wafhing to be touch'd.

SAMSON.

Such ufage as your honourable lords
Afford me' affaffinated and betray'd,
Who durft not with their whole united powers
In fight withftand me fingle and unarm'd,
Nor in the houfe with chamber ambufhes
Clofe-banded durft attack me, no not fleeping,
Till they had hir'd a woman with their gold
Breaking her marriage faith to circumvent me.
Therefore without feign'd fhifts let be affign'd
Some narrow place inclos'd, where fight may give
    thee,
Or rather flight, no great advantage on me;
Then put on all thy gorgeous arms, thy helmet
And brigandine of brafs, thy broad habergeon,
Vaut-brafs and greves, and gauntlet, add thy fpear,

K

A weaver's beam, and fev'n-times-folded fhield,
I only with an oaken-ftaff will meet thee,
And raife fuch outcries on thy clatter'd iron,
Which long fhall not withhold me from thy head,
That in a little time while breath remains thee,
Thou oft fhalt wifh thyfelf at Gath to boaft
Again in fafety what thou wouldft have done
To Samfon, but fhalt never fee Gath more.

HARAPHA.

Thou durft not thus difparage glorious arms,
Which greateft heroes have in battle worn,
Their ornament and fafety, had not fpells
And black inchantments, fome magician's art,
Arm'd thee or charm'd thee ftrong, which thou from
        Heaven
Feign'dft at thy birth was giv'n thee in thy hair,
Where ftrength can leaft abide, though all thy hairs
Were briftles rang'd like thofe that ridge the back
Of chaf'd wild boars, or ruffled porcupines.

SAMSON.

I know no fpells, ufe no forbidden arts;
My truft is in the living God, who gave me
At my nativity this ftrength, diffus'd
No lefs through all my finews, joints, and bones,
Than thine, while I preferv'd thefe locks unfhorn,
The pledge of my unviolated vow.
For proof hereof, if Dagon be thy God,
Go to his temple, invocate his aid
With folemneft devotion, fpread before him
How highly it concerns his glory now
To fruftrate and diffolve thefe magic fpells,

Which I to be the power of Ifrael's God
Avow, and challenge Dagon to the teft,
Offering to combat thee his champion bold,
With th' utmoft of his Godhead feconded:
Then thou fhalt fee, or rather to thy forrow
Soon feel, whofe God is ftrongeft, thine or mine.

### HARAPHA.

Prefume not on thy God, whate'er he be,
Thee he regards not, owns not, hath cut off
Quite from his people, and deliver'd up
Into thy enemies hand, permitted them
To put out both thine eyes, and fetter'd fend thee
Into the common prifon, there to grind
Among the flaves and affes thy comrádes,
As good for nothing elfe, no better fervice
With thofe thy boift'rous locks, no worthy match
For valour to affail, nor by the fword
Of noble warrior, fo to ftain his honour,
But by the barber's razor beft fubdued.

### SAMSON.

All thefe indignities, for fuch they are
From thine, thefe evils I deferve and more,
Acknowledge them from God inflicted on me
Juftly, yet defpair not of his final pardon
Whofe ear is ever open, and his eye
Gracious to re-admit the fuppliant;
In confidence whereof I once again
Defy thee to the trial of mortal fight,
By combat to decide whofe God is God,
Thine or whom I with Ifrael's fons adore.

HARAPHA.

Fair honour that thou doſt thy God, in truſting
He will accept thee to defend his cauſe,
A murderer, a revolter, and a robber.

SAMSON.

Tongue-doughty Giant, how doſt thou prove me
    theſe?

HARAPHA.

Is not thy nation ſubjeƈt to our lords?
Their magiſtrates confeſs'd it, when they took thee
As a league-breaker and deliver'd bound
Into our hands: for hadſt thou not committed
Notorious murder on thoſe thirty men
At Aſcalon, who never did thee harm,
Then like a robber ſtripp'dſt them of their robes?
The Philiſtines, when thou hadſt broke the league,
Went up with armed pow'rs thee only ſeeking,
To others did no violence nor ſpoil.

SAMSON.

Among the daughters of the Philiſtines
I choſe a wife, which argued me no foe;
And in your city held my nuptial feaſt:
But your ill-meaning politician lords,
Under pretence of bridal friends and gueſts,
Appointed to await me thirty ſpies,          .
Who threatening cruel death conſtrain'd the bride
To wring from me and tell to them my ſecret,
That ſolv'd the riddle which I had propos'd.
When I perceiv'd all ſet on enmity,
As on my enemies, wherever chanc'd,

I us'd hoftility, and took their fpoil
To pay my underminers in their coin.
My nation was fubjected to your lords.
It was the force of conqueft; force with force
Is well ejected when the conquer'd can.
But I a private perfon, whom my country
As a league-breaker gave up bound, prefum'd
Single rebellion and did hoftile acts.
I was no private but a perfon rais'd
With ftrength fufficient and command from Heaven
To free my country; if their fervile minds
Me their deliverer fent would not receive,
But to their mafters gave me up for nought,
Th' unworthier they; whence to this day they ferve.
I was to do my part from Heav'n affign'd,
And had perform'd it, if my own offence
Had not difabled me, not all your force:
Thefe fhifts refuted, anfwer thy appellant
Though by his blindnefs maim'd for high attempts,
Who now defies thee thrice to fingle fight,
As a petty enterprife of fmall enforce.

HARAPHA.

With thee, a man condemn'd, a flave inroll'd,
Due by the law to capital punifhment?
To fight with thee no man of arms will deign.

SAMSON.

Cam'ft thou for this, vain boafter, to furvey me,
To defcant on my ftrength, and give thy verdict?
Come nearer, part not hence fo flight inform'd;
But take good heed my hand furvey not thee.

HARAPHA.

O Baal-zebub! can my ears unus'd
Hear thefe difhonours, and not render death?

SAMSON.

No man withholds thee, nothing from thy hand
Fear I incurable; bring up thy van,
My heels are fetter'd, but my fift is free.

HARAPHA.

This infolence other kind of anfwer fits.

SAMSON.

Go baffled coward, left I run upon thee,
Though in thefe chains, bulk without fpirit vaft,
And with one buffet lay thy ftructure low,
Or fwing thee in the air, then dafh thee down
To th' hazard of thy brains and fhatter'd fides.

HARAPHA.

By Aftaroth ere long thou fhalt lament
Thefe braveries in irons loaden on thee.

CHORUS.

His giantfhip is gone fomewhat creft-fall'n,
Stalking with lefs unconfcionable ftrides,
And lower looks, but in a fultry chafe.

SAMSON.

I dread him not, nor all his giant-brood,
Though fame divulge him father of five fons,
All of gigantic fize, Goliah chief.

CHORUS.

He will directly to the lords, I fear,
And with malicious counfel ftir them up
Some way or other yet further to afflict thee.

SAMSON.

He muft allege fome caufe, and offer'd fight
Will not dare mention, left a queftion rife
Whether he durft accept the' offer or not,
And that he durft not plain enough appear'd.
Much more affliction than already felt
They cannot well impofe, nor I fuftain;
If they intend advantage of my labours,
The work of many hands, which earns my keeping
With no fmall profit daily to my owners.
But come what will, my deadlieft foe will prove
My fpeedieft friend, by death to rid me hence,
The worft that he can give, to me the beft.
Yet fo it may fall out, becaufe their end
Is hate, not help to me, it may with mine
Draw their own ruin who attempt the deed.

CHORUS.

Oh how comely it is, and how reviving
To the fpirits of juft men long opprefs'd!
When God into the hands of their deliverer
Puts invincible might
To quell the mighty of the earth, th' oppreffor,
The brute and boift'rous force of violent men
Hardy and induftrious to fupport
Tyrannic pow'r, but raging to purfue
The righteous and all fuch as honour truth;
He all their ammunition
And feats of war defeats
With plain heroic magnitude of mind
And celeftial vigour arm'd,
Their armouries and magazines contemns,

Renders them ufelefs, while
With winged expedition
Swift as the lightning glance he executes
His errand on the wicked, who furpris'd
Lofe their defence diftracted and amaz'd.
　　But patience is more oft the exercife
Of faints, the trial of their fortitude,
Making them each his own deliverer,
And victor over all
That tyranny or fortune can inflict.
Either of thefe is in thy lot,
Samfon, with might indued
Above the fons of men; but fight bereav'd
May chance to number thee with thofe
Whom patience finally muft crown.
　　This idol's day hath been to thee no day of reft,
Labouring thy mind
More than the working day thy hands.
And yet perhaps more trouble is behind,
For I defcry this way
Some other tending, in his hand
A fceptre or quaint ftaff he bears,
Comes on amain, fpeed in his look.
By his habit I difcern him now
A public officer, and now at hand.
His meffage will be fhort and voluble.

OFFICER.

Hebrews, the pris'ner Samfon here I feek.

CHORUS.

His manacles remark him, there he fits.

OFFICER.

Samfon, to thee our lords thus bid me fay;
This day to Dagon is a folemn feaft,
With facrifices, triumph, pomp, and games;
Thy ftrength they know furpaffing human rate,
And now fome public proof thereof require
To honour this great feaft, and great affembly;
Rife therefore with all fpeed and come along,
Where I will fec thee hearten'd and frefh clad
To' appear as fits before th' illuftrious lords.

SAMSON.

Thou know'ft I am an Hebrew, therefore tell them,
Our law forbids at their religious rights
My prefence; for that caufe I cannot come.

OFFICER.

This anfwer, be affur'd, will not content them.

SAMSON.

Have they not fword-players, and every fort
Of gymnic artifts, wreftlers, riders, runners,
Juglers and dancers, antics, mummers, mimics,
But they muft pick me out with fhackles tir'd,
And over-labour'd at their public mill,
To make them fport with blind activity?
Do they not feek occafion of new quarrels
On my refufal to diftrefs me more,
Or make a game of my calamities?
Return the way thou cam'ft, I will not come.

OFFICER.

Regard thyfclf, this will offend them highly.

SAMSON.

Myfelf? my confcience and internal peace.

Can they think me fo broken, fo debas'd
With corporal fervitude, that my mind ever
Will condefcend to fuch abfurd commands?
Although their drudge, to be their fool or jefter,
And in my midft of forrow and heart· grief
To fhow them feats, and play before their god,
The worft of all indignities, yet on me
Join'd with extreme contempt? I will not come.

OFFICER.

My meffage was impos'd on me with fpeed,
Brooks no delay: is this·thy refolution?

SAMSON.

So take it with what fpeed thy meffage needs.

OFFICER.

I am forry what this ftoutnefs will produce.

SAMSON.

Perhaps thou fhalt have caufe to forrow' indeed.

CHORUS.

Confider, Samfon; matters now are ftrain'd
Up to the height, whether to hold or break;
He's gone, and who knows how he may report
Thy words by adding fuel to the flame?
Expect another meffage more imperious,
More lordly thund'ring than thou well wilt bear.

SAMSON.

Shall I abufe this confecrated gift
Of ftrength, again returning with my hair
After my great tranfgreffion, fo requite
Favour renew'd, and add a greater fin
By proftituting holy things to idols;
A Nazarite in place abominable

Vaunting my ſtrength in honour to their Dagon?
Beſides how vile, contemptible, ridiculous,
What act more execrably unclean, profane?

### CHORUS.

Yet with this ſtrength thou ſerv'ſt the Philiſtines,
Idolatrous, uncircumeis'd, unclean.

### SAMSON.

Not in their idol-worſhip, but by labour
Honeſt and lawful to deſerve my food
Of thoſe who have me in their civil power.

### CHORUS.

Where the heart joins not, outward acts defile not.

### SAMSON.

Where outward force conſtrains, the ſentence holds.
But who conſtrains me to the temple' of Dagon,
Not dragging? the Philiſtian lords command.
Commands are no reſtraints.   If I obey them,
I do it freely, vent'ring to diſpleaſe
God for the fear of man, and man prefer,
Set God behind: which in his jealouſy
Shall never, unrepented, find forgiveneſs.
Yet that he may diſpenſe with me or thee
Preſent in temples at idolatrous rites
For ſome important cauſe, thou need'ſt not doubt.

### CHORUS.

How thou wilt here come off ſurmounts my reach.

### SAMSON.

Be of good courage, I begin to feel
Some rouſing motions in me which diſpoſe
To ſomething extraordinary my thoughts.
I with this meſſenger will go along,

Nothing to do, be fure, that may difhonour
Our law, or ftain my vow of Nazarite.
If there be ought of prefage in the mind,
This day will be remarkable in my life
By fome great act, or of my days the laft.

CHORUS.

In time thou haft refolv'd, the man returns.

OFFICER.

Samfon, this fecond meffage from our lords
To thee I am bid fay. Art thou our flave,
Our captive, at the public mill our drudge,
And dar'ft thou at our fending and command
Difpute thy coming? come without delay;
Or we fhall find fuch engines to affail
And hamper thee, as thou fhalt come of force,
Though thou wert firmlier faften'd than a rock.

SAMSON.

I could be well content to try their art,
Which to no few of them would prove pernicious.
Yet knowing their advantages too many,
Becaufe they fhall not trail me through their ftreets
Like a wild beaft, I am content to go.
Mafters commands come with a pow'r refiftlefs
To fuch as owe them abfolute fubjection;
And for a life who will not change his purpofe?
(So mutable are all the ways of men)
Yet this be fure, in nothing to comply
Scandalous or forbidden in our law.

OFFICER.

I praife thy refolution: doff thefe links:
By this compliance thou wilt win the lords
To favour, and perhaps to fet thee free.

### SAMSON.

Brethren, farewell; your company along
I will not wiſh, leſt it perhaps offend them
To ſee me girt with friends; and how the ſight
Of me as of a common enemy,
So dreaded once, may now exaſperate them
I know not: lords are lordlieſt in their wine;
And the well-feaſted prieſt then ſooneſt fir'd
With zeal, if ought religion ſeem concern'd;
No leſs the people on their holy-days
Impetuous, inſolent, unquenchable:
Happen what may, of me expeɕt to hear
Nothing diſhonourable, impure, unworthy
Our God, our law, my nation, or myſelf,
The laſt of me or no I cannot warrant.

### CHORUS.

Go, and the Holy One
Of Iſrael be thy guide
To what may ſerve his glory beſt, and ſpread his name
Great among the heathen round;
Send thee the angel of thy birth, to ſtand
Faſt by thy ſide, who from thy father's field
Rode up in flames after his meſſage told
Of thy conception, and be now a ſhield
Of fire; that Spirit that firſt ruſh'd on thee
In the camp of Dan
Be efficacious in thee now at need.
For never was from Heav'n imparted
Meaſure of ſtrength ſo great to mortal ſeed,
As in thy wondrous aɕtions hath been ſeen.
But wherefore comes old Manoah in ſuch haſte

With youthful fteps? much livelier than ere while
He feems: fuppofing here to find his fon,
Or of him bringing to us fome glad news?

MANOAH.

Peace with you, brethren; my inducement hither ·
Was not at prefent here to find my fon,
By order of the lords new parted hence
To come and play before them at their feaft.
I heard all as I came, the city rings,
And numbers thither flock, I had no will,
Left I fhould fee him forc'd to things unfeemly.
But that which mov'd my coming now, was chiefly
To give ye part with me what hope I have
With good fuccefs to work his liberty.

CHORUS.

That hope would much rejoice us to partake ·
With thee; fay, reverend fire, we thirft to hear.

MANOAH.

I have attempted one by one the lords
Either at home, or through the high ftreet paffing,
With fupplication prone and father's tears,
T' accept of ranfom for my fon their pris'ner.
Some much averfe I found and wond'rous harfh,
Contemptuous, proud, fet on revenge and fpite;
That part moft reverenc'd Dagon and his priefts:
Others more moderate feeming, but their aim
Private reward, for which both God and ftate
They eafily would fet to fale: a third
More generous far and civil, who confefs'd
They had enough reveng'd, having reduc'd
Their foe to mifery beneath their fears,

The reſt was magnanimity to remit,
If ſome convenient ranſom were propos'd.
What noiſe or ſhout was that? it tore the ſky.

CHORUS.

Doubtleſs the people ſhouting to behold ·
Their once great dread, captive, and blind before
        them,
Or at ſome proof of ſtrength before them ſhown.

MANOAH.

His ranſom, if my whole inheritance
May compaſs it, ſhall willingly be paid
And number'd down: much rather I ſhall chooſe
To live the pooreſt in my tribe, than richeſt,
And he in that calamitous priſon left.
No, I am fix'd not to part hence without him.
For his redemption all my patrimony,
If need be, I am ready to forego
And quit: not wanting him I ſhall want nothing.

CHORUS.

Fathers are wont to lay up for their ſons,
Thou for thy ſon art bent to lay out all:
Sons wont to nurſe their parents in old age,
Thou in old age car'ſt how to nurſe thy ſon
Made older than thy age through eye-ſight loſt.

MANOAH.

It ſhall be my delight to tend his eyes,
And view him ſitting in the houſe, ennobled
With all thoſe high exploits by him achiev'd,
And on his ſhoulders waving down thoſe locks,
That of a nation arm'd the ſtrength contain'd:
And I perſuade me God had not permitted

His ftrength again to grow up with his hair
Garrifon'd round about him like a camp
Of faithful foldiery, were not his purpofe
To ufe him further yet in fome great fervice,
Not to fit idle with fo great a gift
Ufelefs, and thence ridiculous about him.
And fince his ftrength with eye-fight was not loft,
God will reftore him eye-fight to his ftrength.

### CHORUS.

Thy hopes are not ill founded nor feem vain
Of his delivery, and thy joy thereon
Conceiv'd, agreeable to a father's love,
In both which we, as next, participate.

### MANOAH.

I know your friendly minds and— O what noife!
Mercy of Heav'n, what hideous noife was that!
Horribly loud, unlike the former fhout.

### CHORUS.

Noife call you it or univerfal groan,
As if the whole inhabitation perifh'd!
Blood, death, and deathful deeds are in that noife,
Ruin, deftruction at the utmoft point.

### MANOAH.

Of ruin indeed methought I heard the noife:
Oh it continues, they have flain my fon.

### CHORUS.

Thy fon is rather flaying them, that outcry
From flaughter of one foe could not afcend.

### MANOAH.

Some difmal accident it needs muft be;
What fhall we do, ftay here or run and fee?

#### CHORUS.

Beſt keep together here, left running thither
We unawares run into danger's mouth.
This evil on the Philiftines is fall'n;
From whom could elſe a general cry be heard?
The ſufferers then will ſcarce moleſt us here,
From other hands we need not much to fear.
What if his eye-fight (for to Iſrael's God
Nothing is hard) by miracle reſtor'd,
He now be dealing dole among his foes,
And over heaps of ſlaughter'd walk his way?

#### MANOAH.

That were a joy preſumptuous to be thought.

#### CHORUS.

Yet God hath wrought things as incredible
For his people of old; what hinders now?

#### MANOAH.

He can I know, but doubt to think he will;
Yet hope would fain ſubſcribe, and tempts belief.
A little ſtay will bring ſome notice hither.

#### CHORUS.

Of good or bad ſo great, of bad the ſooner;
For evil news rides poſt, while good news baits.
And to our wiſh I ſee one hither ſpeeding,
An Hebrew, as I gueſs, and of our tribe.

#### MESSENGER.

O whither ſhall I run, or which way fly
The fight of this ſo horrid ſpectacle,
Which erſt my eyes beheld and yet behold?
For dire imagination ſtill purſues me.

But providence or inftinét of nature feems,
Or reafon though difturb'd, and fcarce confulted,·
To' have guided me aright, I know not how,
To thee firft, reverend Manoah, and to thefe
My countrymen, whom here I knew remaining,
As at fome diftance from the place of horrour,
So in the fad event too much concern'd.

MANOAH.

The accident was loud, and here before thee
With rueful cry, yet what it was we hear not;
No preface needs, thou feeft we long to know.

MESSENGER.

It would burft forth, but I recover breath
And fenfe diftraét, to know well what I utter.

MANOAH.

Tell us the fum, the circumftance defer.

MESSENGER.

Gaza yet ftands, but all her fons are fall'n,
All in a moment overwhelm'd and fall'n.

MANOAH.

Sad, but thou know'ft to Ifraelites not faddeft
The defolation of a hoftile city.

MESSENGER.

Feed on that firft, there may in grief be furfeit.

MANOAH.

Relate by whom.

MESSENGER.

By Samfon.

MANOAH.

That ftill leffens
The forrow, and converts it nigh to joy.

MESSENGER.

Ah Manoah, I refrain, too fuddenly
To utter what will come at laft too foon;
Left evil tidings with too rude irruption
Hitting thy aged ear fhould pierce too deep.

MANOAH.

Sufpenfe in news is torture, fpeak them out.

MESSENGER.

Take then the worft in brief, Samfon is dead.

MANOAH.

The worft indeed, O all my hope's defeated
To free him hence! but death who fets all free
Hath paid his ranfom now and full difcharge.
What windy joy this day had I conceiv'd
Hopeful of his delivery, which now proves
Abortive as the firft-born bloom of fpring
Nipt with the lagging rear of winter's froft!
Yet ere I give the reins to grief, fay firft,
How dy'd he; death to life is crown or fhame.
All by him fell thou fay'ft, by whom fell he?
What glorious hand gave Samfon his death's wound?

MESSENGER.

Unwounded of his enemies he fell.

MANOAH.

Wearied with flaughter then or how? explain.

MESSENGER.

By his own hands.

MANOAH.

Self-violence? what caufe
Brought him fo foon at variance with himfelf
Among his foes?

MESSENGER.

Inevitable caufe
At once both to deftroy and be deftroy'd;
The edifice, where all were met to fee him,
Upon their heads and on his own he pull'd.

MANOAH.

O laftly over-ftrong againft thyfelf!
A dreadful way thou took'ft to thy revenge.
More than enough we know; but while things yet
Are in confufion, give us if thou canft, ?
Eye-witnefs of what firft or laft was done?
Relation more particular and diftinct,

MESSENGER.

Occafions drew me early to this city,
And as the gates I enter'd with fun-rife,
The morning trumpets feftival proclaim'd
Through each high ftreet: little I had difpatch'd,
When all abroad was rumour'd that this day
Samfon fhould be brought forth, to fhow the people
Proof of his mighty ftrength in feats and games;
I forrow'd at his captive ftate, but minded
Not to be abfent at that fpectacle.
The building was a fpacious theatre
Half-round on two main pillars vaulted high,
With feats where all the lords and each degree
Of fort, might fit in order to behold;
The other fide was open, where the throng
On banks and fcaffolds under fky might ftand;
I among thefe aloof obfcurely ftood.
The feaft and noon grew high, and facrifice
Had fill'd their hearts with mirth, high cheer, and wine,

When to their fports they turn'd.   Immediately
Was Samfon as a public fervant brought,
In their ftate livery clad; before him pipes
And timbrels, on each fide went armed guards,
Both horfe and foot, before him and behind
Archers and flingers, cataphraᴄts and fpears.
At fight of him the people with a fhout
Rifted the air, clamouring their God with praife,
Who' had made their dreadful enemy their thrall.
He patient but undaunted where they led him,
Came to the place, and what was fet before him,
Which without help of eye might be affay'd,
To heave, pull, draw, or break, he ftill perform'd
All with incredible, ftupendous force,
None daring to appear antagonift.
At length for intermiffion fake they led him
Between the pillars; he his guide requefted
(For fo from fuch as nearer ftood we heard)
As over-tir'd to let him lean a while
With both his arms on thofe two maffy pillars,
That to the arched roof gave main fupport.
He unfufpicious led him; which when Samfon
Felt in his arms, with head a while inclin'd,
And eyes faft fix'd he ftood, as one who pray'd,
Or fome great matter in his mind revolv'd:
At laft with head ereᴄt thus cry'd aloud,
" Hitherto, lords, what your commands impos'd
I have perform'd, as reafon was, obeying,
Not without wonder or delight beheld:
Now of my own accord fuch other trial
I mean to fhow you of my ftrength, yet greater;

As with amaze ſhall ſtrike all who behold."
This utter'd, ſtraining all his nerves he bow'd,
As with the force of winds and waters pent,
When mountains tremble, thoſe two maſſy pillars
With horrible convulſion to and fro,
He tugg'd, he ſhook, till down they came and drew
The whole roof after them, with burſt of thunder
Upon the heads of all who ſat beneath,
Lords, ladies, captains, counſellors, or prieſts,
Their choice nobility and flow'r, not only
Of this but each Philiſtian city round
Met from all parts to ſolemnize this feaſt.
Samſon with theſe immix'd, inevitably
Pull'd down the ſame deſtruction on himſelf;
The vulgar only ſcap'd who ſtood without.

CHORUS.

O dearly-bought revenge, yet glorious!
Living or dying thou haſt fulfill'd
The work for which thou waſt foretold
To Iſrael, and now ly'ſt victorious
Among thy ſlain ſelf-kill'd
Not willingly, but tangled in the fold
Of dire neceſſity, whoſe law in death conjoin'd
Thee with thy ſlaughter'd foes in number more
Than all thy life had ſlain before.

SEMICHORUS.

While their hearts were jocund and ſublime,
Drunk with idolatry, drunk with wine,
And fat regorg'd of bulls and goats,
Chaunting their idol, and preferring
Before our living Dread who dwells

In Silo his bright fanctuary:
Among them he a fpi'rit of phrenzy fent,
Who hurt their m͟  ͟
And urg'd them on with mad defire
To call in hafte for their deftroyer;
They only fet on fport and play
Unweetingly importun'd
Their own deftruction to come fpeedy upon them.
So fond are mortal men
Fall'n into wrath divine,
As their own ruin on themfelves t' invite,
Infenfate left, or to fenfe reprobate,
And with blindnefs internal ftruck.

SEMICHORUS.

But he though blind of fight,
Defpis'd and thought extinguifh'd quite,
With inward eyes illuminated,
His fiery virtue rous'd
From under afhes into fudden flame,
And as an evening dragon came,
Affailant on the perched roofts,
And nefts in order rang'd
Of tame villatic fowl; but as an eagle
His cloudlefs thunder bolted on their heads.
So virtue giv'n for loft,
Deprefs'd, and overthrown, as feem'd,
Like that felf-begotten bird
In the Arabian woods imboft,
That no fecond knows nor third,
And lay ere while a holocauft,
From out her afhy womb now teem'd,

Revives, reflourifhes, then vigorous moft
When moft inactive deem'd,
And though her body die, he me furvives
A fecular bird ages of lives.

MANOAH.

Come, come, no time for lamentation now,
Nor much more caufe; Samfon hath quit himfelf
Like Samfon, and heroicly hath finifh'd
A life heroic, on his enemies
Fully reveng'd, hath left them years of mourning,
And lamentation to the fons of Caphtor
Through all Philiftian bounds; to Ifrael
Honour hath left, and freedom, let but them
Find courage to lay hold on this occafion;
To' himfelf and father's houfe eternal fame;
And which is beft and happieft yet, all this
With God not parted from him, as was fear'd,
But favouring and affifting to the end,
Nothing is here for tears, nothing to wail
Or knock the breaft, no weaknefs, no contempt,
Difpraife, or blame, nothing but well and fair,
And what may quiet us in a death fo noble.
Let us go find the body where it lies
Soak'd in his enemies blood, and from the ftream
With lavers pure and cleanfing herbs wafh off
The clotted gore.  I with what fpeed the while
(Gaza is not in plight to fay us nay)
Will fend for all my kindred, all my friends,
To fetch him hence, and folemnly attend
With filent obfequy and funeral train
Home to his father's houfe: there will I build him

A monument, and plant it round with fhade
Of laurel ever green, and branching palm,    .
With all his trophies hung, and acts inroll'd
In copious legend, or fweet lyric fong.
Thither fhall all the valiant youth refort,
And from his memory inflame their breafts
To matchlefs valour, and adventures high:
The virgins alfo fhall on feaftful days
Vifit his tomb with flow'rs, only bewailing
His lot unfortunate in nuptial choice,
From whence captivity and lofs of eyes.

CHORUS.

All is beft, though we oft doubt,
What th' unfearchable difpofe
Of higheft wifdom brings about,
And ever beft found in the clofe.
Oft he feems to hide his face,
But unexpectedly returns,
And to his faithful champion hath in place
Bore witnefs glorioufly; whence Gaza mourns
And all that band them to refift
His uncontrollable intent;
His fervants he with new acquift
Of true experience from this great event
With peace and confolation hath difmift
And calm of mind, all paffion fpent.

END OF SAMSON AGONISTES.

# POEMS

UPON

# SEVERAL OCCASIONS,

COMPOSED AT SEVERAL TIMES.

.............. BACCARE FRONTEM
CINGITE, NE VATI NOCEAT MALA LINGUA FUTURO.
VIRGIL, ECLOG. 7.

# POEMS

··ON

# SEVERAL OCCASIONS.

## I.

### ANNO ÆTATIS 17.

###### ON THE DEATH OF A FAIR INFANT, DYING OF A COUGH.

#### 1.

O FAIREST flow'r no fooner blown but blafted,
Soft filken primrofe fading timelefsly,
Summer's chief honour, if thou hadft out-lafted
Bleak Winter's force that made thy bloffom dry;
For he being amorous on that lovely dye
   That did thy cheek envermeil, thought to kifs,
But kill'd, alas, and then bewail'd his fatal blifs.

#### 2.

For fince grim Aquilo his charioteer
By boiftrous rape th' Athenian damfel got,
He thought it touch'd his deity full near,
If likewife he fome fair one wedded not,
Thereby to wipe away th' infámous blot

Of long-uncoupled bed, and childlefs eld,
Which 'mongſt the wanton Gods a foul reproach was
    held.

### 3.

So mounting up in icy-pearlèd car,
Through middle empire of the freezing air
He wander'd long, till thee he fpy'd from far:
There ended waſ his queſt, there ceas'd his care,
Down he defcended from his fnow-foft chair,
    But all unwares with his cold-kind embrace
Unhous'd thy virgin foul from her fair biding place.

### 4.

Yet art thou not inglorious in thy fate;
For fo Apollo, with unweeting hand,
Whilome did flay his dearly-loved mate,
Young Hyacinth born on Eurotas' ſtrand,
Young Hyacinth the pride of Spartan land;
    But then transform'd him to a purple flower:
Alack that fo to change thee Winter had no power.

### 5.

    Yet can I not perfuade me thou art dead,
Or that thy corfe corrupts in earth's dark womb,
Or that thy beauties lie in wormy bed,
Hid from the world in a low delved tomb;
Could Heav'n for pity thee fo ſtriﬅly doom?
    Oh no! for fomething in thy face did ſhine
Above mortality, that ſhow'd thou waſt divine.

### 6.

Refolve me then, oh Soul moſt furely bleſt,
(If fo it be that thou thefe plaints doſt hear)
Tell me bright Spirit where'er thou hovereſt,

Whether above that high firft-moving fphere,
Or in th' Elyfian fields (if fuch there were)
  Oh fay me true, if thou wert mortal wight,
And why from us fo quickly thou didft take thy flight.

### 7.

Wert thou fome ftar which from the ruin'd roof
Of fhak'd Olympus by mifchance didft fall;
Which careful Jove in nature's true behoof
Took up, and in fit place did reinftall?
Or did of late Earth's fons befiege the wall
  Of fheeny Heav'n, and thou fome Goddefs fled
Amongft us here below to hide thy nectar'd head?

### 8.

Or wert thou that juft Maid who once before
Forfook the hated earth, O tell me footh,
And cam'ft again to vifit us once more?
Or wert thou that fweet fmiling Youth?
Or that crown'd matron fage white-robed Truth?
  Or any other of that heav'nly brood
Let down in cloudy throne to do the world fome good?

### 9.

Or wert thou of the golden-winged hoft,
Who having clad thyfelf in human weed,
To earth from thy prefixed feat didft poft,
And after fhort abode fly back with fpeed,
As if to fhow what creatures Heav'n doth breed,
  Thereby to fet the hearts of men on fire
To fcorn the fordid world, and unto Heav'n afpire?

### 10.

But oh why didft thou not ftay here below
To blefs us with thy heav'n-lov'd innocence,

To flake his wrath whom fin hath made our foe,
To turn fwift-rufhing black perdition hence,
Or drive away the flaughtering peftilence,
   To ftand 'twixt us and our deferved fmart?
But thou canft beft perform that office where thou art.

### 11.

Then thou the Mother of fo fweet a Child
Her falfe imagin'd lofs ceafe to lament,
And wifely learn to curb thy forrows wild;
Think what a prefent thou to God haft fent,
And render him with patience what he lent;
   This if thou do, he will an offspring give,
That till the world's laft end fhall make thy name to
   live.

## II.

### ANNO ÆTATIS 19.

AT A VACATION EXERCISE IN THE COLLEGE, PART
LATIN, PART ENGLISH. THE LATIN SPEECHES
ENDED, THE ENGLISH THUS BEGAN.

HAIL native Language, that by finews weak
Didft move my firft endeavouring tongue to fpeak,
And mad'ft imperfect words with childifh trips,
Half unpronounc'd, flide through my infant-lips,
Driving dumb filence from the portal door,
Where he had mutely fat two years before:

Here I falute thee, and thy pardon afk,
That now I ufe thee in my latter tafk:
Small lofs it is that thence can come unto thee,
I know my tongue but little grace can do thee:
Thou need'ft not be ambitious to be firft,
Believe me I have thither packt the worft:
And, if it happen as I did forecaft,
The daintieft difhes fhall be ferv'd up laft.
I pray thee then deny me not thy aid
For this fame fmall negle&t that I have made:
But hafte thee ftraight to do me once a pleafure,
And from thy wardrobe bring thy chiefeft treafure,
Not thofe new fangled toys, and trimming flight
Which takes our late fantaftics with delight,
But cull thofe richeft robes, and gay'ft attire
Which deepeft fpirits, and choiceft wits defire:
I have fome naked thoughts that rove about,
And loudly knock to have their paffage out;
And weary of their place do only ftay
Till thou haft deck'd them in thy beft array;
That fo they may without fufpe&t or fears
Fly fwiftly to this fair affembly's ears;
Yet I had rather, if I were to choofe,
Thy fervice in fome graver fubje&t ufe,
Such as may make thee fearch thy coffers round,
Before thou clothe my fancy in fit found:
Such where the deep tranfported mind may foar
Above the wheeling poles, and at Heav'n's door
Look in, and fee each blifsful Deity
How he before the thunderous throne doth lie,
Lift'ning to what unfhorn Apollo fings
To th' touch of golden wires, while Hebe brings.

M

Immortal nectar to her kingly fire:
Then paffing through the fpheres of watchful fire,
And mifty regions of wide air next under,
And hills of fnow, and lofts of piled thunder,
May tell at length how green-ey'd Neptune raves,
In Heav'n's defiance muftering all his waves;
Then fing of fecret things that came to pafs
When beldam Nature in her cradle was;
And laft of kings, and queens, and heroes old,
Such as the wife Demodocus once told
In folemn fongs at king Alcinous feaft,
While fad Ulyffes foul and all the reft
Are held with his melodious harmony
In willing chains and fweet captivity.
But fie, my wand'ring Mufe, how thou doft ftray!
Expectance calls thee now another way,
Thou know'ft it muft be now thy only bent
To keep in compafs of thy predicament:
Then quick about thy purpos'd bufinefs come,
That to the next I may refign my room.


THEN ENS IS REPRESENTED AS FATHER OF THE
PREDICAMENTS HIS TEN SONS, WHEREOF THE
ELDEST STOOD FOR SUBSTANCE WITH
HIS CANONS, WHICH ENS, THUS
SPEAKING, EXPLAINS.


Good luck befriend thee, Son; for at thy birth
The fairy ladies danc'd upon the earth;
Thy drowfy nurfe hath fworn fhe did them fpie
Come tripping to the room where thou didft lie,

And fweetly finging round about thy bed
Strow all their bleffings on thy fleeping head.
She heard them give thee this, that thou fhouldft ftill
From eyes of mortals walk invifible:
Yet there is fomething that doth force my fear,
For once it was my difmal hap to hear
A Sibyl old, bow-bent with crooked age,
That far events full wifely could prefage,
And in time's long and dark profpective glafs
Forefaw what future days fhould bring to pafs;
Your fon, faid fhe, (nor can you it prevent)
Shall fubject be to many an accident.
O'er all his brethren he fhall reign as king,
Yet every one fhall make him underling;
And thofe that cannot live from him afunder
Ungratefully fhall ftrive to keep him under;
In worth and excellence he fhall out-go them,
Yet being above them, he fhall be below them;
From others he fhall ftand in need of nothing,
Yet on his brothers fhall depend for clothing.
To find a foe it fhall not be his hap,
And peace fhall lull him in her flow'ry lap;
Yet fhall he live in ftrife, and at his door
Devouring war fhall never ceafe to roar:
Yea it fhall be his natural property
To harbour thofe that are at enmity.
What pow'r, what force, what mighty fpell, if not
Your learned hands, can loofe this Gordian knot?

THE NEXT QUANTITY AND QUALITY SPAKE IN
PROSE, THEN RELATION WAS CALLED
BY HIS NAME.

Rivers arife; whether thou be the fon
Of utmoft Tweed, or Oofe, or gulphy Dun,
Or Trent, who like fome earth·born giant fpreads
His thirty arms along th' indented meads,
Or fullen Mole that runneth underneath,
Or Severn fwift, guilty of maiden's death,
Or rocky Avon, or of fedgy Lee,
Or coaly Tine, or ancient hallow'd Dee,
Or Humber loud that keeps the Scythian's name,
Or Medway fmooth, or royal tow'red Thame.

[The reft was Profe.]

## III.

ON

# THE MORNING OF CHRIST'S NATIVITY.

COMPOSED 1629.

1.

This is the month, and this the happy morn,
Wherein the Son of Heav'n's eternal King,
Of wedded maid, and virgin mother born,
Our great redemption from above did bring;
For fo the holy fages once did fing,
    That he our deadly forfeit fhould releafe,
And with his Father work us a perpctual peace.

### 2.

'That glorious form, that light unfufferable,
And that far-beaming blaze of majefty,
Wherewith he wont at Heav'n's high council-table
To fit the midft of Trinal Unity,
He laid afide; and here with us to be,
  Forfook the courts of everlafting day,
And chófe with us a darkfome houfe of mortal clay.

### 3.

Say heav'nly mufe, fhall not thy facred vein
Afford a prefent to the infant God ?
Haft thou no verfe, no hymn, or folemn ftrain,
To welcome him to this his new abode,
Now while the Heav'n by the fun's team untrod,
  Hath took no print of the approaching light,
And all the fpangled hoft keep watch in fquadrons
      bright ?

### 4.

See how from far upon the eaftern road
The ftar-led wizards hafte with odours fweet:
O run, prevent them with thy humble ode,
And lay it lowly at his bleffed feet;
Have thou the honour firft, thy Lord to greet,
  And join thy voice unto the angel quire,
From out his fecret altar touch'd with hallow'd fire.


## THE HYMN.

### 1.

IT was the winter wild,
While the Heav'n-born child
  All meanly wrapt in the rude manger lies;

Nature in awe to him
Hath dofft her gaudy trim,
   With her great Mafter fo to fympathize:
It was no feafon then for her
To wanton with the fun her lufty paramour.

### 2.

Only with fpeeches fair
She woos the gentle air
   To hide her guilty front with innocent fnow,
And on her naked fhame,
Pollute with finful blame,
   The faintly veil of maiden white to throw,
Confounded, that her Maker's eyes
Should look fo near upon her foul deformities.

### 3.

But he her fears to ceafe,
Sent down the meek-ey'd Peace;
   She crown'd with olive green, came foftly fliding
Down through the turning fphere
His ready harbinger,
   With turtle wing the amorous clouds dividing,
And waving wide her myrtle wand,
She ftrikes an univerfal peace through fea and land.

### 4.

No war, or battle's found
Was heard the world around:
   The idle fpear and fhield were high up hung,
The hooked chariot ftood,
Unftain'd with hoftile blood,
   The trumpet fpake not to the armed throng,
And kings fat ftill with awful eye,
As if they furely knew their fovereign Lord was by.

### 5.

But peaceful was the night,
Wherein the Prince of light
  His reign of peace upon the earth began:
The winds with wonder whift
Smoothly the waters kift,
  Whifp'ring new joys to the mild ocean,
Who now hath quite forgot to rave,
While birds of calm fit brooding on the charmed wave.

### 6.

The ftars with deep amaze
Stand fix'd in ftedfaft gaze,
  Bending one way their precious influence,
And will not take their flight,
For all the morning light,
  Or Lucifer that often warn'd them thence;
But in their glimmering orbs did glow,
Until their Lord himfelf befpake, and bid them go.

### 7.

And though the fhady gloom
Had given day her room,
  The fun himfelf withheld his wonted fpeed,
And hid his head for fhame,
As his inferior flame
  The new enlighten'd world no more fhould need;
He faw a greater fun appear
Than his bright throne, or burning axletree could
      bear.

### 8.

The fhepherds on the lawn,
Or ere the point of dawn,

Sat fimply chatting in a ruftic row;
Full little thought they then,
That the mighty Pan
 Was kindly come to live with them below;
Perhaps their loves, or elfe their fheep,
Was all that did their filly thoughts fo bufy keep.

9.

When fuch mufic fweet
Their hearts and ears did greet,
 As never was by mortal finger ftrook,
Divinely-warbled voice
Anfwering the ftringed noife,
 As all their fouls in blifsful rapture took:
The air fuch pleafure loath to lofe,
With thoufand echoes ftill prolongs each heav'nly clofe.

10.

Nature that heard fuch found,
Beneath the hollow round
 Of Cynthia's feat, the aery region thrilling,
Now was almoft won
To think her part was done,
 And that her reign had here its laft fulfilling;
She knew fuch harmony alone
Could hold all Heav'n and Earth in happier union.

11.

At laft furrounds their fight
A globe of circular light,
 That with long beams the fhame-fac'd night array'd;
The helmed Cherubim,
And fworded Seraphim,
 Are feen in glittering ranks with wings difplay'd,

Harping in loud and folemn quire,
With unexpreffive notes to Heav'n's new-born heir.

### 12.

Such mufic (as 'tis faid)
Before was never made,
  But when of old the fons of morning fung,
While the Creator great
His conftellations fet,
  And the well-balanc'd world on hinges hung, .
And caft the dark foundations deep,
And bid the weltring waves their oozy channel keep.

### 13.

Ring out ye cryftal fpheres,
Once blefs our human ears,
  (If ye have pow'r to touch our fenfes fo)
And let your filver chime
Move in melodious time,
  And let the bafe of Heav'n's deep organ blow,
And with your ninefold harmony
Make up full confort to th' angelic fymphony.

### 14.

For if fuch holy fong
Inwrap our fancy long,
  Time will run back, and fetch the age of gold,
And fpeckled Vanity
Will ficken foon and die,
  And leprous Sin will melt from earthly mould,
And Hell itfelf will pafs away,
And leave her dolorous manfions to the peering day.

### 15.

Yea Truth and Juftice then
Will down return to men,

Orb'd in a rainbow; and like glories wearing
Mercy will fit between,
Thron'd in celeftial fheen,
With radiant feet the tiffued clouds down fteering,
And Heav'n, as at fome feftival,
Will open wide the gates of her high palace hall.

### 16.

But wifeft Fate fays no,
This muft not yet be fo,
The babe lies yet in fmiling infancy,
That on the bitter crofs
Muft redeem our lofs;
So both himfelf and us to glorify:
Yet firft to thofe ychain'd in fleep,
The wakeful trump of doom muft thunder through
the deep,

### 17.

With fuch a horrid clang
As on mount Sinai rang,
While the red fire, and fmouldring clouds out brake:
The aged earth aghaft,
With terrour of that blaft,
Shall from the furface to the centre fhake;
When at the world's laft feffion,
The dreadful Judge in middle air fhall fpread his throne.

### 18.

And then at laft our blifs
Full and perfect is,
But now begins; for from this happy day
Th' old Dragon under ground
In ftraiter limits bound,
Not half fo far cafts his ufurped fway,

And wroth to fee his kingdom fail,
Swindges the fcaly horrour of his folded tail.

### 19.

The oracles are dumb,
No voice or hideous hum
  Runs through the arched roof in words deceiving.
Apollo from his fhrine
Can no more divine,
  With hollow fhriek the fteep of Delphos leaving.
No nightly trance, or breathed fpell
Infpires the pale-ey'd prieft from the prophetic cell.

### 20.

The lonely mountains o'er,
And the refounding fhore,
  A voice of weeping heard and loud lament;
From haunted fpring, and dale
Edg'd with poplar pale,
  The parting Genius is wlth fighing fent;
With flow'r-inwoven treffes torn
The nymphs in twilight fhade of tangled thickets mourn.

### 21.

In confecrated earth,
And on the holy hearth,
  The Lars, and Lemures moan with midnight plaint;
In urns, and altars round,
A drear and dying found
  Affrights the flamens at their fervice quaint;
And the chill marble feems to fweat,
While each peculiar pow'r forgoes his wonted feat.

### 22.

Peor and Baälim
Forfake their temples dim,

With that twice batter'd God of Paleſtine;
And mooned Aſhtaroth,
Heav'n's queen and mother both,
　Now ſits not girt with tapers holy ſhine;
The Lybic Hammon ſhrinks his horn,
In vain the Tyrian maids their wounded Thammuz
　　mourn.

### 23.

And ſullen Moloch fled,
Hath left in ſhadows dread
　His burning idol all of blackeſt hue;
In vain with cymbals ring
They call the griſly king,
　In diſmal dance about the furnace blue;
The brutiſh gods of Nile as faſt,
Iſis and Orus, and the dog Anubis haſte.

### 24.

Nor is Oſiris ſeen
In Memphian grove or green,
　Trampling the unſhowr'd graſs with lowings loud:
Nor can he be at reſt
Within his ſacred cheſt,
　Nought but profoundeſt Hell can be his ſhroud;
In vain with timbrel'd anthems dark
The ſable-ſtoled ſorcerers bear his worſhipt ark.

### 25.

He feels from Juda's land
The dreaded infant's hand,
　The rays of Bethlehem blind his duſky eyn
Nor all the gods beſide,
Longer dare abide,
　Not Typhon huge ending in ſnaky twine:

Our babe to fhow his godhead true,
Can in his fwadling bands control the damned crew.

### 26.

So when the fun in bed,
Curtain'd with cloudy red,
   Pillows his chin upon an orient wave,
The flocking fhadows pale
Troop to th' infernal jail,
   Each fetter'd ghoft flips to his feveral grave,
And the yellow-fkirted Fayes
Fly after the night-fteeds, leaving their moon-lov'd
    maze.

### 27.

But fee the virgin bleft
Hath laid her babe to reft,
   Time is our tedious fong fhould here have ending:
Heav'n's youngeft teemed ftar
Hath fix'd her polifh'd car,
   Her fleeping Lord with handmaid lamp attending:
And all about the courtly ftable
Bright-harneft angels fit in order ferviceable.

## IV.

## THE PASSION.

### 1.

EREWHILE of mufic, and ethereal mirth,
Wherewith the ftage of air and earth did ring,
And joyous news of heav'nly infant's birth,

My mufe with angels did divide to fing;
But headlong joy is ever on the wing,
   In wintry folftice like the fhorten'd light
Soon fwallow'd up in dark and long out-living night.
·2.
For now to forrow muft I tune my fong,
And fet my harp to notes of faddeft woe,
Which on our deareft Lord did feize ere long,
Dangers, and fnares, and wrongs, and worfe than fo,
Which he for us did freely undergo:
   Moft perfect hero, try'd in heavieft plight
Of labours huge and hard, too hard for human wight!
3.
He fov'reign Prieft ftooping his regal head,
That dropt with odorous oil down his fair eyes,
Poor flefhly tabernacle entered,
His ftarry front low-rooft beneath the fkies;
O what a mafk was there, what a difguife!
   Yet more; the ftroke of death he muft abide,
Then lies him meekly down faft by his brethren's fide.
4.
Thefe lateft fcenes confine my roving verfe,
To this horizon is my Phœbus bound;
His godlike acts, and his temptations fierce,
And former fufferings other where are found;
Loud o'er the reft Cremona's trump doth found;
   Me fofter airs befit, and fofter ftrings
Of lute, or viol ftill more apt for mournful things.
5.
Befriend me, Night, beft patronefs of grief,
Over the pole thy thickeft mantle throw,
And work my flatter'd fancy to belief,

That Heav'n and Earth are colour'd with my woe;
My forrows are too dark for day to know:
　The leaves fhould all be black whereon I write,
And letters where my tears have wafh'd a wannifh
　　white.

### 6.

See, fee the chariot, and thofe rufhing wheels,
That whirl'd the Prophet up at Chebar flood,
My fpirit fome tranfporting cherub feels,
To bear me where the tow'rs of Salem ftood,
Once glorious tow'rs, now funk in guiltlefs blood;
　There doth my foul in holy vifion fit
In penfive trance, and anguifh, and ecftatic fit.

### 7.

Mine eye hath found that fad fepulchral rock
That was the cafket of Heav'n's richeft ftore,
And here though grief my feeble hands up lock,
Yet on the foften'd quarry would I fcore
My plaining verfe as lively as before;
　For fure fo well inftructed are my tears,
That they would fitly fall in order'd characters.

### 8.

Or fhould I thence hurried on viewlefs wing,
Take up a weeping on the mountains wild,
The gentle neighbourhood of grove and fpring
Would foon unbofom all their echoes mild,
And I (for grief is eafily beguil'd)
　Might think th' infection of my forrows loud
Had got a race of mourners on fome pregnant cloud.

This fubject the Author finding to be above the years he had, when
　he wrote it, and nothing fatisfied with what was begun, left it un-
　finifhed.

## V.

## ON TIME.

FLY, envious Time, till thou run out thy race,
Call on the lazy leaden-ftepping hours,
Whofe fpeed is but the heavy plummet's pace;
And glut thyfelf with what thy womb devours,
Which is no more than what is falfe and vain,
And merely mortal drofs;
So little is our lofs,
So little is thy gain. ·
For when as each thing bad thou haft intomb'd,
And laft of all thy greedy felf confum'd,
Then long Eternity fhall greet our blifs
With an individual kifs;
And Joy fhall overtake us as a flood,
When every thing that is fincerely good
And perfectly divine,
With truth, and peace, and love, fhall ever fhine
About the fupreme throne
Of him, t' whofe happy-making fight alone
When once our heav'nly-guided foul fhall clime,
Then all this earthy groffnefs quit,
Attir'd with ftars, we fhall for ever fit,
   Triumphing over Death, and Chance, and thee,
     O Time.

## VI.

## UPON THE CIRCUMCISION.

Ye flaming Pow'rs, and winged Warriours bright
That erſt with muſic, and triumphant ſong,
Firſt heard by happy watchful ſhepherds ear,
So ſweetly ſung your joy the clouds along
Through the ſoft ſilence of the liſt'ning night;
Now mourn, and if ſad ſhare with us to bear
Your fiery eſſence can diſtil no tear,
Burn in your ſighs, and borrow
Seas wept from our deep ſorrow:
He who with all Heav'n's heraldry whilere
Enter'd the world, now bleeds to give us eaſe;
Alas, how ſoon our ſin
　Sore doth begin
　　His infancy to ſeize!
O more exceeding love or law more juſt?
Juſt law indeed, but more exceeding love!
For we by rightful doom remedileſs
Were loſt in death, till he that dwelt above
High thron'd in ſecret bliſs, for us frail duſt
Emptied his glory, ev'n to nakedneſs;
And that great covenant which we ſtill tranſgreſs
Entirely ſatisfied,
And the full wrath beſide
Of vengeful juſtice bore for our exceſs,
And ſeals obedience firſt with wounding ſmart
This day, but O ere long
Huge pangs and ſtrong
　　Will pierce more near his heart.

### VII.

## AT A SOLEMN MUSIC.

Blest pair of Sirens, pledges of Heav'n's joy,
Sphere-born harmonious fifters, Voice and Verfe,
Wed your divine founds, and mix'd pow'r employ
Dead things with inbreath'd fenfe able to pierce,
And to our high-rais'd phantafy prefent
That undifturbed fong of pure concent,
Aye fung before the fapphire-colour'd throne
To him that fits thereon
With faintly fhout, and folemn jubilee,
Where the bright feraphim in burning row
Their loud up-lifted angel-trumpets blow,
And the cherubic hoft in thoufand quires
Touch their immortal harps of golden wires,
With thofe juft fpirits that wear victorious palms,
Hymns devout and holy pfalms
Singing everlaftingly;
That we on earth with undifcording voice
May rightly anfwer that melodious noife;
As once we did, till difproportion'd fin
Jarr'd againft nature's chime, and with harfh din
Broke the fair mufic that all creatures made
To their great Lord, whofe love their motion fway'd
In perfect diapafon, whilft they ftood
In firft obedience, and their ftate of good.
O may we foon again renew that fong,
And keep in tune with Heav'n, till God ere long
To his celeftial concert us unite,
To live with him, and fing in endlefs morn of light.

## VIII.

## AN EPITAPH

#### ON THE

### MARCHIONESS OF WINCHESTER.

THIS rich marble doth enter
The honour'd wife of Winchefter,
A vifcount's daughter, an earl's heir,
Befides what her virtues fair
Added to her noble birth,
More than fhe could own from earth.
Summers three times eight fave one
She had told; alas too foon,
After fo fhort time of breath,
To houfe with darknefs, and with death.
Yet had the number of her days
Been as complete as was her praife,
Nature and fate had had no ftrife
In giving limit to her life.
Her high birth, and her graces fweet
Quickly found a lover meet;
The virgin quire for her requeft
The god that fits at marriage feaft;
He at their invoking came
But with a fcarce well-lighted flame;
And in his garland as he ftood,
Ye might difcern a cyprefs bud.
Once had the early matrons run
To greet her of a lovely fon,
And now with fecond hope fhe goes,
And calls Lucina to her throes;

But whether by mifchance or blame
Atropos for Lucina came;
And with remorfelefs cruelty
Spoil'd at once both fruit and tree:
The haplefs babe before his birth
Had burial, yet not laid in earth,
And the languifh'd mother's womb
Was not long a living tomb.
So have I feen fome tender flip,
Sav'd with care from winter's nip,
The pride of her carnation train,
Pluck'd up by fome unheedy fwain,
Who only thought to crop the flow'r
New fhot up from vernal fhow'r;
But the fair bloffom hangs the head
Side-ways, as on a dying bed,
And thofe pearls of dew fhe wears,
Prove to be prefaging tears,
Which the fad morn had let fall
On her haft'ning funeral.
Gentle lady, may thy grave
Peace and quiet ever have;
After this thy travel fore
Sweet reft feize thee evermore,
That to give the world increafe,
Short'ned haft thy own life's leafe.
Here, befides the forrowing
That thy noble houfe doth bring,
Here be tears of perfect moan
Wept for thee in Helicon,
And fome flowers, and fome bays,
For thy hearfe, to ftrow the ways,

Sent thee from the banks of Came,
Devoted to thy virtuous name;
Whilft thou, bright faint, high fit'ft in glory
Next her much like to thee in ftory,
That fair Syrian fhepherdefs,
Who after years of barrennefs,
The highly-favour'd Jofeph bore
To him that ferv'd for her before,
And at her next birth much like thee,
Through pangs fled to felicity,
Far within the bofom bright
Of blazing majefty and light:
There with thee, new welcome faint,
Like fortunes may her foul acquaint,
With thee there clad in radiant fheen,
No marchionefs, but now a queen.

## IX.

## SONG.

### ON MAY MORNING.

Now the bright morning ftar, day's harbinger,
Comes dancing from the eaft, and leads with her
The flow'ry May, who from her green lap throws
The yellow cowflip, and the pale primrofe.
   Hail bounteous May that doft infpire
   Mirth and youth and warm defire;

Woods and groves are of thy dreſſing,
Hill and dale doth boaſt thy bleſſing.
Thus we ſalute thee with our early ſong,
And welcome thee, and wiſh thee long.

## X.

### ON SHAKESPEAR. 1630.

WHAT needs my Shakeſpear for his honour'd bones
The labour of an age in piled ſtones,
Or that his hallow'd reliques ſhould be hid
Under a ſtar-ypointing pyramid?
Dear ſon of memory, great heir of fame,
What need'ſt thou ſuch weak witneſs of thy name?
Thou in our wonder and aſtoniſhment
Haſt built thyſelf a live-long monument.
For whilſt to th' ſhame of ſlow-endeavouring art
Thy eaſy numbers flow, and that each heart
Hath from the leaves of thy unvalued book
Thoſe Delphic lines with deep impreſſion took,
Then thou our fancy of itſelf bereaving,
Doſt make us marble with too much conceiving;
And ſo ſepúlchred in ſuch pomp doſt lie,
That kings for ſuch a tomb would wiſh to die.

## XI.

## ON THE UNIVERSITY CARRIER,

WHO SICKENED IN THE TIME OF HIS VACANCY, BEING
FORBID TO GO TO LONDON, BY REASON
OF THE PLAGUE.

HERE lies old Hobfon; Death hath broke his girt,
And here alas, hath laid him in the dirt,
Or elfe the ways being foul, twenty to one,
He's here ftuck in a flough, and overthrown.
'Twas fuch a fhifter, that if truth were known,
Death was half glad when he had got him down;
For he had any time this ten years full,
Dodg'd with him, betwixt Cambridge and the Bull.
And furely Death could never have prevail'd,
Had not his weekly courfe of carriage fail'd;
But lately finding him fo long at home,
And thinking now his journey's end was come,
And that he had ta'en up his lateft inn,
In the kind office of a chamberlain
Show'd him his room where he muft lodge that night,
Pull'd off his boots, and took away the light:
If any afk for him, it fhall be faid,
Hobfon has fupt, and's newly gone to bed.

## XII.

## ANOTHER ON THE SAME.

HERE lieth one, who did moſt truly prove
That he could never die while he could move;
So hung his deſtiny, never to rot
While he might ſtill jog on and keep his trot,
Made of ſphere-metal, never to decay
Until his revolution was at ſtay.
Time numbers motion, yet (without a crime
'Gainſt old truth) motion number'd out his time:
And like an engine mov'd with wheel and weight,
His principles being ceas'd, he ended ſtraight.
Reſt that gives all men life, gave him his death,
And too much breathing put him out of breath;
Nor were it contradiction to affirm
Too long vacation haſten'd on his term.
Merely to drive the time away he ſicken'd,
Fainted, and died, nor would with ale be quicken'd;
" Nay," quoth he, on his ſwooning bed out-ſtretch'd,
" If I mayn't carry, ſure I'll ne'er be fetch'd,
" But vow," though the croſs doctors all ſtood hearers,
" For one carrier put down to make ſix bearers."
Eaſe was his chief diſeaſe, and to judge right,
He dy'd for heavineſs that his cart went light:
His leiſure told him that his time was come,
And lack of load made his life burdenſome,
That ev'n to his laſt breath (there be that ſay't)
As he were preſs'd to death, he cry'd more weight;

*1 v. May 1796, for C. Dilly, in the Poultry, and the rest of the Proprietors.*

But had his doings lafted as they were,
He had been an immortal carrier.
Obedient to the moon he fpent his date
In courfe reciprocal, and had his fate
Link'd to the mutual flowing of the feas,
Yet (ftrange to think) his wain was his increafe:
His letters are deliver'd all and gone,
Only remains this fuperfcription.

## XIII.

## L'ALLEGRO.

HENCE loathed Melancholy,
Of Cerberus and blackeft Midnight born,
In Stygian cave forlorn,
    'Mongft horrid fhapes, and fhrieks, and fights unholy,
Find out fome uncouth cell;
    Where brooding darknefs fpreads his jealous wings,
And the night-raven fings;
    There under ebon fhades, and low-brow'd rocks,
As ragged as thy locks,
    In dark Cimmerian defert ever dwell.
But come thou goddefs fair and free,
In Heav'n yclep'd Euphrofyne,
And by men, heart-eafing Mirth,
Whom lovely Venus at a birth
With two fifter graces more
To ivy-crowned Bacchus bore;

Or whether (as fome fager fing)
The frolic wind that breathes the fpring,
Zephyr with Aurora playing,
As he met her once a maying,
There on beds of violets blue,
And frefh-blown rofes wafh'd in dew,
Fill'd her with thee a daughter fair,
So buxom, blithe, and debonair.
Hafte thee nymph, and bring with thee
·Jeft and youthful Jollity,
Quips and cranks, and wanton wiles,
Nods and becks, and wreathed fmiles,
Such as hang on Hebe's cheek,
And love to live in dimple fleek;
Sport that wrinkled Care derides,
And Laughter holding both his fides.
Come, and trip it as you go
On the light fantaftic toe,
And in thy right hand lead with thee,
The mountain nymph, fweet Liberty;
And if I give thee honour due,
Mirth, admit me of thy crew
To live with her, and live with thee,
In unreproved pleafures free;
To hear the lark begin his flight,
And finging ftartle the dull night,
From his watch-tow'r in the fkies,
Till the dappled dawn doth rife;
Then to come in fpite of forrow,
And at my window bid good morrow,
Through the fweet-briar, or the vine,
Or the twifted eglantine:

While the cock with lively din
Scatters the rear of darknefs thin,
And to the ftack, or the barn-door,
Stoutly ftruts his dames before:
Oft lift'ning how the hounds and horn
Cheerly roufe the flumb'ring morn,
From the fide of fome hoar hill,
Through the high wood echoing fhrill:
Some time walking not unfeen
By hedge-row elms, on hillocks green,
Right againft the eaftern gate,
Where the great fun begins his ftate,
Rob'd in flames, and amber light,
The clouds in thoufand liveries dight,
While the plowman near at hand
Whiftles o'er the furrow'd land,
And the milkmaid fingeth blithe,
And the mower whets his fithe,
And every fhepherd tells his tale
Under the hawthorn in the dale.
Straight mine eye hath caught new pleafures
Whilft the landfcape round it meafures,
Ruffet lawns, and fallows gray,
Where the nibbling flocks do ftray,
Mountains on whofe barren breaft
The lab'ring clouds do often reft,
Meadows trim with daifies pied,
Shallow brooks, and rivers wide.
Towers and battlements it fees
Bofom'd high in tufted trees,
Where perhaps fome beauty lies,
The Cynofure of neighb'ring eyes.

Hard by, a cottage chimney fmokes,
From betwixt two aged oaks,
Where Corydon and Thyrfis met,
Are at their favoury dinner fet
Of herbs, and other country meffcs,
Which the neat-handed Phillis dreffes;
And then in hafte her bow'r fhe leaves,
With Theftylis to bind the fheaves;
Or if the earlier feafon lead
. To the tann'd haycock in the mead.
Sometimes with fecure delight
The upland hamlets will invite,
When the merry bells ring round,
And the jocund rebecs found
To many a youth, and many a maid.
Dancing in the chequer'd fhade;
And young and old come forth to play
On a funfhine holiday,
Till the live-long daylight fail;
Then to the fpicy nut-brown ale,
With ftories told of many a feat,
How fairy Mab the junkets eat,
She was pincht, and pull'd fhe faid,
And he by friar's lantern led
Tells how the drudging Goblin fweat,
To earn his cream-bowl duly fct,
When in one night, ere glimpfe of morn,
His fhadowy flail hath threfh'd the corn,
That ten day-lab'rers could not end;
Then lies him down the lubbar fiend,
And ftretch'd out all the chimney's length,
Bafks at the fire his hairy ftrcngth,

And crop-full out of doors he flings,
Ere the firſt cock his matin rings.
Thus done the tales, to bed they creep,
By whiſp'ring winds ſoon lull'd aſleep.
Tow'red cities pleaſe us then,
And the buſy hum of men,
Where throngs of knights and barons bold
In weeds of peace high triumphs hold,
With ſtore of ladies, whoſe bright eyes
Rain influence, and judge the prize
Of wit, or arms, while both contend
To win her grace, whom all commend.
There let Hymen oft appear
In ſaffron robe, with taper clear,
And pomp, and feaſt, and revelry,
With maſk, and antique pageantry,
Such fights as youthful poets dream
On ſummer eves by haunted ſtream.
Then to the well-trod ſtage anon,
If Johnſon's learned ſock be on,
Or ſweeteſt Shakeſpear, fancy's child,
Warble his native wood-notes wild.
And ever againſt eating cares,
Lap me in ſoft Lydian airs,
Married to immortal verſe,
Such as the meeting ſoul may pierce
In notes, with many a winding bout
Of linked ſweetneſs long drawn out,
With wanton heed, and giddy cunning,
The melting voice through mazes running,
Untwiſting all the chains that tie
The hidden ſoul of harmony;

That Orpheus felf may heave his head
From golden flumber on a bed
Of heapt Elyfian flow'rs, and hear
Such ftrains as would have won the ear
Of Pluto, to have quite fet free
His half regain'd Eurydice.
Thefe delights if thou canft give,
Mirth, with thee I mean to live.

## XIV.

## IL PENSEROSO.

HENCE vain deluding joys,
    The brood of folly without father bred,
How little you befted,
    Or fill the fixed mind with all your toys?
Dwell in fome idle brain,
    And fancies fond with gaudy fhapes poffefs,
As thick and numberlefs
    As the gay motes that people the fun-beams,
Or likeft hovering dreams
    The fickle penfioners of Morpheus train.
But hail thou goddefs, fage and holy,
Hail divineft Melancholy,
Whofe faintly vifage is too bright
To hit the fenfe of human fight,
And therefore to our weaker view
O'erlaid with black, ftaid wifdom's hue;

Published 21 May 1796, for C. Dilly in the Poultry, and the rest of the Proprietors.

Black, but fuch as in efteem
Prince Memnon's fifter might befeem,
Or that ftarr'd Ethiop queen that ftrove
To fet her beauties praife above
The Sea-nymphs, and their pow'rs offended:
Yet thou art higher far defcended,
The bright-hair'd Vefta long of yore
To folitary Saturn bore;
His daughter fhe (in Saturn's reign,
Such mixture was not held a ftain).
Oft in glimmering bow'rs and glades
He met her, and in fecret fhades
Of woody Ida's inmoft grove,
While yet there was no fear of Jove.
Come penfive Nun, devout and pure,
Sober, ftedfaft, and demure,
All in a robe of darkeft grain,
Flowing with majeftic train,
And fable ftole of Cyprus lawn,
Over thy decent fhoulders drawn.
Come, but keep thy wonted ftate,
With even ftep, and mufing gate,
And looks commercing with the fkies,
Thy rapt foul fitting in thine eyes:
There held in holy paffion ftill,
Forget thyfelf to marble, till
With a fad leaden downward caft
Thou fix them on the earth as faft:
And join with thee calm Peace, and Quiet,
Spare Faft, that oft with gods doth diet,
And hears the mufes in a ring
Aye round about Jove's altar fing:

And add to thefe retired Leifure,
That in trim gardens takes his pleafure;
But firft, and chiefeft, with thee bring,
Him that yon foars on golden wing,
Guiding the fiery-wheeled throne,
The cherub Contemplation;
And the mute Silence hift along,
'Lefs Philomel will deign a fong,
In her fweeteft, faddeft plight,
Smoothing the rugged brow of night,
While Cynthia checks her dragon yoke,
Gently o'er th' accuftom'd oak;
Sweet bird that fhunn'ft the noife of folly,
Moft mufical, moft melancholy!
Thee chauntrefs oft the woods among
I woo to hear thy even-fong;
And miffing thee, I walk unfeen
On the dry fmooth-fhaven green,
To behold the wand'ring moon,
Riding near her higheft noon,
Like one that had been led aftray
Through the Heav'n's wide pathlefs way,
And oft, as if her head fhe bow'd,
Stooping through a fleecy cloud.
Oft on a plat of rifing ground,
I hear the far-off Curfeu found,
Over fome wide-water'd fhore,
Swinging flow with fullen roar;
Or if the air will not permit,
Some ftill removed place will fit,
Where glowing embers through the room
Teach light to counterfeit a gloom,

Far from all refort of mirth,
Save the cricket on the hearth,
Or the belman's drowfy charm,
To blefs the doors from nightly harm:
Or let my lamp at midnight hour,
Be feen in fome high lonely tow'r,
Where I may oft out-watch the Bear,
With thrice great Hermes, or unfphere
The fpirit of Plato to unfold
What worlds, or what vaft regions hold
The immortal mind that hath forfook
Her manfion in this flefhly nook:
And of thofe Demons that are found
In fire, air, flood, or under ground,
Whofe power hath a true confent
With planet, or with element.
Sometime let gorgeous tragedy
In fceptred pall come fweeping by,
Prefenting Thebes, or Pelops line,
Or the tale of Troy divine,
Or what (though rare) of later age
Ennobled hath the bufkin'd ftage.
But, O fad Virgin, that thy power
Might raife Mufæus from his bower,
Or bid the foul of Orpheus fing
Such notes, as warbled to the ftring,
Drew iron tears down Pluto's cheek,
And made Hell grant what love did feek.
Or call up him that left half told
The ftory of Cambufcan bold,
Of Camball, and of Algarfife,
And who had Canace to wife,

o

That own'd the virtuous ring and glaſs,
And of the wondrous horſe of braſs,
On which the Tartar king did ride;
And if ought elſe great bards beſide
In ſage and ſolemn tunes have ſung,
Of turneys and of trophies hung,
Of foreſts, and inchantments drear,
Where more is meant than meets the ear.
Thus Night oft ſee me in thy pale career,
Till civil-ſuited Morn appear,
Not trickt and frounct as ſhe was wont
With the Attic boy to hunt,
But kerchieft in a comely cloud,
While rocking winds are piping loud,
Or uſher'd with a ſhower ſtill,
When the guſt hath blown his fill,
Ending on the ruſsling leaves,
With minute drops from off the eaves.
And when the ſun begins to fling
His flaring beams, me goddeſs bring
To arched walks of twilight groves,
And ſhadows brown that Sylvan loves
Of pine, or monumental oak,
Where the rude axe with heaved ſtroke
Was never heard the nymphs to daunt,
Or fright them from their hallow'd haunt.
There in cloſe covert by ſome brook,
Where no profaner eye may look,
Hide me from day's gariſh eye,
While the bee with honied thigh,
That at her flow'ry work doth ſing,
And the waters murmuring,

With fuch concert as they keep,
Entice the dewy feather'd fleep;
And let fome ftrange myfterious dream
Wave at his wings in aery ftream
Of lively portraiture difplay'd,
Softly on my eye-lids laid.
And as I wake, fweet mufic breathe
Above, about, or underneath,
Sent by fome fpirit to mortals good,
Or th' unfeen genius of the wood.
But let my due feet never fail
To walk the ftudious cloifters pale,
And love the high embowed roof,
With antique pillars maffy proof,
And ftoried windows richly dight,
Cafting a dim religious light.
There let the pealing organ blow,
To the full voic'd quire below,
In fervice high, and anthems clear,
As may with fweetnefs, through mine ear,
Diffolve me into ecftafies,
And bring all Heav'n before mine eyes.
And may at laft my weary age
Find out the peaceful hermitage,
The hairy gown and moffy cell,
Where I may fit and rightly fpell
Of every ftar that heav'n doth fhew,
And every herb that fips the dew;
Till old experience do attain
To fomething like prophetic ftrain.
Thefe pleafures Melancholy give,
And I with thee will choofe to live.

## XV.

## ARCADES.

PART OF AN ENTERTAINMENT PRESENTED TO THE
COUNTESS DOWAGER OF DERBY AT HAREFIELD,
BY SOME NOBLE PERSONS OF HER FAMILY,
WHO APPEAR ON THE SCENE IN PAS-
TORAL HABIT, MOVING TOWARD
THE SEAT OF STATE, WITH
THIS SONG.

### 1. SONG.

Look nymphs, and fhepherds look,
What fudden blaze of majefty
Is that which we from hence defcry,
Too divine to be miftook:
   This, this is fhe
To whom our vows and wifhes bend;
Here our folemn fearch hath end.

Fame, that her high worth to raife,
Seem'd erft fo lavifh and profufe,
We may juftly now accufe
Of detraction from her praife;
   Lefs than half we find expreft,
   Envy bid conceal the reft.

Mark what radiant ftate fhe fpreads,
In circle round her fhining throne,
Shooting her beams like filver threads;

This, this is fhe alone,
  Sitting like a goddefs bright,
  In the centre of her light.

Might fhe the wife Latona be,
Or the tow'red Cybele,
Mother of a hundred gods;
Juno dares not give her odds;
  Who had thought this clime had held
  A deity fo unparallel'd?

AS THEY COME FORWARD, THE GENIUS OF THE
WOOD APPEARS, AND TURNING
TOWARD THEM, SPEAKS.

## GENIUS.

STAY, gentle fwains, for though in this difguife,
I fee bright honour fparkle through your eyes;
Of famous Arcady ye are, and fprung
Of that renowned flood, fo often fung,
Divine Alpheus, who by fecret fluice
Stole under feas to meet his Arethufe;
And ye, the breathing rofes of the wood,
Fair filver-bufkin'd nymphs as great and good,
I know this queft of yours, and free intent
Was all in honour and devotion meant
To the great miftrefs of yon princely fhrine,
Whom with low reverence I adore as mine,
And with all helpful fervice will comply
To further this night's glad folemnity;

And lead ye where ye may more near behold
What fhallow-fearching Fame hath left untold;
Which I full oft amidft thefe fhades alone
Have fat to wonder at, and gaze upon:
For know by lot from Jove I am the power
Of this fair wood, and live in oaken bower,
To nurfe the faplings tall, and curl the grove
With ringlets quaint, and wanton windings wove.
And all my plants I fave from nightly ill
Of noifome winds, and blafting vapours chill:
And from the boughs brufh off the evil dew,
And heal the arms of thwarting thunder blue,
Or what the crofs dire-looking planet fmites,
Or hurtful worm with canker'd venom bites.
When evening gray doth rife, I fetch my round
Over the mount, and all this hallow'd ground,
And early ere the odorous breath of morn
Awakes the flumb'ring leaves, or taffel'd horn
Shakes the high thicket, hafte I all about,
Number my ranks, and vifit every fprout
With puiffant words, and murmurs made to blefs;
But elfe in deep of night, when drowfinefs
Hath lock'd up mortal fenfe, then liften I
To the celeftial Sirens harmony,
That fit upon the nine infolded fpheres,
And fing to thofe that hold the vital fhears,
And turn the adamantine fpindle round,
On which the fate of gods and men is wound.
Such fweet compulfion doth in mufic lie,
To lull the daughters of Neceffity,
And keep unfteady Nature to her law,
And the low world in meafur'd motion draw

After the heav'nly tune, which none can hear
Of human mould with grofs unpurged ear;
And yet fuch mufic worthieft were to blaze
The peerlefs height of her immortal praife,
Whofe luftre leads us, and for her moft fit,
If my inferior hand or voice could hit
Inimitable founds, yet as we go,
Whate'er the fkill of leffer gods can fhow,
I will affay, her worth to celebrate,
And fo attend ye toward her glittering ftate;
Where ye may all that are of noble ftem
Approach, and kifs her facred vefture's hem.

## 2. SONG.

O'ER the fmooth enamell'd green,
Where no print of ftep hath been,
Follow me as I fing,
And touch the warbled ftring,
Under the fhady roof
Of branching elm ftar-proof.
Follow me,
I will bring you where fhe fits,
Clad in fplendour as befits
Her deity.
Such a rural Queen
All Arcadia hath not feen.

## 3. SONG.

Nymphs and fhepherds dance no more
 By fandy Ladon's lilied banks,
On old Lycæus or Cyllene hoar
 Trip no more in twilight ranks,
Though Erymanth your lofs deplore,
 A better foil fhall give ye thanks.
From the ftony Mænalus
Bring your flocks, and live with us,
Here ye fhall have greater grace,
To ferve the Lady of this place.
Though Syrinx your Pan's miftrefs were,
Yet Syrinx well might wait on her,
 Such a rural Queen
 All Arcadia hath not feen.

XVI.

A

# M A S K

PRESENTED

## AT LUDLOW CASTLE, 1634,

BEFORE

## *THE EARL OF BRIDGEWATER,*

THEN PRESIDENT OF WALES.

# THE PERSONS.

THE ATTENDANT SPIRIT, AFTERWARDS IN THE
HABIT OF THYRSIS.

COMUS WITH HIS CREW.

THE LADY.

FIRST BROTHER.

SECOND BROTHER.

SABRINA THE NYMPH.

THE CHIEF PERSONS WHO PRESENTED WERE,

THE LORD BRACKLY.

MR. THOMAS EGERTON HIS BROTHER.

THE LADY ALICE EGERTON.

A

# M A S K.

THE FIRST SCENE DISCOVERS A WILD WOOD.

'THE ATTENDANT SPIRIT DESCENDS OR ENTERS.

BEFORE the ſtarry threſhold of Jove's court
My manſion is, where thoſe immortal ſhapes
Of bright aerial Spirits live inſpher'd
In regions mild of calm and ſerene air,
Above the ſmoke and ſtir of this dim ſpot,
Which men call Earth, and with low thoughted care
Confin'd, and peſter'd in this pin-fold here,
Strive to keep up a frail and feveriſh being,
Unmindful of the crown that virtue gives
After this mortal change to her true ſervants
Amongſt the enthron'd Gods on fainted feats.
Yet ſome there be that by due ſteps aſpire,
To lay their juſt hands on that golden key,
That opes the palace of eternity:
To ſuch my errand is; and but for ſuch,

I would not foil thefe pure ambrofial weeds
With the rank vapours of this fin-worn mould.
  But to my talk.   Neptune befides the fway
Of every falt flood, and each ebbing ftream,
Took in by lot 'twixt high and nether Jove
Imperial rule of all the fea-girt ifles,
That like to rich and various gems inlay
The unadorned bofom of the deep,
Which he to grace his tributary Gods
By courfe commits to feveral government,
And gives them leave to wear their faphire crowns,
And wield their little tridents: but this Ifle,
The greateft and the beft of all the main,
He quarters to his blue-hair'd deities;
And all this tract that fronts the falling fun
A noble Peer of mickle truft and power
Has in his charge, with temper'd awe to guide
An old, and haughty nation proud in arms:
Where his fair offspring nurs'd in princely lore
Are coming to attend their father's ftate,
And new-intrufted fceptre; but their way
Lies through the perplex'd paths of this drear wood,
The nodding horrour of whofe fhady brows
Threats the forlorn and wand'ring paffenger;
And here their tender age might fuffer peril,
But that by quick command from fovereign Jove
I was difpatch'd for their defence and guard;
And liften why, for I will tell you now
What never yet was heard in tale or fong,
From old or modern bard, in hall or bower.
  Bacchus, that firft from out the purple grape

Crufh'd the fweet poifon of mifufed wine,
After the Tufcan mariners transform'd,
Coafting the Tyrrhene fhore, as the winds lifted,
On Circe's ifland fell: (Who knows not Circe
The daughter of the fun? whofe charmed cup
Whoever tafted, loft his upright fhape,
And downward fell into a groveling fwine)
This Nymph that gaz'd upon his cluft'ring locks,
With ivy berries wreath'd, and his blithe youth,
Had by him, ere he parted thence, a fon
Much like his father, but his mother more,
Whom therefore fhe brought up, and Comus nam'd,
Who ripe, and frolic of his full grown age,
Roving the Celtic and Iberian fields,
At laft betakes him to this ominous wood,
And in thick fhelter of black fhades imbowr'd
Excels his mother at her mighty art,
Offering to every weary traveller
His orient liquor in a cryftal glafs,
To quench the drowth of Phœbus, which as they tafte,
(For moft do tafte through fond intemp'rate thirft)
Soon as the potion works, their human count'nance,
Th' exprefs refemblance of the Gods, is chang'd
Into fome brutifh form of wolf, or bear,
Or ounce, or tiger, hog, or bearded goat,
All other parts remaining as they were;
And they, fo perfect is their mifery,
Not once perceive their foul disfigurement,
But boaft themfelves more comely than before,
And all their friends and native home forget,
To roll with pleafure in a fenfual ftie.

Therefore when any favour'd of high Jove
Chances to pafs through this advent'rous glade,
Swift as the fparkle of a glancing ftar
I fhoot from Heav'n, to give him fafe convoy,
As now I do: But firft I muft put off
Thefe my fky robes fpun out of Iris woof,
And take the weeds and likenefs of a fwain,
That to the fervice of this houfe belongs,
Who with his foft pipe, and fmooth-dittied fong,
Well knows to ftill the wild winds when they roar,
And hufh the waving woods, nor of lefs faith,
And in this office of his mountain watch,
Likelieft, and neareft to the prefent aid
Of this occafion.   But I hear the tread
Of hateful fteps, I muft be viewlefs now.

COMUS ENTERS WITH A CHARMING ROD IN ONE HAND,
   HIS GLASS IN THE OTHER; WITH HIM A ROUT OF
   MONSTERS, HEADED LIKE SUNDRY SORTS OF WILD
   BEASTS, BUT OTHERWISE LIKE MEN AND WOMEN,
   THEIR APPAREL GLISTERING; THEY COME IN
   MAKING A RIOTOUS AND UNRULY NOISE, WITH
   TORCHES IN THEIR HANDS.

COMUS.

   The ftar that bids the fhepherd fold
Now the top of Heav'n doth hold,
And the gilded car of day
His glowing axle doth allay
In the fteep Atlantic ftream,
And the flope fun his upward beam

Shoots againſt the duſky pole,
Pacing toward the other goal
Of his chamber in the eaſt.
Mean while welcome Joy, and Feaſt,
Midnight Shout, and Revelry,
Tipſy Dance, and Jollity.
Braid your locks with roſy twine,
Dropping odours, dropping wine.
Rigour now is gone to bed,
And Advice with ſcrupulous head,
Strict Age, and ſour Severity
With their grave ſaws in ſlumber lie.
We that are of purer fire
Imitate the ſtarry quire,
Who in their nightly watchful ſpheres,
Lead in ſwift round the months and years.
The ſounds and ſeas, with all their finny drove,
Now to the moon in wavering morrice move;
And on the tawny ſands and ſhelves
Trip the pert fairies and the dapper elves.
By dimpled brook, and fountain brim,
The Wood-Nymphs deck'd with daiſies trim,
Their merry wakes and paſtimes keep:
What hath night to do with ſleep?
Night hath better ſweets to prove,
Venus now wakes, and wakens Love.
Come let us our rites begin,
'Tis only day-light that makes ſin,
Which theſe dun ſhades will ne'er report.
Hail Goddeſs of nocturnal ſport,
Dark-veil'd Cotytto, t' whom the ſecret flame
Of mid-night torches burns; myſterious dame,

That ne'er art call'd, but when the dragon womb
Of Stygian darknefs fpits her thickeſt gloom,
And makes one blot of all the air,
Stay thy cloudy ebon chair,
Wherein thou rid'ſt with Hecat', and befriend
Us thy vow'd prieſts, till utmoſt end
Of all thy dues be done, and none left out,
Ere the blabbing eaſtern fcout,
The nice morn on th' Indian ſteep
From her cabin loophole peep,
And to the tell-tale ſun defcry
Our conceal'd folemnity.
Come, knit hands, and beat the ground
In a light fantaſtic round.

### THE MEASURE.

Break off, break off, I feel the different pace
Of fome chaſte footing near about this ground.
Run to your ſhrouds, within thefe brakes and trees;
Our number may aff'right: Some virgin fure
(For fo I can diſtinguiſh by mine art)
Benighted in thefe woods. Now to my charms,
And to my wily trains; I ſhall ere long
Be well-ſtock'd with as fair a herd as graz'd
About my mother Circe. Thus I hurl
My dazzling fpells into the fpungy air,
Of pow'r to cheat the eye with blear illuſion,
And give it falfe prefentments, left the place
And my quaint habits breed aſtoniſhment,
And put the damfel to fufpicious flight,
Which muſt not be, for that's againſt my courfe;

I under fair pretence of friendly ends,
And well plac'd words of glozing courtefy
Baited with reafons not unplaufible,
Wind me into the eafy-hearted man,
And hug him into fnares. When once her eye
Hath met the virtue of this magic duft,
I fhall appear fome harmlefs villager,
Whom thrift keeps up about his country gear.
But here fhe comes, I fairly ftep afide,
And hearken, if I may, her bufinefs here.

### THE LADY ENTERS.

This way the noife was, if mine ear be true,
My beft guide now; methought it was the found
Of riot and ill manag'd merriment,
Such as the jocund flute, or gamefome pipe
Stirs up among the loofe unletter'd hinds,
When for their teeming flocks, and granges full,
In wanton dance they praife the bounteous Pan,
And thank the Gods amifs. I fhould be loath
To meet the rudenefs, and fwill'd infolence
Of fuch late waffailers; yet O where elfe
Shall I inform my unacquainted feet
In the blind mazes of this tangled wood?
My brothers, when they faw me wearied out
With this long way, refolving here to lodge
Under the fpreading favour of thefe pines,
Stept, as they faid, to the next thicket fide
To bring me berries, or fuch cooling fruit
As the kind hofpitable woods provide.

P

They left me then, when the grey-hooded Even;
Like a fad votarift in palmer's weed,
Rofe from the hindmoft wheels of Phœbus' wain.
But where they are, and why they came not back,
Is now the labour of my thoughts; 'tis likelieft
They had engag'd their wand'ring fteps too far,
And envious darknefs, ere they could return,
Had ftole them from me; elfe, O thievifh Night,
Why fhould'ft thou, but for fome felonious end,
In thy dark lantern thus clofe up the ftars,
That nature hung in Heav'n, and fill'd their lamps
With everlafting oil, to give due light
To the mifled and lonely traveller?
This is the place, as well as I may guefs,
Whence even now the tumult of loud mirth
Was rife, and perfect in my lift'ning ear,
Yet nought but fingle darknefs do I find.
What might this be? A thoufand fantafies
Begin to throng into my memory,
Of calling fhapes, and beck'ning fhadows dire,
And aery tongues, that fyllable men's names
On fands, and fhores, and defert wildernefſes.
Thefe thoughts may ftartle well, but not aftound
The virtuous mind, that ever walks attended
By a ftrong fiding champion, confcience.—
O welcome pure· ey'd Faith, white-handed Hope,
Thou hovering angel girt with golden wings,
And thou unblemifh'd form of Chaftity;
I fee ye vifibly, and now believe
That he, the Supreme Good, to' whom all things ill
Are but as flavifh officers of vengeance,

Would fend a glift'ring guardian if need were
To keep my life and honour unaffail'd.
Was I deceiv'd, or did a fable cloud
Turn forth her filver lining on the night?
I did not err, there does a fable cloud
Turn forth her filver lining on the night,
And cafts a gleam over this tufted grove.
I cannot halloo to my brothers, but
Such noife as I can make to be heard fartheft
I'll venture, for my new enliven'd fpirits
Prompt me; and they perhaps are not far off.


## SONG.


Sweet Echo, fweeteft nymph, that liv'ft unfeen
  Within thy aery fhell,
  By flow Meander's margent green,
And in the violet-embroider'd vale,
  Where the love-lorn nightingale
Nightly to thee her fad fong mourneth well;
Canft thou not tell me of a gentle pair
  That likeft thy Narciffus are?
   O if thou have
  Hid them in fome flow'ry cave,
   Tell me but where,
 Sweet queen of parly, daughter of the fphere,
 So may'ft thou be tranflated to the fkies,
And give refounding grace to all Heav'n's harmonies.

### COMUS.

Can any mortal mixture of earth's mould
Breathe fuch divine inchanting ravifhment?
Sure fomething holy lodges in that breaft,
And with thefe raptures moves the vocal air
To teftify his hidden refidence:
How fweetly did they float upon the wings
Of filence, through the empty-vaulted night,
At every fall fmoothing the raven down
Of darknefs till it fmil'd! I have oft heard
My mother Circe with the Sirens three,
Amidft the flow'ry-kirtled Naiades
Culling their potent herbs, and baleful drugs,
Who as they fung would take the prifon'd foul,
And lap it in Elyfium; Scylla wept,
And chid her barking waves into attention,
And fell Charybdis murmur'd foft applaufe:
Yet they in pleafing flumber lull'd the fenfe,
And in fweet madnefs robb'd it of itfelf;
But fuch a facred, and home-felt delight,
Such fober certainty of waking blifs
I never heard till now.   I'll fpeak to her,
And fhe fhall be my queen.   Hail foreign wonder,
Whom certain thefe rough fhades did never breed,
Unlefs the Goddefs that in rural fhrine
Dwell'ft here with Pan, or Silvan, by bleft fong
Forbidding every bleak unkindly fog
To touch the profp'rous growth of this tall wood.

### LADY.

Nay gentle fhepherd, ill is loft that praife
That is addrefs'd to unattending ears;

Not any boaſt of ſkill, but extreme ſhift
How to regain my ſever'd company,
Compell'd me to awake the courteous Echo
To give me anſwer from her moſſy couch.

### COMUS.

What chance, good lady, hath bereft you thus?

### LADY.

Dim darkneſs, and this leafy labyrinth.

### COMUS.

Could that divide you from near-uſhering guides?

### LADY.

They left me weary on a graſſy turf.

### COMUS.

By falſehood, or diſcourteſy, or why?

### LADY.

To ſeek i' th' valley ſome cool friendly ſpring.

### COMUS.

And left your fair ſide all unguarded, lady?

### LADY.

They were but twain, and purpos'd quick return.

### COMUS.

Perhaps fore-ſtalling night prevented them.

### LADY.

How eaſy my misfortune is to hit!

### COMUS.

Imports their loſs, beſide the preſent need?

### LADY.

No leſs than if I ſhould my brothers loſe.

### COMUS.

Were they of manly prime, or youthful bloom?

LADY.

As fmooth as Hebe's their unrazor'd lips.

COMUS.

Two fuch I faw, what time the abour'd ox
In his loofe traces from the furrow came,
And the fwinkt hedger at his fupper fat;
I faw them under a green mantling vine
That crawls along the fide of yon fmall hill,
Plucking ripe clufters from the tender fhoots;
Their port was more than human, as they ftood:
I took it for a fairy vifion
Of fome gay creatures of the element,
That in the colours of the rainbow live,
And play i'th' plighted clouds. I was awe-ftruck,
And as I paft, I worfhipt; if thofe you feek,
It were a journey like the path to Heaven,
To help you find them.

LADY.

Gentle villager,
What readieft way would bring me to that place?

COMUS.

Due weft it rifes from this fhrubby point.

LADY.

To find out that, good fhepherd, I fuppofe,
In fuch a fcant allowance of ftar-light,
Would overtafk the beft land-pilot's art,
Without the fure guefs of well-practis'd feet.

COMUS.

I know each lane, and every alley green,
Dingle, or bufhy dell of this wild wood,

And every bofky bourn from fide to fide,
My daily walks and ancient neighbourhood;
And if your ftray-attendance be yet lodg'd,
Or fhrowd within thefe limits, I fhall know
Ere morrow wake, or the low-roofted lark
From her thatcht pallat roufe; if otherwife
I can conduct you, lady, to a low
But loyal cottage, where you may be fafe
Till further queft.

### LADY.

Shepherd, I take thy word,
And truft thy honeft offer'd courtefy,
Which oft is fooner found in lowly fheds
With fmoky rafters, than in tap'ftry halls
And courts of princes, where it firft was nam'd,
And yet is moft pretended: In a place
Lefs warranted than this, or lefs fecure,
I cannot be, that I fhould fear to change it.
Eye me, bleft Providence, and fquare my trial
To my proportion'd ftrength. Shepherd, lead on.

### THE TWO BROTHERS.

### ELDER BROTHER.

Unmuffle ye faint Stars, and thou fair Moon,
That wont'ft to love the traveller's benizon,
Stoop thy pale vifage through an amber cloud,
And difinherit Chaos, that reigns here
In double night of darknefs and of fhades;
Or if your influence be quite damm'd up
With black ufurping mifts, fome gentle taper,
Though a rufh-candle from the wicker hole

Of fome clay habitation, vifit us
With thy long levell'd rule of ftreaming light,
And thou fhalt be our ftar of Arcady,
Or Tyrian Cynofure.

SECOND BROTHER.

　　Or if our eyes
Be barr'd that happinefs, might we but hear
The folded flocks penn'd in their wattled cotes,
Or found of paff'ral reed with oaten ftops,
Or whiftle from the lodge, or village cock
Count the night watches to his feathery dames,
'Twould be fome folace yet, fome little cheering
In this clofe dungeon of innumerous boughs.
But O that haplefs virgin, our loft fifter,
Where may fhe wander now, whither betake her
From the chill dew, amongft rude burs and thiftles?
Perhaps fome cold bank is her bolfter now,
Or 'gainft the rugged bark of fome broad elm
Leans her unpillow'd head fraught with fad fears.
What if in wild amazement, and affright,
Or, while we fpeak, within the direful grafp
Of favage hunger, or of favage heat?

ELDER BROTHER.

　　Peace, brother, be not over-exquifite
To caft the fafhion of uncertain evils;
For grant they be fo, while they reft unknown,
What need a man foreftall his date of grief,
And run to meet what he would moft avoid?
Or if they be but falfe alarms of fear,
How bitter is fuch felf-delufion?
I do not think my fifter fo to feek,

Or fo unprincipled in virtue's book,
And the fweet peace that goodnefs bofoms ever,
As that the fingle want of light and noife
(Not being in danger, as I truft fhe is not)
Could ftir the conftant mood of her calm thoughts,
And put them into mif-becoming plight.
Virtue could fee to do what virtue would
By her own radiant light, though fun and moon
Were in the flat fea funk. And wifdom's felf
Oft feeks to fweet retired folitude,
Where with her beft nurfe contemplation
She plumes her feathers, and lets grow her wings,
That in the various buftle of refort
Were all too ruffled, and fometimes impair'd.
He that has light within his own clear breaft
May fit i'th' centre, and enjoy bright day:
But he that hides a dark foul, and foul thoughts,
Benighted walks under the mid-day fun;
Himfelf is his own dungeon.

SECOND BROTHER.

'Tis moft true,
That mufing meditation moft affects
The penfive fecrefy of defert cell,
Far from the cheerful haunt of men and herds,
And fits as fafe as in a fenate houfe;
For who would rob a hermit of his weeds,
His few books, or his beads, or maple difh,
Or do his grey hairs any violence?
But beauty, like the fair Hefperian tree
Laden with blooming gold, had need the guard
Of dragon-watch with uninchanted eye,

To fave her bloffoms, and defend her fruit
From the rafh hand of bold incontinence.
You may as well fpread out the unfunn'd heaps
Of mifers treafure by an outlaw's den,
And tell me it is fafe, as bid me hope
Danger will wink on opportunity,
And let a fingle helplefs maiden pafs
Uninjur'd in this wild furrounding wafte.
Of night, or lonelinefs it recks me not;
I fear the dread events that dog them both,
Left fome ill-greeting touch attempt the perfon
Of our unowned fifter.

ELDER BROTHER.

   I do not, brother,
Infer, as if I thought my fifter's ftate
Secure without all doubt, or controverfy:
Yet where an equal poife of hope and fear
Does arbitrate th' event, my nature is
That I incline to hope, rather than fear,
And gladly banifh fquint fufpicion.
My fifter is not fo defencelefs left
As you imagine: fhe' has a hidden ftrength
Which you remember not.

SECOND BROTHER.

   What hidden ftrength,
Unlefs the ftrength of Heav'n, if you mean that?

ELDER BROTHER.

   I mean that too, but yet a hidden ftrength,
Which if Heav'n gave it, may be term'd her own:
'Tis chaftity, my brother, chaftity:
She that has that, is clad in complete fteel,

And like a quiver'd nymph with arrows keen
May trace huge forefts, and unharbour'd heaths,
Infamous hills, and fandy perilous wilds,
Where through the facred rays of chaftity,
No favage fierce, bandite, or mountaineer
Will dare to foil her virgin purity:
Yea there, where very defolation dwells
By grots, and caverns fhagg'd with horrid fhades,
She may pafs on with unblench'd majefty,
Be it not done in pride, or in prefumption.
Some fay no evil thing that walks by night,
In fog, or fire, by lake, or moorifh fen,
Blue meagre hag, or ftubborn unlaid ghoft,
That breaks his magic chains at Curfeu time,
No goblin, or fwart fairy of the mine,
Hath hurtful pow'r o'er true virginity.
Do ye believe me yet, or fhall I call
Antiquity from the old fchools of Greece .
To teftify the arms of chaftity?
Hence had the huntrefs Dian her dread bow,
Fair filver-fhafted queen, for ever chafte,
Wherewith fhe tam'd the brinded lionefs
And fpotted mountain pard, but fet at nought
The frivolous bolt of Cupid; gods and men
Fear'd her ftern frown, and fhe was queen o'th' woods.
What was that fnaky-headed Gorgon fhield,
That wife Minerva wore, unconquer'd virgin,
Wherewith fhe freez'd her foes to congeal'd ftone,
But rigid looks of chafte aufterity,
And noble grace that dafh'd brute violence

With fudden adoration, and blank awe?
So dear to Heav'n is faintly chaftity,
That when a foul is found fincerely fo,
A thoufand liveried angels lackey her,
Driving far off each thing of fin and guilt,
And in clear dream, and folemn vifion,
Tell her of things that no grofs ear can hear,
Till oft converfe with heav'nly habitants
Begin to caft a beam on th' outward fhape,
The unpolluted temple of the mind,
And turns it by degrees to the foul's effence,
Till all be made immortal: but when luft,
By unchafte looks, loofe geftures, and foul talk,
But moft by lewd and lavifh act of fin,
Lets in defilement to the inward parts,
The foul grows clotted by contagion,
Imbodies, and imbrutes, till fhe quite lofe
The divine property of her firft being.
Such are thofe thick and gloomy fhadows damp
Oft feen in charnel vaults, and fepulchres,
Ling'ring, and fitting by a new made grave, ·
As loath to leave the body that it lov'd,
And link'd itfelf by carnal fenfuality
To a degenerate and degraded ftate.

SECOND BROTHER.

How charming is divine philofophy!
Not harfh, and crabbed, as dull fools fuppofe,
But mufical as is Apollo's lute,
And a perpetual feaft of nectar'd fweets,
Where no crude furfeit reigns.

ELDER BROTHER.

Lift, lift, I hear
Some far off halloo break the filent air.

SECOND BROTHER.

Methought fo too; what fhould it be?

ELDER BROTHER.

For certain
Either fome one like us night-founder'd here,
Or elfe fome neighbour woodman, or, at worft,
Some roving robber calling to his fellows.

SECOND BROTHER.

Heav'n keep my fifter. Again, again, and near;
Beft draw, and ftand upon our guard.

ELDER BROTHER.

I'll halloo;
If he be friendly, he comes well; if not,
Defence is a good caufe, and Heav'n be for us.

THE ATTENDANT SPIRIT, HABITED LIKE

A SHEPHERD.

That halloo I fhould know, what are you? fpeak;
Come not too near, you fall on iron ftakes elfe.

SPIRIT.

What voice is that? my young lord? fpeak again.

SECOND BROTHER.

O brother, 'tis my father's fhepherd, fure.

ELDER BROTHER.

Thyrfis? whofe artful ftrains have oft delay'd
The huddling brook to hear his madrigal,
And fweeten'd every mufkrofe of the dale.

How cam'ſt thou here, good ſwain? hath any ram
Slipt from the fold, or young kid loſt his dam,
Or ſtraggling wether the pent flock forſook?
How could'ſt thou find this dark ſequeſter'd nook?

SPIRIT.

O my lov'd maſter's heir, and his next joy,
I came not here on ſuch a trivial toy
As a ſtray'd ewe, or to purſue the ſtealth
Of pilfering wolf; not all the fleecy wealth
That doth enrich theſe downs is worth a thought
To this my errand, and the care it brought.
But, O my virgin lady, where is ſhe?
How chance ſhe is not in your company?

ELDER BROTHER.

To tell thee ſadly, ſhepherd, without blame,
Or our neglect, we loſt her as we came.

SPIRIT.

Ah me unhappy! then my fears are true.

ELDER BROTHER.

What fears, good Thyrſis? Prithee briefly ſhow.

SPIRIT.

I'll tell ye; 'tis not vain or fabulous,
(Though ſo eſteem'd by ſhallow ignorance)
What the ſage poets, taught by th' heav'nly muſe,
Story'd of old in high immortal verſe,
Of dire chimeras and inchanted iſles,
And rifted rocks whoſe entrance leads to Hell;
For ſuch there be, but unbelief is blind.

Within the navel of this hideous wood,
Immur'd in cypreſs ſhades a ſorcerer dwells,
Of Bacchus and of Circe born, great Comus,

Deep fkill'd in all his mother's witcheries,
And here to every thirfty wanderer
By fly enticement gives his baneful cup,
With many murmurs mix'd, whofe pleafing poifon
The vifage quite transforms of him that drinks,
And the inglorious likenefs of a beaft
Fixes inftead, unmoulding reafon's mintage
Charáctei'd in the face; this have I learnt
Tending my flocks hard by i'th' hilly crofts,
That brow this bottom glade, whence night by night
He and his monftrous rout are heard to howl
Like ftabled wolves, or tigers at their prey,
Doing abhorred rites to Hecate
In their obfcured haunts of inmoft bowers.
Yet have they many baits, and guileful fpells,
To' inveigle and invite th' unwary fenfe
Of them that pafs unweeting by the way.
This evening late, by then the chewing flocks
Had ta'en their fupper on the favoury herb
Of knot-grafs dew-befprent, and were in fold,
I fat me down to watch upon a bank
With ivy canopied, and interwove
With flaunting honey-fuckle, and began,
Wrapt in a pleafing fit of melancholy,
To meditate my rural minftrelfy,
Till fancy had her fill, but ere a clofe
The wonted roar was up amidft the woods,
And fill'd the air with barbarous diffonance;
At which I ceas'd, and liften'd them a while,
Till an unufual ftop of fudden filence
Gave refpite to the drowfy flighted fteeds,

That draw the litter of clofe curtain'd fleep;
At laft a foft and folemn breathing found
Rofe like a fteam of rich diftill'd perfumes,
And ftole upon the air, that even Silence
Was took ere fhe was ware, and wifh'd fhe might
Deny her nature, and be never more,
· Still to be fo difplac'd.  I was all ear,
And took in ftrains that might create a foul
Under the ribs of death: but O ere long
Too well I did perceive it was the voice
Of my moft honour'd lady, your dear fifter.
Amaz'd I ftood, harrow'd with grief and fear,
And O poor haplefs nightingale thought I,
How fweet thou fing'ft, how near the deadly fnare!
Then down the lawns I ran with headlong hafte,
Through paths and turnings often trod by day,
Till guided by mine ear I found the place,
Where that damn'd wizard hid in fly difguife
(For fo by certain figns I knew) had met
Already, ere my beft fpeed could prevent,
The aidlefs innocent lady his wifh'd prey,
Who gently afk'd if he had feen fuch two,
Suppofing him fome neighbour villager.
Longer I durft not ftay, but foon I guefs'd
Ye were the two fhe meant; with that I fprung
Into fwift flight, till I had found you here,
But further know I not.

SECOND BROTHER.

O night and fhades,
How are ye join'd with Hell in triple knot,
Againft th' unarmed weaknefs of one virgin

Alone, and helplefs! Is this the confidence
You gave me, brother?

ELDER BROTHER.

  Yes, and keep it ftill,
Lean on it fafely; not a period
Shall be unfaid for me: againft the threats
Of malice or of forcery, or that power
Which erring men call Chance, this I hold firm,
Virtue may be affail'd, but never hurt,
Surpris'd by unjuft force, but not inthrall'd;
Yea even that which mifchief meant moft harm,
Shall in the happy trial prove moft glory:
But evil on itfelf fhall back recoil,
And mix no more with goodnefs, when at laft
Gather'd like fcum, and fettled to itfelf,
It fhall be in eternal reftlefs change
Self-fed, and felf-confumed: if this fail,
The pillar'd firmament is rottennefs,
And earth's bafe built on ftubble. But come let's on.
Againft th' oppofing will and arm of Heaven
May never this juft fword be lifted up;
But for that damn'd magician, let him be girt
With all the grifly legions that troop
Under the footy flag of Acheron,
Harpies and Hydras, or all the monftrous forms
'Twixt Africa and Ind, I'll find him out,
And force him to reftore his purchafe back,
Or drag him by the curls to a foul death,
Curs'd as his life.

• SPIRIT.

  Alas! good ventrous youth,

.Q

I love thy courage yet, and bold emprife;
But here thy fword can do thee little ftead;
Far other arms, and other weapons muft
Be thofe that quell the might of hellifh charms:
He with his bare wand can unthread thy joints,
And crumble all thy finews.

ELDER BROTHER.

Why prithee, fhepherd,
How durft thou then thyfelf approach fo near,
As to make this relation?

SPIRIT.

Care and utmoft fhifts
How to fecure the lady from furprifal,
Brought to my mind a certain fhepherd lad,
Of fmall regard to fee to, yet well fkill'd
In every virtuous plant and healing herb,
That fpreads her verdant leaf to th' morning ray:
He lov'd me well, and oft would beg me fing,
Which when I did, he on the tender grafs
Would fit, and hearken ev'n to ecftafy,
And in requital ope his leathern fcrip,
And fhow me fimples of a thoufand names,
Telling their ftrange and vigorous faculties:
Amongft the reft a fmall unfightly root,
But of divine effect, he cull'd me out;
The leaf was darkifh, and had prickles on it,
But in another country, as he faid,
Bore a bright golden flow'r, but not in this foil:
Unknown, and like efteem'd, and the dull fwain
Treads on it daily with his clouted fhoon;
And yet more med'cinal is it than that moly

That Hermes once to wife Ulyffes gave;
He call'd it hæmony, and gave it me,
And bad me keep it as of fovereign ufe
'Gainft all inchantments, mildew, blaft, or damp,
Or ghaftly furies apparition.
I purs'd it up, but little reck'ning made,
Till now that this extremity compell'd:
But now I find it true; for by this means
I knew the foul inchanter though difguis'd,
Enter'd the very lime-twigs of his fpells,
And yet came off: if you have this about you,
(As I will give you when we go) you may
Boldly affault the necromancer's hall;
Where if he be, with dauntlefs hardihood,
And brandifh'd blade rufh on him, break his glafs,
And fhed the lufcious liquor on the ground,
But feize his wand; though he and his curs'd crew
Fierce fign of battle make, and menace high,
Or like the fons of Vulcan vomit fmoke,
Yet will they foon retire, if he but fhrink.

ELDER BROTHER.

Thyrfis, lead on apace, I'll follow thee,
And fome good angel bear a fhield before us.

THE SCENE CHANGES TO A STATELY PALACE, SET OUT
 WITH ALL MANNER OF DELICIOUSNESS: SOFT MU-
 SIC, TABLES SPREAD WITH ALL DAINTIES. COMUS
 APPEARS WITH HIS RABBLE, AND THE LADY SET
 IN AN ENCHANTED CHAIR, TO WHOM HE OFFERS
 HIS GLASS, WHICH SHE PUTS BY, AND GOES ABOUT
 TO RISE.

COMUS.

Nay, lady, fit; if I but wave this wand,
Your nerves are all chain'd up in alabafter,
And you a ftatue, or as Daphne was
Root-bound, that fled Apollo.

LADY.

Fool, do not boaft,
Thou canft not touch the freedom of my mind
With all thy charms, although this corporal rind
Thou haft immanacl'd, while Heav'n fees good.

COMUS.

Why are you vex'd, lady? why do you frown?
Here dwell no frowns, nor anger; from thefe gates
Sorrow flies far: fee here be all the pleafures
That fancy can beget on youthful thoughts,
When the frefh blood grows lively, and returns
Brifk as the April buds in primrofe-feafon.
And firft behold this cordial julep here,
That flames, and dances in his cryftal bounds,
With fpi'rits of balm, and fragrant fyrups mix'd.
Not that Nepenthe, which the wife of Thone
In Egypt gave to Jove-born Helena,
Is of fuch pow'r to ftir up joy as this,
To life fo friendly, or fo cool to thirft.
Why fhould you be fo cruel to yourfelf,
And to thofe dainty limbs which Nature lent
For gentle ufage, and foft delicacy?
But you invert the covenants of her truft,
And harfhly deal like an ill-borrower
With that which you receiv'd on other terms,
Scorning the unexempt condition

By which all mortal frailty muſt ſubſiſt,
Refreſhment after toil, eaſe after pain,  ·
That have been tir'd all day without repaſt,
And timely reſt have wanted; but fair virgin,
This will reſtore all ſoon.

LADY.

'Twill not, falſe traitor,
'Twill not reſtore the truth and honeſty
That thou haſt baniſh'd from thy tongue with lies.
.Was this the cottage, and the ſafe abode
Thou toldſt me of? What grim aſpects are theſe,
Theſe ugly-headed monſters? Mercy guard me?
Hence with thy brew'd enchantments, foul deceiver;
Haſt thou betray'd my credulous innocence
.With viſor'd falſehood, and baſe forgery?
And would'ſt thou ſeek again to trap me here
With liquoriſh baits fit to inſnare a brute?
Were it a draught for Juno when ſhe banquets,
I would not taſte thy treaſonous offer; none
But ſuch as are good men can give good things,
And that which is not good, is not delicious
To a well-govern'd and wiſe appetite.

COMUS.

O fooliſhneſs of men! that lend their ears
To thoſe budge doctors of the Stoic fur,
And fetch their precepts from the Cynic tub,
Praiſing the lean and ſallow Abſtinence.
Wherefore did Nature pour her bounties forth,
With ſuch a full and unwithdrawing hand,
Covering the earth with odours, fruits, and flocks, ·
Thronging the ſeas with ſpawn innumerable,   :

But all to pleafe, and fate the curious tafte?
And fet to work millions of fpinning worms,
That in their green fhops weave the fmooth-hair'd filk
To deck her fons, and that no corner might
Be vacant of her plenty, in her own loins
She hutcht th' all-worfhipt ore, and precious gems
To ftore her children with: if all the world
Should in a pet of temp'rance feed on pulfe,
Drink the clear ftream, and nothing wear but frieze,
Th' all-giver would be unthank'd, would be unprais'd,
Not half his riches known, and yet defpis'd,
And we fhould ferve him as a grudging mafter,
As a penurious niggard of his wealth,
And live like Nature's baftards, not her fons,
Who would be quite furcharg'd with her own weight,
And ftrangl'd with her wafte fertility,
Th' earth cumber'd, and the wing'd air darkt with
       plumes,
The herds would over-multitude their lords,
The fea o'erfraught would fwell, and th' unfought
       diamonds
Would fo emblaze the forehead of the deep,
And fo beftud with ftars, that they below
Would grow inur'd to light, and come at laft
To gaze upon the fun with fhamelefs brows.
Lift lady, be not coy, and be not cozen'd
With that fame vaunted name virginity.
Beauty is Nature's coin, muft not be hoarded,
But muft be current, and the good thereof
Confifts in mutual and partaken blifs,
Unfavoury in th' enjoyment of itfelf;

If you let flip time, like a neglected rofe
It withers on the ftalk with languifh'd head.
Beauty is Nature's brag, and muft be fhown
In courts, in feafts, and high folemnities,
Where moft may wonder at the workmanfhip;
It is for homely features to keep home,
They had their name thence; coarfe complexions
And cheeks of forry grain will ferve to ply
The fampler, and to teafe the houfewife's wool.
What need a vermeil-tinctur'd lip for that,
Love-darting eyes, or treffes like the morn?
There was another meaning in thefe gifts,
Think what, and be advis'd, you are but young yet.

### LADY.

    I had not thought to have unlockt my lips
In this unhallow'd air, but that this juggler
Would think to charm my judgment, as mine eyes,
Obtruding falfe rules prankt in reafon's garb.
I hate when vice can bolt her arguments,
And virtue has no tongue to check her pride.
Impoftor, do not charge moft innocent Nature,
As if fhe would her children fhould be riotous
With her abundance; fhe good caterefs
Means her provifion only to the good,
That live according to her fober laws,
And holy dictate of fpare temperance:
If every juft man, that now pines with want,
Had but a moderate and befeeming fhare
Of that which newly pamper'd luxury
Now heaps upon fome few with vaft excefs,
Nature's full bleffings would be well difpens'd

In unfuperfluous even proportion,
And fhe no whit incumber'd with her ftore,
And then the giver would be better thank'd,
His praife due paid; for fwinifh gluttony
Ne'er looks to Heav'n amidft his gorgeous feaft,
But with befotted bafe ingratitude
Crams, and blafphemes his feeder.　Shall I go on?
Or have I faid enough?　To him that dares
Arm his profane tongue with contemptuous words
Againft the fun-clad pow'r of chaftity,
Fain would I fomething fay, yet to what end?
Thou haft nor ear, nor foul to apprehend
The fublime notion, and high myftery,
That muft be utter'd to unfold the fage
And ferious doctrine of virginity,
And thou art worthy that thou fhouldft not know
More happinefs than this thy prefent lot.
Enjoy your dear wit, and gay rhetoric,
That hath fo well been taught her dazzling fence,
Thou art not fit to hear thyfelf convinc'd;
Yet fhould I try, the uncontrolled worth
Of this pure caufe would kindle my rapt fpirits
To fuch a flame of facred vehemence,
That dumb things would be mov'd to fympathize,
And the brute earth would lend her nerves, and
　　　fhake,
Till all thy magic ftructures rear'd fo high,
Were fhatter'd into heaps o'er thy falfe head.

COMUS.

　She fables not, I feel that I do fear
Her words fet off by fome fuperior power;

And though not mortal, yet a cold ſhudd'ring dew
Dips me all o'er, as when the wrath of Jove
Speaks thunder, and the chains of Erebus
To ſome of Satan's crew.   I muſt diſſemble,
And try her yet more ſtrongly.   Come, no more,
This is mere moral babble, and direct
Againſt the canon laws of our foundation;
I muſt not ſuffer this, yet 'tis but the lees
And ſettlings of a melancholy blood:
But this will cure all ſtraight, one ſip of this
Will bathe the drooping ſpirits in delight
Beyond the bliſs of dreams.   Be wiſe, and taſte.—

THE BROTHERS RUSH IN WITH SWORDS DRAWN,
WREST HIS GLASS OUT OF HIS HAND, AND
BREAK IT AGAINST THE GROUND; HIS
ROUT MAKE SIGN OF RESISTANCE,
BUT ARE ALL DRIVEN IN; THE
ATTENDANT SPIRIT
COMES IN.

SPIRIT.

What, have you let the falſe enchanter ſcape?
O ye miſtook, ye ſhould have ſnatcht his wand
And bound him faſt; without his rod revers'd,
And backward mutters of diſſevering power,
We cannot free the Lady that ſits here
In ſtony fetters fix'd, and motionleſs:
Yet ſtay, be not diſturb'd; now I bethink me,
Some other means I have which may be us'd,

Which once of Meliboeus old I learnt,
The foothest shepherd that e'er pip'd on plains.
     There is a gentle nymph not far from hence,
That with moist curb sways the smooth Severn stream,
Sabrina is her name, a virgin pure;
Whilome she was the daughter of Locrine,
That had the sceptre from his father Brute.
She guiltless damsel flying the mad pursuit
Of her enraged stepdame Guendolen,
Commended her fair innocence to the flood,
That stay'd her flight with his cross-flowing course.
The water nymphs that in the bottom play'd,
Held up their pearled wrists and took her in,
Bearing her straight to aged Nereus hall,
Who piteous of her woes rear'd her lank head,
And gave her to his daughters to imbathe
In nectar'd lavers strow'd with asphodil,
And through the porch and inlet of each sense
Dropt in ambrosial oils till she reviv'd,
And underwent a quick immortal change,
Made Goddess of the river; still she retains
Her maiden gentleness, and oft at eve
Visits the herds along the twilight meadows,
Helping all urchin blasts, and ill-luck signs
That the shrewd meddling elf delights to make,
Which she with precious vial'd liquors heals.
For which the shepherds at their festivals
Carol her goodness loud in rustic lays,
And throw sweet garland wreaths into her stream
Of pansies, pinks, and gaudy daffodils.
And, as the old swain said, she can unlock

The clafping charm, and thaw the numbing fpell,
If fhe be right invok'd in warbled fong,
For maidenhood fhe loves, and will be fwift
To aid a virgin, fuch as was herfelf,
In hard-befetting need; this will I try,
And add the pow'r of fome adjuring verfe.

SONG.

Sabrina fair,
   Liften where thou art fitting
Under the glaffy, cool, tranfluccnt wave,
   In twifted braids of lilies knitting
The loofe train of thy amber-dropping hair;
   Liften for dear honour's fake,
   Goddefs of the filver lake,
         Liften and fave.

Liften and appear to us
In name of great Oceanus,
By th' earth-fhaking Neptune's mace,
And Tethys grave majeftic pace,
By hoary Nereus wrinkled look,
And the Carpathian wizard's hook,
By fcaly Triton's winding fhell,
And old footh-faying Glaucus fpell,
By Leucothea's lovely hands,
And her fon that rules the ftrands,
By Thetis tinfel-flipper'd feet,
And the fongs of Sirens fweet,

By dead Parthenope's dear tomb,
And fair Ligea's golden comb,
Wherewith ſhe ſits on diamond rocks,
Sleeking her ſoft alluring locks,
By all the nymphs that nightly dance
Upon thy ſtreams with wily glance,
Riſe, riſe, and heave thy roſy head
From thy coral-paven bed,
And bridle in thy headlong wave,
Till thou our ſummons anſwer'd have.

                    Liſten and ſave.


SABRINA RISES, ATTENDED BY WATER-NYMPHS,
AND SINGS.

By the ruſhy-fringed bank,
Where grows the willow and the oſier dank,
    My ſliding chariot ſtays,
Thick ſet with agate, and the azure ſheen
Of turkis blue, and em'rald green,
      That in the channel ſtrays;
      Whilſt from off the waters fleet
      Thus I ſet my printleſs feet
      O'er the cowſlips velvet head,
        That bends not as I tread;
      Gentle ſwain, at thy requeſt
        I am here.


SPIRIT.

Goddeſs dear,
We implore thy pow'rful hand

To undo the charmed band
Of true virgin here diſtreſt,
Through the force, and through the wile
Of unbleſt inchanter vile.

SABRINA.

Shepherd, 'tis my office beſt
To help inſnared chaſtity:
Brighteſt lady, look on me;
Thus I ſprinkle on thy breaſt
Drops that from my fountain pure
I have kept of precious cure,
Thrice upon thy fingers tip,
Thrice upon thy rubied lip;
Next this marble venom'd feat,
Smear'd with gums of glutinous heat,
I touch with chaſte palms moiſt and cold:
Now the ſpell hath loſt his hold;
And I muſt haſte ere morning hour
To wait in Amphitrite's bow'r.

SABRINA DESCENDS, AND THE LADY RISES OUT
OF HER SEAT.

SPIRIT.

Virgin, daughter of Locrine
Sprung of old Anchiſes line,
May thy brimmed waves for this
Their full tribute never miſs
From a thouſand petty rills,
That tumble down the ſnowy hills:

Summer drowth, or finged air
Never fcorch thy treffes fair,
Nor wet October's torrent flood
Thy molten cryftal fill with mud;
May thy billows roll afhore
The beryl, and the golden ore;
May thy lofty head be crown'd
With many a tow'r and terrace round,
And here and there thy banks upon
With groves of myrrh, and cinnamon.
 Come, lady, while Heav'n lends us grace,
Let us fly this curfed place,
Left the forcerer us entice
With fome other new device.
Not a wafte, or needlefs found,
Till we come to holier ground;
I fhall be your faithful guide
Through this gloomy covert wide,
And not many furlongs thence
Is your Father's refidence,
Where this night are met in ftate
Many a friend to gratulate
His wifh'd prefence, and befide
All the fwains that near abide,
With jigs, and rural dance refort;
We fhall catch them at their fport,
And our fudden coming there
Will double all their mirth and cheer;
Come let us hafte, the ftars grow high,
But night fits monarch yet in the mid fky.

THE SCENE CHANGES, PRESENTING LUDLOW TOWN
AND THE PRESIDENT'S CASTLE; THEN COME
IN COUNTRY DANCERS, AFTER THEM
THE ATTENDANT SPIRIT, WITH
THE TWO BROTHERS AND
THE LADY.

## S O N G.

#### SPIRIT.

Back, Shepherds, back, enough your play,
Till next fun-fhine holiday;
Here be without duck or nod
Other trippings to be trod
Of lighter toes, and fuch court guife
As Mercury did firſt devife
With the mincing Dryades
On the lawns, and on the leas.

THIS SECOND SONG PRESENTS THEM TO THEIR
FATHER AND MOTHER.

Noble lord, and lady bright,
I have brought ye new delight,
Here behold fo goodly grown
Three fair branches of your own;
Heav'n hath timely try'd their youth,
Their faith, their patience, and their truth,

And fent them here through hard affays
With a crown of deathlefs praife,
　　To triumph in victorious dance
O'er fenfual folly, and intemperance.


THE DANCES ENDED, THE SPIRIT EPILOGUIZES.

To the ocean now I fly,
And thofe happy climes that lie
Where day never fhuts his eye,
Up in the broad fields of the fky:
There I fuck the liquid air
All amidft the gardens fair
Of Hefperus, and his daughters three
That fing about the golden tree:
Along the crifped fhades and bowers
Revels the fpruce and jocund Spring,
The Graces, and the rofy-bofom'd Hours,
Thither all their bounties bring;
That there eternal Summer dwells,
And weft-winds with mufky wing
About the cedarn alleys fling
Nard and Caffia's balmy fmells.
Iris there with humid bow
Waters the odorous banks, that blow
Flowers of more mingled hue
Than her purfled fcarf can fhew,
And drenches with Elyfian dew
(Lift mortals, if your ears be true)
Beds of hyacinth and rofes,
Where young Adonis oft repofes,

Waxing well of his deep wound
In flumber foft, and on the ground
Sadly fits th' Affyrian queen;
But far above in fpangled fheen
Celeftial Cupid her fam'd fon advanc'd,
Holds his dear Pfyche fweet entranc'd,
After her wand'ring labours long,
Till free confent the Gods among
Make her his eternal bride,
And from her fair unfpotted fide
Two blifsful twins are to be born,
Youth and Joy; fo Jove hath fworn.

But now my tafk is fmoothly done,
I can fly, or I can run
Quickly to the green earth's end,
Where the bow'd welkin flow doth bend,
And from thence can foar as foon
To the corners of the moon.

Mortals that would follow me,
Love Virtue, fhe alone is free,
She can teach ye how to climb
Higher than the fphery chime;
Or if Virtue feeble were,
Heav'n itfelf would ftoop to her.

R

# XVII.

# LYCIDAS.

IN THIS MOMODY THE AUTHOR BEWAILS A LEARNED
FRIEND, UNFORTUNATELY DROWNED IN HIS
PASSAGE FROM CHESTER ON THE IRISH
SEAS, 1637, AND BY OCCASION FORE-
TELS THE RUIN OF OUR COR-
RUPTED CLERGY, THEN
IN THEIR HEIGHT.

Yᴇᴛ once more, O ye laurels, and once more
Ye Myrtles brown, with Ivy never ſere,
I come to pluck your berries harſh and crude,
And with forc'd fingers rude
Shatter your leaves before the mellowing year.
Bitter conſtraint, and ſad occaſion dear,
Compels me to diſturb your ſeaſon due:
For Lycidas is dead, dead ere his prime,
Young Lycidas, and hath not left his peer:
Who would not ſing for Lycidas? he knew
Himſelf to ſing, and build the lofty rhime.
He muſt not float upon his watery bier
Unwept, and welter to the parching wind,
Without the meed of ſome melodious tear.

Begin then, fifters of the facred well,
That from beneath the feat of Jove doth fpring,
Begin, and fomewhat loudly fweep the ftring.
Hence with denial vain, and coy excufe,
So may fome gentle Mufe
With lucky words favour my deftin'd urn,
And as he paffes turn,
And bid fair peace be to my fable fhrowd.
For we were nurft upon the felf-fame hill,
Fed the fame flock by fountain, fhade, and rill.

Together both, ere the high lawns appear'd
Under the opening eye-lids of the morn,
We drove afield, and both together heard
What time the gray-fly winds her fultry horn,
Batt'ning our flocks with the frefh dews of night,
Oft till the ftar that rofe, at evening, bright,
Tow'rd Heav'n's defcent had flop'd his weft'ring
     wheel.
Mean while the rural ditties were not mute,
Temper'd to th' oaten flute,
Rough Satyrs danc'd, and Fawns with cloved heel
From the glad found would not be abfent long,
And old Damætas lov'd to hear our fong.

But O the heavy change, now thou art gone,
Now thou art gone, and never muft return!
Thee, fhepherd, thee the woods, and defert caves
With wild thyme and the gadding vine o'ergrown,
And all their echoes mourn.
The willows, and the hazel copfes green,
Shall now no more be feen,
Fanning their joyous leaves to thy foft lays.

As killing as the canker to the rofe,
Or taint worm to the weanling herds that graze,
Or froft to flow'rs, that their gay wardrobe wear,
When firft the white-thorn blows;
Such, Lycidas, thy lofs to fhepherds ear.

 Where were ye, nymphs, when the remorfelefs deep
Clos'd o'er the head of your lov'd Lycidas?
For neither were ye playing on the fteep,
Where your old bards, the famous Druids, lie,
Nor on the fhaggy top of Mona high,
Nor yet where Deva fpreads her wizard ftream:
Ah me! I fondly dream
Had ye been there: for what could that have done?
What could the mufe herfelf that Orpheus bore,
The mufe herfelf for her inchanting fon,
Whom univerfal nature did lament,
When by the rout that made the hideous roar,
His gory vifage down the ftream was fent,
Down the fwift Hebrus to the Lefbian fhore?

 Alas! what boots it with inceffant care
To tend the homely flighted fhepherd's trade,
And ftri&ly meditate the thanklefs mufe?
Were it not better done as others ufe,
To fport with Amaryllis in the fhade,
Or with the tangles of Neæra's hair?
Fame is the fpur that the clear fpi'rit doth raife
(That laft infirmity of noble mind)
To fcorn delights, and live laborious days;
But the fair guerdon when we hope to find,
And think to burft out into fudden blaze,
Comes the blind Fury with th' abhorred fhears,

And flits the thin fpun life. But not the praife,
Phœbus reply'd, and touch'd my trembling ears;
Fame is no plant that grows on mortal foil,
Nor in the glift'ring foil
Set off to th' world, nor in broad rumour lies,
But lives and fpreads aloft by thofe pure eyes,
And perfect witnefs of all-judging Jove;
As he pronounces laftly on each deed,
Of fo much fame in Heav'n expect thy meed.

O fountain Arethufe, and thou honour'd flood,
Smooth-fliding Mincius, crown'd with vocal reeds,
That ftrain I heard was of a higher mood:
But now my oat proceeds,
And liftens to the herald of the fea
That came in Neptune's plea;
He afk'd the waves, and afk'd the felon winds,
What hard mifhap hath doom'd this gentle fwain?
And queftion'd every guft of rugged wings
That blows from off each beaked promontory;
They knew not of his ftory,
And fage Hippotades their anfwer brings,
That not a blaft was from his dungeon ftray'd,
The air was calm, and on the level brine
Sleek Panope with all her fifters play'd.
It was that fatal and perfidious bark
Built in th' eclipfe, and rigg'd with curfes dark,
That funk fo low that facred head of thine.

Next Camus, reverend fire, went footing flow,
His mantle hairy, and his bonnet fedge,
Inwrought with figures dim, and on the edge
Like to that fanguine flow'r infcrib'd with woe,

Ah! Who hath reft (quoth he) my deareſt pledge?
Laſt came, and laſt did go,
The pilot of the Galilean lake,
Two maſſy keys he bore of metals twain,
(The golden opes, the iron ſhuts amain)
He ſhook his mitred locks, and ſtern beſpake,
How well could I have ſpar'd for thee, young ſwain,
Enow of ſuch as for their bellies ſake
Creep, and intrude, and climb into the fold?
Of other care they little reck'ning make,
Than how to ſcramble at the ſhearers feaſt,
And ſhove away the worthy bidden gueſt;
Blind mouths! that ſcarce themſelves know how to
        hold
A ſheep-hook, or have learn'd ought elſe the leaſt
That to the faithful herdman's art belongs!
What recks it them? What need they? They are ſped;
And when they liſt, their lean and flaſhy ſongs
Grate on their ſcrannel pipes of wretched ſtraw;
The hungry ſheep look up, and are not fed,
But, ſwoll'n with wind, and the rank miſt they draw,
Rot inwardly, and foul contagion ſpread:
Beſides what the grim wolf with privy paw
Daily devours apace, and nothing ſaid,
But that two-handed engine at the door
Stands ready to ſmite once, and ſmite no more.

    Return, Alpheus, the dread voice is paſt,
That ſhrunk thy ſtreams; return Sicilian muſe,
And call the vales, and bid them hither caſt
Their bells, and flowrets of a thouſand hues.
Ye valleys low, where the mild whiſpers uſe

Of fhades, and wanton winds, and gufhing brooks,
On whofe frefh lap the fwart ftar fparely looks,
Throw hither all your quaint enamel'd eyes,
That on the green turf fuck the honied fhowers,
And purple all the ground with vernal flowers.
Bring the rathe primrofe that forfaken dies,
The tufted crow-toe, and pale jeffamine,
The white pink, and the panfy freakt with jet,
The glowing violet,
The mufk-rofe, and the well-attir'd woodbine,
With cowflips wan that hang the penfive head,
And every flower that fad embroidery wears:
Bid amaranthus all his beauty fhed,
And daffodillies fill their cups with tears,
To ftrow the laureat hearfe where Lycid lies.
For fo to interpofe a little eafe,
Let our frail thoughts dally with falfe furmife.
Ah me! Whilft thee the fhores, and founding feas
Wafh far away, where'er thy bones are hurl'd,
Whether beyond the ftormy Hebrides,
Where thou perhaps under the whelming tide
Vifit'ft the bottom of the monftrous world;
Or whether thou to our moift vows deny'd,
Sleep'ft by the fable of Bellerus old,
Where the great vifion of the guarded mount
Looks tow'rd Namancos and Bayona's hold;
Look homeward angel now, and melt with ruth:
And, O ye dolphins, waft the haplefs youth.

Weep no more, woful fhepherds, weep no more,
For Lycidas your forrow is not dead,
Sunk though he be beneath the watry floor;

So finks the day-ftar in the ocean bed,
And yet anon repairs his drooping head,
And tricks his beams, and with new fpangled ore
Flames in the forehead of the morning fky:
So Lycidas funk low, but mounted high,
Through the dear might of him that walk'd the waves,
Where other groves and other ftreams along,
With nectar pure his oozy locks he laves,
And hears the unexpreffive nuptial fong,
In the bleft kingdoms meek of joy and love.
There entertain him all the faints above,
In folemn troops, and fweet focieties,
That fing, and finging in their glory move,
And wipe the tears for ever from his eyes.
Now, Lycidas, the fhepherds weep no more;
Henceforth thou art the genius of the fhore,
In thy large recompenfe, and fhalt be good
To all that wander in that perilous flood.

Thus fang the uncouth fwain to th' oaks and rills,
While the ftill morn went out with fandals gray,
He touch'd the tender ftops of various quills,
With eager thought warbling his Doric lay:
And now the fun had ftretch'd out all the hills,
And now was dropt into the weftern bay;
At laft he rofe, and twitch'd his mantle blue:
To-morrow to frefh woods and paftures new.

## XVIII.

## THE FIFTH ODE OF HORACE, LIB. I.

QUIS MULTA GRACILIS TE PUER IN ROSA,
RENDERED ALMOST WORD FOR WORD WITHOUT
RHIME, ACCORDING TO THE LATIN MEA-
SURE, AS NEAR AS THE LANGUAGE
WILL PERMIT.

WHAT flender youth bedew'd with liquid odours
Courts thee on rofes in fome pleafant cave,
 Pyrrha? for whom bind'ft thou
 In wreaths thy golden hair,
Plain in thy neatnefs? Oh how oft fhall he
On faith and changed gods complain, and feas
 Rough with black winds and ftorms
 Unwonted fhall admire!
Who now enjoys thee credulous, all gold,
Who always vacant always amiable
 Hopes thee, of flattering gales
 Unmindful. Haplefs they
To whom thou untry'd feem'ft fair. Me in my vow'd
Picture the facred wall declares t' have hung
 My dank and dropping weeds
 To the ftern god of fea.

## AD PYRRHAM.  ODE V.

HORATIUS EX PYRRHÆ ILLECEBRIS TANQUAM
E NAUFRAGIO ENATAVERAT, CUJUS
AMORE IRRETITOS, AFFIRMAT
ESSE MISEROS.


Quis multa gracilis te puer in rosa
Perfusus liquidis urget odoribus,
  Grato, Pyrrha, sub antro?
  Cui flavam religas comam
Simplex munditiis? heu quoties fidem
Mutatosque deos flebit, et aspera
  Nigris æquora ventis
  Emirabitur insolens!
Qui nunc te fruitur credulus aurea,
Qui semper vacuam semper amabilem
  Sperat, nescius auræ
  Fallacis.   Miseri quibus
Intentata nites.   Me tabula sacer
Votiva paries indicat uvida
  Suspendisse potenti
  Vestimenta maris Deo.

## XIX.

## ON THE NEW FORCERS OF CONSCIENCE

UNDER THE LONG PARLIAMENT.

BECAUSE you have thrown off your Prelate Lord,
 And with ſtiff vows renounc'd his Liturgy,
 To ſeize the widow'd whore Plurality
From them whoſe ſin ye envied, not abhorr'd,
Dare ye for this adjure the civil ſword
 To force our conſciences that Chriſt ſet free,
 And ride us with a claſſic hierarchy
Taught ye by mere A. S. and Rotherford?
Men whoſe life, learning, faith, and pure intent
 Would have been held in high eſteem with Paul,
 Muſt now be nam'd and printed Heretics
By ſhallow Edwards and Scotch what d'ye call:
 But we do hope to find out all your tricks,
 Your plots and packing worſe than thoſe of Trent,
     That ſo the Parliament
May with their wholeſome and preventive ſhears
Clip your phylaƈteries, though balk your ears,
     And ſuccour our juſt fears,
When they ſhall read this clearly in your charge,
New Preſbyter is but Old Prieſt writ large.

# SONNETS.

## I.

## TO THE NIGHTINGALE.

O NIGHTINGALE, that on yon bloomy ſpray
    Warbleſt at eve, when all the woods are ſtill,
    Thou with freſh hope the lover's heart doſt fill,
    While the jolly hours lead on propitious May.
Thy liquid notes that cloſe the eye of day,
    Firſt heard before the ſhallow cuckoo's bill,
    Portend ſuccefs in love; O if Jove's will
    Have link'd that amorous pow'r to thy ſoft lay,
Now timely ſing, ere the rude bird of hate
    Foretel my hopelefs doom in ſome grove nigh;
    As thou from year to year haſt ſung too late
For my relief, yet hadſt no reaſon why:
    Whether the muſe, or Love call thee his mate,
    Both them I ſerve, and of their train am I.

## II.

Donna leggiadra il cui bel nome honora
  L'herbofa val di Rheno, e il nobil varco,
  Bene è colui d'ogni valore fcarco
  Qual tuo fpirto gentil non innamora,
Che dolcemente moftra fi di fuora
  De fui atti foavi giamai parco,
  E i don', che fon d'amor faette ed arco,
  La onde l'alta tua virtu s'infiora.
Quando tu vaga parli, o lieta canti
  Che mover poffa duro alpeftre legno
  Guardi ciafcun a gli occhi, ed a gli orecchi
L'entrata, chi de te fi truova indegno;
  Gratia fola di fu gli vaglia, inanti
  Che'l difio amorofo al cuor s'invecchi.

## III.

Qual in colle afpro, al imbrunir di fera
  L'avezza giovinetta paftorella
  Va bagnando l'herbetta ftrana e bella
  Che mal fi fpande a difufata fpera
Fuor di fua natia alma primavera,
  Cofi Amor meco insù la lingua fnella
  Defta il fior novo di ftrania favella,
  Mentre io di te, vezzofamente altera,
Canto, dal mio buon popol non intefo
  E'l bel Tamigi cangio col bel Arno.

Amor lo volfe, ed io a l'altrui pefo
Seppi ch' Amor cofa mai volfe indarno.

Deh! fofs' il mio cuor lento e'l duro feno
A chi pianta dal ciel fi buon terreno.

## CANZONE.

Ridonsi donne e giovani amorofi
  M' accoftandofi attorno, e perche fcrivi,
  Perche tu fcrivi in lingua ignota e ftrana
  Verfeggiando d' amor, e come t'ofi ?
  Dinne, fe la tua fpeme fia mai vana,
  E de penfierilo miglior t' arrivi;
  Cofi mi van burlando, altri rivi
  Altri lidi t'afpettan, et altre onde
  Nelle cui verdi fponde
  Spuntati ad hor, ad hor a la tua chioma
  L' immortal guiderdon d' eterne frondi
  Perche alle fpalle tue foverchia foma ?
    Canzon dirotti, e tu per me rifpondi
  Dice mia Donna, e'l fuo dir, é il mio cuore
  Quefta e lingua di cui fi vanta Amore.

## IV.

Diodati, e te'l dirò con maraviglia,
  Quel ritrofo io ch'amor fpreggiar foléa
  E de fuoi lacci fpeffo mi ridéa
  Gia caddi, ov'huom dabben talhor s'impiglia.
Ne treccie d' oro, ne guancia vermiglia
  M' abbaglian sì, ma fotto nova idea

Pellegrina bellezza che'l cuor bea,
    Portamenti alti honefti, e nelle ciglia
Quel fereno fulgor d' amabil nero,
    Parole adorne di lingua piu d'una,
    E'l cantar che di mezzo l'hemifpero
Traviar ben puo la faticofa Luna,
    E degli occhi fuoi auventa fi gran fuoco
    Che l'incerar gli orecchi mi fia poco.

## V.

PER certo i bei voftr'occhi, Donna mia
    Effer non puo che non fian lo mio fole
    Si mi percuoton forte, come ei fuole
    Per l'arene di Libia chi s'invia,
Mentre un caldo vapor (ne fentì pria)
    Da quel lato fi fpinge ove mi duole,
    Che forfe amanti nelle lor parole
    Chiaman fofpir; io non fo che fi fia:
Parte rinchiufa, e turbida fi cela
    Scoffo mi il petto, e poi n'ufcendo poco
    Quivi d'attorno o s'agghiaccia, o s'ingiela;
Ma quanto a gli occhi giunge a trovar loco
    Tutte le notti a me fuol far piovofe
    Finche mia Alba rivien colma di rofe.

## VI.

GIOVANE piano, e femplicetto amante
    Poi che fuggir me fteffo in dubbio fono,
    Madonna a voi del mio cuor l'humil dono
    Faro divoto; io certo a prove tante

L'hebhi fedele, intrepido, coſtante,
  De penſieri leggiadro, accorto, e buono;
  Quando rugge il gran mondo, e ſcocca il tuono,
  S'arma di ſe, e d' intero diamante,
Tanto del forſe, e d' invidia ſicuro,
  Di timori, e ſperanze al popol uſe
  Quanto d'ingegno, e d'alto valor vago,
E di cetta ſonora, e delle muſe :
  Sol troverete in tal parte men duro
  Ove Amor miſe l'inſanabil ago.

## VII.

### ON HIS BEING ARRIVED TO THE AGE OF TWENTY-THREE.

How ſoon hath time, the ſubtle thief of youth,
  Stoln on his wing my three and twentieth year !
  My haſting days fly on with full career,
  But my late ſpring no bud or bloſſom ſhew'th.
Perhaps my ſemblance might deceive the truth,
  That I to manhood am arriv'd ſo near,
  And inward ripeneſs doth much leſs appear,
  That ſome more timely-happy ſpirits indu'th,
Yet be it leſs or more, or ſoon or ſlow,
  It ſhall be ſtill in ſtricteſt meaſure even
  To that ſame lot, however mean or high,
Toward which Time leads me, and the will of Heaven;
  All is, if I have grace to uſe it ſo,
  As ever in my great Taſk-maſter's eye.

s

## VIII.

## WHEN THE ASSAULT WAS INTENDED TO THE CITY.

CAPTAIN, or Colonel, or Knight in arms,
  Whofe chance on thefe defencelefs doors may feize,
  If deed of honour did thee ever pleafe,
  Guard them, and him within protect from harms.
He can requite thee, for he knows the charms
  That call fame on fuch gentle acts as thefe,
  And he can fpread thy name o'er lands and feas,
  Whatever clime the fun's bright circle warms.
Lift not thy fpear against the Mufe's bow'r:
  The great Emathian conqueror bid fpare
  The houfe of Pindarus, when temple' and tow'r
Went to the ground: And the repeated air
  Of fad Electra's poet had the pow'r
  To fave th' Athenian walls from ruin bare.

## IX.

## TO A VIRTUOUS YOUNG LADY.

LADY that in the prime of earlieft youth
  Wifely haft fhunn'd the broad way and the green;
  And with thofe few art eminently feen,
  That labour up the hill of heav'nly truth,
The better part with Mary and with Ruth

Chofen thou haft; and they that overween,
And at thy growing virtues fret their fpleen,
No anger find in thee, but pity' and ruth.
Thy care is fix'd, and zealoufly attends
To fill thy odorous lamp with deeds of light,
And hope that reaps not fhame. Therefore be fure
Thou, when the bridegroom with his feaftful friends
Paffes to blifs at the mid hour of night,
Haft gain'd thy entrance, Virgin wife and pure.

## X.

### TO THE LADY MARGARET LEY.

DAUGHTER to that good earl, once prefident
Of England's council, and her treafury,
Who liv'd in both, unftain'd with gold or fee,
And left them both, more in himfelf content,
Till fad the breaking of that parliament
Broke him, as that difhoneft victory
At Chæronea, fatal to liberty,
Kill'd with report that old man eloquent.
Though later born than to have known the days
Wherein your father flourifh'd, yet by you,
Madam, methinks I fee him living yet;
So well your words his noble virtues praife,
That all both judge you to relate them true,
And to poffefs them, honour'd Margaret.

## XI.

ON THE

### DETRACTION WHICH FOLLOWED UPON MY WRITING CERTAIN TREATISES.

A BOOK was writ of late call'd Tetrachordon,
  And woven clofe, both matter, form and ftyle;
  The fubjeƈt new: it walk'd the town a while,
  Numb'ring good intelleƈts; now feldom por'd on.
Cries the ftall-reader, Blefs us! what a word on
  A title page is this! and fome in file
  Stand fpelling falfe, while one might walk to Mile-
End Green. Why is it harder, firs, than Gordon,
Colkitto, or Macdonnel, or Galafp?
  Thofe rugged names to our like mouths grow fleek,
  That would have made Quintilian ftare and gafp,
Thy age, like our's, O Soul of fir John Cheek,
  Hated not learning worfe than toad or afp,
    When thou taught'ft Cambridge and king Edward
      Greek.

## XII.

### ON THE SAME.

I DID but prompt the age to quit their clogs
  By the known rules of ancient liberty,
  When ftraight a barbarous noife environs me
  Of owls and cuckoos, affes, apes and dogs:
As when thofe hinds that were transform'd to frogs

Rail'd at Latona's twin-born progeny,
Which after held the fun and moon in fee.
But this is got by cafting pearl to hogs;
That bawl for freedom in their fenfelefs mood,
And ftill revolt when truth would fet them free.
Licence they mean when they cry Liberty;
For who loves that, muft firft be wife and good;
But from that mark how far they rove we fee
For all this wafte of wealth, and lofs of blood.

## XIII.

## TO MR. H. LAWES ON HIS AIRS.

HARRY, whofe tuneful and well meafur'd fong
First taught our Englifh mufic how to fpan
Words with juft note and accent, not to fcan
With Midas ears, committing fhort and long;
Thy worth and fkill exempts thee from the throng,
With praife enough for envy to look wan;
To after age thou fhalt be writ the man,
That with fmooth air could'ft humour beft our
tongue.
Thou honour'ft verfe, and verfe muft lend her wing
To honour thee, the prieft of Phœbus quire,
That turn'ft their happieft lines in hymn, or ftory.
Dante fhall give fame leave to fet thee higher
Than his Cafella, whom he woo'd to fing
Met in the milder fhades of purgatory.

## XIV.

### ON THE

## RELIGIOUS MEMORY OF MRS. CATHARINE THOMSON, MY CHRISTIAN FRIEND,

#### DECEASED 16 DECEM. 1646.

WHEN faith and love, which parted from thee never,
  Had ripen'd thy juſt ſoul to dwell with God,
  Meekly thou didſt reſign this earthy load
  Of death, call'd life; which us from life doth ſever.
Thy works and alms and all thy good endeavour
  Stay'd not behind, nor in the grave were trod;
  But as faith pointed with her golden rod,
  Follow'd thee up to joy and bliſs for ever.
Love led them on, and faith who knew them beſt
  Thy hand-maids, clad them o'er with purple beams
  And azure wings, that up they flew ſo dreſt,
And ſpake the truth of thee on glorious themes
  Before the judge, who thenceforth bid thee reſt
  And drink thy fill of pure immortal ſtreams.

## XV.

### TO THE LORD GENERAL FAIRFAX.

FAIRFAX, whoſe name in arms through Europe rings,
  Filling each mouth with envy or with praiſe,
  And all her jealous monarchs with amaze

And rumours loud, that daunt remoteſt kings,
Thy firm unſhaken virtue ever brings
  Victory home, though new rebellions raiſe
  Their Hydra heads, and the falſe North diſplays
  Her broken league to imp their ſerpent wings.
O yet a nobler taſk awaits thy hand,
  (For what can war, but endleſs war ſtill breed?)
  Till truth and right from violence be freed,
And public faith clear'd from the ſhameful brand
  Of public fraud. In vain doth valour bleed,
  While avarice and rapine ſhare the land.

## XVI.

### TO THE LORD GENERAL CROMWELL.

CROMWELL, our chief of men, who through a cloud,
  Not of war only, but detractions rude,
  Guided by faith and matchleſs fortitude,
  To peace and truth thy glorious way haſt plough'd,
And on the neck of crowned fortune proud
  Haſt rear'd God's trophies, and his work purſued,
  While Darwen ſtream with blood of Scots imbrued,
  And Dunbar field reſounds thy praiſes loud,
And Worceſter's laureat wreath. Yet much remains
  To conquer ſtill; peace hath her victories
  No leſs renown'd than war: new foes ariſe
Threat'ning to bind our ſouls with ſecular chains:
  Help us to ſave free conſcience from the paw
  Of hireling wolves, whoſe goſpel is their maw.

## XVII.

### TO SIR HENRY VANE THE YOUNGER.

VANE, young in years, but in fage counfel old,
    Than whom a better fenator ne'er held
    The helm of Rome, when gowns not arms repell'd
    The fierce Epirot and the African bold,
Whether to fettle peace, or to unfold
    The drift of hollow ftates hard to be fpell'd,
    Then to advife how war may beft upheld
    Move by her two main nerves, iron and gold,
In all her equipage: befides to know
    Both fpiritual pow'r and civil, what each means,
    What fevers each, thou haft learn'd, which few
        have done:
The bounds of either fword to thee we owe:
    Therefore on thy firm hand religion leans
    In peace, and reckons thee her eldeft fon.

## XVIII.

### ON THE LATE MASSACRE IN PIEDMONT.

AVENGE, O Lord, thy flaughter'd faints, whofe bones
    Lie fcatter'd on the Alpine mountains cold;
    Ev'n them who kept thy truth fo pure of old,
    When all our fathers worfhipt ftocks and ftones,
Forget not: in thy book record their groans

Who were thy fheep, and in their ancient fold
Slain by the bloody Piedmontefe that roll'd
Mother with infant down the rocks.   Their moans
The vales redoubled to the hills, and they
 To Heav'n.   Their martyr'd blood and afhes fow
 O'er all th' Italian fields, where ftill doth fway
The triple tyrant; that from thefe may grow
 A hundred fold, who having learn'd thy way
 Early may fly the Babylonian woe.

## XIX.

## ON HIS BLINDNESS.

When I confider how my light is fpent
 Ere half my days, in this dark world and wide,
 And that one talent which is death to hide,
 Lodg'd with me ufelefs, though my foul more bent
To ferve therewith my Maker, and prefent
 My true account, left he returning chide;
 Doth God exact day-labour, light deny'd,
 I fondly afk: But patience to prevent
That murmur, foon replies, God doth not need
 Either man's work or his own gifts; who beft
 Bear his mild yoke, they ferve him beft: his ftate
Is kingly; thoufands at his bidding fpeed,
 And poft o'er land and ocean without reft;
 They alfo ferve who only ftand and wait.

## XX.

### TO MR. LAWRENCE.

Lawrence, of virtuous father virtuous fon,
  Now that the fields are dank, and ways are mire,
  Where fhall we fometimes meet, and by the fire
  Help wafte a fullen day, what may be won
From the hard feafon gaining? time will run
  On fmoother, till Favonius re-infpire
  The frozen earth, and clothe in frefh attire
  The lily' and rofe, that neither fow'd nor fpun.
What neat repaft fhall feaft us, light and choice,
  Of Attic tafte, with wine, whence we may rife
  To hear the lute well touch'd, or artful voice
Warble immortal notes and Tufcan air?
  He who of thofe delights can judge, and fpare
  To interpofe them oft, is not unwife.

## XXI.

### TO CYRIAC SKINNER.

Cyriac, whofe grandfire, on the royal bench
  Of Britifh Themis, with no mean applaufe
  Pronounc'd, and in his volumes taught our laws,
  Which others at their bar fo often wrench;
To day deep thoughts refolve with me to drench
  In mirth, that after no repenting draws;
  Let Euclid reft and Archimedes paufe,
  And what the Swede intends, and what the French.

To meafure life learn thou betimes, and know
  Toward folid good what leads the neareft way;
  For other things mild Heav'n a time ordains,
And difapproves that care, though wife in fhow,
  That with fuperfluous burden loads the day,
  And when God fends a cheerful hour, refrains.


## XXII.

## TO THE SAME.


CYRIAC, this three years day thefe eyes, though clear,
  To outward view, of blemifh or of fpot,
  Bereft of light their feeing have forgot,
  Nor to their idle orbs doth fight appear
Of fun, or moon, or ftar throughout the year,
  Or man, or woman. Yet I argue not
  Againft Heav'n's hand or will, nor bate a jot
  Of heart or hope; but ftill bear up and fteer
Right onward. What fupports me, doft thou afk?
  The confcience, friend, to' have loft them overply'd
  In liberty's defence, my noble tafk,
Of which all Europe talks from fide to fide.
  This thought might lead me through the world's
      vain mafk
  Content though blind, had I no better guide.

## XXIII.

## ON HIS DECEASED WIFE.

Methought I faw my late efpoufed faint
  Brought to me like Alceftis from the grave,
  Whom Jove's great fon to her glad hufband gave,
  Refcued from death by force, though pale and faint.
Mine, as whom wafh'd from fpot of child-bed taint
  Purification in the old law did fave,
  And fuch, as yet once more I truft to have
  Full fight of her in Heav'n without reftraint,
Came vefted all in white, pure as her mind:
  Her face was veil'd, yet to my fancied fight
  Love, fweetnefs, goodnefs, in her perfon fhin'd
So clear, as in no face with more delight.
  But O as to embrace me fhe inclin'd,
  I wak'd, fhe fled, and day brought back my night.

# PSALMS.

## PSALM I.

DONE INTO VERSE 1653.

Bless'd is the man who hath not walk'd aftray
In counfel of the wicked, and i' th' way
Of finners hath not ftood, and in the feat
Of fcorners hath not fat.   But in the great
Jehovah's law is ever his delight,
And in his law he ftudies day and night.
He fhall be as a tree which planted grows
By watry ftreams, and in his feafon knows
To yield his fruit, and his leaf fhall not fall,
And what he takes in hand fhall profper all.
Not fo the wicked, but as chaff which fann'd
The wind drives, fo the wicked fhall not ftand
In judgment, or abide their trial then,
Nor finners in th' affembly of juft men.
For the Lord knows th' upright way of the juft,
And the way of bad men to ruin muft.

## PSALM II.

### DONE AUGUST 8, 1653. TERZETTE.

Why do the Gentiles tumult, and the nations
   Mufe a vain thing,. the kings of th'.earth upftand
   With pow'r, and princes in their congregations
Lay deep their plots together through each land
   Againft the Lord and his Meffiah dear?
   Let us break off, fay they, by ftrength of hand
Their bonds, and caft from us, no more to wear,
   Their twifted cords: He who in Heav'n doth dwell
   Shall laugh, the Lord fhall fcoff them, then fevere
Speak to them in his wrath, and in his fell
   And fierce ire' trouble them; but I, faith he,
   Anointed have my King (though ye rebel)
On Sion my holy' hill.  A firm decree
   I will declare: the Lord to me hath faid
   Thou art my Son, I have begotten thee
This day; afk of me, and the grant is made;
   As thy poffeffion I on thee beftow
   Th' Heathen, and as thy conqueft to be fway'd
Earth's utmoft bounds: them fhalt thou bring full low
   With iron fceptre bruis'd, and them difperfe
   Like to a potter's veffel fhiver'd fo.
And now be wife at length ye Kings averfe,
   Be taught ye Judges of the earth; with fear
   Jehovah ferve, and let your joy converfe
With trembling; kifs the Son left he appear
   In anger and ye perifh in the way,
   If once his wrath take fire like fuel fere.
Happy all thofe who have in him their ftay.

## PSALM III.

AUGUST 9, 1653.

WHEN HE FLED FROM ABSALOM.

Lord how many are my foes!
  How many thofe
   That in arms againft me rife!
  Many are they
That of my life diftruftfully thus fay,
No help for him in God there lies.
But thou Lord art my fhield, my glory,
  Thee through my ftory
   Th' exalter of my head I count;
  Aloud I cry'd
Unto Jehovah, he full foon reply'd
And heard me from his holy mount.
I lay and flept, I wak'd again,
  For my fuftain
   Was the Lord. Of many millions
  The populous rout
I fear not, though incamping round about
They pitch againft me their pavilions.
Rife, Lord, fave me my God, for thou
  Haft fmote ere now
   On the cheek-bone all my foes,
  Of men abhorr'd
Haft broke the teeth. This help was from the Lord;
Thy blefling on thy people flows

## PSALM IV.

### AUGUST 10, 1653.

ANSWER me when I call,
God of my righteoufnefs,
In ftraits and in diftrefs
Thou didft me difinthrall
And fet at large; now fpare,
 Now pity me, and hear my earneft pray'r.
Great ones how long will ye
My glory have in fcorn,
How long be thus forborn
Still to love vanity,
To love, to feek, to prize
 Things falfe and vain, and nothing elfe but lies?
Yet know the Lord hath chofe,
Chofe to himfelf apart,
The good and meek of heart
(For whom to choofe he knows)
Jehovah from on high
 Will hear my voice what time to him I cry.
Be aw'd, and do not fin,
Speak to your hearts alone,
Upon your beds, each one,
And be at peace within.
Offer the offerings juft
 Of righteoufnefs, and in Jehovah truft.
Many there be that fay
Who yet will fhow us good?
Talking like this world's brood;
But, Lord, thus let me pray,

On us lift up the light
    Lift up the favour of thy count'nance bright.
Into my heart more joy    .
And gladnefs thou haft put,
Than when a year of glut
Their ftores doth over-cloy,
And from their plenteous grounds    ·
    With vaft increafe their corn and wine abounds.
In peace at once will I
Both lay me down and fleep,
For thou alone doft keep  ·
Me fafe where'er I lie;
As in a rocky cell
    Thou Lord alone in fafety mak'ft me dwell.


## PSALM V.

### AUG. 12, 1653.

JEHOVAH to my words give ear,
    My meditation weigh,
The voice of my complaining hear
My King and God; for unto thee I pray.
    Jehovah thou my early voice
        Shalt in the morning hear,
    I' th' morning I to thee with choice
Will rank my pray'rs, and watch till thou appear.
    For thou art not a God that takes
        In wickednefs delight,
    Evil with thee no biding makes,
Fools or mad men ftand not within thy fight.

T

All workers of iniquity
    Thou hat'st; and them unblest
Thou wilt destroy that speak a lie;
The bloody' and guileful man God doth detest.
    But I will in thy mercies dear
        Thy numerous mercies go
    Into thy house; I in thy fear
Will tow'rds thy holy temple worship low.
    Lord lead me in thy righteousness,
        Lead me because of those
    That do observe if I transgress,
Set thy ways right before, where my step goes.
    For in his faultring mouth unstable
        No word is firm or sooth;
    Their inside, troubles miserable;
An open grave their throat, their tongue they smooth.
    God, find them guilty, let them fall
        By their own counsels quell'd;
    Push them in their rebellions all
Still on; for against thee they have rebell'd.
    Then all who trust in thee shall bring
        Their joy, while thou from blame
    Defend'st them, they shall ever sing
And shall triumph in thee, who love thy name.
    For thou Jehovah wilt be found
        To bless the just man still,
    As with a shield thou wilt surround
Him with thy lasting favour and good will.

## PSALM VI.

AUG. 13, 1653.

Lord in thine anger do not reprehend me,
  Nor in thy hot difpleafure me correct;
  Pity me, Lord, for I am much deject,
And very weak and faint; heal and amend me:
For all my bones, that ev'n with anguifh ach,
  Are troubled, yea my foul is troubled fore,
  And thou, O Lord, how long? turn Lord, reftore
My foul, O fave me for thy goodnefs fake:
For in death no remembrance is of thee;
  Who in the grave can celebrate thy praife?
  Wearied I am with fighing out my days,
Nightly my couch I make a kind of fea;
My bed I water with my tears; mine eye
  Through grief confumes, is waxen old and dark
  I' th' midft of all mine enemies that mark.
Depart all ye that work iniquity,
Depart from me, for the voice of my weeping
  The Lord hath heard, the Lord hath heard my pray'r,
  My fupplication with acceptance fair
The Lord will own, and have me in his keeping.
Mine enemies fhall all be blank and dafh'd
  With much confufion; then grown red with fhame,
  They fhall return in hafte the way they came,
And in a moment fhall be quite abafh'd.

## PSALM VII.

### AUG. 14, 1653.

#### UPON THE WORDS OF CHUSH THH BENJAMITE
#### AGAINST HIM.

LORD my God to thee I fly,
Save me and fecure me under
Thy protection while I cry,
Left as a lion (and no wonder)
He hafte to tear my foul afunder,
Tearing and no refcue nigh.

Lord my God if I have thought
Or done this, if wickednefs
Be in my hands, if I have wrought
Ill to him that meant me peace,
Or to him have render'd lefs,
And not free'd my foe for nought;

Let th' enemy purfue my foul
And overtake it, let him tread
My life down to the earth, and roll
In the duft my glory dead,
In the duft and there outfpread
Lodge it with difhonour foul.

Rife Jehovah in thine ire,
Roufe thyfelf amidft the rage
Of my foes that urge like fire;

. And wake for me, their fury' affuage;
Judgment here thou didft engage ·
And command which I defire.

So th' affemblies of each nation
Will furround thee, feeking right,
Thence to thy glorious habitation
Return on high and in their fight.
Jehovah judgeth moft upright
All people from the world's foundation,

Judge me Lord, be judge in this
According to my righteoufnefs,
And the innocence which is ·
Upon me: caufe at length to ceafe
Of evil men the wickednefs
And their pow'r that do amifs.

But the juft eftablifh faft,
Since thou art the juft God that tries
Hearts and reins. On God is caft
My defence, and in him lies, ·
In him who both juft and wife
Saves th' upright of heart at laft.

God is a juft judge and fevere,
And God is every day offended;
If the unjuft will not forbear,
His fword he whets, his bow hath bended
Already, and for him intended
The tools of death, that waits him near.

(His arrows purpofely made he
For them that perfecute.)   Behold
He travels big with vanity,
Trouble he hath conceiv'd of old
As in a womb, and from that mould
Hath at length brought forth a lie.

He digg'd a pit, and delv'd it deep,
And fell into the pit he made;
His mifchief that due courfe doth keep,
Turns on his head, and his ill trade
Of violence will undelay'd
Fall on his crown with ruin fteep.

Then will I Jehovah's praife
According to his juftice raife,
And fing the name and deity
Of Jehovah the moft high.

## PSALM VIII.

### AUG. 14, 1653.

O JEHOVAH our Lord, how wondrous great
    And glorious is thy name through all the earth!
So as above the Heav'ns thy praife to fet
    Out of the tender mouths of lateft birth.

Out of the mouths of babes and fucklings thou
    Haft founded ftrength becaufe of all thy foes,
To ftint th' enemy, and flack th' avenger's brow,
    That bends his rage thy providence to' oppofe.

When I behold thy Heav'ns, thy fingers art,
  The moon and ftars which thou fo bright haft fet
In the pure firmament, then faith my heart,
  O what is man that thou remembereft yet,

And think'ft upon him; or of man begot,
  That him thou vifit'ft, and of him art found?
Scarce to be lefs than gods, thou mad'ft his lot,
  With honour and with ftate thou haft him crown'd.

O'er the works of thy hand thou mad'ft him Lord,
  Thou haft put all under his lordly feet,
. All flocks, and herds, by thy commanding word,
  All beafts that in the field or foreft meet,

Fowl of the Heav'ns, and fifh that through the wet
  Sea paths in fhoals do flide, and know no dearth.
O Jehovah our Lord, how wondrous great
  And glorious is thy name through all the earth!

APRIL. 1648.   J. M.

NINE OF THE PSALMS DONE INTO METRE, WHEREIN
ALL, BUT WHAT IS IN A DIFFERENT CHARAC-
TER, ARE THE VERY WORDS OF THE
TEXT, TRANSLATED FROM
THE ORIGINAL.

## PSALM LXXX.

1 THOU shepherd that doft Ifrael *keep*
 · . Give ear *in time of need,*
Who leadeft like a flock of sheep
    *Thy loved* Jofeph's feed, ·
That fit'ft between the Cherubs *bright,*
    *Between their wings out-fpread,*
Shine forth, *and from thy cloud give light,*
    *And on our foes thy dread.*
2 In Ephraim's view and Benjamin's,
    And in Manaffeh's fight,
Awake thy ftrength, come, and *be feen*
    *To* fave us *by thy might.*
3 Turn us again, *thy grace divine*
    *To us* O God *vouchfafe;*
Caufe thou thy face on us to fhine,
    And then we fhall be fafe.
4 Lord God of Hofts, how long wilt thou,
    How long wilt thou declare
Thy fmoking wrath, *and angry brow*
    Againft thy people's prayer!

5 Thou feed'ft them with the bread of tears,
  Their bread with tears they eat,
And mak'ft them largely drink the tears
  *Wherewith their cheeks are wet.*

6 A ftrife thou mak'ft us *and a prey*
  To every neighbour foe,
Among themfelves they laugh, they play,
  And flouts at us they throw.

7 Return us, *and thy grace divine*
  O God of Hofts *vouchfafe,*
Caufe thou thy face on us to fhine,
  And then we fhall be fafe.

8 A vine from Egypt thou haft brought,
  *Thy free love made it thine,*
And drov'ft out nations, *proud and haut,*
  To plant this *lovely* vine.

9 Thou did'ft prepare for it a place,
  And root it deep and faft,
That it *began to grow apace,*
  *And* fill'd the land *at laft.*

10 With her *green* fhade that cover'd *all,*
  The hills were *overfpread,*
Her boughs as *high as* cedars tall
  *Advanc'd their lofty head.*

11 Her branches *on the weftern fide*
  Down to the fea fhe fent,
And *upward* to that river *wide*
  Her other branches *went.*

12 Why haft thou laid her hedges low,
  And broken down her fence,
That all may pluck her, as they go
  *With rudeft violence ?*

13 The *tuſked* boar out of the wood
    Up turns it by the roots,
  Wild beaſts there browſe, and make their food
    *Her grapes and tender ſhoots.*

14 Return now, God of Hoſts, look down
    From Heav'n, thy ſeat divine,
  Behold *us, but without a frown,*
    And viſit this *thy* vine.

15 Viſit this vine, which thy right hand
    Hath ſet, and planted *long*,
  And the young branch, that for thyſelf
    Thou haſt made firm and ſtrong.

16 But now it is conſum'd with fire,
    And cut *with axes* down,
  They periſh at thy dreadful ire,
    At thy rebuke and frown.

17 Upon the man of thy right hand
    Let thy *good* hand be *laid*,
  Upon the Son of Man, whom thou
    Strong for thyſelf haſt made.

18 So ſhall we not go back from thee
    *To ways of ſin and ſhame,*
  Quicken us thou, then *gladly* we
    Shall call upon thy name.

19 Return us, *and thy grace divine*
    Lord God of Hoſts *vouchſafe,*
  Cauſe thou thy face on us to ſhine,
    And then we ſhall be ſafe.

## PSALM LXXXI.

1 To God our ftrength fing loud, *and clear*,
  Sing loud to God *cur King*,
To Jacob's God, *that all may hear*,
  Loud acclamations ring.
2 Prepare a hymn, prepare a fong,
  The timbrel hither bring,
The *cheerful* pfaltry bring along,
  And harp *with* pleafant *ftring*.
3 Blow, *as is wont*, in the new moon
  With trumpets *lofty found*,
Th' appointed time, the day whereon
  Our folemn feaft *comes round*.
4 This was a ftatute *giv'n of old*
  For Ifrael *to obferve*,
A law of Jacob's God, *to hold*,
  *From whence they might not fwerve*.
5 This he a teftimony ordain'd
  In Jofeph, *not to change*,
When as he pafs'd through Egypt land ;
  The tongue I heard was ftrange.
6 From burden, *and from flavifh toil*,
  I fet his fhoulder free :
His hands from pots, *and miry foil*,
  Deliver'd were *by me*.
7 When trouble did thee fore affail,
  *On me then* didft thou call,
And I to free thee *did not fail*,
  *And led thee out of thrall*.

I anſwer'd thee in thunder deep
 With clouds encompaſs'd round;
I try'd thee at the water *ſteep*
 Of Meriba *renown'd.*

8 Hear, O my people, *hearken well,*
 I teſtify to thee,
*Thou ancient ſtock of* Iſrael,
 If thou wilt liſt to me,

9 Throughout the land of thy abode
 No alien god ſhall be,
Nor ſhalt thou to a foreign god
 In honour bend thy knee.

10 I am the Lord thy God which brought
 Thee out of Egypt land;
Aſk large enough, and I, *beſought,*
 Will grant thy full demand.

11 And yet my people would not *hear,*
 *Nor* hearken to my voice;
And Iſrael, *whom I lov'd ſo dear,*
 Miſlik'd me for his choice.

12 Then did I leave them to their will,
 And to their wand'ring mind;
Their own conceits they follow'd ſtill,
 Their own devices blind.

13 O that my people would *be wiſe,*
 *To* ſerve me *all their days,*
And O that Iſrael would *adviſe*
 *To* walk my *righteous* ways.

14 Then would I ſoon bring down their foes,
 *That now ſo proudly riſe,*
And turn my hand againſt *all thoſe*
 *That are* their enemies.

15 Who hate the Lord fhould *then be fain*
　　*To* bow to him and bend,
　　But *they, his people, fhould remain,*
　　Their time fhould have no end.
16 And he would feed them *from the fhock*
　　With flour of fineft wheat,
　　And fatisfy them from the rock
　　With honey *for their meat.*


## PSALM LXXXII.

1 God in the great affembly ftands
　　*Of kings and lordly ftates,*
　　Among the Gods, on both his hands
　　He judges and debates.
2 How long will ye pervert the right
　　With judgment falfe and wrong,
　　Favouring the wicked *by your might,*
　　*Who thence grow bold and ftrong ?*
3 Regard the weak and fatherlefs,
　·　Difpatch the poor man's caufe,
　　And raife the man in deep diftrefs
　　By juft and equal laws.
4 Defend the poor and defolate,
　　And refcue from the hands
　　Of wicked men the low eftate
　　Of him *that help demands.*
5 They know not, nor will underftand, ·
　　In darknefs they walk on,
　　The earth's foundations all are mov'd,
　　And out of order gone.

6 I faid that ye were Gods, yea all
    The fons of God moft high;
7 But ye fhall die like men, and fall
    As other princes *die.*
8 Rife God, judge thou the earth *in might,*
    This *wicked* earth redrefs,
    For thou art he who fhalt by right
    The nations all poffefs.

## PSALM LXXXIII.

1 BE not thou filent *now at length,*
    O God hold not thy peace,
    Sit thou not ftill O God of *ftrength,*
    *We cry, and do not ceafe.*
2 For lo thy *furious* foes *now* fwell,
    And ftorm outrageoufly,
    And they that hate thee *proud and fell*
    Exalt their heads full high.
3 Againft thy people they contrive
    Their plots and counfels deep,
    Them to infnare they chiefly ftrive,
    Whom thou doft hide and keep.
4 Come let us cut them off, fay they,
    Till they no nation be,
    That Ifrael's name for ever may
    Be loft in memory.
5 For they confult with all their might;
    And all as one in mind
    Themfelves againft thee they unite,
    And in firm union bind.

6 The tents of Edom, and the brood
  Of *scornful* Ishmael,
  Moab, with them of Hagar's blood,
  *That in the desert dwell,*

7 Gebal and Ammon *there conspire,*
  And *hateful* Amalek,
  The Philistims, and they of Tyre,
  *Whose bounds the Sea doth check.*

8 With them *great* Ashur also bands
  *And doth confirm the knot:*
  *All these have lent their armed hands*
  To aid the sons of Lot.

9 Do to them as to Midian *bold,*
  *That wasted all the coast,*
  To Sisera, and as *is told*
  *Thou didst* to Jabin's *host,*
  *When* at the brook of Kishon *old*
  *They were repuls'd and slain,*

10 At Endor quite cut off, and roll'd
  As dung upon the plain.

11 As Zeb and Oreb evil *sped,*
  So let their princes *speed,*
  As Zeba, and Zalmunna *bled,*
  So let their princes *bleed.*

12 *For they amidst their pride* have said,
  By right now shall we seize
  God's houses, and *will now invade*
  Their stately palaces.

13 My God, oh make them as a wheel,
  *No quiet let them find,*
  Giddy and *restless* let *them reel*
  Like stubble from the wind.

14 As *when* an *aged* wood takes fire
 *Which on a fudden ftrays,*
 The *greedy* flame runs higher and higher
 Till all the mountains blaze,
15 So with thy whirlwind them purfue,
 And with thy tempeft chafe;
16 And till they yield thee honour due;
 Lord fill with fhame their face.
17 Afham'd, and troubled let them be,
 Troubled, and fham'd for ever,
 Ever confounded, and fo die
 With fhame, *and fcape it never.*
18 Then fhall they know that thou whofe name
 Jehovah is alone,
 Art the moft high, *and thou the fame*
 O'er all the earth *art one.*

## PSALM LXXXIV.

1 How lovely are thy dwellings fair!
 O Lord of Hofts, how dear
 The *pleafant* tabernacles are,
 *Where thou doft dwell fo near!*
2 My foul doth long and almoft die
 Thy courts O Lord to fee,
 My heart and flefh aloud do cry,
 O living God, for thee.
3 There ev'n the fparrow *freed from wrong*
 Hath found a houfe of *reft.*
 The fwallow there, to lay her young
 Hath built her *brooding* neft,

Ev'n by thy altars, Lord of Hosts,
*They find their safe abode,*
*And home they fly from round the coasts*
*Toward thee,* my King, my God.

4 Happy, who in thy house reside,
Where thee they ever praise,

5 Happy, whose strength in thee doth bide,
And in their hearts thy ways.

6 They pass through Baca's *thirsty* vale,
*That dry and barren ground,*
As through a fruitful watry dale
Where springs and show'rs abound.

7 They journey on from strength to strength
*With joy and gladsome cheer,*
*Till* all before *our* God *at length*
In Sion do appear.

8 Lord God of Hosts hear *now* my prayer,
O Jacob's God give ear,

9 Thou God our shield look on the face
Of thy anointed *dear.*

10 For one day in thy courts *to be*
Is better, *and more blest,*
Than *in the joys of vanity*
A thousand days *at best.*
I in the temple of my God
Had rather keep a door,
Than dwell in tents, *and rich abode,*
With sin *for evermore.*

11 For God the Lord both sun and shield
Gives grace and glory *bright,*
No good from them shall be withheld
Whose ways are just and right.

U

12 Lord *God* of Hofts *that reign'ſt on high,*
 That man is *truly* bleſt,
Who *only* on thee doth rely,
 And in thee only reſt.


## PSALM LXXXV.

1 Thy land to favour gracioufly
 Thou haſt not Lord been ſlack,
Thou haſt from *hard* captivity
 Returned Jacob back.
2 Th' iniquity thou didſt forgive
 *That wrought* thy people woe,
And all their ſin, *that did thee grieve,*
 Haſt hid *where none ſhall know.*
3 Thine anger all thou hadſt remov'd,
 And *calmly* didſt return
From thy fierce wrath which we had prov'd
 Far worſe than fire to burn.
4 God of our ſaving health and peace,
 Turn us, and us reſtore,
Thine indignation cauſe to ceaſe
 Toward us, *and chide no more.*
5 Wilt thou be angry without end,
 For ever angry thus,
Wilt thou thy frowning ire extend
 From age to age on us?
6 Wilt thou not turn, and *hear our voice,*
 And us again revive,
That ſo thy people may rejoice
 By thee preſerv'd alive.

7 Caufe us to fee thy goodnefs, Lord,
    To us thy mercy fhew,
  Thy faving health to us afford,
    *And life in us renew.*

8 *And now* what God the Lord will fpeak,
    I will *go ftraight and* hear,
  For to his people he fpeaks peace,
    And to his faints *full dear,*
  To his dear faints he will fpeak peace,
    But let them never more
  Return to folly, *but furceafe*
    *To trefpafs as before.*

9 Surely to fuch as do him fear
    Salvation is at hand,
  And glory fhall *ere long appear*
    *To* dwell within our land.

10 Mercy and Truth *that long were mifs'd*
    Now *joyfully* are met,
  *Sweet* Peace and Righteoufnefs have kifs'd,
    *And hand in hand are fet.*

11 Truth from the earth, *like to a flow'r,*
    Shall bud and bloffom *then,*
  And Juftice from her heav'nly bow'r
    Look down *on mortal men.*

12 The Lord will alfo then beftow
    Whatever thing is good,
  Our land fhall forth in plenty throw
    Her fruits *to be our food.*

13 Before him Righteoufnefs fhall go
    *His royal harbinger,*
  Then will he come, and not be flow,
    His footfteps cannot err.

## PSALM LXXXVI.

1 THY *gracious* ear, O Lord, incline,
    O hear me *I thee pray*,
For I am poor, and almoſt pine
    With need, *and ſad decay*.
2 Preſerve my ſoul, for I have trod
    Thy ways, and love the juſt,
Save thou thy ſervant, O my God,
    Who *ſtill* in thee doth truſt.
3 Pity me, Lord, for daily.thee
    I call;  4. O make rejoice
Thy ſeryant's ſoul; for Lord to thee
    I lift my ſoul *and voice*.
5 For thou art good, thou Lord art prone
    To pardon, thou to all
Art full of mercy, thou *alone*
    To them that on thee call.
6 Unto my ſupplication, Lord,
    Give ear, and to the cry
Of my *inceſſant* pray'rs afford
    Thy hearing gracioufly.
7 I in the day of my diſtreſs
    Will call on thee *for aid*;
For thou wilt *grant* me *free acceſs*,
    *And* anſwer *what I pray'd*.
8 Like thee among the gods is none,
    O Lord, nor any works
*Of all that other gods have done*
    Like to thy *glorious* works.

9 The nations all whom thou haſt made
  Shall come, *and all ſhall frame*
To bow them low before thee, Lord,
  And glorify thy name.

10 For great thou art, and wonders great
  By thy ſtrong hand are done,
Thou *in thy everlaſting ſeat*
  Remaineſt God alone.

11 Teach me, O Lord, thy way *moſt right,*
  I in thy truth will bide,
To fear thy name my heart unite,
  *So ſhall it never ſlide.*

12 Thee will I praiſe, O Lord my God,
  *Thee honour and adore*
With my whole heart, and blaze abroad
  Thy name for evermore.

13 For great thy mercy is tow'rd me,
  And thou haſt free'd my ſoul,
Ev'n from the loweſt Hell ſet free,
  *From deepeſt darkneſs foul.*

14 O God the proud againſt me riſe,
  And violent men are met
To ſeek my life, and in their eyes
  No fear of thee have ſet.

15 But thou, Lord, art the God moſt mild,
  Readieſt thy grace to ſhew,
Slow to be angry, and *art ſtyl'd*
  Moſt merciful, moſt true.

16 O turn to me *thy face at length,*
  And me have mercy on,
Unto thy ſervant give thy ſtrength,
  And ſave thy handmaid's ſon.

17 Some sign of good to me afford,
　　And let my foes *then* see,
　　And be asham'd, because thou Lord
　　Dost help and comfort me.


## PSALM LXXXVII.

1 AMONG the holy mountains *high*
　　Is his foundation fast,
　　*There seated is his sanctuary,*
　　*His temple there is plac'd.*

2 Sion's *fair* gates the Lord loves more
　　Than all the dwellings *fair*
　　Of Jacob's *land, though there be store,*
　　*And all within his care.*

3 City of God, most glorious things
　　Of thee *abroad* are spoke;

4 I mention Egypt, *where proud kings*
　　*Did our forefathers yoke.*

　　I mention Babel to my friends,
　　Philistia *full of scorn,*
　　And Tyre with Ethiops *utmost ends,*
　　Lo this man there was born:

5 But *twice that praise shall in our ear*
　　Be said of Sion *last,*
　　This and this man was born in her,
　　High God shall fix her fast.

6 The Lord shall write it in a scroll
　　That ne'er shall be out-worn,
　　When he the nations doth inroll,
　　That this man there was born.

7 Both they who fing, and they who dance,
    *With facred fongs are there,*
In thee *fresh brooks, and foft ftreams glance,*
    *And* all my fountains *clear.*

## PSALM LXXXVIII.

1 LORD God that doft me fave and keep,
    All day to thee I cry;
And all night long before thee *weep,*
Before thee *proftrate lie.*

2 Into thy prefence let my pray'r
    *With fighs devout afcend,*
And to my cries, that *ceafelefs are,*
    Thine ear with favour bend.

3 For cloy'd with woes and trouble ftore
    Surcharg'd my foul doth lie,
My life *at death's uncheerful door*
    Unto the grave draws nigh.

4 Reckon'd I am with them that pafs
    Down to the *difmal* pit,
I am a man, but weak alas,
    And for that name unfit.

5 From life difcharg'd and parted quite
    Among the dead to *fleep,*
And like the flain *in bloody fight*
    That in the grave lie *deep.*
Whom thou rememberest no more,
    Doft never more regard,
Them from thy hand deliver'd o'er
    *Death's hideous houfe hath barr'd.*

6 Thou in the loweſt pit *profound*
  Haſt ſet me *all forlorn,*
Where thickeſt darkneſs *hovers round,*
  In horrid deeps *to mourn.*

7 Thy wrath, *from which no ſhelter ſaves,*
  . Full ſore doth preſs on me;
Thou break'ſt upon me all thy ways,
  And all thy waves break me.

8 Thou doſt my friends from me eſtrange,
  And mak'ſt me odious,
Me to them odious, *for they change,*
  And I here pent up thus.

9 Through ſorrow, and affliction great,
  Mine eye grows dim and dead,      .
Lord, all the day I thee intreat,
  My hands to thee I ſpread.

10 Wilt thou do wonders on the dead,
  Shall the deceas'd ariſe
And praiſe thee *from their loathſome bed*
  *With pale and hollow eyes ?*

11 Shall they thy loving kindneſs tell
  On whom the grave *hath hold,*
Or they who in perdition *dwell,*
  Thy faithfulneſs *unfold?*

12 In darkneſs can thy mighty *hand*
  *Or* wondrous acts be known,
Thy juſtice in the *gloomy* land
  Of *dark* oblivion?

13 But I to thee, O Lord, do cry,
  *Ere yet my life be ſpent,*
And *up to thee* my pray'r *doth hie,*
  Each morn, and thee prevent.

14 Why wilt thou, Lord, my foul forfake,
  And hide thy face from me?
15 That am already bruis'd, and fhake
  With terrour fent from thee?
  Bruis'd, and afflicted, and *fo low*
  As ready to expire,
  While I thy terrours undergo
  Aftonifh'd with thine ire.
16 Thy fierce wrath over me doth flow,
  Thy threatnings cut me through:
17 All day they round about me go,
  Like waves they me purfue.
18 Lover and friend thou haft remov'd,
  And fever'd from me far:
  They *fly me now* whom I have lov'd,
  And as in darknefs are.


## A PARAPHRASE ON PSALM CXIV.

THIS AND THE FOLLOWING PSALM WERE
DONE BY THE AUTHOR AT
FIFTEEN YEARS OLD.

When the bleft feed of Terah's faithful fon
After long toil their liberty had won,
And paft from Pharian fields to Canaan land,
Led by the ftrength of the Almighty's hand,
Jehovah's wonders were in Ifrael fhown,
His praife and glory was in Ifrael known.
That faw the troubled Sea, and fhivering fled,
And fought to hide his froth-becurled head

Low in the earth; Jordan's clear ftreams recoil,
As a faint hoft that hath receiv'd the foil.
The high, huge-bellied mountains fkipt like rams
Amongft their ewes, the little hills like lambs.
Why fled the ocean? And why fkipt the mountains?
Why turned Jordan tow'rd his cryftal fountains?
Shake Earth, and at the prefence be aghaft
Of him that ever was, and aye fhall laft,
That glaffy floods from rugged rocks can crufh,
And make foft rills from fiery flint ftones gufh.

## PSALM CXXXVI.

Let us with a gladfome mind
Praife the Lord, for he is kind,
  For his mercies aye endure,
  Ever faithful, ever fure.

Let us blaze his name abroad,
For of gods he is the God;
  For his, &c.

O let us his praifes tell,
Who doth the wrathful tyrants quell.
  For his, &c.

Who with his miracles doth make
Amazed Heav'n and Earth to fhake.
  For his, &c.

Who by his wifdom did create
The painted Heav'ns fo full of ftate.
   For his, &c.

Who did the folid earth ordain
To rife above the watry plain.
   For his, &c.

Who by his all-commanding might
Did fill the new-made world with light.
   For his, &c.

And caus'd the golden-treffed fun,
All the day long his courfe to run.
   For his, &c.

The horned moon to fhine by night,
Amongft her fpangled fifters bright.
   For his, &c.

He with his thunder-clafping hand
Smote the firft-born of Egypt land.
   For his, &c.

And in defpite of Pharaoh fell,
He brought from thence his Ifrael.
   For his, &c.

The ruddy waves he cleft in twain
Of the Erythræan main.
   For his, &c.

The floods ſtood ſtill like walls of glaſs,
While the Hebrew bands did paſs.
　For his, &c.


But full ſoon they did devour
The tawny king with all his power.
　For his, &c.


His choſen people he did bleſs
In the waſteful wilderneſs.
　For his, &c.


In bloody battle he brought down
Kings of proweſs and renown.
　For his, &c.


He foil'd bold Seon and his hoſt,
That rul'd the Amorrean coaſt.
　For his, &c.


And large-limb'd Og he did ſubdue,
With all his over-hardy crew.
　For his, &c.


And to his ſervant Iſrael
He gave their land therein to dwell.
　For his, &c.


He hath with a piteous eye
Beheld us in our miſery.
　For his, &c.

And freed us from the flavery
Of the invading enemy.
   For his, &c,

.

All living creatures he doth feed,
And with full hand fupplies their need.
   For his, &c.

Let us therefore warble forth
His mighty majefty and worth.
   For his, &c.

That his manfion hath on high
Above the reach of mortal eye.
   For his mercies aye endure,
    Ever faithful, ever fure.

# JOANNIS MILTONI,

## LONDINENSIS,

# POEMATA.

QUORUM PLERAQUE INTRA ANNUM ÆTATIS
VIGESIMUM CONSCRIPSIT.

Hæc quæ fequuntur de authore teftimonia, tametfi
ipfe intelligebat non tam de fe quam fupra fe effe
dicta, eò quod præclaro ingenio viri, nec non amici
ita ferè folent laudare, ut omnia fuis potius virtutibus, quam veritati congruentia nimis cupidè affin-
gant, noluit tamen horum egregiam in fe voluntatem
non effe notam; cum alii præfertim ut id faceret
magnopere fuaderent. Dum enim nimiæ laudis in-
vidiam totis ab fe viribus amolitur, fibique quod plus
æquo eft non attributum effe mavult, judicium inte-
rim hominum cordatorum atque illuftrium quin fummo fibi honori ducat, negare non poteft.

## JOANNES BAPTISTA MANSUS,

### MARCHIO VILLENSIS, NEAPOLITANUS,

#### AD

## JOANNEM MILTONIUM, ANGLUM.

Ut mens, forma, decor, facies, mos, fi pietas fic,
Non anglus, veràm hercle Angelus ipfe fores.

#### AD

## JOANNEM MILTONEM, ANGLUM,

### TRIPLICI POESEOS LAUREA CORONANDUM,

### GRÆCA NIMIRUM, LATINA, ATQUE

### HETRUSCA, EPIGRAMMA

## JOANNIS SALSILLI, ROMANI.

Cede Meles, cedat depreffa Mincius urna;
Sebetus Taffum definat ufque loqui;
At Thamefis victor cunctis ferat altior undas,
Nam per te, Milto, par tribus unus erit.

x

## AD JOANNEM MILTONUM.

Græcia Mæonidem, jactet fibi Roma Maronem,
Anglia Miltonum jactat utrique parem.

SELVAGGI.

AL

# SIGNIOR GIO. MILTONI,

### NOBILE INGLESE.

## ODE.

Ergimi all' Etra ò Clio
Perche di ftelle intreccierò corona
Non più del Biondo Dio
La Fronde eterna in Pindo, e in Elicona
Dienfi a merto maggior, maggiori i fregi,
A' celefte virtù celefti pregi.

Non puo del tempo edace
Rimaner preda, eterno alto valore
Non puo l' oblio rapace
Furar dalle memorie eccelfo onore,
Su l' arco di mia cetra un dardo forte
Virtù m'adatti, e ferirò la morte.

Del Ocean profondo
Cinta dagli ampi gorghi Anglia rifiede
Separata dal mondo,
Però che il fuo valor l'umana eccede:
Quefta feconda sà produrre Eroi,
Ch' hanno a ragion del fovruman tra noi.

Alla virtù fbandita
Danno ne i petti lor fido ricetto,
Quella gli è fol gradita,
Perche in lei fan trovar gioia, e diletto;
Ridillo tu, Giovanni, e moftra in tanto
Con tua vera virtù, vero il mio Canto.

Lungi dal Patrio lido
Spinfe Zeufi l' induftre ardente brama;
Ch' udio d'Helena il grido
Con aurea tromba rimbombar la fama,
E per poterla effigiare al paro
Dalle più belle Idee traffe il più raro.

Cofi l'Ape Ingegnofa
Trae con induftria il fuo liquor pregiato
Dal giglio e dalla rofa,
E quanti vaghi fiori ornano il prato;
Formano un dolce fuon diverfe Chorde,
Fan varie voci melodia concorde.

Di bella gloria amenta
Milton dal Ciel natio per varie parti
Le peregrine piante

Volgesti a ricercar scienze, ed arti;
Del Gallo regnator vedesti i Regni,
E dell' Italia ancor gl' Eroi piu degni.

Fabro quasi divino
Sol virtù rintracciando il tuo pensiero
Vide in ogni confino
Chi di nobil valor calca il sentiero;
L' ottimo dal miglior dopo scegliea
Per fabbricar d'ogni virtu l'Idea.

Quanti nacquero in Flora
O in lei del parlar Tosco apprésar l'arte,
La cui memoria onora
Il mondo fatta eterna in dotte carte,
Volesti ricercar per tuo tesoro,
E parlasti con lor nell' opre loro.

Nell' altera Babelle
Per te il parlar confuse Giove in vano,
Che per varie favelle
Di se stessa trofeo cadde su'l piano:
Ch' Ode oltr' all Anglia il suo piu degno Idioma
Spagna, Francia, Toscana, e Grecia e Roma.

I piu profondi arcani
Ch' occulta la natura e in cielo e in terra
Ch' à Ingegni sovrumani
Troppo avaro tal' hor gli chiude, e serra,
Chiaromente conosci, e giungi al fine
Della moral virtude al gran confine.

Non batta il Tempo l'ale,
Fermifi immoto, e in un fermin fi gl' anni,
Che di virtù immortale
Scorron di troppo ingiuriofi a i danni;
Che s'opre degne di Poema o ftoria
Furon gia, l'hai prefenti alla memoria.

Dammi tua dolce Cetra
Se vuoi ch'io dica del tuo dolce canto,
Ch' inalzandoti all' Etra
Di' farti huomo celefte ottiene il vanto,
Il Tamigi il dirà che gl' e conceffo
Per te fuo cigno parreggiar Permeffo.

I o che in riva del Arno
Tento fpiegar tuo merto alto, e preclaro
So che fatico indarno,
E ad ammirar, non a lodarlo imparo;
Freno dunque la lingua, e afcolto il core
Che ti prende a lodar con lo ftupore.

DEL SIG. ANTONIO FRANCINI, GENTILHUOMO

FIORENTINO.

# JOANNI MILTONI

## LONDINENSI,

JUVENI PATRIA, VIRTUTIBUS EXIMIO,

VIRO qui multa peregrinatione, studio cuncta orbis terrarum loca perspexit, ut novis Ulysses omnia ubique ab omnibus apprehenderet:

Polyglotto, in cujus ore linguæ jam deperditæ sic reviviscunt, ut idiomata omnia sint in ejus laudibus infacunda; Et jure ea percallet, ut admirationes et plausus populorum ab propria sapientia excitatos intelligat:

Illi, cujus animi dotes corporisque sensus ad admirationem commovent, et per ipsam motum cuique auferunt; cujus opera ad plausus hortantur, sed venustate vocem laudatoribus adimunt.

Cui in memoria totus orbis; in intellectu sapientia; in voluntate ardor gloriæ; in ore eloquentia; harmonicos cœlestium sphærarum sonitus astronomia duce audienti; characteres mirabilium naturæ per quos Dei magnitudo describitur magistra philosophia le-

genti; antiquitatum latebras, vetuſtatis excidia, eru-
ditionis ambages, comite aſſidua autorum lectione,

Exquirenti, reſtauranti, percurrenti.
At cur nitor in arduum?

Illi in cujus virtutibus evulgandis ora Famæ non
ſufficiant, nec hominum ſtupor in laudandis ſatis eſt,
reverentiæ et amoris ergo hoc ejus meritis debitum
admirationis tributum offert Carolus Datus, Patricius
Florentinus,

TANTO HOMINI SERVUS, TANTÆ VIRTUTIS AMATOR.

# ELEGIARUM

## LIBER PRIMUS.

## ELEGIA PRIMA

### AD CAROLUM DEODATUM.

T<small>ANDEM</small>, chare, tuæ mihi pervenere tabellæ,
   Pertulit et voces nuncia charta tuas;
Pertulit occiduâ Devæ Ceftrenfis ab orâ
   Vergivium prono quâ petit amne falum.
Multùm crede juvat terras aluiffe remotas
   Pectus amans noftri, tamque fidele caput,
Quòdque mihi lepidum tellus longinqua fodalem
   Debet, at unde brevi reddere juffa velit.
Me tenet urbs refluâ quam Thamefis alluit undâ,
   Meque nec invitum patria dulcis habet.
Jam nec arundiferum mihi cura revifere Camum,
   Nec dudum vetiti me laris angit amor.
Nuda nec arva placent, umbrafque negantia molles,
   Quàm male Phœbicolis convenit ille locus!

Nec duri libet ufque minas preferre magiftri
 Cæteraque ingenio non fubeunda meo.
Si fit hoc exilium patrios adiiffe penates,
 Et vacuum curis otia grata fequi,
Non ego yel profugi nomen, fortemve recufo
 Lætus et exilii conditione fruor.
O utinam vates nunquam graviora tuliffet
 Ille Tomitano flebilis exul agro;
Non tunc Ionio quicquam ceffiffet Homero,
 Neve foret victo laus tibi prima Maro.
Tempora nam licet hic placidis dare libera Mufis,
 Et totum rapiunt me mea vita libri.
Excipit hinc feffum finuofi pompa theatri,
 Et vocat ad plaufus garrula fcena fuos.
Seu catus auditur fenior, feu prodigus hæres,
 Seu procus, aut pofitâ caffide miles adeft,
Sive decennali fœcundus lite patronus
 Detonat inculto barbara verba foro;
Sæpe vafer gnato fuccurrit fervus amanti,
 Et nafum rigidi fallit ubique patris;
Sæpe novos illic virgo mirata calores
 Quid fit amor nefcit, dum quoque nefcit, amat.
Sive cruentatum furiofa Tragœdia fceptrum
 Quaffat, et effufis crinibus ora rotat,
Et dolet, et fpecto, juvat et fpectaffe dolendo,
 Interdum et lacrymis dulcis amaror ineft:
Seu puer infelix indelibata reliquit
 Gaudia, et abrupto flendus amore cadit,
Seu ferus è tenebris iterat Styga criminis ultor
 Confcia funereo pectora torre movens,
Seu mœret Pelopeia domus, feu nobilis Ili,
 Aut luit inceftos aula Creontis avos.

Sed neque fub tecto femper nec in urbe latemus,
 Irrita nec nobis tempora veris eunt.
Nos quoque lucus habet vicinâ confitus ulmo,
 Atque fuburbani nobilis umbra loci.
Sæpius hic blandas fpirantia fidera flammas
 Virgineos videas præteriiffe choros.
Ah quoties dignæ ftupui miracula formæ
 Quæ poffit fenium vel reparare Jovis!
Ah quoties vidi fuperantia lumina gemmas,
 Atque faces quotquot volvit uterque polus;
Collaque bis vivi Pelopis quæ brachia vincant,
 Quæque fluit puro nectare tincta via,
Et decus eximium frontis, tremulofque capillos,
 Aurea quæ fallax retia tendit Amor;
Pellacefque genas, ad quos hyacinthina fordet
 Purpura, et ipfe tui floris, Adoni, rubor!
Cedite laudatæ toties Heroides olim,
 Et quæcunque vagum cepit amica Jovem.
Cedite Achæmeniæ turritâ fronte puellæ,
 Et quot Sufa colunt, Memnoniamque Ninon.
Vos etiam Danaæ fafces fubmittite Nymphæ,
 Et vos Iliacæ, Romuleæque nurus.
Nec Pompeianas Tarpëia Mufa columnas
 Jactet, et Aufoniis plena theatra ftolis.
Gloria Virginibus debetur prima Britannis,
 Extera fat tibi fit fœmina poffe fequi.
Tuque urbs Dardaniis Londinum ftructa colonis
 Turrigerum latè confpicienda caput,
Tu nimium felix intra tua mœnia claudis
 Quicquid formofi pendulus orbis habet.
Non tibi tot cœlo fcintillant aftra fereno
 Endymioneæ turba miniftra deæ,

Quot tibi conſpicuæ formáque auróque puellæ
   Per medias radiant turba videnda vias.
Creditur huc geminis veniſſe invecta columbis
   Alma pharetrigero milite cincta Venus,
Huic Cnidon, et riguas Simoentis flumine valles,
   Huic Paphon, et roſeam poſt habitura Cypron.
Aſt ego, dum pueri ſinit indulgentia cæci,
   Mœnia quàm ſubitò linquere fauſta paro;
Et vitare procul maleſidæ infamia Circes
   Atria, divini Molyos uſus ope.
Stat quoque juncoſas Cami remeare paludes,
   Atque iterum raucæ murmur adire Scholæ.
Interea fidi parvum cape munus amici,
   Paucaque in alternos verba coacta modos.


## ELEGIA SECUNDA,

### ANNO ÆTATIS 17.

#### IN OBITUM PRÆCONIS ADADEMICI
#### CANTABRIGIENSIS.

Te, qui conſpicuus baculo fulgente ſolebas
   Palladium toties ore ciere gregem,
Ultima præconum præconem te quoque ſæva
   Mors rapit, officio nec favet ipſa ſuo.
Candidiora licet fuerint tibi tempora plumis
   Sub quibus accipimus delituiſſe Jovem,
O dignus tamen Hæmonio juveneſcere ſucco,
   Dignus in Æſonios vivere poſſe dies,
Dignus quem Stygiis medicâ revocaret ab undis
   Arte Coronides, ſæpe rogante dea.

Tu fi juſſus eras acies accire togatas,
    Et celer à Phœbo nuntius ire tuo,
Talis in Iliacâ ſtabat Cyllenius aula
    Alipes, ætherea miſſus ab arce Patris.
Talis et Eurybates ante ora furentis Achillei
    Rettulit Atridæ juſſa ſevera ducis.
Magna ſepulchrorum regina, ſatelles Averni
    Sæva nimis Muſis, Palladi ſæva nimis,
Quin illos rapias qui pondus inutile terræ,
    Turba quidem eſt telis iſta petenda tuis.
Veſtibus hunc igitur pullis ·Academia luge,
    Et madeant lachrymis nigra feretra tuis.
Fundat et ipſa modos querebunda Elegëia triſtes,
    Perſonet et totis mœnia mœſta ſcholis.

## ELEGIA TERTIA,

### ANNO ÆTATIS 17.

#### IN OBITUM PRÆSULIS WINTONIENSIS.

Mœstus eram, et tacitùs nullo comitante ſedebam,
    Hærebantque animo triſtia plura meo,
Protinus en ſubiit funeſtæ cladis imago
    Fecit in Angliaco quam Libitina ſolo;
Dum procerum ingreſſa eſt ſplendentes marmore turres,
    Dira ſepulchrali mors metuenda face;
Pulſavitque auro gravidos et jaſpide muros,
    Nec metuit ſatrapum ſternere falce greges.
Tunc memini clarique ducis, fratriſque verendi
    Intempeſtivis oſſa cremata rogis:

Et memini Heroum quos vidit ad æthera raptos,
　　Flevit et amiſſos Belgia tota duces.
At te præcipuè luxi digniſſime Præſul,
　　Wintoniæque olim gloria magna tuæ;
Delicui fletu, et triſti ſic ore querebar,
　　Mors fera Tartareo diva ſecunda Jovi,
Nonne ſatis quod ſylva tuas perſentiat iras,
　　Et quod in herboſos jus tibi detur agros,
Quodque afflata tuo marceſcant lilia tabo,
　　Et crocus, et pulchræ Cypridi ſacra roſa,
Nec ſinis ut ſemper fluvio contermina quercus
　　Miretur lapſus prætereuntis aquæ?
Et tibi ſuccumbit liquido quæ plurima cœlo
　　Evehitur pennis quamlibet augur avis,
Et quæ mille nigris errant animalia ſylvis,
　　Et quod alunt mutum Proteos antra pecus.
Invida, tanti tibi cum ſit conceſſa poteſtas;
　　Quid juvat humanâ tingere cæde manus?
Nobileque in pectus certas acuiſſe ſagittas,
　　Semideamque animam ſede fugâſſe ſuâ?
Talia dum lacrymans alto ſub pectore volvo,
　　Roſcidus occiduis Heſperus exit aquis,
Et Tarteſſiaco ſubmerſerat æquore currum
　　Phœbus, ab eöo littore menſus iter.
Nec mora, membra cavo poſui refovenda cubili,
　　Condiderant oculos noxque ſoporque meos:
Cum mihi viſus eram lato ſpatiarier agro,
　　Heu nequit ingenium viſa referre meum.
Illic puniceâ radiabant omnia luce,
　　Ut matutino cum juga ſole rubent.
Ac veluti cum pandit opes Thaumantia proles,
　　Veſtitu nituit multicolore ſolum.

Non dea tam variis ornavit floribus hortos
    Alcinoi, Zephyro Chloris amata levi.
Flumina vernantes lambunt argentea campos,
    Ditior Hefperio flavet arena Tago.
Serpit odoriferas per opes levis aura Favoni,
    Aura fub innumeris humida nata rofis,
Talis in extremis terræ Gangetidis oris
    Luciferi regis fingitur effe domus.
Ipfe racimiferis dum denfas vitibus umbras
    Et pellucentes miror ubique locos,
Ecce mihi fubito Præful Wintonius aftat,
    Sidereum nitido fulfit in ore jubar;
Veftis ad auratos defluxit candida talos,
    Infula divinum cinxerat alba caput.
Dumque fenex tali incedit venerandus amiĉtu,
    Intremuit læto florea terra fono.
Agmina gemmatis plaudunt cœleftia pennis,
    Pura triumphali perfonat æthra tubâ.
Quifque novum amplexu comitem cantuque falutat,
    Hofque aliquis placido mifit ab ore fonos;
Nate veni, et patri felix cape gaudia regni,
    Semper ab hinc duro, nate, labore vaca.
Dixit, et aligeræ tetigerunt nablia turmæ,
    At mihi cum tenebris aurea pulfa quies.
Flebam turbatos Cephaleiâ pellice fomnos,
    Talia contingant fomnia fæpe mihi.

# ELEGIA QUARTA,

ANNO ÆTATIS 18.

AD THOMAM JUNIUM, PRÆCEPTOREM SUUM, APUD
MERCATORES ANGLICOS, HAMBURGÆ
AGENTES, PASTORIS MUNERE
FUNGENTEM.

CURRE per immenſum ſubitò mea littera pohtum,
　　I, pete Teutonicos læve per æquor agros;
Segnes rumpe moras, et nil, precor, obſtet eunti,
　　Et feſtinantis nil remoretur iter.
Ipſe ego Sicanio frænantem carcere ventos
　　Æolon, et virides ſollicitabo Deos,
Cæruleamque ſuis comitatam Dorida Nymphis,
　　Ut tibi dent placidam per ſua regna viam.
At tu, ſi poteris, celeres tibi ſume jugales,
　　Vecta quibus Colchis fugit ab ore viri;
Aut queis Triptolemus Scythicas devenit in oras
　　Gratus Eleuſinâ miſſus ab urbe puer.
Atque ubi Germanas flavere videbis arenas
　　Ditis ad Hamburgæ mœnia flecte gradum,
Dicitur occiſo quæ ducere nomen ab Hamâ,
　　Cimbrica quem fertur clava dediſſe neci.
Vivit ibi antiquæ clarus pietatis honore
　　Præſul Chriſticolas paſcere doctus oves;
Ille quidem eſt animæ pluſquam pars altera noſtræ,
　　Dimidio vitæ vivere cogor ego.
Hei mihi quot pelagi, quot montes interjecti
　　Me faciunt aliâ parte carere mei!

Charior ille mihi quàm tu doctiffime Graium
    Cliniadi, pronepos qui Telamonis erat;
Quàmque Stagirites generofo magnus alumno,
    Quem peperit Lybico Chaonis alma Jovi.
Qualis Amyntorides, qualis Philyrëius Heros
    Myrmidonum regi, talis et ille mihi.
Primus ego Aonios illo præeunte receffus
    Luftrabam, et bifidi facra vireta jugi,
Pieriofque haufi latices, Clioque favente,
    Caftalio fparfi læta ter ora mero.
Flammeus at fignum ter viderat arietis Æthon,
    Induxitque auro lanea terga novo,
Bifque novo terram fparfifti Chlori fenilem
    Gramine, bifque tuas abftulit Aufter opes:
Necdum ejus licuit mihi lumina pafcere vultu,
    Aut linguæ dulces aure bibiffe fonos.
Vade igitur, curfuque Eurum præverte fonorum,
    Quàm fit opus monitis res docet, ipfa vides.
Invenies dulci cum conjuge fortè fedentem,
    Mulcentem gremio pignora chara fuo,
Forfitan aut veterum prælarga volumina patrum
    Verfantem, aut veri biblia facra Dei,
Cæleftive animas faturantem rore tenellas,
    Grande falutiferæ religionis opus.
Utque folet, multam fit dicere cura falutem,
    Dicere quam decuit, fi modo adeffet, herum.
Hæc quoque paulum oculos in humum defixa modeftos
    Verba verecundo fis memor ore loqui:
Hæc tibi, fi teneris vacat inter prælia Mufis,
    Mittit ab Angliaco littore fida manus.
Accipe finceram, quamvis fit fera, falutem;
    Fiat et hoc ipfo gratior illa tibi.

Scra quidem, fed vera fuit, quam cafta recepit
　　Icaris à lento Penelopeia viro.
Aft ego quid volui manifeftum tollere crimen,
　　Ipfe quod ex omni parte levare nequit?
Arguitur tardus meritò, noxamque fatetur,
　　Et pudet officium deferuiffe fuum.
Tu modò da veniam faffo, veniamque roganti,
　　Crimina diminui, quæ patuere, folent.
Non ferus in pavidos rictus diducit hiantes
　　Vulnifico pronos nec rapit ungue leo.
Sæpe fariffiferi crudelia pectora Thracis
　　Supplicis ad mœftas delicuere preces.
Extenfæque manus avertunt fulminis ictus,
　　Placat et iratos hoftia parva Deos.
Jamque diu fcripfiffe tibi fuit impetus illi,
　　Neve moras ultra ducere paffus Amor.
Nam vaga Fama refert, heu nuntia vera malorum!
　　In tibi finitimis bella tumere locis,
Teque tuamque urbem truculento milite cingi,
　　Et jam Saxonicos arma paraffe duces.
Te circum latè campos populatur Enyo,
　　Et fata carne virûm jam cruor arva rigat;
Germanifque fuum conceffit Thracia Martem,
　　Illuc Odryfios Mars pater egit equos;
Perpetuòque comans jam deflorefcit oliva,
　　Fugit et ærifonam Diva perofa tubam,
Fugit io terris, et jam non ultima virgo
　　Creditur ad fuperas jufta volaffe domos.
Te tamen intereà belli circumfonat horror,
　　Vivis et ignoto folus inopfque folo;
Et, tibi quam patrii non exhibuere penates,
　　Sede peregrinâ quæris egenus opem.

Patria dura parens, et faxis fævior albis
    Spumea quæ pulfat littoris unda tui,
Siccine te decet innocuos exponere fœtus,
    Siccine in externam ferrea cogis humum,
Et finis ut terris quærant alimenta remotis
    Quos tibi profpiciens miferat ipfe Deus,
Et qui læta ferunt de cœlo nuntia, quique
    Quæ via poft cineres ducat ad aftra, docent?
Digna quidem Stygiis quæ vivas claufa tenebris,
    Æternâque animæ digna perire fame!
Haud aliter vates terræ Thefbitidis olim
    Preffit inaffueto devia tefqua pede,
Defertafque Arabum falebras, dum regis Achabi
    Effugit atque tuas, Sidoni dira, manus.
Talis et horrifono laceratus membra flagello,
    Paulus ab Æmathiâ pellitur urbe Cilix.
Pifcofæque ipfum Gergeffæ civis Iëfum
    Finibus ingratus juffit abire fuis.
At tu fume animos, nec fpes cadat anxia curis,
    Nec tua concutiat decolor offa metus.
Sis etenim quamvis fulgentibus obfitus armis,
    Intententque tibi millia tela necem,
At nullis vel inerme latus violabitur armis,
    Deque tuo cufpis nulla cruore bibet.
Namque eris ipfe Dei radiante fub ægide tutus,
    Ille tibi cuftos, et pugil ille tibi;
Ille Sionææ qui tot fub mœnibus arcis
    Affyrios fudit nocte filente viros;
Inque fugam vertit quos in Samaritidas oras
    Mifit ab antiquis prifca Damafcus agris,
Terruit et denfas pavido cum rege cohortes,
    Aere dum vacuo buccina clara fonat,

Cornea pulvereum dum verberat ungula campum,
   Currus arenofam dum quatit actus humum,
Auditurque hinnitus equorum ad bella ruentûm,
   Et ftrepitus ferri, murmuraque alta virûm.
Et tu (quod fupereft miferis) fperare memento,
   Et tua magnanimo pectore vince mala;
Nec dubites quandoque frui melioribus annis,
   Atque iterum patrios poffe videre lares.


# ELEGIA QUINTA,

## ANNO ÆTATIS 20.

# IN ADVENTUM VERIS.

In fe perpetuo Tempus revolubile gyro
   Jam revocat Zephyros vere tepente novos;
Induiturque brevem Tellus reparata juventam,
   Jamque foluta gelu dulce virefcit humus.
Fallor? an et nobis redeunt in carmina vires,
   Ingeniumque mihi munere veris adeft?
Munere veris adeft, iterumque vigefcit ab illo
   (Quis putet) atque aliquod jam fibi pofcit opus.
Caftalis ante oculos, bifidumque cacumen oberrat,
   Et mihi Pyrenen fomnia nocte ferunt;
Concitaque arcano fervent mihi pectora motu,
   Et furor, et fonitus me facer intùs agit.
Delius ipfe venit, video Penëide lauro
   Implicitos crines, Delius ipfe venit.
Jam mihi mens liquidi raptatur in ardua cœli,
   Perque vagas nubes corpore liber eo;

Perque umbras, perque antra feror penetralia vatum,
    Et mihi fana patent interiora Deûm;
Intuiturque animus toto quid agatur Olympo,
    Nec fugiunt oculos Tartara cæca meos.
Quid tam grande fonat diftento fpiritus ore?
    Quid parit hæc rabies, quid facer ifte furor?
Ver mihi, quod dedit ingenium, cantabitur illo;
    Profuerint ifto reddita dona modo.
Jam Philomela tuos foliis adoperta novellis
    Inftituis modulos, dum filet omne nemus:
Urbe ego, tu fylvâ fimul incipiamus utrique,
    Et fimul adventum veris uterque canat.
Veris io rediere vices, celebremus honores
    Veris, et hoc fubeat Mufa perennis opus.
Jam fol Æthiopas fugiens Tithoniaque arva,
    Flectit ad Arctoas aurea lora plagas.
Eft breve noctis iter, brevis eft mora noctis opacæ,
    Horrida cum tenebris exulat illa fuis.
Jamque Lycaonius plauftrum cœlefte Bootes
    Non longâ fequitur feffus ut ante viâ;
Nunc etiam folitas circum Jovis atria toto
    Excubias agitant fidera rara polo.
Nam dolus, et cædes, et vis cum nocte receffit,
    Neve Giganteum Dii timuere fcelus.
Forte aliquis fcopuli recubans in vertice paftor,
    Rofcida cum primo fole rubefcit humus,
Hac, ait, hac certè caruifti nocte puellâ
    Phœbe tuâ, celeres quæ retineret equos.
Læta fuas repetit fylvas, pharetramque refumit
    Cynthia, Luciferas ut videt alta rotas,
Et tenues ponens radios gaudere videtur
    Officium fieri tam breve fratris ope.

Defere, Phœbus ait, thalamos Aurora feniles,
    Quid juvat effœto procubuiffe toro?
Te manet Æolides viridi venator in herba,
    Surge, tuos ignes altus Hymettus habet.
Flava verecundo dea crimen in ore fatetur,
    Et matutinos ocius urget equos.
Exuit invifam Tellus rediviva feneĉtam,
    Et cupit amplexus Phœbe fubire tuos;
Et cupit, et digna eft, quid enim formofius illâ,
    Pandit ut omniferos luxuriofa finus,
Atque Arabum fpirat meffes, et ab ore venufto
    Mitia cum Paphiis fundit amoma rofis!
Ecce coronatur facro frons ardua luco,
    Cingit ut Idæam pinea turris Opim;
Et vario madidos intexit flore capillos,
    Floribus et vifa eft poffe placere fuis.
Floribus effufos ut erat redimita capillos
    Tenario placuit diva Sicana Deo.
Afpice Phœbe tibi faciles hortantur amores,
    Mellitafque movent flamina verna preces.
Cinnameâ Zephyrus leve plaudit odorifer alâ,
    Blanditiafque tibi ferre videntur aves.
Nec fine dote tuos temeraria quærit amores
    Terra, nec optatos pofcit egena toros,
Alma falutiferum medicos tibi gramen in ufus
    Præbet, et hinc titulos adjuvat ipfa tuos.
Quòd fi te pretium, fi te fulgentia tangunt
    Munera, (muneribus fæpe coemptus Amor)
Illa tibi oftentat quafcunque fub æquore vafto,
    Et fuperinjeĉtis montibus abdit opes.
Ah quoties cum tu clivofo feffus Olympo
    In verfpertinas præcipitaris aquas,

Cur te, inquit, curfu languentem Phœbe diurno
　Hefperiis recipit Cærula mater aquis?
Quid tibi cum Tethy! Quid cum Tarteflide lym-
　　phâ,
　Dia quid immundo perluis ora falo?
Frigora Phœbe meâ melius captabis in umbrâ,
　Huc ades, ardentes imbue rore comas.
Mollior egelidâ veniet tibi fomnus in herbâ,
　Huc ades, et gremio lumina pone meo.
Quáque jaces circum mulcebit lene fufurrans
　Aura per humentes corpora fufa rofas.
Nec me (crede mihi) terrent Semeléia fata,
　Nec Phætonteo fumidus axis equo;
Cum tu Phœbe tuo fapientius uteris igni,
　Huc ades, et gremio lumina pone meo.
Sic Tellus lafciva fuos fufpirat amores;
　Matris in exemplum cætera turba ruunt.
Nunc etenim toto currit vagus orbe Cupido,
　Languentefque fovet folis ab igne faces.
Infonuere novis lethalia cornua nervis,
　Trifte micant ferro tela corufca novo.
Jamque vel invictam tentat fuperaffe Dianam,
　Quæque fedet facro Vefta pudica foco.
Ipfa fenefcentem reparat Venus annua formam,
　Atque iterum tepido creditur orta mari.
Marmoreas juvenes clamant Hymenæe per urbes,
　Littus io Hymen, et cava faxa fonant.
Cultior ille venit tunicâque decentior aptâ,
　Puniceum redolet veftis odora crocum.
Egrediturque frequens ad amœni gaudia veris
　Virgineos auro cincta puella finus.

Votum eft cuique fuum, votum eft tamen omnibus
   unum,
  Ut fibi quem cupiat, det Cytherea virum.
Nunc quoque feptenâ modulatur arundine paftor,
  Et fua quæ jungat carmina Phyllis habet.
Navita noɕturno placat fua fidera cantu,
  Delphinafque leves ad vada fumma vocat.
Jupiter ipfe alto cum conjuge ludit Olympo,
  Convocat et famulos ad fua fefta Deos.
Nunc etiam Satyri cum fera crepufcula furgunt,
  Pervolitant celeri florea rura choro,
Sylvanufque fuâ cyparifli fronde revinɕtus,
  Semicaperque Deus, femideufque caper.
Quæque fub arboribus Dryades latuere vetuftis
  Per juga, per folos expatiantur agros.
Per fata luxuriat fruticetaque Mænalius Pan,
  Vix Cybele mater, vix fibi tuta Ceres;
Atque aliquam cupidus prædatur Oreada Faunus,
  Confulit in trepidos dum fibi nympha pedes,
Jamque latet, latitanfque cupit male teɕta videri,
  Et fugit, et fugiens pervelit ipfa capi.
Dii quoque non dubitant cœlo præponere fylvas,
  Et fua quifque fibi numina lucus habet.
Et fua quifque diu fibi numina lucus habeto,
  Nec vos arborea dii precor ite domo.
Te referant miferis te Jupiter aurea terris
  Sæcla, quid ad nimbos afpera tela redis?
Tu faltem lentè rapidos age Phœbe jugales
  Quà potes, et fenfim tempora veris eant;
Brumaque produɕtas tardè ferat hifpida noɕtes,
  Ingruat et noftro ferior umbra polo.

## ELEGIA SEXTA.

AD

# CAROLUM DEODATUM

RURI COMMORANTEM,

QUI CUM IDIBUS DECEMB. SCRIPSISSET, ET SUA CAR-
MINA EXCUSARI POSTULASSET SI SOLITO MINUS
ESSENT BONA, QUOD INTER LAUTITIAS QUIBUS
ERAT AB AMICIS EXCEPTUS, HAUD SATIS FELICEM
OPERAM MUSIS DARE SE POSSE AFFIRMABAT, HOC
HABUIT RESPONSUM.

Mitto tibi fanam non pleno ventre falutem,
   Qua tu diftento fortè carere potes.
At tua quid noftram prolectat Mufa camœnam,
   Nec finit optatas poffe fequi tenebras?
Carmine fcire velis quàm te redamemque colamque,
   Crede mihi vix hoc carmine fcire queas.
Nam neque nofter amor modulis includitur arctis,
   Nec venit ad claudos integer ipfe pedes.
Quàm bene folennes epulas, hilaremque Decembrim,
   Feftaque cœlifugam quæ coluere Deum,
Deliciafque refers, hyberni gaudia ruris,
   Hauftaque per lepidos Gallica mufta focos!
Quid quereris refugam vino dapibufque poefin?
   Carmen amat Bacchum, carmina Bacchus amat.
Nec puduit Phœbum virides geftaffe corymbos,
   Atque hederam lauro præpofuiffe fuæ.
Sæpius Aoniis clamavit collibus Euœ
   Mifta Thyoneo turba novena choro.
Nafo Corallæis mala carmina mifit ab agris:
   Non illic epulæ, non fata vitis erat.

Quid nifi vina, rofafque racemiferumque Lyæum
　　Cantavit brevibus Tëia Mufa modis?
Pindaricofque inflat numeros Teumefius Euan,
　　Et redolet fumptum pagina quæque merum;
Dum gravis everfo currus crepat axe fupinus,
　　Et volat Eleo pulvere fufcus eques.
Quadrimoque madens Lyricen Romanus Iaccho
　　Dulce canit Glyceran, flavicomamque Chloen.
Jam quoque lauta tibi generofo menfa paratu
¨　Mentis alit vires, ingeniumque fovet.
Maffica fœcundam defpumant pocula venam,
　　Fundis et ex ipfo condita metra cado.
Addimus his artes, fufumque per intima Phœbum
　　Corda, favent uni Bacchus, Apollo, Ceres.
Scilicet haud mirum tam dulcia carmina per te
　　Numine compofito tres peperiffe Deos.
Nunc quoque Threffa tibi cælato barbitos auro
　　Infonat argutâ molliter ifta manu;
Auditurque chelys fufpenfa tapetia circum,
　　Virgineos tremulâ quæ regat arte pedes.
Illa tuas faltem teneant fpeftacula Mufas,
　　Et revocent, quantum crapula pellit iners.
Crede mihi dum pfallit ebur, comitataque pleftrum
　　Implet odoratos fefta chorea tholos,
Percipies tacitum per peftora ferpere Phœbum,
　　Quale repentinus permeat offa calor,
Perque puellares oculos digitumque fonantem
　　Irruet in totos lapfa Thalia finus.
Namque Elegia levis multorum cura Deorum eft,
　　Lt vocat ad numeros quemlibet illa fuos;
Liber adeft, elegis, Eratoque, Cerefque, Venufque,
　　Et cum purpureâ matre tenellus Amor.

Talibus inde licent convivia larga poetis,
  Sæpius et veteri commaduiffe mero.
At qui bella refert, et adulto fub Jove cœlum,
  Heroafque pios, femideofque duces,
Et nunc fancta canit fuperum confulta deorum,
  Nunc latrata fero regna profunda cane,
Ille quidem parcè Samii pro more magiftri
  Vivat, et innocuos præbeat herba cibos ;
Stet prope fagineo pellucida lympha catillo,
  Sobriaque è puro pocula fonte bibat.
Additur huic fcelerifque vacans, et cafta juventus,
  Et rigidi mores, et fine labe manus.
Qualis vefte nitens facrâ, et luftralibus undis
  Surgis ad infenfos augur iture Deos.
Hoc ritu vixiffe ferunt poft rapta fagacem
  Lumina Tirefian, Ogygiumque Linon,
Et lare devoto profugum Calchanta, fenemque
  Orpheon edomitis fola per antra feris ;
Sic dapis exiguus, fic rivi potor Homerus
  Dulichium vexit per freta longa virum,
Et per monftrificam Perfeiæ Phœbados aulam,
  Et vada fœmineis infidiofa fonis,
Perque tuas rex ime domos, ubi fanguine nigro
  Dicitur umbrarum detinuiffe greges.
Diis etenim facer eft vates, divûmque facerdos,
  Spirat et occultum pectus, et ora Jovem.
At tu fiquid agam fcitabere (fi modò faltem
  Effe putas tanti nofcere fiquid agam)
Paciferum canimus cœlefti femine regem,
  Fauftaque facratis fæcula pacta libris,
Vagitumque Dei, et ftabulantem paupere tecto
  Qui fuprema fuo cum patre regna colit,

Stelliparumque polum, modulantefque æthere turmas,
  Et fubitò elifos ad fua fana Deos.
Dona quidem dedimus Chrifti natalibus illa,
  Illa fub auroram lux mihi prima tulit.
Te quoque preffa manent patriis meditata cicutis,
  Tu mihi, cui recitem, judicis inftar eris.


# ELEGIA SEPTIMA,

### ANNO ÆTATIS 19.

Nondum blanda tuas leges Amathufia nôram,
  Et Paphio vacuum pectus ab igne fuit.
Sæpe cupidineas, puerilia tela, fagittas,
  Atque tuum fprevi maxime numen Amor.
Tu puer imbelles dixi transfige columbas,
  Conveniunt tenero mollia bella duci.
Aut de pafferibus tumidos age, parve, triumphos,
  Hæc funt militiæ digna trophæa tuæ.
In genus humanum quid inania dirigis arma?
  Non valet in fortes ifta pharetra viros.
Non tulit hoc Cyprius, (neque enim Deus ullus ad iras
  Promptior) et duplici jam ferus igne calet.
Ver erat, et fummæ radians per culmina villæ
  Attulerat primam lux tibi Maie diem:
At mihi adhuc refugam quærebant lumina noctem,
  Nec matutinum fuftinuere jubar.
Aftat Amor lecto, pictis amor impiger alis,
  Prodidit aftantem mota pharetra Deum:
Prodidit et facies, et dulce minantis ocelli,
  Et quicquid puero dignum et Amore fuit.

Talis in æterno juvenis Sigeius Olympo
    Mifcet amatori pocula plena Jovi;
Aut qui formofas pellexit ad ofcula nymphas
    Thiodamantæus Naiade raptus Hylas.
Addideratque iras, fed et has decuiffe putares,
    Addideratque truces, nec fine felle minas.
Et mifer exemplo fapuiffes tutiùs, inquit,
    Nunc mea quid poffit dextera teftis eris.
Inter et expertos vircs numerabere noftras,
    Et faciam vero per tua damna fidem.
Ipfe ego fi nefcis ftrato Pythone fuperbum
    Edomui Phœbum, ceffit et ille mihi;
Et quoties meminit Peneidos, ipfe fatetur
    Certiùs et graviùs tela nocere mea.
Me nequit adductum curvare peritiùs arcum,
    Qui poft terga folet vincerc Parthus eques:
Cydoniufque mihi cedit venator, et ille
    Infcius uxori qui necis author erat.
Eft etiam nobis ingens quoque victus Orion,
    Herculeæque manus, Herculeufque comes.
Jupiter ipfe licet fua fulmina torqueat in me,
    Hærebunt lateri fpicula noftra Jovis.
Cætera quæ dubitas meliùs mea tcla docebunt,
    Et tua non leviter corda petenda mihi.
Nec te ftulte tuæ poterunt defendere Mufæ,
    Nec tibi Phœbæus porriget anguis opem.
Dixit, et aurato quatiens mucrone fagittam,
    Evolat in tepidos Cypridos ille finus.
At mihi rifuro tonuit ferus ore minaci,
    Et mihi de puero non metus ullus erat.
Et modò quà noftri fpatiantur in urbe Quirites,
    Et modò villarum proxima rura placent.

Turba frequens, faciéque fimillima turba dearum
   Splendida per medias itque reditque vias.
Auctaque luce dies gemino fulgore corufcat,
   Fallor? an et radios hinc quoque Phœbus habet.
Hæc ego non fugi fpectacula grata feverus,
   Impetus et quò me fert juvenilis, agor.
Lumina luminibus malè providus obvia mifi,
   Neve oculos potui continuiffe meos.
Unam fortè aliis fupereminuiffe notabam,
   Principium noftri lux erat illa mali.
Sic Venus optaret mortalibus ipfa videri,
   Sic regina Deûm confpicienda fuit.
Hanc memor objecit nobis malus ille Cupido,
   Solus et hos nobis texuit antè dolos.
Nec procul ipfe vafer latuit, multæque fagittæ,
   Et facis à tergo grande pependit onus.
Nec mora, nunc ciliis hæfit, nunc virginis ori,
   Infilit hinc labiis, infidet inde genis:
Et quafcunque agilis partes jaculator oberrat,
   Hei mihi, mille locis pectus inerme ferit.
Protinus infoliti fubierunt corda furores,
   Uror amans intùs, flammaque totus eram.
Interea mifero quæ jam mihi fola placebat,
   Ablata eft oculis non reditura meis.
Aft ego progredior tacitè querebundus, et excors,
   Et dubius volui fæpe referre pedem.
Findor, et hæc remanet, fequitur pars altera votum,
   Raptaque tam fubitò gaudia flere juvat.
Sic dolet amiffum proles Junonia cælum,
   Inter Lemniacos præcipitata focos.
Talis et abreptum folem refpexit, ad Orcum
   Vectus ab attonitis Amphiaraus equis.

Quid faciam infelix, et luctu victus? amores
  Nec licet inceptos ponere, neve fequi.
O utinam fpectare femel mihi detur amatos
  Vultus, et coràm triftia verba loqui;
Forfitan et duro non eft adamante creata,
  Forte nec ad noftras furdeat illa preces.
Crede mihi nullus fic infeliciter arfit,
  Ponar in exemplo primus et unus ego.
Parce precor teneri cum fis Deus ales amoris,
  Pugnent officio nec tua facta tuo.
Jam tuus O certè eft mihi formidabilis arcus,
  Nate deâ, jaculis nec minus igne potens:
Et tua fumabunt noftris altaria donis,
  Solus et in fuperis tu mihi fummus eris.
Deme meos tandem, verùm nec deme furores,
  Nefcio cur, mifer eft fuaviter omnis amans:
Tu modo da facilis, pofthæc mea fiqua futura eft,
  Cufpis amaturos figat ut una duos.


Hæc ego mente olim lævâ, ftudioque fupino
  Nequitiæ pofui vana trophæa meæ.
Scilicet abreptum fic me malus impulit error,
  Indocilifque ætas prava magiftra fuit.
Donec Socraticos umbrofa Academia rivos
  Præbuit, admiffum dedocuitque jugum.
Protinus extinctis ex illo tempore flammis,
  Cincta rigent multo pectora noftra gelu.
Unde fuis frigus metuit puer ipfe fagittis,
  Et Diomedéam vim timet ipfa Venus.

## IN PRODITIONEM BOMBARDICAM.

Cum fimul in regem nuper fatrapafque Britannos
    Aufus es infandum perfide Fauxe nefas,
Fallor? an et mitis voluifti ex parte videri,
    Et penfare malâ cum pietate fcelus?
Scilicet hos alti miffurus ad atria cœli,
    Sulphureo curru flammivolifque rotis.
Qualiter ille feris caput inviolabile Parcis
    Liquit Iördanios turbine raptus agros.

## IN EANDEM.

Siccine tentafti cœlo donâffe Iäcobum
    Quæ feptemgemino Bellua monte lates?
Ni meliora tuum poterit dare munera numen,
    Parce precor donis infidiofa tuis.
Ille quidem fine te confortia ferus adivit
    Aftra, nec inferni pulveris ufus ope.
Sic potiùs fœdos in cœlúm pelle cucullos,
    Et quot habet brutos Roma profana Deos,
Namque hac aut aliâ nifi quemque adjuveris arte,
    Crede mihi cœli vix bene fcandet iter.

## IN EANDEM.

Purgatorem animæ derifit Iäcobus ignem,
    Et fine quo fuperûm non adeunda domus.
Frenduit hoc trinâ monftrum Latiale coronâ,
    Movit et horrificum cornua dena minax.

Et nec inultus ait temnes mea facra Britanne,
　　Supplicium fpreta relligione dabis.
Et fi ftelligeras unquam penetraveris arces,
　　Non nifi per flammas trifte patebit iter.
O quàm funefto cecinifti proxima vero,
　　Verbaque ponderibus vix caritura fuis!
Nam prope Tartareo fublime rotatus ab ignl
　　Ibat ad æthereas umbra perufta plagas.

## IN EANDEM.

Quem modò Roma fuit devoverat impia diris,
　　Et Styge damnârat Tænarioque finu,
Hunc vice mutâtâ jam tollere geftit ad aftra,
　　Et cupit àd fuperos evehere ufque Deos.

## IN INVENTOREM BOMBARDÆ.

Iapetionidem laudavit cæca vetuftas,
　　Qui tulit ætheream folis ab axe facem:
At mihi major erit, qui lurida creditur arma,
　　Et trifidum fulmen furripuifle Jovi.

AD
## LEONORAM ROMÆ CANENTEM.

Angelus unicuique fuus (fic credite gentes)
　　Obtigit æthereis ales ab ordinibus.
Quid mirum? Leonora tibi fi gloria major,
　　Nam tua præfentem vox fonat ipfa Deum.

z

Aut Deus, aut vacui certè mens tertia cœli
 Per tua secretò guttura serpit agens;
Serpit agens, facilisque docet mortalia corda
 Sensim immortali assuescere posse sono.
Quòd si cuncta quidem Deus est, per cunctaque fusus,
 In te unâ loquitur, cætera mutus habet.


## AD EANDEM.

ALTERA Torquatum cepit Leonora poetam,
 Cujus ab insano cessit amore furens.
Ah miser ille tuo quantò feliciùs ævo
 Perditus, et propter te Leonora foret!
Et te Pieriâ sensisset voce canentem
 Aurea maternæ fila movere lyræ,
Quamvis Dircæo torsisset lumina Pentheo
 Sævior, aut totus desipuisset iners,
Tu tamen errantes cæcâ vertigine sensus
 Voce eadem poteras composuisse tuâ;
Et poteras ægro spirans sub corde quietem
 Flexanimo cantu restituisse sibi.


## AD EANDEM.

CREDULA quid liquidam Sirena Neapoli jactas,
 Claraque Parthenopes fana Achelöiados,
Littoreamque tuâ defunctam Naiada ripâ
 Corpore Chalcidico sacra dedisse rogo?
Illa quidem vivitque, et amœnâ Tibridis undâ
 Mutavit rauci murmura Pausilipi.
Illic Romulidûm studiis ornata secundis,
 Atque homines cantu detinet atque Deos.

## APOLOGUS DE RUSTICO ET HERO.

Rusticus ex malo fapidiffima poma quotannis
  Legit, et urbano lecta dedit Domino:
Hinc incredibili fructûs dulcedine captus
  Malum ipfam in proprias tranftulit areolas.
Hactenus illa ferax, fed longo debilis ævo,
  Mota folo affueto, protenùs aret iners.
Quod tandem ut patuit Domino, fpe lufus inani,
  Damnavit celeres in fua damna manus.
Atque ait, heu quantò fatius fuit illa Coloni
  (Parva licet) grato dona tuliffe animo!
Poffem ego avaritiam frænare, gulamque voracem:
  Nunc periere mihi et fœtus et ipfe parens.

ELEGIARUM FINIS.

# SYLVARUM LIBER.

ANNO ÆTATIS 16.

IN

## OBITUM PROCANCELLARII MEDICI. ·

PARERE fati difcite legibus,
Manufque Parcæ jam date fupplices,
   Qui pendulum telluris orbem
     Iäpeti colitis nepotes.

Vos fi relicto mors vaga Tænaro
Semel vocârit flebilis, heu moræ
   Tentantur incafsùm dolique;
     Per tenebras Stygis ire certum eft.

Si deftinatam pellere dextera
Mortem valeret, non ferus Hercules
   Neffi venenatus cruore
     Æmathiâ jacuiffet Oetâ.

Nec fraude turpi Palladis invidæ
Vidiffet occifum Ilion Hectora, aut
   Quem larva Pelidis peremit
     Enfe Locro, Jove lacrymante.

Si trifte fatum verba Hecatëia
Fugare poffint, Telegoni parens
   Vixiffet infamis, potentique
     Ægiali foror ufa virgâ.

Numenque trinum fallere fi queant
Artes medentûm, ignotaque gramina,
   Non gnarus herbarum Machaon
     Eurypyli cecidiffet haftâ.

Læfiffet et nec te Philyreie
Sagitta echidnæ perlita fanguine,
   Nec tela te fulmenque avitum
     Cæfe puer genetricis alvo.

Tuque O alumno major Apolline,
Gentis togatæ cui regimen datum,
   Frondofa quem nunc Cirrha luget,
     Et mediis Helicos in undis,

Jam præfuiffes Palladio gregi
Lætus, fuperftes, nec fine gloria,
   Nec puppe luftraffes Charontis
     Horribiles barathri receffus.

At fila rupit Perfephone tua
Irata, cum te viderit artibus
   Succoque pollenti tot atris
     Faucibus eripuiffe mortis.

Colende Præfes, membra precor tua
Molli quiefcant cefpite, et ex tuo

Crefcant rofæ, calthæque bufto,
Purpureoque hyacinthus ore.

Sit mite de te judicium Æaci,
Subrideatque Ætnæa Proferpina,
Interque felices perennis
Elyfio fpatiere campo.

## IN QUINTUM NOVEMBRIS,

### ANNO ÆTATIS 17.

JAM pius extremâ veniens Iäcobus ab arĉto
Teucrigenas populos, latéque patentia regna
Albionum tenuit, jamque inviolabile fœdus
Sceptra Caledoniis conjunxerat Anglica Scotis:
Pacificúfque novo felix'divefque fcdebat
In folio, occultique doli fecurus et hoftis:
Cum ferus ignifluo regnans Acheronte tyrannus,
Eumenidum pater, æthero vagus exul Olympo,
Forte per immenfum terrarum erraverat orbem,
Dinumerans fceleris focios, vernafque fidcles,
Participes regni poft funera mœfta futuros;
Hic tempeftates medio ciet aëre diras,
Illic unanimes odium ftruit inter amicos,
Armat et invictas in mutua vifcera gentes;
Regnaque olivifera vertit florentia pace,
Et quofcunque videt puræ virtutis amantes,
Hos cupit adjicere imperio, fraudumque magifter
Tentat inaccefTum fceleri corrumpere pectus,
Infidiafque locat tacitas, caffefque latentes

Tendit, ut incautos rapiat, feu Cafpia tigris
Infequitur trepidam deferta per avia prædam.
Noĉte fub illuni, et fomno niĉantibus aftris.
Talibus infeftat populos Summanus et urbes
Cinĉtus cæruleæ fumanti turbine flammæ.
Jamque fluentifonis albentia rupibus arva
Apparent, et terra Deo dileĉta marino,
Cui nomen dederat quondam Neptunia proles,
Amphitryoniaden qui non dubitavit atrocem
Æquore tranato furiali pofcere bello,
Ante expugnatæ crudelia fæcula Trojæ.

At fimul hanc opibufque et feftâ pace beatam
Afpicit, et pingues donis Cerealibus agros,
Quodque magis doluit, venerantem numina veri
Sanĉta Dei populum, tandem fufpiria rupit
Tartareos ignes et luridum olentia fulphur;
Qualia Trinacria trux ab Jove claufus in Ætna
Efflat tabifico monftrofus ob ore Tiphœus.
Ignefcunt oculi, ftridetque adamantinus ordo
Dentis, ut armorum fragor, iĉtaque cufpide cufpis.
Atque pererrato folum hoc lacrymabile mundo
Inveni, dixit, gens hæc mihi fola rebellis,
Contemtrixque jugi, noftraque potentior arte.
Illa tamen, mea fi quicquam tentamina poffunt,
Non feret hoc impune diu, non ibit inulta.
Haĉtenus; et piceis liquido natat aëre pennis;
Quà volat, adverfi præcurfant agmine venti,
Denfantur nubes, et crebra tonitrua fulgent.

Jamque pruinofas velox fuperaverat Alpes,
Et tenet Aufoniæ fines, à parte finiftra
Nimbifer Appenninus erat, prifcique Sabini,

Dextra veneficiis infamis Hetruria, nec non
Te furtiva Tibris Thetidi videt ofcula dantem;
Hinc Mavortigenæ confiftit in arce Quirini.
Reddiderant dubiam jam fera crepufcula lucem,
Cum circumgreditur totam Tricoronifer urbem,
Panificofque Deos portat, fcapulifque virorum
Evehitur, præeunt fubmiffo poplite reges,
Et mendicantum feries longiffima fratrum;
Cereaque in manibus geftant funalia cæci,
Cimmeriis nati in tenebris, vitamque trahentes.
Templa dein multis fubeunt lucentia tædis
(Vefper erat facer ifte Petro) fremitufque canentum
Sæpe tholos implet vacuos, et inane locorum.
Qualiter exululat Bromius, Bromiique caterva,
Orgia cantantes in Echionio Aracyntho,
Dum tremit attonitus vitreis Afopus in undis,
Et procul ipfe cavâ refponfat rupe Cithæron.

His igitur tandem folenni more peraƈtis,
Nox fenis amplexus Erebi taciturna reliquit,
Præcipitefque impellit equos ftimulante flagello,
Captum oculis Typhlonta, Melanchætemque ferocem,
Atque Acherontæo prognatam patre Siopen
Torpidam, et hirfutis horrentem Phrica capillis.
Interea regum domitor, Phlegetontius hæres
Ingreditur thalamos (neque enim fecretus adulter
Producit fteriles molli fine pellice noƈtes)
At vix compofitos fomnus claudebat ocellos,
Cum niger umbrarum dominus, reƈtorque filentum,
Prædatorque hominum falfâ fub imagine teƈtus
Aftitit, affumptis miçuerunt tempora canis,
Barba finus promiffa tegit, cineracea longo

Syrmate verrit humum veſtis, pendetque cucullus
Vertice de raſo, et ne quicquam deſit ad artes,
Cannabeo lumbos conſtrixit fune ſalaces,
Tarda feneſtratis figens veſtigia calceis.
Talis, uti fama eſt, vaſtâ Franciſcus eremo
Tetra vagabatur ſolus per luſtra ferarum,
Sylveſtrique tulit genti pia verba ſalutis
Impius, atque lupos domuit, Lybicoſque leones.

    Subdolus at tali Serpens velatus amiĉtu
Solvit in has fallax ora execrantia voces;
Dormis nate? Etiamne tuos ſopor opprimit artus?
Immemor O fidei, pecorumque oblite tuorum!
Dum cathedram venerande tuam, diademaque triplex
Ridet Hyperboreo gens barbara nata ſub axe,
Dumque pharetrati ſpernunt tua jura Britanni:
Surge, age, ſurge piger, Latius quem Cæſar adorat,
Cui reſerata patet convexi janua cœli,
Turgentes animos, et faſtus frange procaces,
Sacrilegique ſciant, tua quid malediĉtio poſſit,
Et quid Apoſtolicæ poſſit cuſtodia clavis;
Et memor Heſperiæ disjeĉtam ulciſcere claſſem,
Merſaque Iberorum lato vexilla profundo,
Sanĉtorumque cruci tot corpora fixa probofæ,
Thermodoontea nuper regnante puella.
At tu ſi tenero mavis torpeſcere leĉto,
Creſcenteſque negas hoſti contundere vires,
Tyrrhenum implebit numeroſo milite pontum,
Signaque Aventino ponet fulgentia colle:
Relliquias veterum franget, flammiſque cremabit,
Sacraque calcabit pedibus tua colla profanis,
Cujus gaudebant ſoleis dare baſia reges.

Nec tamen hunc bellis et aperto Marte laceſſes,
Irritus ille labor, tu callidus utere fraude,
Quælibet hæreticis diſponere retia fas eſt;
Jamque ad conſilium extremis rex magnus ab oris
Patricios vocat, et procerum de ſtirpe creatos,
Grandævoſque patres trabeâ, caniſque verendos;
Hos tu membratim poteris conſpergere in auras,
Atque dare in cineres, nitrati pulveris igne
Ædibus injeɛto, quà convenere, ſub imis.
Protinus ipſe igitur quoſcunque habet Anglia fidos
Propoſiti, faɛtique mone, quiſquámne tuorum
Audebit ſummi non juſſa faceſſere Papæ?
Perculſoſque metu ſubito, caſúque ſtupentes
Invadat vel Gallus atrox, vel ſævus Iberus.
Sæcula ſic illic tandem Mariana redibunt,
Tuque in belligeros iterum dominaberis Anglos.
Et nequid timeas, divos divaſque ſecundas
Accipe, quotque tuis celebrantur numina faſtis.
Dixit et adſcitos ponens malefidus amiɛtus
Fugit ad infandam, regnum illætabile, Lethen.
    Jam roſea Eoas pandens Tithonia portas
Veſtit inauratas redeunti lumine terras;
Mœſtaque adhuc nigri deplorans funera nati
Irrigat ambroſiis montana cacumina guttis;
Cum ſomnos pepulit ſtellatæ janitor aulæ,
Noɛturnos viſus, et ſomnia grata revolvens.
    Eſt locus æternâ ſeptus caligine noɛtis,
Vaſta ruinoſi quondam fundamina teɛti,
Nunc torvi ſpelunca Phoni, Prodotæque bilinguis,
Effera quos uno peperit Diſcordia partu.
Hic inter cæmenta jacent præruptaque ſaxa,

Offa inhumata virûm, et trajecta cadavera ferro;
Hic Dolus intortis femper fedet ater ocellis,
Jurgiaque, et ftimulis armata Calumnia fauces,
Et Furor, atque viæ moriendi mille videntur,
Et Timor, exanguifque locum circumvolat Horror,
Perpetuoque leves per muta filentia Manes
Exululant, tellus et fanguine confcia ftagnat.
Ipfi etiam pavidi latitant penetralibus antri
Et Phonos, et Prodotes, nulloque fequente per antrum,
Antrum horrens, fcopulofum, atrum feralibus umbris
Diffugiunt fontes, et retrò lumina vortunt;
Hos pugiles Romæ per fæcula longe fideles
Evocat antiftes Babylonius, atque ita fatur.
Finibus occiduis circumfufum incolit æquor
Gens exofa mihi, prudens natura negavit
Indignam penitus noftro conjungere mundo:
Illuc, fic jubeo, celeri contendite greffu,
Tartareoque leves difflentur pulvere in auras
Et rex et pariter fatrapæ, fcelerata propago,
Et quotquot fidei caluere cupidine veræ
Confilii focios adhibete, operifque miniftros.
Finierat, rigidi cupidè paruere gemelli.

    Interea longo flectens curvamine cœlos
Defpicit æthereâ dominus qui fulgurat arce,
Vanaque perverfæ ridet conamina turbæ,
Atque fui caufam populi volet ipfe tueri.

    Effe ferunt fpatium, quà diftat ab Afide terra
Fertilis Europe, et fpectat Mareotidas undas;
Hic turris pofita eft Titanidos ardua Famæ
Ærea, lata, fonans, rutilis vicinior aftris
Quàm fuperimpofitum vel Athos vel Pelion Offæ.

Mille fores aditufque patent, totidemque feneftræ,
Amplaque per tenues tranflucent atria muros:
Excitat hic varios plebs agglomerata fufurros;
Qualiter inftrepitant circum mulctralia bombis
Agmina mufcarum, aut texto per ovilia junco,
Dum Canis æftivum cœli petit ardua culmen.
Ipfa quidem fummâ fedet ultrix matris in arce,
Auribus innumeris cinctum caput eminet olli,
Queis fonitum exiguum trahit, atque leviffima captat
Murmura, ab extremis patuli confinibus orbis.
Nec tot, Ariftoride fervator inique juvencæ
Ifidos, immiti volvebas lumina vultu,
Lumina non unquam tacito nutantia fomno,
Lumina fubjectas late fpectantia terras.
Iftis illa folet loca luce carentia fæpe
Perluftrare, etiam radianti impervia foli:
Millenifque loquax auditaque vifaque linguis
Cuilibet effundit temeraria, veraque mendax
Nunc minuit, modo confictis fermonibus auget.
Sed tamen à noftro meruifti carmine laudes
Fama, bonum quo non aliud veracius ullum,
Nobis digna cani, nec te memoraffe pigebit
Carmine tam longo, fervati fcilicet Angli
Officiis vaga diva tuis, tibi reddimus æqua.
Te Deus, æternos motu qui temperat ignes,
Fulmine præmiffo alloquitur, terrâque tremente:
Fama files? an te latet impia Papiftarum
Conjurata cohors in meque meofque Britannos,
Et nova fceptigero cædes meditata Iäcobo?
Nec plura, illa ftatim fenfit mandata Tonantis,
Et fatis ante fugax ftridentes induit alas,

Induit et variis exilia corpora plumis;
Dextra tubam geſtat Temeſæo ex ære ſonoram.
Nec mora jam pennis cedentes remigat auras,
Atque parum eſt curſu celeres prævertere nubes,
Jam ventos, jam ſolis equos poſt terga reliquit:
Et primo Angliacas ſolito de more per urbes
Ambiguas voces, incertaque murmura ſpargit,.
Mox arguta dolos, et deteſtabile vulgat
Proditionis opus, nec non faƈta horrida diƈtu,
Authoreſque addit ſceleris, nec garrula cæcis
Inſidiis loca ſtruƈta ſilet; ſtupuere relatis,
Et pariter juvenes, pariter tremuere puellæ,
Effœtique ſenes pariter, tantæque ruinæ
Senſus ad ætatem ſubito penetraverat omnem.
Attamen interea populi miſereſcit ab alto
Æthereus pater, et crudelibus obſtitit auſis
Papicolûm; capti pœnas raptantur ad acres;
At pia thura Deo, et grati ſolvuntur honores;
Compita læta focis genialibus omnia fumant;
Turba choros juvenilis agit: Quintoque Novembris
Nulla dies toto occurrit celebratior anno.


ANNO ÆTATIS 17.

## IN OBITUM PRÆSULIS ELIENSIS.

Adhuc madentes rore ſqualebant genæ,
   Et ſicƈa nondum lumina
Adhuc liquentis imbre turgebant ſalis,
   Quem nuper effudi pius,

Dum mœsta charo jufta perfolvi rogo
 Wintonienfis Præfulis.
Cum centilinguis Fama (proh femper mali
 Cladifque vera nuntia)
Spargit per urbes divitis Britanniæ,
 Populofque Neptuno fatos,
Ceffiffe morti, et ferreis fororibus
 Te generis humani decus,
Qui rex facrorum illâ fuifti in infulâ
 Quæ nomen Anguillæ tenet.
Tunc inquietum pectus irâ protinus
 Ebulliebat fervidâ,
Tumulis potentem fæpe devovens deam:
 Nec vota Nafo in Ibida
Concepit alto diriora pectore,
 Graiufque vates parcius
Turpem Lycambis execratus eft dolum,
 Sponfamque Neobolen fuam.
At ecce diras ipfe dum fundo graves,
 Et imprecor neci necem,
Audiffe tales videor attonitus fonos
 Leni, fub aurâ, flamine:
Cæcos furores pone, pone vitream
 Bilemque et irritas minas,
Quid temerè violas non nocenda numina,
 Subitoque ad iras percita?
Non eft, ut arbitraris elufus mifer,
 Mors atra Noctis filia,
Erebóve patre creta, five Erinnye,
 Vaftove nata fub Chao:
Aft illa cœlo miffa ftellato, Dei
 Meffes ubique colligit;

Animafque mole carneâ reconditas
   In lucem et auras evocat;
Ut cum fugaces excitant Horæ diem
   Themidos Jovifque filiæ;
Et fempiterni ducit ad vultus patris;
   At jufta raptat impios
Sub regna furvi luctuofa Tartari,
   Sedefque fubterraneas.

Hanc ut vocantem lætus audivi, cito
   Fœdum reliqui carcerem,
Volatilefque fauftus inter milites
   Ad aftra fublimis feror:
Vates ut olim raptus ad cœlum fenex
   Auriga currus ignei.

Non me Bootis terruere lucidi
   Sarraca tarda frigore, aut
Formidolofi Scorpionis brachia,
   Non enfis Orion tuus.
Prætervolavi fulgidi folis globum,
   Longéque fub pedibus deam
Vidi triformem, dum coërcebat fuos
   Frænis dracones aureis.

Erraticorum fiderum per ordines,
   Per lacteas vehor plagas,
Velocitatem fæpe miratus novam,
   Donec nitentes ad fores
Ventum eft Olympi, et regiam cryftallinam, et
   Stratum fmaragdis atrium.

Sed hic tacebo, nam quis effari queat
   Oriundus humano patre
Amœnitates illius loci? mihi
   Sat eft in æternum frui.

## NATURAM NON PATI SENIUM.

Heu quàm perpetuis erroribus acta fatifcit
Avia mens hominum, tenebrifque immerfa profundis
Oedipodioniam volvit fub pectore noctem!
Quæ vefana fuis metiri facta deorum
Audet, et incifas leges adamante perenni
Affimilare fuis, nulloque folubile fæclo
Confilium fati perituris alligat horis.
  Ergóne marcefcet fulcantibus obfita rugis
Naturæ facies, et rerum publica mater
Omniparum contracta uterum fterilefcet ab ævo?
Et fe faffa fenem malè certis paffibus ibit
Sidereum tremebunda caput? num tetra vetuftas
Annorumque æterna fames, fqualorque fitufque
Sidera vexabunt? an et infatiabile Tempus
Efuriet Cœlum, rapietque in vifcera patrem?
Heu, potuitne fuas imprudens Jupiter arces
Hoc contra muniffe nefas, et Temporis ifto
Exemiffe malo, gyrofque dediffe perennes?
Ergo erit ut quandoque fono dilapfa tremendo
Convexi tabulata ruant, atque obvius ictu
Stridat uterque polus, fuperàque ut Olympius aulâ
Decidat, horribilifque retectâ Gorgone Pallas;
Qualis in Ægeam proles Junonia Lemnon
Deturbata facro cecidit de limine cœli?
Tu quoque Phœbe tui cafus imitabere nati
Præcipiti curru, fubitâque ferere ruinâ
Pronus, et extinctâ fumabit lampade Nereus,

Et dabit attonito feralia fibila ponto.
Tunc etiam aërei divulfis fedibus Hæmi
Diffultabit apex, imoque allifa barathro
Terrebunt Stygium dejecta Ceraunia Ditem,
In fuperos quibus ufus erat, fraternaque bella.
   At pater omnipotens fundatis fortius aftris
Confuluit rerum fummæ, certoque peregit
Pondere fatorum lances, atque ordine fummo
Singula perpetuum juffit fervare tenorem.
Volvitur hinc lapfu mundi rota prima diurno;
Raptat et ambitos fociâ vertigine cœlos.
Tardior haud folito Saturnus, et acer ut olim
Fulmineum rutilat criftatâ caffide Mavors.
Floridus æternùm Phœbus juvenile corufcat,
Nec fovet effœtas loca per declivia terras
Devexo temone Deus; fed femper amicâ
Luce potens eadem currit per figna rotarum.
Surgit odoratis pariter formofus ab Indis
Æthereum pecus albenti qui cogit Olympo
Mane vocans, et ferus agens in pafcua cœli,
Temporis et gemino difpertit regna colore.
Fulget, obitque vices alterno Delia cornu,
Cæruleumque ignem paribus complectitur ulnis.
Nec variant elementa fidem, folitoque fragore
Lurida perculfas jaculantur fulmina rupes.
Nec per inane furit leviori murmure Corus,
Stringit et armiferos æquali horrore Gelonos
Trux Aquilo, fpiratque hyemem, nimbofque volutat.
Utque folet, Siculi diverberat ima Pelori
Rex maris, et raucâ circumftrepit æquora conchâ
Oceani Tubicen, nec vaftâ mole minorem

Ægeona ferunt dorſo Balearica cete.
Sed neque Terra tibi ſæcli vigor ille vetuſti
Priſcus abeſt, ſervatque ſuum Narciſſus odorem,
Et puer ille ſuum tenet et puer ille decorem
Phœbe tuuſque et Cypri tuus, nec ditior olim
Terra datum ſceleri ˙cclavit montibus aurum
Conſcia, vel ſub aquis gemmas. Sic denique in ævum
Ibit cunctarum ſeries juſtiſſima rerum,
Donec flamma orbem populabitur ultima, latè
Circumplexa polos, et vaſti culmina cœli;
Ingentique rogo flagrabit machina mundi.

## DE IDEA PLATONICA QUEMADMODUM
## ARISTOTELES INTELLEXIT.

Dicite ſacrorum præſides nemorum deæ,
Tuque O noveni perbeata numinis
Memoria mater, quæque in immenſo procul⸴
Antro recumbis otioſa Æternitas,
Monumenta ſervans, et ratas leges Jovis,
Cœlique faſtos atque ephemeridas Deûm,
Quis ille primus cujus ex imagine
Natura ſolers finxit humanum genus,
Æternus, incorruptus, æquævus polo,
Unuſque et univerſus, exemplar Dei?
Haud ille Palladis gemellus innubæ
Interna proles inſidet menti Jovis;
Sed quamlibet natura ſit communior,
Tamen ſeorsùs extat ad morem unius,
Et, mira, certo ſtringitur ſpatio loci;

Seu fempiternus ille fiderum comes
Cœli pererrat ordines decemplicis,
Citimúmve terris incolit lunæ globum :
Sive inter animas corpus adituras fedens
Obliviofas torpet ad Lethes aquas:
Sive in remôtâ forte terrarum plaga
Incedit ingens hominis archetypus gigas,
Et diis tremendus erigit celfum caput
Atlante major portitore fiderum.
Non cui profundum cæcitas lumen dedit
Dircæus augur vidit hunc alto finu;
Non hunc filenti nocte Plëiones nepos
Vatum fagaci præpes oftendit choro;
Non hunc facerdos novit Affyrius, licet
Longos vetufti commemoret atavos Nini,
Prifcumque Belon, inclytumque Ofiridem.
Non ille trino gloriofus nomine
Ter magnus Hermés (ut fit arcani fciens)
Talem reliquit Ifidis cultoribus.
At tu perenne ruris Academi decus
(Hæc monftra fi tu primus induxit fcholis)
Jam jam poetas urbis exules tuæ
Revocabis, ipfe fabulator maximus,
Aut inftitutor ipfe migrabis foras.


## AD PATREM.

Nunc mea Pierios cúpiam per pectora fontes
Irriguas torquere vias, totumque per ora
Volvere laxatum gemino de vertice rivum;

Ut tenues oblita fonos audacibus alis
Surgat in officium venerandi Mufa parentis.
Hoc utcunque tibi gratum pater optime carmen
Exiguum meditatur opus, nec novimus ipfi
Aptiùs à nobis quæ poffint munera donis
Refpondere tuis, quamvis nec maxima poffint
Refpondere tuis, nedum ut par gratia donis
Effe queat, vacuis quæ redditur arida verbis.
Sed tamen hæc noftros oftendit pagina cenfus,
Et quod habemus opum chartâ numeravimus iftâ,
Quæ mihi funt nullæ, nifi quas dedit aurea Clio,
Quas mihi femoto fomni peperere fub antro,
Et nemoris laureta facri Parnaffides umbræ.

Nec tu vatis opus divinum defpice carmen,
Quo nihil æthereos ortus, et femina cœli,
Nil magis humanam commendat origine mentem,
Sanĉta Promethéæ retinens veftigia flammæ.
Carmen amant fuperi, tremebundaque Tartara carmen
Ima ciere valet, divofque ligare profundos,
Et triplici duros Manes adamante coercet.
Carmine fepofiti retegunt arcana futuri
Phœbades, et tremulæ pallentes ora Sibyllæ;
Carmina facrificus follennes pangit ad aras,
Aurea feu fternit motantem cornua taurum;
Seu cùm fata fagax fumantibus abdita fibris
Confulit, et tepidis Parcam fcrutatur in extis.
Nos etiam patrium tunc cum repetemus Olympum,
Æternæque moræ ftabunt immobilis ævi,
Ibimus auratis per cœli templa coronis,
Dulcia fuaviloquo fociantes carmina pleĉtro,
Aftra quibus, geminique poli convexa fonabunt.

Spiritus et rapidos qui circinat igneus orbes,
Nunc quoque fidereis intercinit ipfe choreis
Immortale melos, et inenarrabile carmen;
Torrida dum rutilus compefcit fibila ferpens,
Demiffoque ferox gladio manfuefcit Orion;
Stellarum nec fentit onus Maurufius Atlas.
Carmina regales epulas ornare folebant,
Cum nondum luxus, vaftæque immenfa vorago
Nota gulæ, et modico fpumabat cœna Lyæo.
Tum de more fedens fefta ad convivia vates
Æfculeâ intonfos redimitus ab arbore crines,
Heroumque actus, imitandaque gefta canebat,
Et chaos, et pofiti latè fundamina mundi,
Reptantefque deos, et alentes numina glandes,
Et nondum Ætneo quæfitum fulmen ab antro.
Denique quid vocis modulamen inane juvabit,
Verborum fenfufque vacans, numerique loquacis?
Silveftres decet ifte choros, non Orphea cantus,
Qui tenuit fluvios et quercubus addidit aures
Carmine, non citharâ, fimulachraque functa canendo
Compulit in lacrymas; habet has à carmine laudes.
    Nec tu perge precor facras contemnere Mufas,
Nec vanas inopefque puta, quarum ipfe peritus
Munere, mille fonos numeros componis ad aptos,
Millibus et vocem modulis variare canoram
Doctus, Arionii meritò fis nominis hæres.
Nunc tibi quid mirum, fi me genuiffe poëtam
Contigerit, charo fi tam propè fanguine juncti
Cognatas artes, ftudiumque affine fequamur?
Ipfe volens Phœbus fe difpertire duobus,
Altera dona mihi, dedit altera dona parenti,

Dividuumque Deum genitorque puerque tenemus.

    Tu tamen ut fimules teneras odiffe Camœnas,
Non odiffe reor, neque enim, pater, ire jubebas
Quà via lata patet, quà pronior area lucri,
Certaque condendi fulget fpes aurea nummi:
Nec rapis ad leges, malè cuftoditaque gentis
Jura, nec infulfis damnas clamoribus aures.
Sed magis excultam cupiens ditefcere mentem,
Me procul urbano ftrepitu, feceffibus altis
Abductum Aoniæ jucunda per otia ripæ
Phœbæo lateri comitem finis ire beatum.
Officium chari taceo commune parentis,
Me pofcunt majora, tuo pater optime fumptu
Cùm mihi Romuleæ patuit facundia linguæ,
Et Latii veneres, et quæ Jovis ora decebant
Grandia magniloquis elata vocabula Graiis,
Addere fuafifti quos jactat Gallia flores,
Et quam degeneri novus Italus ore loquelam
Fundit, barbaricos teftatus voce tumultus,
Quæque Palæftinus loquitur myfteria vates.
Denique quicquid habet cœlum, fubjectaque cœlo
Terra parens, terræque et cœlo interfluus aer,
Quicquid et unda tegit, pontique agitabile marmor,
Per te noffe licet, per te, fi noffe libebit.
Dimotâque venit fpectanda fcientia nube,
Nudaque confpicuos inclinat ad ofcula vultus,
Ni fugiffe velim, ni fit libâffe moleftum.

    I nunc, confer opes quifquis malefanus avitas
Auftriaci gazas, Perüanaque regna præoptas.
Quæ potuit majora pater tribuiffe, vel ipfe
Jupiter, excepto, donâffet ut omnia, cœlo?

Non potiora dedit, quamvis et tuta fuiſſent,
Publica qui juveni commiſit lumina nato
Atque Hyperionios currus, et fræna diei,
Et circum undantem radiatâ luce tiaram.
Ergo ego jam doꞔtæ pars quamlibet ima catervæ
Viꞔtrices hederas inter, laurofque fedebo,
Jamque nec obfcurus populo mifcebor inerti,
Vitabuntque oculos veſtigia noſtra profanos.
Eſte procul vigiles curæ, procul eſte querelæ,
Invidiæque acies tranſverſo tortilis hirquo,
Sæva nec anguiferos extende calumnia riꞔtus;
In me triſte nihil fœdiſſima turba poteſtis,
Nec veſtri fum juris ego; fecuraque tutus
Peꞔtora, vipereo gradiar fublimis ab iꞔtu.

At tibi, chare pater, poſtquam non æqua merenti
Poſſe referre datur, nec dona rependere faꞔtis,
Sit memorâſſe fatis, repetitaque munera grato
Percenfere animo, fidæque reponere menti.

Et vos, O noſtri, juvenilia carmina, lufus,
Si modo perpetuos fperare audebitis annos,
Et domini fupereſſe rogo, lucemque tueri,
Nec fpiſſo rapient oblivia nigra fub Orco,
Forſitan has laudes, decantatumque parentis
Nomen, ad exemplum, fero fervabitis ævo.

## PSALM CXIV.

ΙΣΡΑΗΛ ὁτε παιδες, ἱτ' αγλαα φυλ' Ιακωϐ̃ε
Αιγυπλιον λιπε δημον, απεχθεα, βαρϐαροφωνον,
Δη τοτε μεννον εγν ὁσιον γενος υιες Ιεδα.

Εν δε Θεος λαοισι μεγα κρειων βασιλευεν.

Ειδε και εντροπαδην φυγαδ᾽ ερρωησε θαλασσα

Κυματι ειλυμενη ροθιω, οδ᾽ αρ᾽ εστυφελιχθη

Ιρος Ιορδανης ποτι αργυροειδεα πηγην.

Εκ δ᾽ ορεα σκαρθμοισιν απειρεσια κλονεονlo,

Ως κριοι σφριγόωνlες εὔτραφερῳ εν αλωη.

Βαιοτεραι δ᾽ ἁμα πασαι ανασκιρτησαν εριπναι,

Οια παραι συριlγι φιλη ὑπο μητερι αρνες.

Τιπlε συγ᾽ αινα θαλασσα πελωρ φυγαδ᾽ ερρωησας

Κυματι ειλυμενη ροθιω; τι δ᾽ αρ εστυφελιχθης

Ιρος Ιορδανη ποτι αργυροειδεα πηγην;

Τιπl᾽ ορεα σκαρθμοισιν απειρεσια κλονεεσθε

Ως κριοι σφριγοωνlης εὔτραφερῳ εν αλωη;

Βαιοτεραι τι δ᾽ αρ ὑμμες ανασκιρτησατ᾽ εριπναι,

Οια παραι συριlγι φιλη ὑπο μητερι αρνες;

Σειεο γαια τρεϋσα θεον μεγαλ᾽ εκτυπεονlα

Γαια θεον τρειϋσ᾽ ὑπατον σεβας Ισσακιδαο,

Ος τε και εκ σπιλαδων ποταμυς χεε μορμυρονlας,

Κρηγηγντ᾽ αεναον πετρης απο δακρυοεσσης.

PHILOSOPHUS AD REGEM QUENDAM, QUI EUM IGNO-
TUM ET INSONTEM INTER REOS FORTE CAPTUM
INSCIUS DAMNAVERAT, την επι θανατῳ πορευομενος
HÆC SUBITO MISIT.

Ω ανα ει ολεσης με τον εννομον, ϋδε τιν᾽ ανδρων

Δεινον ὁλως δρασανlα, σοφωτατον ισθι καρηνον

Ρηϊδιως αφελοιο, το δ᾽ ὑστερον αυθι νοησεις,

Μαψιδιως δ᾽ αρ επειτα τεον προς θυμον οδυρη,

Τοιον δ᾽ εκ πολιος περιωνυμον αλκαρ ολεσσας.

IN EFFIGIEI EJUS SCULPTOREM.

Αμαθει γεγραφθαι χειρι τηνδε μεν εικονα
Φαιης ταχ' αν, προς ειδος αυτοφυες βλεπων.
Τον δ' εκλυπωτον εκ επιγνοτες φιλοι
Γελατε φαυλε δυσμιμηνμα ζωγραφε.

## AD SALSILLUM POETAM ROMANUM
## ÆGROTANTEM.

### SCAZONTES.

O Musa gressum quæ volens trahis claudum;
Vulcanioque tarda gaudes incessu,
Nec sentis illud in loco minus gratum,
Quàm cùm decentes flava Dëiope suras
Alternat aureum ante Junonis lectum,
Adesdum et hæc s'is verba pauca Salsillo
Refer, Camœna nostra cui tantum est cordi,
Qamque ille magnis prætulit immeritò divis.
Hæc ergo alumnus ille Londini Milto,
Diebus hisce qui suum linquens nidum
Polique tractum, (pessimus ubi ventorum,
Insanientis impotensque pulmonis
Pernix anhela sub Jove exercet flabra)
Venit feraces Itali soli ad glebas,
Visum superbâ cognitas urbes famâ
Virosque doctæque indolem juventutis,
Tibi optat idem hic fausta multa Salfille,
Habitumque fesso corpori penitùs sanum;

Cui nunc profunda bilis infeſtat renes,
Præcordiiſque fixa damnoſum ſpirat.
Nec id pepercit impia quòd tu Romano
Tam cultus ore Leſbium condis melos.
O dulce divûm munus, O ſalus Hebes
Germana! Tuque Phœbe morborum terror
Pythone cæſo, ſive tu magis Pæan
Libenter audis, hic tuus ſacerdos eſt.
Querceta Fauni, voſque rore vinoſo
Colles benigni, mitis Evandri ſedes,
Siquid ſalubre vallibus frondet veſtris,
Levamen ægro ferte certatim vati.
Sic ille charis redditus rursùm Muſis
Vicina dulci prata mulcebit cantu.
Ipſe inter atros emirabitur lucos
Numa, ubi beatum degit otium æternum,
Suam reclivis ſemper Ægeriam ſpectans.
Tumiduſque et ipſe Tibris hinc delinitus
Spei favebit annuæ colonorum:
Nec in ſepulchris ibit obſeſſum reges
Nimiùm ſiniſtro laxus irruens loro:
Sed fræna melius temperabit undarum,
Aduſque curvi ſalſa regna Portumni.

## MANSUS.

Joannes Baptiſta Manſus, Marchio Villenſis, vir in-
genii laude, tum litterarum ſtudio, nec non et bel-
lica virtute apud Italos clarus in primis eſt. Ad
quem Torquati Taſſi dialogus extat de Amicitia
ſcriptus; erat enim Taſſi amiciſſimus; ab quo etiam
inter Campaniæ principes celebratur, in illo poe-
mate cui titulus Geruſalemme Conquiſtata, lib. 20.

> Fra cavalier magnanimi, è corteſi
> Riſpléndé il Manſo . . . .

Is authorem Neapoli commorantem ſummâ benevo-
lentiâ proſecutus eſt, multaque ei detulit humani-
tatis officia. Ad hunc itaque hoſpes ille antequam
ab ea urbe diſcederet, ut ne ingratum ſe oſtenderet,
hoc carmen miſit.

Hæc quoque Manſe tuæ meditantur carmina laudi
Pierides, tibi Manſe choro notiſſime Phœbi,
Quandoquidem ille alium haud æquo eſt dignatus ho-
    nore,
Poſt Galli cineres, et Mecænatis Hetruſci.
Tu quoque, ſi noſtræ tantum valet aura Camœnæ,
Victrices hederas inter, lauroſque ſedebis.
Te pridem magno felix concordia Taſſo
Junxit, et æternis inſcripſit nomina chartis.
Mox tibi dulciloquum non inſcia Muſa Marinum
Tradidit, ille tuum dici ſe gaudet alumnum,

Dum canit Affyrios divûm prolixus amores;
Mollis et Aufonias ftupefecit carmine nymphas.
Ille itidem moriens tibi foli debita vates
Offa tibi foli,` fupremaque vota reliquit.
Nec manes pietas tua chara fefellit amici,
Vidimus arridentem operofo ex ære poetam.
Nec fatis hoc vifum eft in utrumque, et nec pia ceffaut
Officia in tumulo, cupis integros rapere Orco,
Quà potes, atque avidas Parcarum eludere leges:
Amborum genus, et varia fub forte peraĉtam
Defcribis vitam, morefque, et dona Minervæ;
Æmulus illius Mycalen qui natus ad altam
Rettulit Æolii vitam facundus Homeri.
Ergo ego te Cliûs et magni nomine Phœbi,
Manfe pater, jubeo longum falvere per ævum
Miffus Hyperboreo juvenis peregrinus ab axe.
Nec tu longinquam bonus afpernabare Mufam,
Quæ nuper gelidâ vix enutrita fub Arĉto
Imprudens Italas aufa eft volitare per urbes.
Nos etiam in noftro modulantes flumine cygnos
Credimus obfcuras noĉtis fenfiffe per umbras,
Quà Thamefis late puris argenteus urnis
Oceani glaucos perfundit gurgite crines.
Quin et in has quondam pervenit Tityrus oras.
Sed neque nos genus incultum, nec inutile Phœbo,
Quà plaga fepteno mundi fulcata Trione
Brumalem patitur longâ fub noĉte Boöten.
Nos etiam colimus Phœbum, nos munera Phœbo
Flaventes fpicas, et lutea mala caniftris,
Halantemque crocum (perhibet nifi vana vetuftas)
Mifimus, et leĉtas Druidum de gente choreas.

(Gens Druides antiqua facris operata deorum
Heroum laudes imitandaque gefta canebant)
Hinc quoties fefto cingunt altaria cantu
Delo in herbofâ Graiæ de more puellæ
Carminibus lætis memorant Corinëida Loxo,`
Fatidicamque Upin, cum flavicomâ Hecaërge,
Nuda Caledonio variatas pectora fuco.
Fortunate fenex, ergo quacunque per orbem
Torquati decus, et nomen celebrabitur ingens,
Claraque perpetui fuccrefcet fama Marini,
Tu quoque in ora frequens venies plaufumque viro-
    rum,
Et parili carpes iter immortale volatu.
Dicetur tum fponte tuos habitaffe penates
Cynthius, et famulas veniffe ad limina Mufas:
At non fponte domum tamen idem, et regis adivit
Rura Pheretiadæ cœlo fugitivus Apollo;
Ille licet magnum Alciden fufceperat hofpes;
Tantùm ubi clamofos placuit vitare bubulcos,
Nobile manfueti ceffit Chironis in antrum,
Irriguos inter faltus frondofaque tecta
Peneium prope rivum: ibi fæpe fub ilice nigrâ
Ad citharæ ftrepitum blandâ prece victus amici
Exilii duros lenibat voce labores.
Tum neque ripa fuo, barathro nec fixa fub imo
Saxa ftetere loco, nutat Trachinia rupes,
Nec fentit folitas, immania pondera, filvas,
Emotæque fuis properant de collibus orni,
Mulcenturque novo maculofi carmine lynces.
Diis dilecte fenex, te Jupiter æquus oportet
Nafcentem, et miti luftrarit lumine Phœbus,

Atlantifque nepos; neque enim nifi charus ab ortu
Diis fuperis poterit magno faviffe poetæ.
Hinc longæva tibi lento fub flore feneétus
Vernat, et Æfonios lucratur vivida fufos,
Nondum deciduos fervans tibi frontis honores,
Ingeniumque vigens, et adultum mentis acumen.
O mihi fi mea fors talem concedat amicum
Phœbæos decoraffe viros qui tam bene nòrit,
Si quando indigenas revocabo in carmina reges,
Arturumque etiam fub terris bella moventem;
Aut dicam inviétæ fociali fœdere menfæ
Magnanimos Heroas, et (O modo fpiritus adfit)
Frangam Saxonicas Britonum fub Marte phalanges.
Tandem ubi non tacitæ permenfus tempora vitæ,
Annorumque fatur cineri fua jura relinquam,
Ille mihi leéto madidis aftaret ocellis,
Aftanti fat erit fi dicam fim tibi curæ;
Ille meos artus livènti morte folutos
Curaret parva componi molliter urna.
Forfitan et noftros ducat de marmore vultus,
Neétens aut Paphia myrti aut Parnaffide lauri
Fronde comas, at ego fecura pace quiefcam.
Tum quoque, fi qua fides, fi præmia certe bonorum,
Ipfe ego cælicolûm femotus in æthera divûm,
Quò labor et mens pura vehunt, atque ignea virtus,
Secreti hæc aliqua mundi de parte videbo
(Quantum fata finunt) et tota mente ferenùm
Ridens purpureo fuffundar lumine vultus,
Et fimul æthereo plaudam mihi lætus Olympo.

# EPITAPHIUM DAMONIS.

### ARGUMENTUM.

Thyrfis et Damon ejufdem viciniæ paftores, eadem ftudia fequuti à
pueritiâ amici erant, ut qui plurimum. Thyrfis animi causâ pro-
fectus peregrè de obitu Damonis nuncium accepit. Domum pof-
tea reverfus, et rem ita effe comperto, fe, fuamque folitud nem
hoc carmine deplorat. Damonis autem fub perfonâ hîc intelligi-
tur Carolus Deodatus ex urbe Hetruriæ Luca paterno genere oriundus, cætera Anglus; ingenio, doctrinâ, clariffimifque cæteris
virtutibus, dum viveret, juvenis egregius.

HIMERIDES nymphæ (nam vos et Daphnin et Hylan,
Et plorata diu meminiftis fata Bionis)
Dicite Sicelicum Thamefina per oppida carmen:
Quas mifer effudit voces, quæ murmura Thyrfis,
Et quibus affiduis exercuit antra querelis,
Fluminaque, fontefque vagos, nemorumque receffus,
Dum fibi præreptum queritur Damona, neque altam
Luctibus exemit noctem loca fola pererrans.
Et jam bis viridi furgebat culmus arifta,
Et totidem flavas numerabant horrea meffes,
Ex quo fumma dies tulerat Damona fub umbras,
Nec dum aderat Thyrfis; paftorem fcilicet illum
Dulcis amor Mufæ Thufca retinebat in urbe.
Aft ubi mens expleta domum, pecorifque relicti
Cura vocat, fimul affuetâ fedetque fub ulmo,
Tum verò amiffum tum denique fentit amicum,
Cœpit et immenfum fic exonerare dolorem.
  Ite domum impafti, domino jam nou vocat, agni.
Hei mihi! quæ terris, quæ dicam numina cœlo,

Poftquam te immiti rapuerunt funere, Damon!
Siccine nos linquis, tua fic fine nomine virtus
Ibit, et obfcuris numero fociabitur umbris?
At non ille, animas virgâ qui dividit aureâ,
Ifta velit, dignumque tui te ducat in agmen,
Ignavumque procul pecus arceat omne filentûm.
  Ite domum impafti, domino jam non vacat, agni.
Quicquid erit, certè nifi me lupus antè videbit,
Indeplorato non comminuere fepulchro,
Conftabitque tuus tibi honos, longumque vigebit
Inter paftores: Illi tibi vota fecundo
Solvere poft Daphnin, poft Daphnin dicere laudes,
Gaudebunt, dum rura Pales, dum Faunus amabit:
Si quid id eft, prifcamque fidem coluiffe, piúmque,
Palladiáfque artes, fociúmque habuiffe canorum.
  Ite domum impafti, domino jam non vacat, agni.
Hæc tibi certa manent, tibi erunt hæc præmia, Damon,
At mihi quid tandem fiet modò? quis mihi fidus
Hærebit lateri comes, ut tu fæpe folebas
Frigoribus duris, et per loca fœta pruinis,
Aut rapido fub fole, fiti morientibus herbis?
Sive opus in magnos fuit eminùs ire leones,
Aut avidos terrere lupos præfepibus altis;
Quis fando fopire diem, cantuque folebit?
  Ite domum impafti, domino jam non vacat, agni.
Pectora cui credam? quis me lenire docebit
Mordaces curas, quis longam fallere noctem
Dulcibus alloquiis, grato cùm fibilat igni
Molle pyrum, et nucibus ftrepitat focus, at malus
      aufter
Mifcet cuncta foris, et defuper intonat ulmo?

2 B

Ite domum impafti, domino jam non vacat, agni.
Aut æftate, dies medio dum vertitur axe,
Cum Pan æfculeâ fomnum capit abditus umbrâ,
Et repetunt fub aquis fibi nota fedilia nymphæ,
Paftorefque latent, ftertit fub fepe colonus;
Quis mihi blanditiáfque tuas, quis tum mihi rifus,
Cecropiofque fales referet, cultofque lepores?

Ite domum impafti, domino jam non vacat, agni.
At jam folus agros, jam pafcua folus oberro,
Sicubi ramofæ denfantur vallibus umbræ,
Hic ferum expecto, fupra caput imber et Eurus
Trifte fonant, fractæque agitata crepufcula fylvæ.

Ite domum impafti, domino jam non vacat, agni,
Heu quam culta mihi priùs arva procacibus herbis
Involvuntur, et ipfa fitu feges alta fatifcit!
Innuba neglecto marcefcit et uva racemo,
Nec myrteta juvant; ovium quoque tædet, at illæ
Mœrent, inque fuum convertunt ora magiftrum.

Ite domum impafti, domino jam non vacat, agni.
Tityrus ad corylos vocat, Alphefibœus ad ornos,
Ad falices Aegon, ad flumina pulcher Amyntas,
" Hîc gelidi fontes, hîc illita gramina mufco,
" Hîc Zephyri, hîc placidas interftrepit arbutus undas;"
Ifta canunt furdo, frutices ego nactus abibam.

Ite domum impafti, domino jam non vacat, agni.
Mopfus ad hæc, nam me redeuntem forte notârat,
(Et callebat avium linguas, et fidera Mopfus)
Thyrfi quid hoc? dixit, quæ te coquit improba bilis?
Aut te perdit amor, aut te malè fafcinat aftrum,
Saturni grave fæpe fuit paftoribus aftrum,
Intimaque obliquo figit præcordia plumbo.

Ite domum impafti, domino jam non vacat, agni.
Mirantur nymphæ, et quid te, Thyrfi, futurum eft?
Quid tibi vis? aiunt, non hæc folet effe juventæ
Nubila frons, oculique truces, vultufque feveri,
Illa choros, lufufque leves, et femper amorem
Jure petit; bis ille mifer qui ferus amavit.

Ite domum impafti, domino jam non vacat, agni.
Venit Hyas, Dryopéque, et filia Baucidis Aegle,
Docta modos, citharæque fciens, fed perdita faftu,
Venit Idumanii Chloris vicina fluenti;
Nil me blanditiæ, nil me folantia verba,
Nil me, fi quid adeft, movet, aut fpes ulla futuri.

Ite domum impafti, domino jam non.vacat, agni.
Hei mihi quam fimiles ludunt per prata juvenci,
Omnes unanimi fecum fibi lege fodales!
Nec magis hunc alio quifquam fecernit amicum
Dè grege, fic denfi veniunt ad pabula thoes,
Inque vicem hirfuti paribus junguntur onagri;
Lex eadem pelagi, deferto in littore Proteus
Agmina phocarum numerat; vilifque volucrum
Paffer habet femper quicum fit, et omnia circum
Farra libens volitat, ferò fua tecta revifens,
Quem fi fors letho objecit, feu milvus adunco
Fata tulit, roftro, feu ftravit arundine foffor,
Protinus ille alium focio petit inde volatu.
Nos durum genus, et diris exercita fatis
Gens homines aliena animis, et pectore difcors,
Vix fibi quifque parem de millibus invenit unum,
Aut fi fors dederit tandem non afpera votis,
Illum inopina dies, quâ non fperaveris horâ
Surripit, æternum linquens in fæcula damnum.

Ite domum impafti, domino jam non vacat, agni.
Heu quis me ignotas traxit vagus error in oras
Ire per aëreas rupes, Alpemque nivofam!
Ecquid erat tanti Romam vidiffe fepultam,
(Quamvis illa foret, qualem dum viferet olim,
Tityrus ipfe fuas et oves et rura reliquit;)
Ut te tam dulci poffem caruiffe fodale,
Poffem tot maria alta, tot interponere montes,
Tot fylvas, tot faxa tibi, fluviofque fonantes!
Ah certè extremùm licuiffet tangere dextram,
Et bene compofitos placidè morientis ocellos,
Et dixiffe, " vale, noftri memor ibis ad aftra."
   Ite domum impafti, domino jam non vacat, agni.
Quamquam etiam veftri nunquam meminiffe pigebit,
Paftores Thufci, Mufis operata juventus,
Hic Charis, atque Lepos; et Thufcus tu quoque Da-
      mon,
Antiquâ genus unde petis Lucumonis ab urbe.
O ego quantus eram, gelidi cum ftratus ad Arni
Murmura, populeumque nemus, quà mollior herba,
Carpere nunc violas, nunc fummas carpere myrtos,
Et potui Lycidæ certantem audire Menalcam.
Ipfe etiam tentare aufus fum, nec puto multùm
Difplicui, nam funt et apud me munera veftra
Fifcellæ, calathique, et cerea vincla cicutæ:
Quin et noftra fuas docuerunt nomina fagos
Et Datis, et Francinus, erant et vocibus ambo
Et ftudiis noti, Lydorum fanguinis ambo.
   Ite domum impafti, domino jam non vacat, agni.
Hæc mihi tum læto dictabat rofcida luna,
Dum folus teneros claudebam cratibus hœdos.

Ah quoties dixi, cùm te cinis ater habebat,
Nunc canit, aut lepori nunc tendit retia Damon,
Vimina nunc texit, varios fibi quod fit in ufus!
Et quæ tum facili fperabam mente futura
Arripui voto levis, et præfentia finxi,
Heus bone numquid agis? nifi te quid forte retardat,
Imus? et argutâ paulùm recubamus in umbrâ,
Aut ad aquas Colni, aut ubi jugera Caffibelauni?
Tu mihi percurres medicos, tua gramina, fuccos,
Helleborúmque, humiléfque crocos, foliúmque hya-
    cinthi,
Quafque habet ifta palus herbas, artefque medentûm.
Ah pereant herbæ, pereant artefque medentûm,
Gramina, poftquam ipfi nil profecêre magiftro.
Ipfe etiam, nam nefcio quid mihi grande fonabat
Fiftula, ab undecimâ jam lux eft altera noĉte,
Et tum forte novis admôram labra cicutis,
Diffiluere tamen ruptâ compage, nec ultra
Ferre graves potuere fonos, dubito quoque ne fim
Turgidulus, tamen et referam, vos cedite, fylvæ.
    Ite domum impafti, domino jam non vacat, agni.
Ipfe ego Dardanias Rutupina per æquora puppes
Dicam, et Pandrafidos regnum vetus Inogeniæ,
Brennúmque Arvigarúmque duces, prifcúmque Beli-
    num,
Et tandem Armoricos Britonum fub lege colonos;
Tum gravidam Arturo fatali fraude Iögernen,
Mendaces vultus, affumptaque Gorlöis arma,
Merlini dolus. O mihi tum fi vita fuperfit,
Tu procul annofa pendebis, fiftula, pinu
Multùm oblita mihi, aut patriis mutata Camœnis

Brittonicum ſtrides, quid enim? omnia non licet uni
Non ſperâſſe uni licet omnia, mi ſatis ampla
Merces, et mihi grande decus (ſim ignotus in ævum
Tum licet, externo penituſque inglorius orbi)
Si me flava comas legat Uſa, et potor Alauni,
Vorticibuſque frequens Abra, et nemus omne Treantæ,
Et Thameſis meus ante omnes, et fuſca metallis
Tamara, et extremis me diſcant Orcades undis.
　　Ite domum impaſti, domino jam non vacat, agni.
Hæc tibi ſervabam lentâ ſub cortice lauri,
Hæc, et plura ſimul, tum quæ mihi pocula Manſus,
Manſus, Chalcidicæ non ultima gloria ripæ,　.
Bina dedit, mirum artis opus, mirandus et ipſe,
Et circum gemino cælaverat argumento:
In medio rubri maris unda, et odoriferum ver,
Littora longa Arabum, et ſudantes balſama ſylvæ,
Has inter Phœnix, divina avis, unica terris
Cæruleûm fulgens diverſicoloribus alis
Auroram vitreis ſurgentem reſpicit undis.
Parte alia polus omnipatens, et magnus Olympus,
Quis putet? hic quoque Amor, pictæque in nube pha-
　　　retræ,
Arma coruſca faces, et ſpicula tincta pyropo;
Nec tenues animas, pectúſque ignobile vulgi
Hinc ferit, at circûm flammantia lumina torquens,
Semper in erectum ſpargit ſua tela per orbes
Impiger, et pronos nunquam collimat ad ictus,
Hinc mentes ardere ſacræ, formæque deorum.
　　Tu quoque in his, nec me fallit ſpes lubrica, Damon,
Tu quoque in his certè es, nam quò tua dulcis abiret
Sanctáque ſimplicitas, nam quò tua candida virtus?

Nec te Lethæo fas quæfiviffe fub orco,
Nec tibi conveniunt lacrymæ, nec flebimus ultrà,
Ite procul lacrymæ, purum colit æthera Damon,
Æthera purus habet, pluvium pede reppulit arcum;
Heroúmque animas inter, divófque perennes,
Æthereos haurit latices et gaudia potat
Ore facro. Quin tu, cœli poft jura recepta,
Dexter ades, placidúfque fave quicunque vocaris,
· Seu tu nofter eris Damon, five æquior audis
Diodotus, quo te divino nomine cunéti
Cœlicolæ nôrint, fylvifque vocabere Damon.
, Quòd tibi purpureus pudor, et fine labe juventus
Grata fuit, quòd nulla tori libata voluptas,
En etiam tibi virginei fervantur honores;
Ipfe caput nitidum cinétus rutilante corona,
Lætáque frondentis geftans umbracula palmæ
Æternum perages immortales hymenæos;
Cantus ubi, choreifque furit lyra mifta beatis,
Fefta Sionæo bacchantur et Orgia thyrfo.

JAN. 23, 1646.

AD

# JOANNEM ROUSIUM,

OXONIENSIS ACADEMIÆ BIBLIOTHECARIUM.

DE LIBRO POEMATUM AMISSO, QUEM ILLE SIBI DE-
NUO MITTI POSTULABAT, UT CUM ALIIS
NOSTRIS IN BIBLIOTHECA PUB-
LICA REPONERET, ODE.

STROPHE 1.

GEMELLE cultu fimplici gaudens liber,
Fronde licet geminâ,
Munditiéque nitens non operofâ,
Quam manus attulit
Juvenilis olim,
Sedula tamen haud nimii poetæ;
Dum vagus Aufonias nunc per umbras,
Nunc Britannica per vireta lufit
Infons populi, barbitóque devius
Indulfit patrio, mox itidem pectine Daunio
Longinquum intonuit melos
Vicinis, et humum vix tetigit pede;

ANTISTROPHE.

Quis te, parve liber, quis te fratribus
Subduxit reliquis dolo?
Cum tu miffus ab urbe,
Docto jugiter obfecrante amico,

Illuſtre tendebas iter
Thameſis ad incunabula
Cærulei patris,
Fontes ubi limpidi
Aonidum, thyaſuſque ſacer
Orbi notus per immenſos
Temporum lapſus redeunte cœlo,
Celeberque futurus in ævum;

### STROPHE II.

Modò quis deus, aut editus deo
Priſtinam gentis miſeratus indolem
(Si ſatis noxas luimus priores,
Mollique luxu degener otium)
Tollat nefandos civium tumultus,
Almaque revocet ſtudia ſanctus,
Et relegatas ſine ſede Muſas
Jam penè totis finibus Angligenûm;
Immundaſque volucres
Unguibus imminentes
Figat Apollineâ pharetrâ,
Phinéamque abigat peſtem procul amne Pegaſéo.

### ANTISTROPHE.

Quin tu, libelle, nuntii licet malâ
Fide, vel oſcitantiâ
Semel erraveris agmine fratrum,
Seu quis te teneat ſpecus,
Seu qua te latebra, forſan unde vili
Callo teréris inſtitoris inſulſi,
Lætare felix, en iterum tibi
Spes nova fulget, poſſe profundam
Fugere Lethen, vehique ſuperam
In Jovis aulam, remige pennâ;

Nam te Roüfius fui
Optat peculî, numcróque jufto
Sibi pollicitum queritur abeffe,
Rogatque venias ille, cujus inclyta
Sunt data virûm monumenta curæ:
Téque adytis etiam facris
Voluit reponi, quibus et ipfe præfidet
Æternorum operum cuftos fidelis,
Quæftorque gazæ nobilioris,
Quàm cui præfuit Iön,
Clarus Erechtheides,
Opulenta dei per templa parentis,
Fulvofque tripodas, donaque Delphica,
Ion Aĉtææ genitus Creufâ.

Ergo, tu vifere lucos
Mufarum ibis amœnos;
Dianique Phœbi rurfus ibis in domum,
Oxoniâ quam valle colit
Delo pofthabitâ,
Bifidòque Parnaffi jugo:
Ibis honeftus,
Poftquam egregiam tu quoque fortem
Naĉtus abis, dextri prece follicitatus amici.
Illic legéris inter alta nomina
Authorum, Graiæ fimul et Latinæ
Antiqua gentis lumina, et verum decus.

Vos tandem haud vacui mei labores,
Quicquid hoc fterile fudit ingenium,
Jam ferò placidam fperare jubeo

Perfunctam invidiâ requiem, fedefque beatas
Quas bonus Hermes,
Et tutela dabit folers Roüfi,
Quo neque lingua procax vulgi penetrabit, atque
    longè
Turba legentum prava faceffet;
At ultimi nepotes,
Et cordatior ætas
Judicia rebus æquiora forfitan
Adhibebit integro finu.
Tum, livore fepulto,
Si quid meremur fana pofteritas fciet
Roüfio favente.


Ode tribus conftat Strophis, totidémque Antiftro-
phis, unâ demum Epodo claufis, quas, tametfi omnes
nec verfuum numero, nec certis ubique colis exactè
refpondeant, ita tamen fecuimus, commodè legendi
potiùs, quàm ad antiquos concinendi modos rationem
fpectantes. Alioquin hoc genus rectiùs fortaffe dici
monoftrophicum debuerat. Metra partim funt κατα
σχεσιν, partim απολελυμενα. Phaleucia quæ funt,
Spondæum tertio loco bis admittunt, quod idem in
fecundo loco Catullus ad libitum fecit.

AD

# CHRISTINAM,

SUECORUM REGINAM NOMINE CROMWELLI.

BELLIPOTENS Virgo, feptem Regina Trionum,
  Chriftina, Arɛtoï lucida ftella poli,
Cernis quas merui dura fub caffide rugas,
  Utque fenex armis impiger ora tero;
Invia fatorum dum per veftigia nitor,
  Exequor et populi fortia juffa manu.
Aft tibi fubmittit frontem reverentior umbra;
  Nec funt hi vultus Regibus ufque truces.

# SELECT NOTES

## PARADISE REGAINED.

In order to introduce to more general notice this *elegant* Poem, which has been ftrangely neglected, though it abounds with MORAL inftruction peculiarly adapted to the juvenile age, it has been judged proper to infert NOTES upon it, illuftrative of its Beauties, and explanatory of its more difficult or obfcure paffages.

The limits of our volume will not allow us to *continue* the comment through the other Poems, nor is it indeed fo requifite, as their Beauties are generally felt, and as they are read and ftudied by thofe who pafs over the PARADISE REGAINED with a careleffnefs bordering on contempt.

# PARADISE REGAINED*.

## BOOK I.

"MILTON,* " fays Mr. Hayley, " had already executed one ex-
" tenſive divine poem, peculiarly diſtinguiſhed by richneſs and ſub-
" limity of deſcription: in framing a ſecond he naturally wiſhed to
" vary its effect; to make it rich in moral ſentiment, and ſublime in
" its mode of unfolding the higheſt wiſdom that man can learn; for
" this purpoſe it was neceſſary to keep all the ornamental parts of the
" poem in due ſubordination to the precept. This delicate and difficult
" point is accompliſhed with ſuch felicity, they are blended together
" with ſuch exquiſite harmony and mutual aid, that, inſtead of ar-
" raigning the plan, we might rather doubt if any poſſible change could
" improve it. Aſſuredly there is no poem of an epic form, where the
" ſublimeſt moral is ſo forcibly and ſo abundantly united to poetical
" delight: the ſplendor of the poet does not blaze indeed ſo intenſely
" as in his larger production; here he reſembles the Apollo of Ovid,
" ſoftening his glory in ſpeaking to his ſon, and avoiding to dazzle the
" fancy that he may deſcend into the heart."

*Hayley's Life of Milton.*

" To cenſure the PARADISE REGAINED, becauſe it does not more
" reſemble the PARADISE LOST, is hardly leſs abſurd, than it would
" be to condemn the Moon for not being a Sun, inſtead of admiring
" the two different luminaries, and feeling that both the greater and the
" leſs are equally the work of the ſame divine and inimitable power."

*Ibid.*

*line 1. page 3. I, who ere while the happy garden ſung*
*By one man's diſobedience loſt,—*]

The ſun of Milton's genius appears to be ſetting in this poem; but
the ſunſet is a beautiful object, when the evening clouds are tinged with
gold and purple. *Knox.*

*l.* 3. *p.* 3. *Recover'd Paradise*—]

It may feem a little odd that Milton fhould impute the recovery of Paradife to this fhort fcene of our Saviour's life upon earth, and not ra-ther extend it to his agony, crucifixion, &c. But the reafon no doubt was, that Paradife, *regained* by our Saviour's refifting the temptations of Satan, might be a better contraft to Paradife, *left* by our firft parents too eafily yielding to the fame feducing fpirit. Befides he might, very probably, and indeed very reafonably, be apprehenfive, that a fubject, fo extenfive as well as fublime, might be too great a burden for his de-clining conftitution, and a tafk too long for the fhort term of years he could then hope for. Even in his Paradife Loft he expreffes his fears, left he had begun too late, and left *an age too late, or cold climate, or years, fhould have damp'd his intended wing*; and furely he had much greater caufe to dread the fame now, and to be very cautious of launch-ing out too far.               *Thyer.*

*l.* 8. *p.* 3. ———— *who ledft this glorious eremite*
         *Into the defert,*—]

It is faid, Mat. iv. 1. *Then was Jefus led up of the fpirit into the wildernefs, to be tempted of the devil.* And from the Greek original ερημ**◉** the defert, and ερημιτης an inhabitant of the defert, is rightly formed the word *eremite*; which was ufed before by Milton in his Pa-dife Loft, iii. 474.

And by Fairfax, in his tranflation of Taffo, Cant. 11. St. 4.

And in Italian, as well as in Latin, there is *eremita,* which the French, and we after them, contract into *hermite, hermit.*    *Newton.*

*l.* 11. *p.* 3. ————————————*infpire,*
        *As thou art wont, my prompted fong, elfe mute,*]

In the very fine opening of the NINTH book of the PARADISE LOST, Milton thus fpeaks of *the infpiration of the mufe:*

> If anfwerable ftill I can obtain
>
> Of my celeftial patronefs, who deigns
>
> Her nightly vifitation, unimplor'd,
>
> And DICTATES TO ME SLUMBERING, OR INSPIRES
>
> EASY MY UNPREMEDITATED VERSE.

So alfo in his invocation of *Urania,* at the beginning of the SEVENTH book.

More fafe I fing with mortal voice, unchang'd
To hoarfe or mute, though fall'n on evil days,
On evil days though fall'n, and evil tongues;
In darkneſs, and with dangers compaſs'd round,
And folitude; yet not alone, WHILE THOU
VISIT'ST MY SLUMBERS NIGHTLY, OR WHEN MORN
PURPLES THE EAST; ftill govern thou my fong,
URANIA.——

And in the introduction to the fecond book of *The Reafon of Church
Government urged againſt Prelacy,* where he promiſes to undertake
fomething, he yet knows not what, that may be of uſe and honour to
his country, he adds, " This is not to be obtained but by devout prayer
" to that Eternal Spirit, who can enrich with all utterance and know-
" ledge, and fends out his Seraphim, with the hallowed fire of his
" altar, to touch and purify whom he pleaſes."——Here then we fee,
that Milton's invocations of the Divine Spirit were not merely *exordia
pro formâ.*——Indeed his profe works are not without their invocations.

12. *p.* 3. ———————— *my prompted fong, elſe mute,*]
Milton's third wife, who furvived him many years, related of him,
that he uſed to compofe his poetry chiefly in winter; and on his waking in a morning would make her write down fometimes twenty or
thirty verfes. Being afked, whether he did not often read Homer and
Virgil, fhe underſtood it as an imputation upon him for ftealing from
thoſe authors, and anfwered with eagerneſs, " he ftole from nobody
" but the Mufe who infpired him;" and, being afked by a lady prefent who the Mufe was, replied, " IT WAS GOD's GRACE AND THE
" HOLY SPIRIT THAT VISITED HIM NIGHTLY."
*Newton's Life of Milton.*

Mr. Richardfon alfo fays, that " Milton would fometimes lie awake
" whole nights, but not a verfe could he make; and on a fudden his
" poetical fancy would rufh upon him with an *impetus* or *æſtrum.*"
*Johnfon's Life of Milton.*

14. *p.* 3. *With profperous wing full fumm'd,*——]
We have the like expreſſion in Paradife Loſt, vii. 421.

'They SUMM'D their pens ——

It is a term in falconry. A hawk is faid to be *full fumm'd*, when all his feathers are grown, when he wants nothing of the *fum* of his feathers, *cui nihil de* SUMMA *pennarum deeft*, as Skinner fays.

*Newton.*

44. *p.* 4. *O ancient powers of air, and this wide world,*]

So the devil is called in fcripture *the prince of the power of the air*, Eph. ii. 2. and evil fpirits are termed the *rulers of the darknefs of this world*, Eph. vi. 12. Satan here fummons a council, and opens it as he did in the PARADISE LOST: but here is not that copioufnefs and variety which is in the other; here are not different fpeeches and fentiments adapted to the different charaΩers; it is a council without a debate; Satan is the only fpeaker. And the author, as if confcious of this defeΩ, has artfully endeavoured to obviate the objeΩion, by faying that their danger

——— admits no long debate,
But muft with fomething fudden be oppos'd.

And afterwards,

——— no time was then
For long indulgence to their fears or grief.

The true reafon is, he found it impoffible to exceed or equal the fpeeches in his former council, and therefore has affigned the beft reafon he could for not making any in this. *Newton.*

83. *p.* 6. *A perfeΩ dove defcend,*—]

Vida, like Milton, defcribes the Holy Ghoft defcending as a " perfeΩ dove;"

Protinus aurifluo Jordanes gurgite fulfit,
Et fuperûm vafto intonuit domus alta fragore :
Infuper et cœli claro delapfa columba eft
Vertice per purum, candenti argentea pluma
Terga, fed auratis circum et rutilantibus alis :
Jamque viam late fignans fuper aftitit ambos,
Cœleftique aurâ pendens afflavit utrumque.
Vox fimul et magni rubrâ genitoris ab æthrâ
Audita eft, nati dulcem teftantis amorem.

*Chriftiad.* iv. 214.

*l.* 131. *p.* 7. *Thou and all Angels converfant on earth,*
    *With man or men's affairs,—*]

This feems to be taken from the verfes attributed to Orpheus;

Αγγελοι, ὁισι μεμηλε βροτοις ὡς παντα τελειται.

*Newton.*

*l.* 168. *p.* 8. *So fpake the eternal Father, and all Heaven*
    *Admiring flood a fpace,—*]

We cannot but take notice of the great art of the poet in fetting forth
the dignity and importance of his fubject.   He reprefents all beings as
interefted one way or other in the event.   A council of devils is fum-
moned; an affembly of angels is held.   Satan is the fpeaker in the one;
the Almighty in the other.   Satan expreffes his diffidence, but ftill re-
folves to make trial of this Son of God; the Father declares his purpofe
of proving and illuftrating his Son.   The infernal crew are diftracted
and furprifed with deep difmay; all Heaven ftands a while in admiration.   The fiends are filent through fear and grief; the angels burft
forth into finging with joy and the affured hopes of fuccefs.   And their
attention is thus engaged, the better to engage the attention of the
reader.                                                *Newton.*

*l.* 182. *p.* 9. ——————————— *vigils tun'd:*]

This is a very uncommon expreffion, and not eafy to be underftood,
unlefs we fuppofe, that by *vigils* the poet means thofe fongs which they
fung while they kept their watches.   Singing of hymns is their manner of keeping their *wakes* in Heaven.   And I fee no reafon why their
evening fervice may not be called *vigils,* as their morning fervice is
called *matins.*                                          ·*Newton.*

*l.* 189. *p.* 9. *One day walk'd forth alone, the Spirit leading,*
    · *And his deep thoughts,—*]

In what a fine light does Milton here place that text of Scripture,
where it is faid that *Jefus was led up of the Spirit into the wildernefs!*
He adheres ftrictly to the infpired hiftorian, and at the fame time gives
it a turn·which is extremely poetical.                      *Thyer.*

*l.* 201. *p.* 9. *When I was yet a child, no childifh play*
    *To me was pleafing';—*]

How finely and confiftently does Milton here imagine the youthful
meditations of our Saviour!   How different from, and fuperiour to, that

superftitious trumpery, which one meets with in the *Evangelium In-*
*fantiæ,* and other fuch apocryphal trafh! Vid. Fabricii Cod. Apoc.
N. Teft.                                                    *Thyer.*

He feems to allude to Callimachus, who fays elegantly of young Jupiter, Hymn. in Jov. 56.

    Οξυ δ' αναϹησας, ταχινοι δε τοι ηλθον ιυλοι.
    Αλλ' ετι παιδνῷ εων εφρασσαο παντα τελεια.

    Swift was thy growth, and early was thy bloom,
    But earlier wifdom crown'd thy infant days.

                                 *Jortin.*

Henry Stephens's tranflation of the latter verfe is very much to our
purpofe.

    Verum ætate puer, digna es meditatus adulta:

or rather his more paraphraftical tranflation,

    Verum ætate puer, puerili haud more folebas
    Ludere; fed jam tum tibi feria cunĉta placebant,
    Digna ætate animus jam tum volvebat adulta.

And Pindar in like manner praifes Demophilus. Pyth. Od. iv. 501.
Κεινῷ γαρ εν παισι νεῷ, εν δι βυλαις πρεσϹυς. Our author might
allude to thefe paffages, but he certainly did allude to the words of the
Apoftle, 1 Cor. xiii. 11. only inverting the thought, *When I was a*
*child, I fpake as a child, &c.*                           *Newton.*

  *l.* 218. *p.* 10. *Then to fubdue and quell, o'er all the earth,*
             *Brute violence, and proud tyrannic power,* ]

    Thus in his Samfon Agoniftes,

        O! how comely it is, and how reviving
        To the fpirits of JUST men long OPPRESS'D,
        When God into the hands of their DELIVERER
        Puts INVINCIBLE might
        To quell the mighty of the earth, the OPPRESSOR,
        The brute and boifterous force of VIOLENT men
        Hardy and induftrious to fupport
        TYRANNIC POWER, but raging to purfue
        The RIGHTEOUS and all fuch as honour TRUTH;
        He all their ammunition
        And feats of war defeats,

With PLAIN HEROIC MAGNITUDE OF MIND
And celeſtial vigour arm'd.——

*l.* 221. *p.* 10. *Yet held it more humane, more heavenly, firſt, &c.*]

The true ſpirit of toleration breathes in theſe lines, and the ſentiment is very fitly put into the mouth of him, who *came not to deſtroy
men's lives, but to ſave them.* *Newton.*

*l.* 222. *p.* 10. *By winning words to conquer willing hearts,*]
Virgil GEORG. iv. 561.

—————— victorque volentes

Per populos dat jura ———————

which expreſſion of Virgil ſeems to be taken from Xenophon, Oecono-
mic. xxi. 12. Ου γαρ πανυ μοι δοκει ολον τυὶι το αγαθον ανθρωπινον
ειναι, αλλα θειον, το εθελονίων αρχειν. *Jortin.*

*l.* 227. *p.* 10. —————————— *my mother ſoon perceiving*
————————————— *inly rejoic'd,*]
Virgil, ÆN. i. 502.

Latonæ TACITUM pertentant gaudia pectus. *Jortin.*

*l.* 255. *p.* 11. *Juſt Simeon and prophetic Anna,—*]

It may not be improper to remark how ſtrictly our author adheres
to the Scripture hiſtory, not only in the particulars which he relates,
but alſo in the very epithets which he affixes to the perſons; as here
*Juſt Simeon,* becauſe it is ſaid, Luke ii. 25, *and the ſame man was juſt:*
and *prophetic Anna,* becauſe it is ſaid, Luke ii. 36, *and there was one
Anna a propheteſs.* The like accuracy may be obſerved in all the reſt
of this ſpeech. *Newton.*

*l.* 262. *p.* 11. ——— *and ſoon found of whom they ſpake
I am—*]

The Jews thought that the Meſſiah, when he came, would be without all power and diſtinction, and *unknown even to himſelf,* till Elias
had anointed and declared him. Χριϲ☉ δε ει και γεγενηίαι, και ιϲι
πυ, αγνωϲ☉ ιϲι, και υδε αυτος σω ἑαυτον επιϲαται, υδε ιχει δυναμιν
τινα, μεχρις αν ελθεν Ηλιας χριση αυτον, και φανερον παϲι ποιηση.
Juſt. Mart. Dial. cum Tryph. p. 266. Ed. Col. *Calton.*

*l.* 294. *p.* 12. *So ſpake our Morning Star—*]

So our Saviour is called in the Revelation, xxii. 16, *the bright and
morning ſtar.* *Newton.*

And thus Spenſer, in his HYMN OF HEAVENLY LOVE,

> O bleſſed well of love ! O flowre of grace !
> O glorious MORNING STAR ! O lamp of light !
> Moſt lively image of thy Father's face,
> Eternal king of glory, Lord of might,
> Meek Lamb of God before all worlds behight,
> How can we thee requite for all this good ?
> Or what can prize that thy moſt precious blood ?

*l. 302. p. 13. Full forty days he paſſ'd, whether on hill*
*Sometimes, anon on ſhady vale, &c.*]

Here the Poet of Paradiſe Loſt breaks out in his meridian ſplendour. There is ſomething particularly piƈtureſque in this deſcription.

*l. 312. p. 13. The fiery ſerpent fled and noxious worm,*]

The word *worm*, though joined with the epithet noxious, may give too low an idea to ſome readers; but, as we obſerved upon the Paradiſe Loſt, IX. 1068, where Satan is called *falſe worm*, it is a general name for the reptile kind; and a ſerpent is called the mortal worm, by Shakeſpear, 2 HENRY SIXTH, Aƈt III. *Newton.*

*l. 458. p. 18. ——————— Delphos,—*]

In the famous controverſy about ancient and modern learning, Mr. Wotton reproves Sir William Temple for putting *Delphos* for *Delphi* every where in his Eſſays. Mr. Boyle juſtifies it, and ſays that it is uſed by all the fineſt writers of our tongue, and beſt judges of it, particularly Waller, Dryden, Creech, &c. If theſe authorities may juſtify Sir William Temple, they may alſo juſtify Milton; but certainly the true way of writing it is not *Delphos* in the accuſative caſe, but *Delphi* in the nominative. *Newton.*

# BOOK II.

*l. 1. p. 23. Mean while the new baptis'd, &c.—*]

The greatest, and indeed justest, objection to this Poem is the nar-
rowness of its plan, which, being confined to that single scene of our
Saviour's life on earth, his Temptation in the Desert, has too much
sameness in it, too much of the reasoning, and too little of the descrip-
tive part; a defect most certainly in an epic poem, which ought to
consist of a proper and happy mixture of the instructive and the de-
lightful. Milton was himself, no doubt, sensible of this imperfection,
and has therefore very judiciously contrived and introduced all the little digressions that could with any sort of propriety connect with his
subject, in order to relieve and refresh the reader's attention. The following conversation betwixt Andrew and Simon upon the missing of
our Saviour so long, with the Virgin's reflections on the same occasion,
and the council of the Devils how best to attack their enemy, are in-
stances of this sort, and both very happily executed in their respective
ways. The language of the former is cool and unaffected, correspond-
ing most exactly to the humble pious character of the speakers: that
of the latter is full of energy and majesty, and not inferiour to their
most spirited speeches in the Paradise Lost. *Thyer.*

*l. 42. p. 24. ——————— God of Israel,
Send thy Messiah forth, &c.*]

This sudden turn and breaking forth into prayer to God is beautiful. The prayer itself is conceived very much in the spirit of the
Psalms, and almost in the words of some of them. *Newton.*

*l. 153. p. 28. Set women in his eye, &c.*]

As this temptation is not mentioned in the Gospels, it could not with
any propriety have been proposed to our Saviour; it is much more fitly
made the subject of debate among the wicked spirits themselves. All
that can be said in praise of the power of beauty, and all that can be
alleged to depreciate it, is here summed up with greater force and ele-
gance, than I ever remember to have seen in any other author.
*Newton.*

*l.* 186. *p.* 29. ———————— *Califlo, Clymene,*
            *Daphne, or Semele, Antiopa,*
            Or *Amymone, Syrinx,*—]

All thefe miftreffes of the gods might have been furnifhed from
Ovid, who is faid to have been our Author's favourite Latin Poet. Indeed that he was fo at an early period of life, appears from Milton's
frequent imitations of him in his juvenile Latin Poems.—For *Califlo,*
fee Ovid. MET. ii. 409. et FAST. ii. 155.—For *Clymene,* the mother
of *Phaeton,* MET. i. *ad finem.*—*Daphne*; MET. i. 452.—*Semele*;
MET. iii. 253.—*Antiopa*; MET. vi. 110.—*Amymone*; EPIST. xix.
131. et 1. AMOR. x. 5.—*Syrinx*; MET. i. 690.

The ftory of Califlo is recorded alfo by Milton's favourite tragic poet
Euripides.

> Ω μαχαρ Αρκαδια πολι παρθενι
> Καλλιςοι, Διος 'α λιχεων επε-
> -ϛας, τετραβαμοσι γυιοις
> 'Ως πολυ ματρος εμας ελαχες πλεον.
>
> Euripid. HELEN. 381.

  Happy Califlo, thou Arcadian nymph,
  That didft afcend the couch of Jove; transform'd
  To a four-footed favage, far more bleft
  Art thou, than fhe to whom I owe my birth.
                                                  *Wodhull.*

And Semele is mentioned in his HYPPOLITUS, v. 456.

> 'Οσοι μεν ουν γραφας τι των παλαιτερων
> Εχουσιν, αυτοι τ' εισιν εν μουσαις αει,
> Ισασι μεν, Ζευς 'ως πόϊ' ηρασθη γαμων
> Σεμελης. ————————

They who with ancient writings have convers'd,
And ever dwell among the tuneful Nine,
Know how to Theban Semele's embrace
Flew amorous Jove. ————                         *Wodhull.*

The ftory of Antiopa, or Antiope, is recorded likewife by Proper-
tius, (L. iii. EL. 14.) a Poet whom (as Mr. Warton obferves) Milton
has occafionally imitated. Antiope is alfo mentioned in a Greek Epi-
gram, in the Anthologia, where four of Jupiter's principal amours,

and the difguifes under which he accomplifhed them, are recited with
the ufual Greek epigrammatic brevity.

Ζευς, Κυκνος, Ταυρος, ΣΑΤΥΡΟΣ, χρυσος δι' ερωτης

Ληδης, Ευρωπης, ΑΝΤΙΟΠΗΣ, Δαναης.      *Dunfter.*

*l.* 190. *p.* 29. *Apollo, Neptune, Jupiter, or Pan,*]

*Califto, Semele,* and *Antiopa,* were miftreffes to Jupiter; *Clymene*
and *Daphne* to *Apollo;* and *Syrinx* to *Pan.*—Both here and elfewhere
Milton confiders the gods of the heathens as demons or devils.    Thus,
in the Septuagint verfion of the Pfalms; Παντες οι θεοι των εθνων δαιμο-
νια. Pfalm xcvi. 5. (and likewife in the Vulgate Latin, *Quoniam
omnes Dii gentium dæmonia.)*    And the notion of the demons having
commerce with women in the fhape of the heathen gods is very ancient, and is exprefsly afferted by Juftin Martyr. *See* Apol. i. P. 10.
et 33. edit. Thirlbii.                                      *Newton.*

*l.* 190. *p.* 29. ——————————— *Pan,*
                *Satyr, or Faun, or Sylvan ?—*]

        Unlefs the goddefs that in rural fhrine

        Dwell'ft here with PAN, OR SYLVAN,—   COMUS, 267.

Milton notices all thefe rural demi-gods and their amours, in his
beautiful Latin Elegy, IN ADVENTUM VERIS.

*l.* 196. *p.* 29. *Remember that Pellean conqueror,*]

Alexander the Great was born at *Pella* in Macedonia: his continence and clemency to Darius's queen and daughters, and the other
Perfian ladies whom he took captive after the battle of Iffus, are commended by the hiftorians.    Tum quidem ita fe geffit, ut omnes ante
eum reges et continentia et clementia vincerentur. Virgines enim re-
gias excellentis formæ tam fanéte habuit, quam fi eodem quo ipfe pa-
rente genitæ forent: conjugem ejufdem, quam nulla ætatis fuæ pul-
chritudine corporis vicit, adeo ipfe non violavit, ut fummam adhi-
buerit curam, ne quis captivo corpori illuderet, &c. Quint. Curt.
lib. iii. cap. 9.    He was then a young conqueror, of about twenty-
three years of age, *a youth,* as Milton expreffes it.        *Newton.*

*l.* 199. *p.* 29. *How he firnam'd of Africa difmifs'd,*
                *In his prime youth, the fair Iberian maid.*]

The continence of Scipio Africanus at the age of twenty-four, and
his generofity in reftoring a beautiful Spanifh lady to her hufband and

friends, are celebrated by Polybius, Livy, Valerius Maximus, and various other authors.                                           *Newton.*

l. 214. *p.* 30. ———— *(as the zone of Venus once*
                    *Wrought that effect on Jove, so fables tell,)*]

Η, και απο ϛηθεσφιν ελυσατο κεϛον ιμανϊα,
Ποικιλον· ενθα δε οι θελκηρια πανϊα τετυκϊο·
Ενθ’ ενι μεν φιλοτης, εν δ’ ιμερος, εν δ’ οαριϛυς,
Παρφασις, ἡ τ’ εκλεψε νοον ϖυκα ϖερ φρονεονϊων.

                                              Iliad. xiv. 214.

She said. With awe divine the queen of love
Obey’d the sister and the wife of Jove :
And from her fragrant breast the zone unbrac’d,
With various skill and high embroidery grac’d.
In this was every art, and every charm,
To win the wisest, and the coldest warm :
Fond love, the gentle vow, the gay desire,
The kind deceit, the still-reviving fire,
Persuasive speech, and more persuasive sighs,
Silence that spoke, and eloquence of eyes.          *Pope.*

l. 215. *p.* 30. ——————————*so fables tell,*]

The words *so fables tell* look as if the Poet had forgot himself, and
spoke in his own person rather than in the character of Satan.
                                                        *Newton.*

l. 216. *p.* 30. ———— *one look from his majestic brow,*
                    *Seated as on the top of virtue’s hill,*]

Here is the construction that we often meet with in Milton : from
his majestic brow, that is, from the majestic brow *of him* seated as on
the top of virtue’s hill : and the expression of *virtue’s hill* was probably in allusion to the rocky eminence on which the virtues are placed
in the table of Cebes, or the arduous ascent up the hill to which virtue is represented pointing in the best designs of *the judgment of Hercules.*                                                    *Newton.*

Milton’s meaning here is best illustrated by a passage in Shakespeare ;
which most probably he had in his mind.—Hamlet, in the scene with
his mother, pointing to the picture of his father, says,

See what a GRACE was SEATED ON THAT BROW !

Hyperion's curls, the front of Jove himſelf;
An eye, like Mars to threaten or command, &c.

Thus alſo, in Love's Labour Lost,

What peremptory eagle-ſighted eye,
Dares look upon THE HEAVEN OF HER BROW,
That is not BLINDED BY HER MAJESTY?

Act III. Sc. 4.

*l. 266. p. 32. Him thought,—*]

We ſay now, and more juſtly, *he thought*; but *him thought* is of the ſame conſtruction as *me thought*, and is uſed by our old writers, as by Fairfax, Cant. 13. St. 40.

HIM THOUGHT he heard the ſoftly whiſtling wind.

*Newton.*

*l. 308. p. 33. The fugitive bond-woman, with her ſon
Outcaſt Nebaioth,—*]

Hagar, who fled from the face of her miſtreſs, Gen. xvi. 6, is therefore called a *fugitive*: her ſon was not a fugitive, but an *out-caſt*; ſo exact was our author in the uſe of his epithets.

*l. 313. p. 33. Native of Thebez,—*]

*Thebez* is the ſame as *Theſbe*, or *Thiſbe*, or *Tiſhbe*, the birth-place of the prophet Elijah. *Newton.*

*l. 313. p. 33. ————————— wandering here was fed*]

It appears that Milton conceived the wilderneſs, where Hagar wandered with her ſon, and where the Iſraelites were fed with manna, and where Elijah retreated from the rage of Jezebel, to be the ſame with the wilderneſs where our Saviour was tempted. And yet it is certain, that they were very different places; for the wilderneſs where Hagar wandered was *the wilderneſs of Beer-ſheba*, Gen. xxi. 14; and where the Iſraelites were fed with manna was *the wilderneſs of Sin*, Exod. xvi. 1; and where Elijah retreated was *in the wilderneſs, a day's journey from Beer-ſheba*, 1 Kings, xix. 4; and where our Saviour was tempted was *the wilderneſs near Jordan*. But our author conſiders all that tract of country as one and the ſame wilderneſs, though diſtinguiſhed by different names from the different places adjoining. *Newton.*

*l. 340. p. 34. A table richly ſpread, &c.*]

This temptation is not recorded in Scripture, but is however in-

vented with great confiftency, and very aptly fitted to the prefent condition of our Saviour.  This way of embellifhing his fubject is a privilege which every poet has a juft right to, provided he obferves harmony and decorum in his hero's character; and one may further add,
that Milton had in this particular place ftill a ftronger claim to an indulgence of this kind, fince it was a pretty general opinion among the
Fathers, that our Saviour underwent many more temptations than
thofe which are mentioned by the Evangelifts; nay, Origen goes fo far
as to fay, that he was every day, whilft he continued in the wildernefs,
attacked by a frefh one.  The beauties of this defcription are too obvious to efcape any reader of tafte.  It is copious, and yet expreffed
with a very elegant concifenefs.  Every proper circumftance is mentioned, and yet it is not at all clogged or incumbered, as is often the
cafe, with too tedious a detail of particulars.  It was a fcene entirely
frefh to our author's imagination, and nothing like it had before oc-
curred in his Paradife Loft, for which reafon he has been the more dif-
fufe, and laboured it with greater care, with the fame good judgment
that makes him in other places avoid expatiating on fcenes which he
had before defcribed.  In a word, it is in my opinion worked up with
great art and beauty, and plainly fhews the crudity of that notion
which fo much prevails among fuperficial readers, that Milton's genius was upon the decay when he wrote his Paradife Regained.

*Thyer.*

  The banquet here furnifhed by Satan, Bifhop Newton obferves, is
like that prepared by Armida for her lovers.  Taffo, C. x. 64.

> Appreftar fù l' herbetta, ov' è più denfa
>  L' ombra, e vicino al fuon de l'acque chiare,
> Fece di fculti vafi altera menfa,
> E ricca di vivande elette e care.
> Era quì ciò ch' ogni ftagion difpenfa,
> Ciò che dona la terra, ò manda il mare,
> Ciò che l' arte condifce, e cento belle
> Servivano al convito accorte ancelle.

> Under the curtain of the green-wood fhade,
> Befide the brook upon the velvet grafs,

In maſſy veſſel of pure ſilver made,
A banquet rich and coſtly furniſh'd was;
All beaſts, all birds beguil'd by fowler's trade,
All fiſh were there in floods or ſeas that paſs;
All dainties made by art : and at the table
An hundred virgins ſerv'd ———————    *Fairfax.*

In COMUS, where the Lady is tempted by the Enchanter, the ſcene is laid in " *a ſtately palace ſet out with all manner of delicioufneſs, ſoft* " *muſic, and tables ſpread with all dainties.*"

*l.* 343. *p.* 34. *In paſtry built*—]

The paſtry in the beginning of the laſt century was frequently of conſiderable magnitude and ſolidity. Of ſuch kind muſt have been the pye in which Jeoffrey Hudſon, afterwards King James's Dwarf, when eight years old was ſerved up to table at an entertainment given by the Duke of Buckingham. We may ſuppoſe this pye was not conſiderably larger than was uſual on ſuch occaſions, otherwiſe the joke would have loſt much of its effect from ſomething extraordinary being expected. A ſpecies of *mural* paſtry ſeems to have prevailed in ſome of the preceding centuries, when artificial repreſentations of caſtles, towers, &c. were very common at all great feaſts, and were called *ſuttleties, ſubtilties,* or *ſotilties.*—Leland, in his account of the entertainment at the inthronization of Archbiſhop Warham in 1504, (*Collectanea,* Vol. 6) mentions " a ſuttlety of three ſtages, with vanes and towres " embattled," and " a warner with eight towres embattled, and made " with *flowres*;" which poſſibly meant *made in paſtry.*—In the catalogue of the expences at this feaſt there is a charge for wax and ſugar, *in operatione de le ſotilties.* Probably the wax and ſugar were employed to render the paſte of flour more adheſive and tenacious, the better to ſupport itſelf when moulded into ſuch a variety of forms.

*l.* 344. *p.* 34. *Gris-amber-ſteam'd;*—]

Ambergris, or grey-amber, is eſteemed the beſt, and uſed in perfumes and cordials. A curious lady communicated the following remarks upon this paſſage to Mr. Peck, which we will here tranſcribe. " *Grey* amber is the amber our author here ſpeaks of, and melts like " butter. It was formerly a main ingredient in every concert for a " banquet; viz. to fume the meat with, and that whether boiled,

" roaſted, or baked; laid often on the top of a baked pudding; which
" laſt I have eat of at an old courtier's table. And I remember in an
" old chronicle there is much complaint of the nobilities being made
" ſick at Cardinal Wolſey's banquets, with rich ſcented cakes and
" diſhes moſt coſtly dreſſed with ambergris. I alſo recollect I once
" ſaw a little book writ by a gentlewoman of Queen Elizabeth's court,
" where ambergris is mentioned as the hautgout of that age. I fancy
" Milton tranſpoſed the word for the ſake of his verſe; to make it
" read more poetically." And Beaumont and Fletcher in the CUS-
TOM OF THE COUNTRY, Act III. Scene 2.

———————— Be ſure

The wines be luſty, high, and full of ſpirit,
And AMBER'D ALL.                                    *Newton.*

Mr. Warton, in his Note on COMUS, V. 863, cites ſeveral curious
paſſages, which ſhew that amber was formerly a favourite in cookery;
among others, one from Maſſinger's CITY MADAM, where " phea-
ſants DRENCH'D WITH AMBERGRIS" are ſpoken of as a prime
delicacy; and another from Marmion's ANTIQUARY, which mentions " a fat nightingale ſeaſoned with pepper and AMBERGRIS."

*l.* 346. *p.* 34. *And exquiſiteſt name,*—]

This alludes to that ſpecies of Roman luxury, which gave *exquiſite
names* to fiſh of exquiſite taſte, ſuch as that they called *cerebrum Jovis.*
They extended this even to a very capacious diſh, as that they called
*clypeum Minervæ.* The modern Italians fall into the ſame wanton-
neſs of luxurious impiety, as when they call their exquiſite wines by
the names of *lacrymæ Chriſti* and *lac Virginis.*          *Warburton.*

*l.* 346. *p.* 34. ———————— *for which was drain'd
Pontus, and Lucrine bay, and Afric coaſt.*]

The fiſh are brought to furniſh this banquet from all the different
parts of the world then known; from *Pontus,* or the Euxine Sea, in
Aſia; from the *Lucrine Bay,* in Italy; and from the *coaſt of Africa;*
all which places are celebrated for different kinds of fiſh by the authors
of antiquity.                                            *Newton.*

*l.* 349. *p.* 34. ———————— *that diverted Eve!*]

*Diverted* is here uſed in the Latin ſignification of diverto, *to turn
aſide.*                                                 *Newton.*

*l.* 353. *p.* 34. *Than Ganymed or Hylas* ;—]

Thefe were two moft beautiful youths, cup-bearers; Ganymede to
Jupiter, and Hylas to Hercules. *Newton.*

*l.* 359. *p.* 35. ——— *faery damfels met in foreft wide*
*By knights of Logres, or of Lyones,*
*Lancelot, or Pelleas, or Pellenore.*]

Sir *Lancelot, Pelleas,* and *Pellenore,* (the latter by the title of *King*
Pellenore) are *Perfons* in the old Romance of MORTE ARTHUR, or
*The Lyf of King Arthur, of his noble Knyghtes of the round table, and*
*in thende the dolorous deth of them all;* written originally in French, and
tranflated into Englifh by Sir Thomas Malleory, Knt. printed by
William Caxton, 1484.—From this old Romance, Mr. Warton (OB-
SERVATIONS ON SPENSER, Sect. 2) fhews that Spenfer borrowed
much. Sir Lancelot is there called of *Logris*; and Sir Triftram is
named of *Lyones,* under which title he appears alfo in the Faery Queen.
*Logris* is the fame with *Loegria* (according to the more fabulous hiftorians, and amongft them Milton), an old name for England. Hol-
linfhed calls it both Loegria and Logiers. In his *Hiftory of England,*
B. ii. 4. 5, having related the conqueft of our Ifland by Brute, or
Brutus, a Trojan, and his building the city of Troynovant, he thus
proceeds. " When Brutus had builded this city and brought it under
" his fubjection, he by the advice of his nobles commanded this ifle
" (which before hight Albion) to be called Britain, and the inhabi-
" tants Britons after his name, for a perpetual memorie that he was
" firft bringer of them into the land. In this mean while alfo he had
" by his wife three fons, the firft named Locrinus cr Locrine, the fe-
" cond Cambris or Camber, the third Albanactus or Albanact. Now
" when the time of his death drew neere, to the firft he betooke the
" government of that part of the land now known by the name of
" England, fo that the fame was long after called LOEGRIA or Lo-
" GIERS of this Locrinus," &c. &c.—The fame author, in his *De-*
*fcription of Britain,* inftead of *Loegria,* or *Logiers,* writes it LHOE-
GRES. The Title of his TWENTY-SECOND Chapter is, *after what*
*manner the fovereigntie of this ifle doth remaine to the princes of Lhoegres*
*or kings of England.* Spenfer, in his FAERY QUEEN, where he gives

the *Chronicle of the early Briton Kings from Brute to Uther's reign*, calls
it *Logris*.

> Locrine was left the fovereign lord of all,
> But Albanact had all the northern part
> Which of himfelf Albania he did call ;
> And Camber did poffefs the weftern quart
> Which Severn now from LOGRIS doth depart.
>
> B. II. C. x. 14.

*Lyones* was an old name for Cornwall, or at leaft for a part of that
county.   Camden (in his BRITANNIA), fpeaking of the *Land's End*,
fays, " the inhabitants are of opinion that this promontory did once
" reach farther to the weft, which the feamen pofitively conclude from
" the rubbifh they draw up.   The neighbours will tell you too, from
" a certain old tradition, that the land there drowned by the incurfions
" of the fea was called *Lioneffe*."   Sir Triftram of Lyones, or Lioneffe,
is well known to the readers of the old romances.   In the *French* tranflation of the ORLANDO INAMORATO of Boiardo,  he is termed *Trif-*
*tran de Leonnois,* although in the original he is only mentioned by the
fingle name of Triftran.   In the Orlando Inamorato alfo, among the
knights, who defend Angelica in the fortrefs of Albracca againft
Agrican, is Sir Hubert of Lyones, *Uburto dal Lione.*—Triftram, in his
account of himfelf in the FAERY QUEEN, B. VI. C. ii. 28, fays,

> And Triftram is my name, the only heir
> Of good king Meliogras, which did reign
> In Cornwall, till that he through life's defpair
> Untimely died. ———

He then relates how his Uncle feized upon the crown, whereupon
his Mother, conceiving great fears for her fon's perfonal fafety, deter-
mined to fend him into " fome foreign land."

> So, taking counfel of a wife man read,
> She was by him advis'd to fend me quite
> Out of the country wherein I was bred,
> The which the fertile LIONESSE is hight,
> Into the land of Faery. ———

Thefe particulars, Mr. Warton fhews, are drawn from the MORTE

ARTHUR, where it is faid, " there was a knight Meliodas, and he was
" Lord and King of the county of Lyones, and he wedded King Marke's
" fifter of Cornewale."—The iffue of this marriage was Sir Triftram.
Thefe Knights, he alfo obferves, are there often reprefented as meeting beautiful damfels in defolate forefts.—Indeed a foreft was almoft as
neceffary in an old romance as a valorous knight, or a beautiful damfel, whofe beauty and prowefs were feverally to be endangered and
proved by the difficulties and dangers they underwent amidft

> —— forefts and inchantments drear,
>
> PENSEROSO, 119.

Milton's later thoughts could not, we find, but rove at times where,
as he himfelf told us, " his younger feet wandered," when he " be-
" took him among thofe lofty fables and romances, which recount in
" folemn cantos the deeds of knighthood founded by our victorious
" kings, and from hence had in renowne over all Chriftendome."—
APOL. FOR SMECTYMN. p. 177. Profe Works. ed. Amft. 1698.

Sir Pelleas, " a very valorous knight of Arthur's round table," is
one of thofe who purfue the Blatant beaft, when, after having been con-
quered and chained up by Sir Calidore, it " broke its iron chain," and
again " ranged through the world." FAERY QUEEN, B. VI. C. xii.
39.                                                                             *Warton.*

*l. 365. p. 35.* ————————————— *Flora's earlieft fmells.*]
We may collect from many paffages in our Author's poems, that he
was habitually acquainted with the beauties of the early morning, and
particularly fenfible of them. Mr. Warton fays that he " has delineated
them with the lively pencil of a lover." *Note on* LYCIDAS, 27.

In his ARCADES, 56, he fpeaks of

> —— the ODOROUS BREATH OF MORN.

In the PARADISE LOST, iv. 641. he likewife alludes to the peculiar fragrance of flowers at " that fweet hour of prime;

> Sweet is the BREATH OF MORN, her rifing fweet—

And in the beginning of the FIFTH Book, Adam thus concludes the
fpeech in which he comforts Eve, on her waking in the morning, refpecting her troublefome dream;

> Be not difhearten'd then, nor cloud thofe looks,
> That wont to be more cheerful and ferene

2 D

> Than when fair morning first smiles on the
> world;
> And let us to our fresh employments rise
> Among the groves, the fountains, and the flowers,
> That open now their choicest bosom'd smells.

Philips, the imitator of our author, has most beautifully, and in a manner perfectly worthy of his master, copied the idea expressed in the last line:

> ———— when the kind early dew
> .Unlocks embosom'd odors, ————
>
> Cider, ii. 59.

But to revert to Milton, where he speaks more at large, and perfectly *con amore*;

> Now when as sacred light began to dawn
> In Eden on the humid flowers that breath'd
> Their morning incense, when all things that breathe
> From the earth's great altar send up silent praise
> To the Creator, and his nostrils fill
> With grateful smell, forth came the human pair,
> And join'd their vocal worship to the quire
> Of creatures wanting voice; that done, partake
> The season prime for sweetest scents and airs:
>
> Paradise Lost, ix. 192.

To the first part of which passage we may trace Mr. Gray, in a highly-finished line of his Elegy;

> . The breezy call of incense-breathing morn,———

We find a semblance of " Flora's earliest smells" in the following very picturesque and poetical stanza of Spenser.

> Thus being enter'd they behold around
> A large and spacious plain, on every side
> Strowed with pleasance, whose fair grassy ground
> Mantled with green, and goodly beautifide
> With all the ornaments of Flora's pride,
> Wherewith her mother Art, as half in scorn
> Of niggard Nature, like a pompous bride
> Did deck her, and too lavishly adorn,

WHEN FORTH FROM VIRGIN BOWER SHE COMES IN TH'
EARLY MORN.                         F. Q. B. II. 12. 50.
                                                *Warton.*

*l.* 423. *p.* 37. *What rais'd Antipater the Edomite,*
      *And his son Herod plac'd on Judah's throne,*]

This appears to be the fact from hiftory. When Jofephus intro-
duces Antipater upon the ftage, he fpeaks of him as abounding with great
riches. Φιλ☉ δε τις Υρκανε Ιδυμαι☉, Αντιπατρ☉ λεγομεν☉, πολ-
λων μεν ευποραν χρηματων, κ. τ. λ. Antiq. lib. xiv. cap. 1. And his
fon Herod was declared king of Judea by the favour of Mark Antony,
partly for the fake of the money which he promifed to give him;—
τα δε και υπο χρηματων ων αυτω Ηρωδης υπεσχετο δωσειν ει γενοιτο βα-
σιλευς. Ibid. cap. 14.                         *Newton.*

*l.* 439. *p.* 37. *Gideon, and Jephtha, and the shepherd lad,*]

Our Saviour is rightly made to cite his firft inftances from Scripture, and of his own nation, as being the beft known to him; but it
is with great art that the poet alfo fuppofes him not to be unacquainted
with heathen hiftory, for the fake of introducing a greater variety of
examples. Gideon faith of himfelf, *O my Lord, wherewith shall I fave
Ifrael? behold my family is poor in Manaffeh, and I am the leaft in my
father's houfe.* Judges, vi. 15. And Jephtha *was the fon of an harlot,*
and his brethren *thruft him out, and faid unto him, Thou shalt not inherit
in our father's houfe, for thou art the fon of a ftrange woman.* Judges, xi.
1, 2. And the exaltation of David from a fheep-hook to a fceptre is
very well known. *He chofe David alfo his fervant, and took him from
the sheep-folds: From following the ewes great with young, he brought
him to feed Jacob his people, and Ifrael his inheritance.* Pfalm lxxviii.
70, 71.                                         *Newton.*

*l.* 446. *p.* 37. *Quintius, Fabricius, Curius, Regulus,*]

*Quintius Cincinnatus* was twice invited from following the plough to
be conful and dictator of Rome; and after he had fubdued the enemy,
when the fenate would have enriched him with public lands and private contributions, he rejected all thefe offers, and retired again to his
cottage and old courfe of life. *Fabricius* could not be bribed by all the
large offers of king Pyrrhus to aid him in negotiating a peace with the
Romans: and yet he lived and died fo poor, that he was buried at the

public expenſe, and his daughters fortunes were paid out of the trea-
ſury. *Curius Dentatus* would not accept of the lands which the ſenate
had aſſigned him for the reward of his victories; and when the ambaſſadors of the Samnites offered him a large ſum of money as he was ſitting at the fire and roaſting turnips with his own hands, he nobly re-
fuſed to take it, ſaying that it was his ambition not to be rich, but to
command thoſe who were ſo. And *Regulus*, after performing many
great exploits, was taken priſoner by the Carthaginians, and ſent with
the ambaſſadors to Rome to treat of peace, upon oath to return to Car-
thage, if no peace or exchange of priſoners ſhould be agreed upon : but
was himſelf the firſt to diſſuade a peace, and choſe to leave his country, family, friends, every thing, and return a glorious captive to
certain tortures and death, rather than ſuffer the ſenate to conclude a
diſhonourable treaty. Our Saviour cites theſe inſtances of noble Romans in order of time, as he did thoſe of his own nation : and, as Mr.
Calton obſerves, the Romans in the moſt degenerate times were fond
of theſe (and ſome other like) examples of ancient virtue; and their
writers of all ſorts delight to introduce them : but the greateſt honour
that poetry ever did them is here, by the praiſe of the Son of God.

*Newton.*

*l.* 453. *p.* 38. *Extol not riches then, &c.*—]

Milton concludes this book and our Saviour's reply to Satan with a
ſeries of thoughts as noble and juſt, and as worthy of the ſpeaker, as
can poſſibly be imagined. I think one may venture to affirm, that,
as the Paradiſe Regained is a poem entirely moral and religious, the ex-
cellency of which does not conſiſt ſo much in bold figures and ſtrong
images, as in deep and virtuous ſentiments expreſſed with a becoming
gravity, and a certain decent majeſty, this is as true an inſtance of the
ſublime, as the battles of the Angels in the Paradiſe Loſt. *Thyer.*

*l.* 466. *p.* 38. *Yet he, who reigns within himſelf, &c.*—]

" The Paradiſe Regained," Mr. Hayley very juſtly obſerves, " is
" a poem that particularly deſerves to be recommended to ardent and
" ingenuous youth, as it is admirably calculated to inſpire that ſpirit
" of ſelf-command, which is, as Milton eſteemed it, the trueſt heroiſm,
" and the triumph of Chriſtianity."

*Life of Milton,* p. 126.

*l.* 476. *p.* 38. *Is yet more kingly* ;—]

In this fpeech concerning riches and realms, our poet has culled all the choiceft, fineft flowers out of the heathen poets and philofophers who have written upon thefe fubjects. It is not fo much their words, as their fubftance fublimed and improved. But here he foars above them, and nothing could have given him fo complete an idea of a divine teacher, as the life and character of our Bleffed Saviour.

*Newton.*

# BOOK III.

*l.* 13. *p.* 43. —————— *as the oracle*
*Urim and Thummim, thofe oraculous gems*
*On Aaron's breaft* ;—]

Aaron's breaft-plate was a piece of cloth doubled, of a fpan fquare, in which were fet in fockets of gold twelve precious ftones bearing the names of the twelve tribes of Ifrael engraven on them, which being fixed to the ephod, or upper veftment of the high prieft's robes, was worn by him on his breaft on all folemn occafions. In this breaft-plate the *Urim* and *Thummim*, fay the Scriptures, were put. And the learned Prideaux, after giving fome account of the various opinions concerning *Urim* and *Thummim*, fays it will be fafeft to hold, that the words *Urim* and *Thummim* meant only the divine virtue and power, given to the breaft-plate in its confecration, of obtaining an oraculous anfwer from God, whenever counfel was afked of him by the high-prieft with it on, in fuch manner as his words did direct; and that the names of *Urim* and *Thummim* were given hereto only to denote the clearnefs and perfection which thefe oracular anfwers always carried with them. For *Urim* fignifieth *light*, and *Thummim*, *perfection*. *Newton.*

*l.* 25. *p.* 44. —————— *glory the reward*]

Our Saviour having withftood the allurement of riches, Satan attacks him in the next place with the charms of glory. I have fometimes thought that Milton might poſſibly take the hint of thus connecting theſe two temptations from Spenſer, who, in his ſecond book of the Faery Queen, repreſenting the virtue of temperance under the character of Guyon, and leading him through various trials of his conſtancy, brings him to the houſe of riches, or *Mammon's delve*, as he terms it, and immediately after to the palace of glory, which he deſcribes, in his allegorical manner, under the figure of a beautiful woman called *Philotimè*.               .           · *Thyer.*

*l. 31. p. 44. Thy years are ripe, and over-ripe;—*]
Our Saviour's temptation was ſoon after his baptiſm; and he was baptized when he was *about thirty years of age.* Luke iii. 23. *Newton.*

*l. 71. p. 45. They err, who count it glorious to ſubdue*
        *By conqueſt far and wide, to over-run*
        *Large countries, and in field great battles win,*
        *Great cities by aſſault: &c.—*]

Here might be an alluſion intended to Lewis THE FOURTEENTH, who at this time began to diſturb Europe, and whoſe vanity and ambition were gratified by titles, ſuch as are here mentioned, from his numerous paraſites.

We may here compare PARADISE LOST, xi. 691.
      To overcome in battle, and ſubdue
      Nations, and bring home ſpoils with infinite
      Manſlaughter, ſhall be held the higheſt pitch
      Of human glory, and for glory done
      Of triumph, to be ſtyl'd great conquerors,
      Patrons of mankind, gods, and ſons of gods,
      Deſtroyers rightlier call'd, and plagues of men.
And again, ver. 789 of the ſame book.
      —— in acts of proweſs eminent
      And great exploits, but of true virtue void;
      Who having ſpilt much blood, and done much waſte,
      Subduing nations, and achiev'd thereby
      Fame in the world, high titles and rich prey,
      Shall change their courſe to pleaſure, eaſe, and ſloth. *Dunſter.*

*l. 74. p. 45. ——————— what do theſe worthies,*
        *But rob and ſpoil, &c.—*]

Thus Drummond, in his SHADOW OF THE JUDGMENT;

All live on earth by fpoil  *   *   *   *

*   *   *   *   *   *   *   *   *   *

Who moft can ravage, rob, ranfack, blafpheme,

Is held moft virtuous, hath a WORTHY's name:—

And Thucydides, defcribing the ancient inhabitants of Greece, fays,
" They betook themfelves to robbing under the direction of perfons by
" no means defpicable, and fpent their lives chiefly in plundering de-
" fencelefs towns and villages ; thefe practices being fo far from difcre-
" ditable, that they were attended with a certain degree of honour."—

ετραπεντο προς ληςειαν, ηγυμενων ανδρων μ των αδυνατωτατων  —   —
—  —  και προσπιπ]οντες πολεσιν ατειχιςοις, και κατα κωμας οικυμε-
ναις, ηρπαζεν, και τον πλειςον τυ βιυ εντευθεν εποιυν]ο· ουκ εχοντος πω
αισχυνην τουτυ τυ εργυ, φεροντος δε τι και δοξης μαλλον. L. i. C. 5.

Dunfter.

*l.* 75. *p.* 45. *But rob and fpoil, burn, flaughter, and inflave*
*Peaceable nations, neighb'ring, or remote,*
*Made captive,*—]

This defcription of the ravages of conquerors may have been copied
from fome of the accounts of the barbarous nations that invaded Rome.
Ovid defcribes the Getæ thus *fpoiling*, *robbing*, *flaying*, *enflaving*, and
*burning*.

Hoftis, equo pollens longèque volante fagittâ,
  Vicinam latè depopulatur humum.

Diffugiunt alii ; nullifque tuentibus agros
  Incuftoditæ diripiuntur opes ;

Ruris opes parvæ, pecus et ftridentia plauftra,
  Et quas divitias incola pauper habet.

Pars agitur vinctis poft tergum capta lacertis,
  Refpiciens fruftrà rura laremque fuum.

Pars cadit hamatis miferè confixa fagittis ;
  Nam volucri ferro tinctile virus ineft.

Quæ nequeunt fecum ferre aut abducere, perdunt :
  Et cremat infontes hoftica flamma cafas.

TRIST. iii. El. x. 55.
Dunfter.

*l. 78. p. 45.* ——— ————— *who leave behind*
          *Nothing but ruin—*]

Thus, Joel ii. 3. *The land is as the garden of Eden before them, and*
BEHIND THEM A DESOLATE WILDERNESS.

And Mr. Gray, in his BARD, has a fimilar defcription finely expreffed, where he fpeaks of the conquefts of Edward the Black Prince
in France.

          ——— What terrors round him wait!
Amazement in his van, with flight combin'd,
And Sorrow's faded form, and Solitude behind.

                                        *Dunfter.*

*l. 81. p. 46.* ——— ————— *and muft be titled Gods,*
          *Great Benefactors of mankind, Deliverers,*]

The fecond Antiochus king of Syria was called Antiochus ΘεΘ,
or *the God:* and the learned author De Epoch. Syro-Macedonum,
p. 109, fpeaks of a coin of Epiphanes infcribed Θευ Επιφανυς. The
Athenians gave Demetrius Poliorcetes, and his father Antigonus, the
titles of Ευεργεται, *Benefactors,* and Σωτηρες, *Deliverers.*

                                        *Calton.*

In Froelick's *Annales regum et rerum Syriæ* there are prints of five
different coins of Antiochus Epiphanes, with the infcription ΒΑΣΙΛΕ-
ΩΣ ΑΝΤΙΟΧΟΥ ΘΕΟΥ ΕΠΙΦΑΝΟΥΣ. The firft Antiochus was called
ΣΩΤΗΡ; as was the firft Ptolemy king of Egypt. Two of the Ptole-
mies affumed the title of ΕΥΕΡΓΕΤΗΣ.—Diodorus Siculus relates that
the Syracufans with one voice faluted Gelon by the titles of Benefac-
tor, Deliverer, and King.—μια φωνη παντας αποκαλειν ΕΥΕΡΓΕΤΗΝ,
και ΣΩΤΗΡΑ, και ΒΑΣΙΛΕΑ. L. ii. 26.

The title of ευεργετης, as affumed by tyrants, is referred to, Luke
xxii. 25.—*And they that exercife authority over them* ARE CALLED
BENEFACTORS.

When Demetrius Poliorcetes returne* from his expedition to Cor-
cyra, the Athenians received him with divine honours, and in their
hymns and choruffes celebrated him as " the only true God, for that
" all other Gods were afleep, or were gone abroad, or did not exift."—
ως αιη μονος θεος αληθινος, οι δε αλλοι καθευδουσιν, η απεδημησιν, η ουκ
εισιν. Demochares ap. Athenæn. L. 6.          *Dunfter.*

*l.* 84. *p.* 46. (*One is the son of Jove, of Mars the other,*)]

Alexander is particularly intended by the one, and Romulus by the other, who, though better than Alexander, founded his empire in the blood of his brother, and for his over-grown tyranny was at last destroyed by his own senate. *Newton.*

*l.* 109. *p.* 46. *Think not so slight of glory;—*]

There is nothing throughout the whole poem more expressive of the true character of the Tempter than this reply. There is in it all the falsehood of *the father of lies,* and the glozing subtlety of an insidious deceiver. The argument is false and unsound, and yet it is veiled over with a certain plausible air of truth. The poet has also, by introducing this, furnished himself with an opportunity of explaining that great question in divinity, why God created the world, and what is meant by that glory which he expects from his creatures. This may be no improper place to observe to the reader the author's great art in weaving into the body of so short a work so many grand points of the Christian theology and morality. *Thyer.*

*l.* 158. *p.* 48. *Reduc'd a province under Roman yoke,*]

Judæa was reduced to the form of a Roman province, in the reign of Augustus, by Quirinius, or Cyrenius, then governor of Syria; and Coponius, a Roman of the equestrian order, was appointed to govern it, under the title of Procurator. *Newton.*

*l.* 159. *p.* 48. ———————— *nor is always rul'd*
　　　　　　*With temperate sway—*]

The Roman government indeed was not always the most temperate. At this time Pontius Pilate was procurator of Judea, and, it appears from history, was a most corrupt and flagitious governor. See particularly Philo, *de Legatione ad Caium.* *Newton.*

*l.* 160. *p.* 48. ———————— *oft have they violated*
　　　　　　*The temple, &c.—*]

Pompey, with several of his officers, entered not only into the holy place, but also penetrated into the holy of holies, where none were permitted by the law to enter, except the high priest alone, once in a year, on the great day of expiation. Antiochus Epiphanes had before been guilty of a similar profanation. See 2 Macab. C. v.

*Newton.*

*l.* 165. *p.* 48. *So did not Maccabeus, &c.—*]

The Tempter had noticed the profanation of the temple by the Romans, as well as that by Antiochus Epiphanes, king of Syria; and now he would infer, that Jesus was to blame for not vindicating his country against the one, as *Judas Maccabeus* had done against the other. He fled indeed into the wilderness from the persecutions of Antiochus, but there he took up arms against him, and obtained so many victories over his forces, that he recovered the city and sanctuary out of their hands, and his family was in his brother Jonathan advanced to the high priesthood, and in his brother Simon to the principality, and so they continued for several descents sovereign pontiffs and sovereign princes of the Jewish nation till the time of Herod the great: though their father Mattathias, (the son of John, the son of Simon, the son of Asmonæus, from whom the family had the name of Asmoneans,) was no more than a priest of the course of Joarib, and dwelt at Modin, which is famous for nothing so much as being the country of the Maccabees. See 1 Maccab. Josephus, Prideaux, &c.

*Newton.*

*l.* 242. *p.* 51. *(As he who seeking asses found a kingdom,)*]

Saul, seeking his father's asses, came to Samuel, and by him was anointed king. 1 Sam. ix.          *Newton.*

*l.* 284. *p.* 52. ——————— *Persepolis,*
          *His city,—*]

The city of Cyrus; if not built by him, yet by him made the capital city of the Persian Empire.          *Newton.*

*l.* 285. *p.* 52. ——————— *Bactra there;—*]

The chief city of Bactriana a province of Persia, famous for its fruitfulness; mentioned by Virgil, GEORG. ii. 136.          *Newton.*

*l.* 286. *p.* 52. *Ecbatana her structure vast there shows,*]

Ancient historians speak of *Ecbatana*, the metropolis of Media, as a very large city. Herodotus compares it to Athens, L. i. C. 98; Strabo calls it a great city, μεγαλη πολις, L. ii; and Polybius, L. 10. says it greatly excelled other cities in riches and magnificence of buildings.          *Newton.*

*l.* 287. *p.* 52. *And Hecatompylos her hundred gates;—*]

The names signifies *a city with an hundred gates*; and so the capital city of Parthia was called, 'Εκατομπυλον το των Παρθυαιων βασιλειον. Strabo. L. xi. p. 514. *Newton.*

*l.* 288. *p.* 52. *Sufa by Choafpes,—*]

Sufa, the Shuſhan of the holy ſcriptures, and the royal ſeat of the kings of Perſia, who reſided here in the winter and at Ecbatana in the ſummer, was ſituated on the river *Choafpes,* or Eulœus, or Ulai as it is called in Daniel; or rather on the confluence of theſe two rivers, which meeting at Sufa form one great river, ſometimes called by one name, and ſometimes by the other. *Newton.*

Dionyſius deſcribes the Choaſpes flowing by Sufa,

—— παρα τε ρειαν χθονα Σωσων. 1074.

*l.* 288. *p.* 52. ——————— *amber ſtream,*]

Thus in the PARADISE LOST, iii. 358.

And where the river of bliſs through midſt of heaven

Rolls o'er Elyſian flowers her AMBER STREAM ;—

where Bp. Newton obſerves that the clearneſs of amber was proverbial with the ancients, and cites

—— ΑΔΕΚΤΡΙΝΟΝ υδωρ.

Callimach. HYMN AD CER. 29.

And Virgil. GEORG. iii. 522.

—— non qui per ſaxa volutus

PURIOR ELECTRO campum petit amnis :——

Sabrina the River-Goddeſs, in COMUS, is addreſſed, Ver. 863, as having

—— AMBER-DROPPING hair;

where Mr. Warton obſerves that her hair *drops amber,* becauſe, in the poet's idea, her ſtream was ſuppoſed to be tranſparent.

*l.* 289. *p.* 52. *The drink of none but kings;—*]

It may be granted, and it is not at all improbable, that none beſides the king might drink of that water of *Choafpes,* which was boiled and barreled up for his uſe in his military expeditions. Solinus indeed, who is a frivolous writer, ſays " *Choafpes* ita dulcis eſt, ut Per-" ſici reges quamdiu intra ripas Perſidis fluit ſolis ſibi ex eo pocula " vindicarint." Milton therefore, conſidered as a poet, with whoſe purpoſe the fabulous ſuited beſt, is by no means to be blamed for what he has advanced ; as even the authority of Solinus is ſufficient to juſtify him. *Jortin.*

*l.* 289. *p.* 52. ───────── *of later fame,*
    *Built by Emathian, or by Parthian hands,*
    *The great Seleucia, Nisibis, and there*
    *Artaxata, Teredon, Ctesiphon,*]

Cities of later date, *built by Emathian hands,* that is, Macedonian; by the successors of Alexander in Asia. *The great Seleucia,* built near the river Tigris by Seleucus Nicator, one of Alexander's captains, and called *great* to distinguish it from others of the same name; *Nisibis,* another city upon the Tigris, called also Antiocha, *Antiochia quam Nisibin vocant.* Plin. vi. 16. *Artaxata,* the chief city of Armenia, seated upon the river Araxes, *juxta Araxem Artaxate.* Plin. vi. 10. *Teredon,* a city near the Persian bay, below the confluence of Euphrates and Tigris, *Teredon infra confluentem Euphratis et Tigris.* Plin. vi. 28. *Ctesiphon,* near Seleucia, the winter residence of the Parthian kings, Strabo. L. xvi. p. 743.     *Newton.*

 *l.* 292. *p.* 52. *Artaxata*—]

Strabo, L. xi. p. 528. says that Artaxata was built by Hannibal, for Artaxas; who, after being general to Antiochus the Great, became king of Armenia.

 *l.* 294. *p.* 52. *All these the Parthian, now some ages past*
    *By great Arsaces led, who founded first*
    *That empire, under his dominion holds,*
    *From the luxurious kings of Antioch won.*]

*All these* cities, which before belonged to the Seleucidæ or Syro-Macedonian princes, sometimes called *kings of Antioch,* from their usual place of residence, were now under the dominion of the Parthians, whose empire was founded by *Arsaces,* who revolted from Antiochus Theus, according to Prideaux, two hundred and fifty years before Christ. This view of the Parthian empire is much more agreeably and poetically described than Adam's prospect of the kingdoms of the world from the mount of vision in the Paradise Lost, xi. 385— 411: but still the anachronism in this is worse than in the other: in the former Adam is supposed to take a view of cities many years before they were built, and in the latter our Saviour beholds cities, as Nineveh, Babylon, &c. in this flourishing condition many years after they were laid in ruins; but it was the design of the former vision to

exhibit what was future, it was not the defign of the latter to exhibit
what was paft. *Newton.*

*l.* 298. *p.* 53. *And juſt in time thou com'ſt to have a view*
*Of his great power ; &c.*—]

Milton, confidering very probably that a geographic defcription of
kingdoms, however varied in the manner of expreffion and diverfi-
fied with little circumftances, muft foon grow tedious, has very judi-
cioufly thrown in this digreffive picture of an army muftering for an
expedition, which he has executed in a very mafterly manner. The
fame conduct he has obferved in the fubfequent defcription of the Roman empire, by introducing into the fcene prætors and proconfuls
marching out to their provinces with troops, lictors, rods, and other
enfigns of power, and ambaffadors making their entrance into that
imperial city from all parts of the world. There is great art and defign in this contrivance of our Author's, and the more as there is no
appearance of any, fo naturally are the parts connected. *Thyer.*

*l.* 315. *p.* 53. *Of many provinces from bound to bound ;*—]

He had before mentioned the principal cities of the Parthians, and
he now recounts feveral of their provinces. *Newton.*

*l.* 316. *p.* 53. *Arachoſia,*—]

This was one of the largeft provinces of the Parthian Empire, and,
as Bp. Newton obferves, is defcribed by Strabo extending to the river
Indus, μεχρι τυ Ινδυ πόλαμυ τεταμενη. L. xi. p. 516.

*l.* 316. *p.* 53. ——————————— *Candaor*—]

In the Edition of 1680 it is written *Gandaor.* Pliny, defcribing
this country, fpeaks of the *Gandari,* L. vi. 16. where Father Harduin
would read *Candari,* and fays, (as Bp. Newton obferves,) that they
are different from the *Gandari.* Pomponius Mela notices the fame
people, L. i. C. 2. where the commentators are divided between the
readings of Candari or Gandari. Voffius, in a note on the place,
clearly fhows they were a different people from the Indian Gandari,
and that they were the *Candari* of Ptolemy, and the people meant
by Pliny, in the paffage already referred to.—Thefe provinces lay
eaftward. Candahar, or Kandahar, is the modern name of Arachoſia.

*l.* 317. *p.* 53. —— *Margiana to the Hyrcanian cliffs*
   *Of Caucasus, and dark Iberian dales,*]

Margiana and Hyrcania lay northward of Arachosia towards the
Caspian Sea. Margiana is mentioned by Pliny, L. vi. 16.——The
Hyrcanian " cliffs of Caucasus" and " the Iberian dales" are joined
together by Strabo, who says, that the highest part of the Caucasus
bordered on Albania, Iberia, and Colchis.—τα μεν ουν υψηλοτατα
τȣ οντως Καυκασȣ τα νοτιȣτατα εςι, τα προς Αλβανια και Ιβηρια και
Κολχοις. L. xi. p. 506.—The Iberian dales are termed dark, as the
country abounded in forests. Tacitus describes the Iberians " saltuosos
" locos incolentes." ANNAL. vi. 34.

*l.* 319. *p.* 53. *From Atropatia and the neighb'ring plains,*
   *Of Adiabene, Media, and the south*
   *Of Susiana, to Balsara's haven.*]

This description of the Parthian provinces moves nearly in a circle.
It begins with Arachosia east; then advances northward to Margiana;
and from thence, turning westward, proceeds to Hyrcania, Iberia, and
the Atropatian or northern division of Media. Here it turns again
southward, and carries us to Adiabene, or the western part of Baby-
lonia, which, as Bp. Newton observes, Strabo (L. xvi. p. 745,) describes as a *plain country*, της μεν ȣν Αϑιαβηνης ἡ πλειςη πεδιας εςι;
then, passing through part of Media, it concludes with Susiana, which
extended southward to the Persian Gulph, called *Balsara's haven*,
from the Port of Balsera, Bassorah, or Bussorah.

*l.* 333. *p.* 54. ———————————— *or overlay*
   *With bridges rivers proud, as with a yoke;*]

Alluding probably to Æschylus's description of Xerxes's bridge
over the Hellespont. PERSÆ, 71.

   Πολυγομφον ὁδισμα
   Ζυγον αμφιβαλων αυχενι ποντȣ.    *Thyer.*

*l.* 337. *p.* 54. *Such forces met not, nor so wide a camp,*
   *When Agrican with all his northern powers*
   *Besieg'd Albracca, &c.*—]

What Milton here alludes to is related in Boiardo's Orlando Inamorato, L. i. Cant. 10. The number of forces said to be there
assembled is incredible, and extravagant even beyond the common

extravagancy of romances. Agrican the Tartar king brings into the field no lefs than two millions two hundred thoufand;

> Ventidua centinaia di migliara
> Di caualier hauea quel Rè nel campo,
> Cofa non mai udita———

and Sacripante the king of Circaffia, who comes to the affiftance of Gallaphrone, three hundred and eighty-two thoufand. It muft be acknowledged, I think, by the greateft admirers of Milton, that the impreffion which romances had made upon his imagination in his youth, has in this place led him into a blameable excefs. Not to mention the notorious fabuloufnefs of the fact alluded to, which I doubt fome people will cenfure in a poem of fo grave a turn, the number of the troops of Agrican, &c. is by far too much difproportioned to any army, which the Parthian king by an hiftorical evidence could be fuppofed to bring into the field. *Thyer.*

*l.* 341. *p.* 54. *The faireft of her fex Angelica,*]

This is that Angelica who afterwards made her appearance in the fame character in Ariofto's Orlando Furiofo, which was intended as a continuation of the ftory, which Boiardo had begun. As Milton fetches his fimile from a romance, he adopts the terms ufed by thefe writers, viz. *proweft* and *Paynim.* *Thyer.*

*l.* 374. *p.* 55. ——————— *thofe ten tribes*
> *Whofe offspring in his territory yet ferve,*
> *In Habor, and among the Medes difpers'd;*]

Thefe were the ten tribes, whom Shalmanefer, king of Affyria, carried captive into Affyria, *and put them in Halab and in Habor by the river of Gozan, and in the cities of the Medes.* 2 Kings, xviii. 11. which cities were now under the dominion of the Parthians.

*Newton.*

*l.* 428. *p.* 57. *Who, freed, as to their ancient patrimony,*
> *Unhumbled, unrepentant, unreform'd,*
> *Headlong would follow; and to their Gods perhaps*
> *Of Bethel and of Dan ?—*]

There is fome difficulty and obfcurity in this paffage; and feveral conjectures and emendations have been offered to clear it but none, I think, entirely to fatisfaction. Mr. Sympfon would read *Headlong*

*would fall off, and &c.* or *Headlong would fall, &c.* But Mr. Calton
seems to come nearer the poet's meaning. Whom or what would
they follow, says he? There wants an accusative case; and what
must be understood to complete the sense can never be accounted for
by an ellipsis, that any rules or use of language will justify. He
therefore suspects by some accident a whole line may have been lost;
and proposes one, which he says may serve at least for a commentary
to explain the sense, if it cannot be allowed for an emendation.

> *Their fathers in their old iniquities*
> Headlong would follow, &c.——

Or is not the construction thus, *Headlong would follow as to their ancient patrimony, and to their Gods perhaps, &c. ?*            *Newton.*

# BOOK IV.

*l. 27. p. 62. Another plain, &c.—*]
The learned reader need not be informed that the country here
meant is Italy, which indeed is long but not broad, and is washed by
the Mediterranean on the south, and screened by the Alps on the
north, and divided in the midst by the river Tiber.            *Newton.*

*l. 66. p. 63. ————— turms of horse—*]
Troops of horse; as Bp. Newton observes, from the Latin, *turma.*
Virg. *Æn.* v. 560.

> ————— equitum TURMÆ,——

*l. 68. p. 63. ————— on the Appian road,*
> Or on the Emilian,—]

The Appian road from Rome led towards the south of Italy, and
the Emilian towards the north. The nations on the Appian road are
included in ver. 69—76, those on the Emilian in ver. 77—79.

Newton.

*l.* 69. *p.* 63. ———————————— *from fartheft fouth,*
  *Syene, and where the fhadow both way falls, &c.*—]

He firft mentions places in *Africa*; *Syene,* a city of Egypt on the confines of Ethiopia; Ditionis Ægypti effe incipit a fine Æthiopiæ Syene; Plin. Lib. v. Sect. 9; *Meroe,* an ifland and city of Ethiopia, in the river Nile, therefore called *Nilotic ifle, where the fhadow both way falls;* Rurfus in Meroe, (infula hæc caputque gentis Æthiopum—in amne Nilo habitatur,) bis anno abfumi umbras; Plin. Lib. ii. Sect. 73; *the realm of Bocchus,* Mauritania. Then *Afian* nations; among thefe *the golden Cherfonefe,* Malacca the moft fouthern promontory of the Eaft Indies, (fee Paradife Loft, xi. 392; *and utmoft Indian ifle Taprobane,* wherefore Pliny fays it is " extra orbem a " natura relegata ;" Lib. vi. Sect. 22. Then the *Europæan* nations as far as to *the Tauric pool,* that is the palus Mæotis; " Lacus ipfe " Mæotis, Tanain amnem ex Riphæis montibus defluentem accipiens, " noviffimum inter Europam Afiamque finem, &c." Plin. Lib. iv. Sect. 12.              *Newton.*

*l.* 115. *p.* 65. *On citron tables or Atlantic ftone,*]

Tables made of *citron* wood were in fuch requeft among the Romans, that Pliny calls it *menfarum infania.* They were beautifully veined and fpotted. See his account of them, Lib. xiii. Sect. 29. I do not find that the *Atlantic ftone* or marble was fo celebrated : the *Numidicus lapis* and *Numidicum marmor* are often mentioned in Roman authors.              *Newton.*

*l.* 145. *p.* 66. *Or could of inward flaves make outward free ?*]

This noble fentiment Milton explains more fully, and expreffes more diffufively, in his PARADISE LOST, xii. 90.

  ——— therefore fince he permits
  Within himfelf unworthy pow'rs to reign
  Over free reafon, God in judgment juft
  Subjects him from without to violent lords; &c.

So alfo again, in his xiith Sonnet,

  Licence they mean, when they cry Liberty ;
  FOR WHO LOVES THAT, MUST FIRST BE WISE AND GOOD.

No one had ever more refined notions of true liberty than Milton.
              *Thyer.*

*l. 230. p. 68. Ruling them by perfuafion as thou mean'ft.*]

Alluding to thofe charming lines, i. 221.

> Yet held it more humane, more heavenly, firſt
> By winning words to conquer willing hearts,
> And make perfuafion do the work of fear.　　*Newton.*

*l. 239. p. 69. ———— pure the air, and light the foil ;*]

Attica being a mountainous country, the foil was light, and the air ſharp and pure; and therefore faid to be productive of ſharp wits. ——τεν ευκρασιαν των ορων εν αυτω κατιδυσα, ὅτι φρονιμωτατυς ανδρας εισι. Plato in Timæo. p. 24. Vol. 3. Ed. Serr.——" Athenis tenue " cœlum, ex quo acutiores etiam putantur Attici."——Cicero, Dᴇ Fᴀᴛᴏ, 4.　　　　　　　　　　　　　　　*Newton.*

*l. 244. p. 69. ———— the olive grove of Academe,*]

The Academy is always defcribed as a woody, ſhady, place. Diogenes Laertius calls it προαςειν ΑΛΣΩΔΕΣ; and Horace fpeaks of the sʏʟvᴀs Academi, 2 Epiſt. ii. 45. But Milton diſtinguiſhes it by the particular name of *the olive grove of Academe*, becaufe the olive was particularly cultivated about Athens, being facred to Minerva the goddefs of the city : he has befides the exprefs authority of Ariſtophanes, Nᴜʙ. 1001.

Αλλ' εις Ακαδημιαν κατιων, ὑπο ταις μοριαις αποθριξεις.

Sed in Academiam defcendens fub facris olivis fpatiaberis.

　　　　　　　　　　　　　　　　　　　　　*Newton.*

This whole defcription of the Academe is infinitely charming. Bp. Newton has juſtly obferved that " Plato's Academy was never more " beautifully defcribed." " Cicero," he adds, " who has laid the " fcene of one of his dialogues (De Fin. 1.. v.) there, and who had " been himfelf on the fpot, has not painted it in more lively co- " lours."

*l. 245. p. 69. ———————— where the Attic bird*
　　　　　　　*Trills her thick-warbled notes &c.—*]

Philomela, who according to the fables, was changed into a nightingale, was the daughter of Pandion king of Athens. Hence the nightingale is called *Atthis* in Latin, quaſi Attica avis ; thus Martial, L. i. Ep. 54.

Sic ubi multifonâ fervet facer Aᴛᴛʜɪᴅᴇ lucus, &c. *Newton.*

*l.* 247. *p.* 69.  *There flow'ry hill Hymettus with the sound*
            *Of bees industrious murmur oft invites*
            *To studious musing ;—*]

Valerius Flaccus calls it *Florea juga Hymetti*, Argonaut. V. 344;
and the honey was so much esteemed and celebrated by the ancients,
that it was reckoned the best of the Attic honey, as the Attic honey
was said to be the best in the world. The poets often speak of the
murmur of the bees as inviting to sleep, Virg. Ecl. i. 56.

     Sæpe levi somnum suadebit inire susurro :

but Milton gives a more elegant turn to it, and says that it *invites to
studious musing*, which was more proper indeed for his purpose, as he is
here describing the Attic learning.                           *Newton.*

     *l.* 249. *p.* 69.  ——————————— *Ilissus—*]

Mr. Calton and Mr. Thyer have observed with me, that Plato hath
laid the scene of his Phædrus on the banks, and at the spring, of
this pleasant river.—χαριεντα γυν και καθαρα και διαφανη τα υδατια
φαινεται.  " Nonne hinc aquulæ puræ ac pellucidæ jocundo mur-
" mure confluunt?" Ed. Serr. Vol. iii. p. 229.  The philosophical
retreat at the spring-head is beautifully described by Plato, in the next
page, where Socrates and Phædrus are represented sitting on a green
bank, shaded with a spreading platane, of which Cicero hath said very
prettily, that it seemeth not to have grown so much by the water
which is described, as by Plato's eloquence ;  " quæ mihi videtur non
" tam ipsa aquula, quæ describitur, quam Platonis oratione crevisse."
De Orat. i. 7.                                              *Newton.*

     *l.* 253. *p.* 69.  *Lyceum there,—*]

The *Lyceum* was the school of Aristotle, who had been tutor to
Alexander the Great, and was the founder of the sect of the Peripatetics, so called, απο τυ περιπατειν, from his *walking*, and teaching
philosophy.  But there is some reason to question, whether the *Lyceum* was *within the walls*, as Milton asserts.  For Suidas says ex-
pressly, that it was a place in the suburbs, built by Pericles for the
exercising of soldiers : and I find the scholiast upon Aristophanes in
the Irene, speaks of going into the Lyceum, and going out of it again,
and *returning back into the city :*——εις το Λυκειον εισιονες —— και
παλιν εξιονιες εκ τυ Λυκειυ, και απιονιες εις την πολιν.       *Newton.*

*l.* 253. *p.* 69. ——————— *painted Stoa*—]

*Stoa* was the school of Zeno, whose disciples from the place had the name of Stoics; and this Stoa, or portico, being adorned with variety of paintings, was called in Greek Ποικιλη, or *various*, and here by Milton the *painted Stoa*. See Diogenes Laertius, in the lives of Aristotle and Zeno.                                                                *Newton.*

*l.* 257. *p.* 69. *Æolian charms,*—]

*Æolia carmina*, verses such as those of Alcæus and Sappho, who were both of Mitylene in Lesbos, an island belonging to the Æolians.

> Princeps ÆOLIUM CARMEN ad Italos
> Deduxisse modos, ——————     Hor. L. iii. ODE XXX. 13.
> Fingent ÆOLIO CARMINE nobilem,—   IBID. L. iv. ODE iii. 12.
>                                                                            *Newton.*

Our English word *charm* is derived from *carmen*; as are *inchant*, and *incantation*, from *canto*.

*l.* 257. *p.* 69. ——————— *Dorian Lyric odes,*]

Such as those of Pindar; who calls his lyre Δωριαν φορμιγγα. OLYMP. i. 26, &c.                                                                *Newton.*

*l.* 258. *p.* 69. *And his who gave them breath, &c.*—]

Our Author agrees with those writers, who speak of Homer as the father of all kinds of poetry. Dionysius the Halicarnassean, and Plutarch, have attempted to show that poetry in all its forms, tragedy, comedy, ode, and epitaph, are included in his works.     *Newton.*

" *l.* 259. *p.* 69. *Blind Melesigenes, thence Homer call'd,*]

Our Author here follows Herodotus, in his life of Homer, where it is said that he was born near the river Meles, and that from thence his mother named him at first Melesigenes,—τιθεται ονομα τω παιδι Μελισιγενεα, απο τυ ποταμυ την επωνυμιαν λαβυσα,—and that afterwards when he was blind and settled at Cuma, he was called *Homer*, quasi ὁ μη ορων, from the term by which the Cumæans distinguished blind persons;—εντευθεν δε και τυνομα Ὁμηρος επεκρατησε τω Μελησιγενει, απο της συμφορης. ὁι γαρ Κυμαιοι τους τυφλυς ὁμηρυς λεγυσιν.                                                                *Newton.*

*l.* 262. *p.* 69. ——— *Chorus or Iambic,*—]

: The two constituent parts of the ancient tragedy were the dialogue, written chiefly in the IAMBIC measure, and the CHORUS, which con-

fifted of various meafures.—The character here given by our author
of the ancient tragedy, is very juft and noble; and the Englifh reader
cannot form a better idea of it in its higheft beauty and perfection,
than by reading our author's SAMSON AGONISTES. *Newton.*

*l. 267. p. 70. Thence to the famous orators repair, &c.—*]

How happily does Milton's verfification in this, and the following
lines, concerning the Socratic philofophy, exprefs what he is defcribing ! In the firft we feel, as it were the nervous rapid eloquence of
Demofthenes, and the latter have all the gentlenefs and foftnefs of the
humble modeft character of Socrates. *Thyer.*

*l. 268. p. 70. ———— whofe refiftlefs eloquence*
*Wielded at will that fierce democratie,*
*Shook the arfenal, and fulmin'd over Greece,*]

———— ΠΕΡΙΚΛΕΗΣ ΟΥΛΥΜΠΙΟΣ
ΗΣΤΡΑΠΤΕΝ, ΕΒΡΟΝΤΑ, ΞΥΝΕΚΥΚΑ ΤΗΝ ΕΛΛΑΔΑ.

523.

*l. 271. p. 70. To Macedon and Artaxerxes throne :*]

As Pericles and others *fulmin'd over Greece to Artaxerxes throne*
againft the Perfian king, fo Demofthenes was the orator particularly,
who *fulmin'd over Greece to Macedon* againft king Philip, in his Ora-
tions, therefore denominated Philippics. *Newton.*

*l. 276. p. 70. ———————— from whofe mouth iffu'd forth*
*Mellifluous ftreams, that water'd all the fchools*
*Of Academics &c.—*]

Thus Quintilian calls Socrates *fons philofophorum.* L. i. C. 10. As
the ancients looked upon Homer to be the father of poetry, fo they
efteemed Socrates the father of moral philofophy.

*l. 285. p. 70. To whom our Saviour fagely thus reply'd.*]

This anfwer of our Saviour is as much to be admired for folid rea-
foning, and the many fublime truths contained in it, as the preceding
fpeech of Satan is for that fine vein of poetry which runs through it :
and one may obferve in general, that Milton has quite throughout
this work thrown the ornaments of poetry on the fide of errour, whether it was that he thought great truths beft exprefled in a grave, unaffected ftyle, or intended to fuggeft this fine moral to the reader, that
fimple naked truth will always be an over-match for falfehood,

though recommended by the gayest rhetoric, and adorned with the most bewitching colours.                                      *Thyer.*

> *l.* 288. *p.* 70. ——————————— *he who receives*
> *Light from above, from the fountain of light,*
> *No other doctrine needs, though granted true;*]

*St. James,* C. i. V. 17. *Every good and every perfect gift is from above, and* COMETH DOWN FROM THE FATHER OF LIGHTS; which refers to what the apostle had said in the 5th verse of the same chapter; *If any of you lack wisdom, let him ask of God, that giveth to all men liberally,* &c.

> *l.* 296. *p.* 70. *A third sort doubted all things, though plain sense;*]

These were the Sceptics or Pyrrhonians, the disciples of Pyrrho, who asserted nothing to be either honest or dishonest, just or unjust; that men do all things by law and custom; and that in every thing *this* is not preferable to *that.* This was called the Sceptic philosophy from its continual inspection, and never finding; and Pyrrhonian from Pyrrho. (See Stanley's Life of Pyrrho, who takes this account from Diogenes Laertius.)                                 *Newton.*

> *l.* 297. *p.* 70. *Others in virtue plac'd felicity,*
> *But virtue join'd with riches and long life;*]

These were the old Academics, and the Peripatetics the scholars of Aristotle.

> *l.* 299. *p.* 70. *In corporal pleasure he, and careless ease;*]

EPICURUS. The HE is here contemptuously emphatical.

> *l.* 341. *p.* 72. ——————————— *personating*]

This is in the Latin sense of *persono,* to celebrate loudly, to publish or proclaim.

> *l.* 354. *p.* 72. ——————————— *statists*—]

Or statesmen. A word in more frequent use formerly, as in Shakspeare, CYMBELINE, Act II. Sc. 5.

> —— I do believe,
> (STATIST though I am none, nor like to be ı)

and HAMLET, Act V. Sc. 3.

> I once did hold it, as our STATISTS do, &c.        *Newton.*

> *l.* 421. *p.* 75. *Infernal ghosts and hellish furies round*
> *Environ'd thee, some howl'd, some yell'd,* &c.—]

With that, methought, A LEGION OF FOUL FIENDS
ENVIRON'D ME, AND HOWLED IN MINE EARS .
Such hideous cries, that with the very noife
I trembling wak'd; and for a feafon after
Could not believe but that I was in Hell:
Such terrible impreffion made my dream.

> K. RICHARD III. ACT I. Sc. 5.

*l.* 427. *p.* 75. ————— *with pilgrim fteps—*]
With the flow folemn pace of a pilgrim on a journey of devotion.

> *Newton.*

*l.* 427. *p.* 75. ————————— *amice gray,*]
*Amice gray* is gray clothing. Amice, a fignificant word, is derived
from the Latin *amicio*, to clothe: and is ufed by Spenfer, FAERY
QUEEN, Book I. C. iv. St. 18.

> Array'd in habit black, and AMICE THIN,
> Like to an holy monk the fervice to begin. *Newton.*

*l.* 428. *p.* 75. *Who with her radiant finger ftill'd the roar*
> *Of thunder, chac'd the clouds, and laid the winds, &c.*]

This is an imitation of a paffage in the firft Æneid of Virgil, where
Neptune is reprefented with his trident laying the ftorm which Æolus
had raifed. ver. 142.

> Sic ait, et dicto citius tumida æquora placat,
> COLLECTASQUE FUGAT NUBES, folemque reducit.

There is the greater beauty in the Englifh poet, as the fcene he is defcribing under this charming figure is perfectly confiftent with the
courfe of nature; nothing being more common than to fee a ftormy
night fucceeded by a pleafant, ferene morning. *Thyer.*

*l.* 430. *p.* 75. *And grifly fpectres, which the Fiend had rais'd,*]
> So when the fun in bed,
> Curtain'd with cloudy red,
> Pillows his chin upon an orient wave,
> The flocking fhadows pale,
> Troop to the infernal jail,
> Each fetter'd ghoft flips to his feveral grave,

> And the yellow-fkirted Fayes
> Fly after the night fteeds, leaving their moon-lov'd maze.

This popular fuperftition, refpecting the evanefcence of fpirits at the crowing of the cock, Shakfpeare, as Mr. Warton obferves, has finely availed h'mfelf of in his HAMLET, where the Ghoft vanifhes at this circumftance.

> It faded on the crowing of the cock.
> Some fay that ever 'gainft that feafon comes,
> Wherein our Saviour's birth is celebrated,
> The bird of dawning fingeth all night long :
> And then, fay they, no fpirit dares walk abroad ;
> The nights are wholefome, then no planets ftrike,
> No fairy takes, no witch has power to charm ;
> So hallow'd and fo gracious is the time.

The fuppofed effect of day-break, in this refpect, is alfo defcribed very poetically by the fame great mafter in his MIDSUMMER NIGHT'S DREAM, Act. III. Scene *the laft.*

> And yonder fhines Aurora's harbinger ;
> At whofe approach ghofts wandering here and there
> Troop home to churchyards : damned fpirits all,
> That in croffways and floods have burial,
> Already to their wormy beds are gone.

Thus alfo Cowley, in his HYMN TO LIGHT, Stanz. 10.

> Night and her ugly fubjects thou doft fright, &c.

And Stanz. 17.

> The ghofts, and monfter fpirits, that did prefume
> A body's privilege to affume,
> Vanifh again invifibly.——

But perhaps no poet has more happily availed himfelf of this old fuperftition, or has introduced it more poetically than the late Mr. Gray, in his PROGRESS OF POETRY, where the relief, which the Mufe affords to the real and imaginary ills of life, is compared to the day difpelling the gloom and terrours of the night.

Night, and all her fickly dews,
Her SPECTRES WAN, and birds of boding cry,
He gives to range the dreary fky;
Till down the eaftern cliffs afar
Hyperion's march they fpy, and glittering fhafts of war.

STANZA ii. I.—

*Dunfter.*

*l.* 432. *p.* 75. *And now the fun with more effectual beams*
*Had chear'd the face of earth, and dry'd the wet*
*From drooping plant, or dropping tree ; the birds,*
*Who all things now behold more frefh and green*
*After a night of ftorm fo ruinous,*
*Clear'd up their choiceft notes in bufh and fpray,*
*To gratulate the fweet return of morn.*]

There is in this defcription all the bloom of Milton's youthful
fancy. We may compare an evening fcene of the fame kind, PARA-
DISE LOST, ii. 488.

As, when from mountain tops the dufky clouds
Afcending, while the north-wind fleeps, o'erfpread
Heaven's chearful face, the lowering element
Scowls o'er the darken'd landfcape fnow or fhower ;
If chance the radiant fun with farewell fweet
Extend his evening beam, the fields revive,
The birds their notes renew, and bleating herds
Atteft their joy, that hill and valley ring.      *Thyer.*

*l.* 454. *p.* 76. ——————— *thefe flaws,*—]      (From *Flo.*)
*Flaw* is a fea term for a fudden ftorm, or guft of wind.

In the PARADISE LOST, among the changes produced in the natural world are violent ftorms, which are defcribed

—— arm'd with ice,

And fnow and hail, and STORMY GUST AND FLAW;

x. 697.

where Bp. Newton cites two verfes from Shakfpeare's VENUS and
ADONIS;

Like a red morn that ever yet betoken'd
GUST, and foul FLAWS to herdfmen and to herds.

*l.* 455. *p.* 76. *As dangerous to the pillar'd frame of Heaven,*]
So alſo, Comus, 597;

—— if this fail,
The PILLAR'D FIRMAMENT is rottenneſs.
In both, no doubt, alluding to Job, xxvi. 11. *The* PILLARS OF
HEAVEN *tremble, and are aſtoniſh'd at his reproof.* *Thyer.*

*l.* 541. *p.* 78. ———————————— *without wing*
*Of hippogrif*—]
An *hippogrif* is an imaginary creature, part like an horſe, and part
like a gryphon.

Arioſto frequently makes uſe of this creature to convey his heroes
from place to place. *Newton.*

*l.* 564. *p.* 79. ———————— *in Iraſſa*—]
*Iraſſa* is a place in Lybia, mentioned by Herodotus.

*l.* 572. *p.* 79. *And as that Theban monſter, &c.*—]
The Sphinx, who, on her riddle being ſolved by Œdipus, threw
herſelf into the ſea. Statius, THEB. i. 66.

—— Si Sphingos iniquæ
Callidus ambages, te præmonſtrante, reſolvi. *Newton.*

*l.* 572. *p.* 79. ———— *that Theban monſter that propos'd*
*Her riddle, and him, who ſolved it not, devour'd,*
*That once found out and ſolv'd, for grief and ſpite*
*Caſt herſelf headlong from the Iſmenian ſteep;*]
*Iſmenian ſteep,* from the river Iſmenus, which ran by Thebes;
ο γαρ Ασωπος, και Ὁ ΙΣΜΗΝΟΣ δια τη πολιν ρευσι τη προ των Θηβων.
Strabo. ix. p. 408.—*Iſmenus* is thus frequently uſed by the Latin
poets for *Theban.*

*l.* 581. *p.* 80. ———————— *and ſtrait a fiery globe*
*Of Angels on full ſail of wing flew nigh,*
*Who on their plumy vans &c.*—]
There is a peculiar ſoftneſs and delicacy in this deſcription, and
neither circumſtances nor words could be better ſelected to give the
reader an idea of the eaſy and gentle deſcent of our Saviour, and to
take from the imagination that horrour and uneaſineſs which it is naturally filled with in contemplating the dangerous and uneaſy ſituation
he was left in. *Thyer.*

So Pſyche was carried down from the rock by zephyrs, and laid lightly on a green and flowery bank, and there entertained with inviſible muſic.   See Apuleius, Lib. iv.                    *Richardſon.*

Mr. Richardſon might have added that Pſyche was alſo entertained with a banquet miniſtered by Spirits.   The paſſages from Apuleius, (at the end of the FOURTH Book of the METAMORPHOSES, and the beginning of the FIFTH,) are well worth citing.

" Pſychem autem paventem ac trepidam, et in ipſo ſcopuli vertice
" deflentem, mitis aura molliter ſpirantis Zephyri, vibratis hinc inde
" laciniis et reflato ſinu ſenſim levatam, ſuo tranquillo ſpiritu vehens
" paulatim per devexa rupis excelſæ, vallis ſubditæ florentis ceſpitis
" gremio leniter delapſam reclinat."————————————

—" Et illico vini nectarei eduliorumque variorum fercula copioſa,
" nullo ſerviente, ſed tantum ſpiritu quodam impulſa, ſubminiſtran-
" tur.   Nec quemquam tamen illa videre poterat, ſed verba tantum
" audiebat excidentia et ſolas voces famulas habebat.   Poſt opimas
" dapes quidam intro ceſſit, et cantavit inviſus; et alius citharam
" pulſavit, quæ non videbatur, nec ipſe.   Tunc modulatæ multitu-
" dinis conferta vox aures ejus affertur; ut quamvis hominum nemo
" pareret, chorum tamen eſſe pateret."                   *Dunſter.*

*l.* 596. *p.* 80. *True image of the Father, &c.*—]
    Cedite Romani ſcriptores, cedite Graii.

All the poems that ever were written muſt yield, even PARADISE LOST muſt yield, to the REGAINED in the grandeur of its cloſe. Chriſt ſtands triumphant on the pointed eminence.   The Demon falls with amazement and terrour, on this full proof of his being that very Son of God, whoſe thunder forced him out of Heaven.   The bleſſed Angels receive new knowledge.   They behold a ſublime truth eſtabliſhed, which was a ſecret to them at the beginning of the Temptation; and the great diſcovery gives a proper opening to their hymn on the victory of Chriſt, and the defeat of the Tempter.        *Calton.*

*l.* 605. *p.* 81. *Thou didſt debel,*—]
    *i. e.* Subdue in Battle.

Virgil, ÆN. vi. 853;
    ———— DEBELLARE ſuperbos.

And Ibid, v. 730;

       —— gens dura atque aspera cultu

     DEBELLANDA tibi Latio est;——

*l.* 624. *p.* 81. ————————— *Abaddon*—]

    The name of the Angel of the bottomless pit, Rev. ix. 11; here applied to the bottomless pit itself.                   *Newton.*

## THE END.